Dark Peak

First published in 2012
by Stonewood Press
97 Benefield Road, Oundle PE8 4EU
Tel: 0845 456 4838
Email: books@stonewoodpress.co.uk
Web: www.stonewoodpress.co.uk

Paperback ISBN: 978-0-9569122-2-2
Hardback ISBN: 978-0-9569122-4-4

Printed and bound in the UK by Imprintdigital, Exeter

Designed and typeset in Stone Print 11pt/13pt
by Martin Parker at www.silbercow.co.uk
Cover illustration by Martin Parker

For more information about JG Parker and Dark Peak,
please visit www.theelementals.net

For M: the first reader

ACKNOWLEDGMENTS

I would like to thank Martin for his inspiring reading and guidance throughout writing DARK PEAK, Preetha Leela Chockalingam for her evergreen support, Lucy Hamilton for her insightful comments, and David and Steven for a place to write.

JG PARKER has lived and written in London, Sheffield, Edinburgh and Houston, and now lives in the quiet depths of Northamptonshire surrounded by rolling fields and forests that go on forever and are likely to be home to any number of natural (and possibly supernatural) creatures. DARK PEAK is Parker's first novel.

DARK PEAK

BY

J G PARKER

Stonewood PRESS

A Prologue of Sorts

Whoooomph!

The tail crashed into the wall inches from his face. Bricks and weak cement jerked and crumbled as the solid muscle pulled away and struck once more. Jake sank to the floor. His stomach wrenched and heaved and he was dizzy from the blood pounding in his head. He was riddled with adrenaline, useful enough when he'd started this fight, fizzing and cocky as a summer storm. Now it only made him shake, rapid and uncontrollable.

The tail paused mid-air and pulled sharply away. It was replaced by the sounds of heavy feet moving over debris. Above him, Jake heard the wet snort he'd grown used to from his nightmares. He wiped his face with a bloodied hand and stared up.

Through the gaps in the derelict roof he could see the comfort of the early evening sky; plums and oranges, and in the distance, the moon already rising. Then nothing but solid shadow.

Then a face, thin and grey and longer than the whole of Jake's young body. It was covered in dust and smoke, and it leaned down until its eyes were level with the crumpled boy. It didn't blink even once and Jake thought, not for the first time, how the eyes reminded him of the colour of mountains in winter. In the centre, they were filled with fire.

And disappointment.

Jake was dog-tired. He coughed, his throat ragged and dry, and held his hand against the pains in his chest.

A voice spoke.

It went beyond deep.

It was every sound ever made by stone: the clacking of pebbles on a beach, the trickling of sand in an egg-timer, the wreck of valleys in a landslide. It was the havoc of volcanoes singing in the smallest hours.

And Jake could feel it in his bones, his brain, his blood. In his heart. The voice entered and occupied him. He would never quite get used to it.

'There, lad,' it said, calm as a glacial lake. '*Now* do you understand?'

Chapter 1

It wasn't as if she was going to keep it. She'd borrowed it only for the journey but, jeeze, he could be so touchy about his things. And anyway he wasn't using it, it was just lying there on top of the drawer in his bedroom. An old comb.

This is just crap, she grumbled to herself. I get a bawling off Mam and he gets to stomp around acting betrayed and righteous! It's different when he goes through my things (not that he ever really does but that's not important right now) but when *I* do it *once* – okay maybe twice – it's like the world's gunna end! It wouldn't be like this if dad was still alive. Oh, yeah!

Elizabeth Walker sat on an unfamiliar bed running her hands over the thin quilt. It had little flowers on it. Her red suitcase lay half-unzipped beside her next to her guitar. She picked at a loose thread on the quilt's stitching, rolled it into a little ball and tried to push it back into the fabric.

That comb! She wished she'd never took it. It would have been easier to pop to the poundshop and pick up half a dozen cheapo ones. Definitely a lot less stress, anyway.

It wasn't even a very good comb! It was too fine for her hair and stiff. Fair enough, it could get lugs out quickly (like a hot knife through butter) but it took forever just to give her hair a proper comb. All that static. By the end, she'd looked like a Troll-doll, and no amount of patting it down with a dampened hand worked. She didn't even know why she'd kept it!

Opposite the bed was a long, discoloured mirror fastened to an ancient wardrobe. Elizabeth caught her reflection in it. Her face was still red and blotchy but she was calmer now. She sat for a few minutes staring at the yellowish figure looking back at her. She looked older than her eleven years, as if she carried the weight of the world on her back. And in a way she did because she'd grown up a lot in the last year or so. She'd had to. They all had, even Mam.

Grown up and faced the world differently.

She sighed and ran her fingers through her soft, brown hair. Her mother liked to call it auburn, but she knew it was brown. A long bob. She'd thought recently about cutting it short but she'd miss the way she could hide her face if she needed to. She pulled her hair back and up, holding it tight at the crown. No, she didn't have the face for short hair.

A small knock sounded on her door and she looked up to see her brother holding on to the frame. She stared at him and sucked at her teeth.

'What?' she said, flatly. A shaft of sunlight cut across the room, dividing it in half. The boy sagged a little and started to step over the threshold.

'Don't you come in 'ere,' snapped Elizabeth. 'No way, get lost! *My* room!'

Her brother hesitated, frozen to the door frame.

'Look, Bett–'

'Don't *Bett* me! My name's Elizabeth!' It was a defence she retreated to when she was upset with Jake, as if she could hide behind the name her father had given her like it was a shield or a talisman.

'I got a gobfull coz of you and that comb, Jake, so go on! Sod off!'

For a minute, her brother looked smaller and younger than she was, even though he was neither. He scratched his arm and stammered, 'I- I know, but look–'

He edged in and sat on the bed, carefully, sliding the suitcase to one side. Elizabeth slapped his hands away and pulled her case towards her.

'Get off my *stuff*. I can't touch your *stuff*, you keep off mine! Go on! I mean it! Freg off!'

Jake twiddled with the same piece of thread Elizabeth had and said, 'Eyup, I'm trying to apologize.'

His sister was stubborn. It was the one trait Elizabeth had inherited from her father while Jake got the rest: his quietness, his determination, his intolerance of selfish, foolish people.

He pulled a face as if it would make everything better. It was something his father would do when Elizabeth sulked and it had always worked for him.

Not for Jake.

'Whaddya doing?' she said, solid as a rock. Jake sighed and tried again.

'Look Bett...'

Elizabeth shoved two fingers in her ears and turned her back to her brother. Through the window she could see a gathering of sheep in the field opposite the cottage. Great, she thought, six and a half weeks of sheep and Jake. Oh, God!

'La-la-la-la-laa. La-la-la-la,' she sang tunelessly, wishing her brother would go away.

Downstairs their mother was rearranging the furniture in the room that would be her study during the holiday. Elizabeth and Jake could hear the huffing and tugging and not so subtle hints for help. The boy looked from his sister to the door.

'If you're gunna be stupid, I'm going,' he said, glancing back. Elizabeth raised her elbows higher and the volume of her voice followed.

'LaalaaLAAAAAA!!!'

Jake stood up and headed for the door saying as he went, 'I'm gunna go help Mam. But look, I *am* sorry.'

Elizabeth stopped singing and Jake forged on with his apology.

'Earlier. Y'know. I was a bit of a... a...'

'Pillock,' suggested Elizabeth, sweetly. Jake was caught off guard; his sister hardly ever swore and when she did it always sounded both serious and ridiculously funny at the same time. He laughed, a strong genuine laugh.

'I was going to say *spoon* but yeah, pillock'll do.'

The moment of Elizabeth being angry had almost passed. Almost.

'Huh, you were. Spoon *and* pillock,' she said.

'Yeah, I know. But about that comb...'

Elizabeth suddenly flared.

'What about it Jake? What's so *special*, huh? You freaked, Jake, freaked!'

Jake bit his lip and held on to the door. He should have let it lie.

'Yeah, I know I did. But, I don't know...'

'Yeah, whateva,' said Elizabeth peevishly. She watched her brother leave and shook her head. Out of the two of them, she thought, you'd never guess he was the older. Freaking over a comb, for crying out loud. A stupid comb.

There!

Heat.

History.

He felt the stark rush of power. But weak, weaker than it should have been.

The muscles of his shoulders rippled in agitation.

Was he wrong? Had someone else found it? Used it?

Impossible. Only the blood-line could cause any kind of surge.

The stone floor was covered by a rectangle, its carvings pulsating. He circled it slowly eight, nine times, and as he did so, the glow of the cave brightened. Everything was alive, even the stones surrounding him.

He smiled grimly and uncoiled his ancient body.

It was time to leave.

Jake left after lunch to check out the best areas. He'd followed the deer tracks and the sounds of birds until he came to the river. If he was quiet enough he'd catch something. Something good.

Already he'd caught a water vole and a low-flying barn owl. It was probably too late for kingfishers, and too early for bats but he could come back later for them.

He settled back, the weight of his old camera taken up by a waist-high tripod nestled at the front of his make-shift hide. His father had bought the camera six years ago. *It's the best way to catch animals, Jakey,* he'd said after he'd haggled the shopkeeper down. Now the Minolta's gaze was fixed firmly on the water's edge.

It really was beautiful here. Keep your beaches and your resorts, thought Jake, this is what I want in a holiday. Quiet, forests, mountains, valleys. And rivers.

He loved rivers.

Elizabeth always called him a nature nerd but he didn't care. He wouldn't think twice about getting up at the crack of dawn, taking his camera, some sandwiches and a bottle of Lucozade and see what he could find.

He had a fantasy that he'd enter the photographic competition run by the Natural History Museum in London. He'd never been to London, but he'd go one day.

He sat watching the rippling water and fantasized about the prize he'd win and the ceremony he'd attend. In his mind's eye he saw his photos in magazines and on T.V. where a grey-haired man was talking about his exciting use of colour and inspiring composition. Jake smiled behind the camera. He could see a cloud of midges above the water, darting in and out of a faint rainbow from the river's spray. He snapped the shutter.

He had hundreds of photographs already, and had won one or two competitions, but he was looking for the perfect shot; something his father would have been proud of.

He heard a splash, more like a memory of a splash, and saw the reeds tussle one another. Otters? It was a bit too early for otters, wasn't it? Jake smiled. His father had loved otters. Yes, *they'd* be perfect. And this spot was perfect too. He'd checked on the internet before they'd set off. The rivers were full of otter sightings after years of clean-up programmes. Otters and their complex, chattering families. It was the families his father had loved the most, the way they looked after one another. It gives hope, he'd told Jake, when otters come back to a river.

Safe in his hide, Jake quietly unwrapped an egg sandwich. You can't go wrong with an egg sandwich. Lunch had been toast and beans but that was hours ago and he was hungry again. Tomorrow they'd have to go shopping for more supplies but at least they had bread, butter and eggs. He smiled and bit his sandwich, and put the fantasy of the competition to the back of his mind to focus on the river.

Nothing was happening. The stuffiness of the hide made him drowsy and an image of the comb flashed into his head.

Elizabeth was still sulking, he knew. Not even he could understand what had happened so how could he expect his sister to? He really *had* just freaked. As soon as he'd found out she'd taken it, and he only found out because she'd dropped her bag in the filling station and it had fallen out with all her other junk, he'd gone – what did Elizabeth call it? – *ballistic*! He'd called her every name he could think of and snatched it off the floor, as if the only thing that mattered was the comb.

When their mother came rushing out of the public toilets threatening to bang their heads together, Jake spewed out some angry rubbish about Elizabeth before he stormed off to fume on a bench outside the burger bar. He could hear the stifled row in the background and knew Elizabeth, angry and embarrassed amongst all the strangers, was close to tears. But he didn't really care. The rest of the journey, short as it was, had been unbearable.

What was it about the comb? It was just a *thing*. A thing from his father, but even then, not really; it was in a box of things his grandfather had left Jake's father when he'd died. An odd assortment: a jet marble, a small book of random words, a vial of sea-water (Jake had opened and sniffed it) a posy of dried but perfectly formed flowers (daisies, flag and baby's breath), a leaf carved out of wood. And the comb.

And now, because it was one of those things that had to be passed on, Jake owned the box. He'd had it for more than a year now. A year three months ago.

It was made of thin, four-plied wood, deep red and shiny as chestnuts. The lid was hinged and had a brass clasp. It was lined with green velvet soft as spring moss. And that was all. It had no markings, no decorations. No secret drawers – Jake had checked it over enough times to be sure of that. It was just a handsome box about the size of a chocolate box with a mess of items inside.

Jake had been drawn to the comb. A curious looking thing, about eight inches long, half comb-head, half handle. The head had once been white but was now creamy yellow and its teeth were so finely spaced you couldn't even force a thumb nail between them without the risk of snapping one or the other. He hadn't tried using it – it looked sharp, and anyway his hair was too short. The whole head had been carved, perfectly carved, from an ancient piece of bone or antler, but it was flat as any comb could be.

The handle was even more unusual. Where it joined the blade there was no seam. It was as if the two materials had bonded together naturally: no scorch marks, no filing scratches. There was a small symbol, a circle bisected by an outlined arrow, covering the join, but that was all. The handle was pointed and plain. And it was made of stone. Jake didn't know what kind – he wasn't a born geologist – but it was smooth as if it had been weathered rather than sculptured. It reminded him of the tip of a finger.

He'd been given the box three days after his father's funeral when he helped his mother sort through his father's office. She'd found a cardboard box of knick-knacks: a painting Jake had made, a nursery rhyme Elizabeth had written, a stack of letters from his grandfather. And the wooden box.

Jake had taken out a couple of the handscrawled letters, then put them away waiting for a day when he was really bored. Then he'd started on the junk in the box. He'd asked his mother, Lucy, about it a few days later.

'Your dad...' she said, stirring spaghetti sauce for supper, '...had a strange relationship with your grandfather. He could be a tough old beggar when he wanted to be. Stubborn. And your dad, well, so could he. I don't remember a wooden box though. Anything in it?'

Jake had mumbled something about junk, and his mother had smiled not unkindly, and said, 'That'd be about right. He liked collecting odd stuff, your dad. Here put these on the table.' And she'd passed him four large, white china plates.

There was the briefest moment that lasted three lifetimes. Jake carefully took the top plate and gave it back to his mother.

'We only need three, Mam,' he said gently.

Lucy looked small, badly coloured in. She laughed, half-embarrassed and said, 'Of course. Yes.'

That all seemed like it was a century ago. And now they were in the Peak district for six weeks. Their first holiday since the funeral. Jake had brought the box and the letters with him, he didn't really know why. And he'd forgotten about the comb.

Until today.

Now, he chewed on his bottom lip and dismissed any thoughts of combs, then stretched his cramped spine. Except for the midges, and the occasional brown bird, there was nothing to photograph yet. He stifled a yawn. It was so warm–

What was that?!

Jake flicked the camera round to the water's far edge.

Rustling.

Heavy.

Loud.

Otters?

He pressed the shutter automatically then stopped, listening closely for the chatter of otters.

Ten seconds, thirty, almost a whole minute.

Not even a glimpse of a tail. He peered through the camera lens. He *had* heard something, seen the leaves moving in the light. But... there wasn't anything there.

He realized he was holding his breath and started to let it out in slow silence. Maybe he'd imagined it then? He was hot, sleepy; sometimes you did imagine things– *That! There!*

What was that*?*

In the rushes. He saw something! A glimpse!

Grey. Golden? Big! Click! Click, click, click! Big!

The sound of running, then the heavy flap of beating wings. Click!

And it was gone.

Jake ran down to the river. Broken rush canes scattered fluff into the air and water. The ground had been flattened. Jake patted it – it was as warm as a dry stone wall in summer.

He pulled out his phone and checked his apps for what he might have seen. Not a heron; too white. A buzzard? Much too big. An eagle? Not this far down the country. What the hell else? Large. Golden. Can fly. His phone was out of answers. Who else could he ask?

Dad would have known, he said to himself. *And he'd have got the photo. He would have.*

Putting his phone away, he took his father's watch out of his top pocket. Its round face was white under the trees' gloom. Its numbers, luminous and glowing faintly golden, showed the time as a quarter to five. But the second hand had stopped moving.

Jake held the watch up to his ear. He shook it. Held it up again. Not even the faintest tick. This is weird, Jake said to the watch, I only wound you up this morning.

He realized he was holding his breath again. He listened. There was no sound. No birds, no river, no aeroplanes, no distant tractors.

True silence.

But Jake could hear the din of his blood pounding through his skull. If lonliness was a sound, this is what it would sound like.

Then, the ticking of his father's watch and the noises flooded in.

'What just happened?' Jake said out loud, and even the sound of his own voice made him jump. Nothing answered. Did he really expect it to? He ran back to the hide, and packed up his things as quickly as possible leaving nothing but the shelter to say he'd been there.

But what *else* had been there?

He slung his bag over his shoulder and looked up nervously, then set off, thinking about the warm depression in the reeds and the exposed camera film on its reel waiting to be developed.

'So we're being civilized again, are we?' Lucy said sweetly as she poured water into three glasses. Her children sat down, opposite one another. Jake looked unusually distracted and Elizabeth still had her earphones clamped firmly in her ears. Their mother tugged some kitchen towel off the roll and passed it over to them for napkins.

'Made up yet?' she added. The children shrugged and nodded, glancing at each other before picking up their forks and starting on the chips and egg in front of them. Lucy sat down, mimicked their shrugs and reached for the brown sauce.

'I thought we were having pizza today,' said Jake hopefully.

'I've not found a number, yet. We'll have pizza tomorrow. After I've looked around a bit more.'

Lucy smiled and looked at her children. It was all good, she thought. They fought. They made up. It never lasted long, neither the fighting nor the truces, but that was fine; they were teenagers. Hers. And Bill's. Now just hers...

Lucy watched Jake polishing off his chips. He eats like a horse that boy, no – like an elephant! Why isn't he fat? He's like his dad that way. Bill could eat anything and stayed skinny as a rake. Look at Elizabeth, just like me, barely eating and working too hard.

Jake wiped his plate with a thick slice of bread and licked his thumb. Lucy studied him. No, Jake's not skinny, he's – what's the word? an old word – *lean*. Yes, lean. Lean means underneath it all he's tough. And in some ways he was very tough; he could lift most things – he'd lugged the furniture around like it was for a doll's house. And he had stamina too. How many times had he gone out on a trip with his dad and come back in the evening practically carrying him? People were always surprised by how strong Jake was. But strength is hard to measure.

Lucy remembered how quiet he'd grown after his father's death. And then came the time with all the truanting, and when he'd stopped his karate classes, the ones Bill had insisted on. Jake had been good at them. He'd made fighting look easy; he was so calm he almost floated.

Bill had wanted his son to be prepared for anything, but in truth he was worried about bullying at school. He was always worrying about the boy. As if he needed to protect him. But he needn't have worried, Jake was fine. He got on with everybody. He was easy to like. But after the funeral, Lucy thought she could see anger under her son's skin; she could certainly see it behind his eyes.

He'd said it wasn't fair. He'd screamed it.

It wasn't fair. How could it be? They were just children…

Lucy swallowed and looked at her son now as he mopped up the last bit of egg yolk on his plate and, still chewing, asked if there was going to be any pudding. She smiled.

'There's some cake in the fridge, but wait until your sister's finished first.' Lucy pointed to her daughter's half-finished plate, then flicked her long fringe out of her eyes.

'Bett, have you got any hairgrips? My fringe's getting too long.'

Elizabeth, her earphones dangling around her neck, reached behind her head and pulled out a thin, silver pin with one hand. She passed it over to her mother and continued eating the last of her chips.

'Here, borrow this one. What sort of cake?' she added.

'Ta. Plain cake,' Lucy mumbled, the hairpin wedged between her teeth as she pulled back her fringe with both hands. 'There's cream too if you want it.'

Jake took the cake out of the fridge and three small plates from the draining board by the sink.

'You done?' he asked his sister. 'Clear up then and I'll get the cream.'

'Any custard?' asked Elizabeth.

'No,' answered Lucy. 'Honestly, you'd have custard for breakfast if I let you. You're lucky I brought cream.'

'You can't have this kind of cake without custard, though!' laughed Elizabeth, pulling a face. 'I mean, euww!'

Lucy passed her empty plate over to her daughter, who took it to the old stone sink, and wiped some crumbs from the table with her hand.

'Yes you can,' she said, 'you have *cream*. Anyway, when I was a kid we had plain cake on its own or with butter.'

'Yeah, but custard wasn't invented when you wa' a kid, Mam,' said Jake, thickly slicing the square cake. 'Who wants a big bit?'

'Me!' squealed Elizabeth, waving both hands in the air.

'No surprise there, then,' he said and passed his sister a plate full of cake dripping with cream. He held the knife up. 'Mam?'

'I'll have half of that, love, no, a bit less... perfect...'

For any passing stranger looking in, it *was* perfect – a homely, normal family scene.

Outside the large kitchen windows, rain started to fall, readying itself for a proper summer storm. In the hedges bordering the garden something moved low to the ground, and snorted. Then it turned away from the window and left the perfect scene of a family happily finishing its evening meal. Thunder rumbled and it sounded like a thousand wings beating in tandem. Then soft rain began to fall.

⊘

The storm was heavy and noisy, and Jake kept dozing off then waking up. He'd asked for the attic room because it was furthest away from Elizabeth's incessant music, but the bed was little more than a camp bed. The mattress was inflatable, and he was sure it had a slow puncture. He'd see if he could bring up a decent bed tomorrow. Now, he'd just have to put up with it.

He turned onto his back, trying to get comfortable. Rain belted the roof as though it was cardboard and not slate at all.

Jake sighed and beat up his pillow once more.

The weather here was wrong. Jake had slept through hundreds of thunderstorms without so much as a grunt from him, but this one? The rhythm was messed up. The lightning and thunder didn't know what they were doing – either both came at the same time or they zagged and crashed independently of one another. And *that* isn't how it works in nature! Thunder comes out of lightning – one after the other – everyone knows that! Everyone except the weather here!

A streak of lightning seared across Jake's closed eyelids. He growled. It must be, what three, four o'clock? He leaned over to the small bedside table for his father's watch. It was working perfectly now. In fact, it seemed shinier and its tick was louder than it had been. Loud and healthy, each *tock* following its *tick* like, well, clockwork.

Reluctant to turn on the light, Jake fumbled around in the dark, patting the surface of the rickety table and half expecting it to collapse just like the bed was doing.

His watch was missing.

He fumbled some more. The only things he'd put on the table were a glass of water, an ugly brass lamp, a book, and his watch.

Where was it!? He'd put it down safely on top of a book he'd found downstairs – old, cloth-bound and musty smelling, all about the history of the cottage and the Peaks. *Where* was his father's watch?!

More lightning. In the strips of light from the random flashes, he fumbled for the brass chain of the ancient lamp and pulled hard screwing up his eyes to save them from pain.

He opened them slowly but still couldn't see the watch anywhere. His stomach started to turn – *I can't have lost Dad's watch, I* can't *have!* – he felt a thick heat rising in his chest, and panic took hold of him.

It wasn't the *only* thing he had of his father's but it was the most *important*. It was the Watch. The one they'd take out on trips together. The one that told them when it was time to eat, time to leave, time for Jake to have a bath, to go to bed. It was the watch that was always there, and even when one blue leather strap wore so thin it snapped it didn't stop his father taking it everywhere with him. 'I'll have to sort this strap out' he kept saying, but never did.

When Jake was four, his father had put the watch on the boy's wrist, tightening the straps so the buckle folded back on itself. The watch's face was almost as big as Jake's hand.

And now he'd lost it.

Jake looked behind the table knowing he was wasting his time. Time. Hah! He rooted through the rest of the objects and knocked the book onto the floor. And there, as if marking the page, was Jake's watch.

He breathed out deeply and laughed, relieved. A bookmark! He must have put it in when he'd finished reading. He'd been more tired than he thought. He picked up the book and read the page that the watch had been guarding. He turned the book over.

Stone House.

On the worn-out spine was a small symbol Jake could almost make out as a circle with a line running through it. A publisher's logo, probably.

Jake shut the book and put it away. He slid the watch under his pillow for safety, and clicked off the light. His hand closed over the watch's round face and he found himself stroking its strap with this thumb. The gentle ticking somehow drowned out the persistent hammering of the rain as he settled into the deflating bed. He started to nod off, slowly turning a passage from the book over and over in his head like a strange, tuneless lullaby: *Geological composition of area. 1). Carboniferous Limestone...*

CHAPTER 2

*T*he cave roof dripped water onto the carved shapes at his feet. He closed his ancient eyes. The day had been filled with busyness. He had seen enough. He was certain.

This one was his.

Darkness, unctuous and ripe, clung to the cave walls, barely relieved by the soft phosphorescence of prehistoric algae.

He hunkered down and mumbled something low and terrible. The darkness, as if looking for somewhere to hide, slunk back into the cave, seeping into what cracks it could find. The algae glowed.

The gloom comforted him.

He circled his cave once, twice, like a cat beside a fire, until he was satisfied that he was alone. Then he lay down and slept.

Jake lay in bed, sloping to one side, his feet uncovered. The mattress was almost flat now. When he moved it was like moving in jelly. His head ached and his neck was stiff. He could hear the noises of the new day downstairs: Elizabeth's hair-drier, the cottage's ancient kettle whistling on the stove, his mother chattering on the landline.

He should get up, but he felt dog-tired.

It wasn't just the rain, the mattress or the panic over the watch (once he'd finally settled down he was out like a light) it was the dreams. Hundreds, it seemed, of childish dreams.

Dreams he'd not had for years.

In one there was an invisible thing chasing him through the forests until he slipped through a fissure in the path and ended up, bruised, bleeding and covered in slime, in an underground cave the size of a warehouse.

In another he was in a house he didn't recognise and his grandfather went from room to room opening every door he could find while his father followed him in anger, slamming the doors shut in Jake's face. Everywhere was pitch black and the only light came from a flaming torch his grandfather carried.

Dreams melting into each other. And always a presence: not exactly terrifying, but formidable. Jake could feel it in everyday things: a large rock on a cliff, a derelict concrete building.

The dream that woke him – made him drag himself from his sleep – was an old one. He'd been plagued by it until he was seven. He stretched his aching back and tried to put it out of his mind, but images – fire, darkness, the blotted out sun – flashed like the snapping of his camera. They seemed so real, so *now*!

– He's on holiday with his father. They're walking in the hills. The sun shines. They're comfortable, happy, chatting. Then Jake hears a loud snort behind him. Bill hears it too. They turn and see, blotting out the sun, the enormous shape of a mediaeval dragon, its eyes flaming, its skin black and slimy. It fills the air with smoke. It charges.

Bill grabs his son's hand and they run as fast as they can. But the boy stumbles and falls. The dragon flicks its head, lifts off in one bound and soars up. Bill stands guard, one hand tugging at his son, the other shielding his eyes as he tries to keep the dragon in sight. Jake almost makes it to his knees before the creature lunges like a falcon and, snorting fire, wrenches the screaming man from his son. And lifts him over the trees. Leaving the boy bawling and desperate. And lost. –

Jake had woken up with his throat dry from trying to scream, his eyes sore and itchy. For a minute he'd expected his father to come running into his room. But this *wasn't* his room. This was the attic of some old stone house in the Peak district. And his father wouldn't come running.

The dream had been so familiar – he couldn't tell you how many times he'd dreamt it before – but this time it was wrong. He should have been a boy of three or four, not his own age now. And the hills. In the dreams he'd had as a child he'd never known where they were, but these ones he recognized. They were the same hills he'd passed yesterday on his way home from the river.

⌖

'You look tired, are you okay?' asked Jake's mother as her son slouched into the kitchen. 'It's a bit late for you, isn't it? I expected you to be up with the larks, snapping away...' Lucy smiled brightly and put a fresh pot of hot tea on the table.

'I din't sleep well,' Jake growled, slumping onto a chair as his mother rummaged through the cupboards.

'Where did we put the bread?' Lucy said to the air, to her son she said, 'Was it the rain? God, it was loud wasn't it?'

'Left cupboard,' said Jake numbly, slouching over the table with his head resting on one hand. 'Yeah, it was the rain,' he said.

'Oh, ta. Now, jam, jam...?' murmured Lucy, opening the same cupboard doors. Jake smiled and poured himself a cup of tea from the pot.

'Fridge,' he said. 'Door, top shelf, next to the butter.'

Lucy nodded and took the butter, jam and marmalade from the fridge door. She slipped two slices of bread into the toaster and pressed the button down twice before the bread stayed put. 'You're a star,' she said sweetly. 'What are you up to today?'

'Not much,' said Jake. The tea was good, he thought cradling the cup. A bit hot, but good. Strong. It had been ages since they'd had tea from a real pot. His father had loved his tea from a pot. Jake looked for a tea-towel to use as a cosy. He couldn't see one, and gave up.

'I thought I'd swap the bed in my room,' he said, yawning. 'That mattress's got a slow puncture.'

'It's an airbed?' Lucy said, glancing over her shoulder. She found the honey in the cupboard and brought it to the table. The toast popped behind her. She flicked it onto a plate. The butter melted in yellow blobs as she ran a knife across it.

'Yeah. On a camp-bed.'

'I'll talk to the agency people. We've paid enough for this place, we should at least all have decent beds.' Lucy filled the toaster again.

'It's okay,' Jake said. 'It'll take ages to get someone to come and sort it, don't worry. I'll get Bett to help me. She's forgiven me, I think. Afterwards we can go down town.' Jake pulled a face at the thought of shopping with his sister. 'We can take the bed from the room next to yours,' he added.

'Why don't you just move rooms?'

'I like the attic. It's big. Quiet. We'll manage. It won't be heavy – it's only a single bed.'

Lucy looked doubtfully at her son, her eyebrows raised.

'Our Elizabeth? Move a whole bed? Into an attic?'

Jake shrugged, his sleepy eyes sparkling a little.

'I'd pay good money to see that!' said Lucy, laughing as she passed her son a slice of jammy toast. 'Here, eat this. If you do go in town, can you get me an ink cartridge from that stationers? Mine's nearly run out.'

'Alright,' said Jake through mouthfuls of toast.

'Thanks. How're you getting to town?' Lucy filled the toaster again and slid onto a chair.

'There's a bus every half hour. I saw a sign yesterday.'

'Okay. Good.' Lucy bit down on her toast and chewed thoughtfully. Eventually she said, 'Y'know there's a couple of bikes in the back-shed?'

Now it was Jake's turn to look doubtful.

'Yeah? Really? Bett move a bed *and* ride a bike? You'd have to pay *her* good money to do that.' He finished his toast and took another from the small pile.

'Right,' laughed Lucy.

Jake liked it when his mother laughed. She was doing it a little more nowadays. It was as if she'd forgotten how to and it was starting to come back.

'What will you do in town?'

'Not much. Have a look round. I need to take in a film in to be developed. Check out the library.'

'On holiday?'

'I found a book about this place. Its history and stuff. I thought it might be interesting to find out more.'

Lucy looked around the room and smiled, nodding. 'It's special this place, Jake. Look at how it's built. It's almost all stone. Even the kitchen counter's marble. And the sink's stone too, look.'

Jake did so. Lucy was right. Except for the wooden beams and a bit of an extension, it was all stone.

'Anyway,' said Lucy, breaking the spell. 'You'll just end up shopping, it *is* your sister you know. If there isn't a New Look or a Claire's, then the world'll explode.'

'Yeah!' Jake tutted. 'Make up and shoes! Girls!'

'Get you, you old man!' teased Lucy before draining her mug. Behind her the door opened and her daughter, under a haze of hairspray and teenage perfume, bounced in.

'Who's an old man? Oh, you? Well, yeah, of course. Born old you were,' she said with a casual tone.

'Do you always ask your own questions then answer them?' asked Jake smartly.

'Only way I'll get an intelligent answer,' replied his sister, her smile so sweet she made cherubs blush.

'Ah, here's my lovely *schlafmutze*! Did you sleep well?' Lucy reached out and wrapped her arms around Elizabeth's waist. The girl struggled then finally gave in.

'All right, yeah. I've slept better... *why*?'

'No need to be suspicious, I'm just asking... Anyway, I'm sure you've got a ton of stuff to do today...' Lucy was grinning as she released her daughter. She nodded to Jake, placed her mug and plate in the sink and headed out the door. 'I'll leave both of you to it. Bett, there's toast or cereal, whatever you want. The honey's nice.'

'Ta, I'll just have a coffee.'

'No coffee! It's tea or juice. Or hot chocolate. Jake, don't let her have coffee. I mean it! This is not some American soap!'

'*You* drink coffee!'

'Grown up!' called Lucy over her shoulder. Elizabeth pulled a face at her mother's retreating back.

'I saw that! Eyes in the back of my head as well, remember?!' And then she was gone, retreating into her makeshift office.

'Huh,' said Elizabeth sulkily, reaching for the coffee jar.

'You can't have that,' said Jake seizing it from her resisting hands.

'Food fascist!'

'Eyup! Watch what you're saying!' he said sharply, then softer, 'Here, look, I'll get you a nice cuppa tea.'

Jake tested the sides of the tea-pot for heat. It was...warm...ish. He scooped a spoon of sugar up on a plastic spoon and dropped it into the cup, then added the milk slowly.

Elizabeth teamed cornflakes into a bowl and stared at her brother.

'Alright,' she said. 'What're you *after*?'

'Why do I have to be after anything?'

'When did you last make me tea?'

She had a point. 'I need a favour,' Jake said simply.

'...And *there* it is. What is it and what's in it for me?'

'I'll take you to the pickies.' said Jake stirring the tea casually.

Elizabeth thought about it for less than a second. 'Okay, deal,' she said. She held a spoon up to her mouth and shovelled in cornflakes. 'Wmssplwsizzzihh?'

'Eh?' asked Jake.

'I 'ed, wha'izzzih?' she swallowed and scooped up more cornflakes.

'D'you mean 'what is it?'?'

'Huhummm... wha'izzzit?' She took a long swig from the mug of tea. 'Urgh, this is cold!'

Jake stood up and said, 'Nuke it then.'

Elizabeth looked suspiciously at the hulking microwave pushed to the back of the kitchen counter.

'Does that thing actually work? It looks ancient,' she said.

Nervously she opened the door, put the mug on the tray, closed it and turned the large white knob to 'drinks'. Jake left the room before anything could explode.

'It is,' he said, then over his shoulder added, 'See you in a bit.'

Elizabeth looked at the microwave and pleaded, 'please don't blow up.' She pushed the 'on' button and crossed her fingers. It buzzed and whirred. In the hallway, Jake fiddled with his camera.

'Eyup!' Elizabeth shouted through the wall. 'What's this favour? Jake? ...I said, what's this favour? I'm not climbing anything, y'know! No trees or mountains!'

'Don't worry,' Jake shouted. 'We can do it when you've had your cornflakes.'

'Do what? Jake!? Jaaaake!'

The microwave pinged. The tea was hot.

Elizabeth was sulking. As far as she was concerned, it had been not so much a favour as a part-time labourer's job. She'd bent her finger back and two of her nails had broken down to the quick. They'd had to dismantle some of the bed frame to get it into the attic, and they only had one screwdriver and a rusted hammer. Elizabeth reminded Jake about this at every opportunity. And even made up some opportunities to be sure.

The bus was old and smelled of diesel and socks. A drinks can was wedged down between their seats and it was sticky and gathering fluff. They changed seats again. Jake had heard of the phrase 'round the houses' but he didn't know what it meant until now. The road wound like a millipede and every so often the bus shook and grumbled in and out of potholes the size of open graves.

'It was a very bad winter.' This came from an old woman sitting in front of them. 'That's why the potholes are so bad, love.'

Jake and Elizabeth just nodded as politely as possible.

'Yes,' the woman went on. 'It freezes the road and then the juggernauts come and they're too heavy for it. It breaks up, look.'

Jake looked to where she was pointing.

'Yeah, that's a big one,' he said, absently. He caught the woman's eye and she smiled.

'It gets very cold here, in winter. Good job you've come for summer,' she laughed. 'The weather's changing, love. Everyone says so – ooh, this is my stop.' She pressed the button, hoisted herself off the seat and waited for the bus to stop with a judder. Its doors stuck half-way open so she had to squeeze through.

'Bye,' she said happily.

'Bye,' said Jake.

He watched her as she shuffled along the path then reached down to dislodge something from her shoe. Then she carried on, talking to herself.

'She's a bit weird,' whispered Elizabeth.

'She probably just wanted a chat.'

They left it at that and sat back, chatting aimlessly until the bus pulled into the station. Elizabeth had almost forgiven Jake, again. For now.

Jake was bored. He'd dropped his film in at the local chemists, and found out it would be three or four days before he got it back. He wasn't sure he could wait that long!

He'd forgotten how boring shopping with Elizabeth really was. She could spend hours raking through rails of brightly coloured tea-shirts and jeans. And anything with sparkles on it. And he'd ended up carrying most of it!

'Okay,' he said, stopping opposite a stone building. 'I need to pop to the library over there–'

'– Oh God, no, Jaaake. We're on holiday!'

'Jeeze! I've just been traipsing after you for the last million years!

'This is because of *your* favour, remember?' said Elizabeth hotly.

Jake did a quick scan of the remaining shops and said as calmly as he could muster, 'Listen, you go and look in whatever shops you haven't emptied out already –' Elizabeth stuck out her tongue – 'And I'll get you at that coffee shop over there in an hour. Yeah?' he added.

'That's not long,' Elizabeth whined.

'It'll do. Now, here,' Jake took out his wallet and selected a note.

'A fi-ver!' moaned Elizabeth derisively. Jake didn't know the word 'derision' but he did know the word 'ungrateful', and as he tried to snatch the money back out of his sister's hand, she clutched it to her.

'Thanks. Can I have a coffee?' she said.

'No, you know you can't,' Jake called, walking over the road. 'An hour, okay? *And no coffee!*'

The library building was an architectural mixture of old, re-built and add-on. The main archway was huge and carved from limestone. Jake didn't like fussy things and he wasn't big on ornamentation, so he liked the archway - simple and elegant. He walked through it and felt curiously safe. If he'd had his mother's eye for detail, he might have noticed, at floor level, a carved mark: a circle bisected by an arrow.

He awoke suddenly from a dream-filled sleep.

Energy. There was energy stirring. Threshold!

He heard the drip, drip from the cavern roof echo as he uncoiled his body and stirred.

31

'Hey, you'll never guess what I found out!' Jake threw down a folder of photocopied pages with a satisfying thwack. Ordnance Survey maps and photographs peeked out, free of the gloom of books and archive drawers.

The library had been a gold mine and Jake's excitement glowed like gold-dust. His sister looked up from her magazine and looked at him as if nothing could be more interesting than Hollywood.

'You're late!' she said sweetly, sipping her coffee.

'Yeah, I'm sorry. I tried to call but I din't have a signal. They kicked me out! Early closing on Mondays. Mad! Anyway, I ran out of photocopying change and – Eyup, are you drinking *coffee*?'

'Ha ha... what's a few minutes between friends, eh?' Elizabeth hurried. 'So what have you found out then?'

'This place... this town...' Jake spread his arms wide and paused for effect.

Elizabeth rolled her eyes. 'What about it?'

'Granddad built it!'

Jake grinned like a magician showing a new trick. Ta-daahhh...

'What? Have *you* been drinking coffee?' laughed Elizabeth.

'No, seriously! Most of it, anyway. Cool, in't it?' said Jake.

'Which one?' asked Elizabeth. Jake's train of thought was derailed.

'This one,' he said pointing down at the pages.

Elizabeth sighed. It wasn't so hard to understand her, was it?

'Which *Granddad*, stupid. Not which town.'

'Oh. Oh right,' Jake barely noticed his sister's pained look. 'Granddad Stanley.'

'*Dad's* dad?'

'Yeah...'

'Dad's *dad*? The one in Scotland.'

'Yeah. Hang on...'

Jake went to fetch himself a hot chocolate and a muffin the size of his fist, leaving his sister mouthing like a goldfish *Dad's dad...?* When he returned, Elizabeth was riffling through his papers.

There in black and white, newly photocopied, was the stone

archway of the library. The picture was from an old newspaper article and the archway looked smaller than in real life, as if the photograph had somehow stripped it of something, something like power.

Elizabeth started to read the article. It didn't mention her grandfather anywhere, which seemed somehow wrong to her, but she couldn't say why. It was all about the opening of the library's new wing.

'What was he?' she asked, thoughtfully. 'An architect?'

'No,' said Jake. 'Not an architect. I mean he *literally* built it. He was a mason. A master mason.'

Elizabeth looked up from the paper to see her brother breaking up chunks of muffin and shovelling a piece into his mouth.

'What...' she said, 'like with the handshakes and stuff. All the secret messages in church windows and things?'

'Wha?' said Jake, the muffin sticking to his tongue.

'Y'know... in that film? With the priests and the masons and all that running all over the place. The Illiterati!' Elizabeth was getting almost as excited as Jake; she could now imagine a holiday filled with intrigue and dark strangers and near-death experiences... adventure! With *her* at the heart of it!

'Noooo,' said Jake, slowly. 'A proper mason, not a *freemason*. He built things out of stone. With his hands. And it's *Illuminati*, you numpty.'

Elizabeth's interest dropped like a stone in a pond.

'Oh.' she said, flatly. 'Is that all?'

Jake faltered... wasn't it *enough*?

'He carved things too. Out of stone.'

Elizabeth pulled a soap opera face and pursed her lips.

'So?' she said and sipped her coffee. A thick layer of froth spilled down the side of her oversized cup.

'So?' Jake said, incredulously. 'So, *this* place, *this* town, is where *our dad* was born! Where he grew up!'

His sister's eyes widened. She tilted her head, thinking.

'Here? But I thought he was born in Scotland.'

'So did I,' interrupted Jake. 'But I think he must have just studied there or summats.'

'But Granny May and Granddad Stanley lived in Edinburgh. We had holidays there! In summer!'

'I know, I know but when they were younger they lived *here*. Look.'

Jake pulled out a page filled with meticulous columns of names and addresses. The hand-writing was delicate and precise. *84 Long Lane: Stanley Jacob and Elizabeth May Walker and their two year old son, William.*

Jake grinned at his sister who was squinting to read the writing.

'Parish records. Everywhere has them,' he said.

'*Why*, though? And I mean, why didn't he tell us, not why are there Parish records, before you say anything,' said Elizabeth.

Jake closed his mouth, then said in a careful tone, 'I don't know. There's some more. See this...' He pulled out a sheet filled with odd symbols:

⊘	†	≠
Walker	Mason	Williamson
↗	Φ	◈
Stanyer	Lewis	Perry
✳	∿	₵
Sawyer	Manton	Wilson
⁂	▲	Δ
Eaton	Carver	Macun

Elizabeth looked blankly at the page. Squiggles and names that meant nothing to her.

'Seriously, *why* didn't Dad say something?' she said.

Jake forced the symbols under her nose. 'Focus!' he said.

Elizabeth came back from her private thoughts, took a hold of the paper and held it up to her face.

'What *are* they?' she said, peering curiously at the symbols. 'And what are all these names for?'

'Recognize any?' said Jake, a tinge of glee in his voice. Elizabeth bit her bottom lip and looked over the table again.

'Well, that's our name, there, and there's Williams and Jones and Wilson, but so what. They're common names.'

She passed the sheet back to Jake. His eyes glistened.

He was beaming.

'No, and yes. That name. That name *there*,' he said stabbing the paper with his finger, 'is *not* common...'

'There's loads of Walkers, Jake.'

'Yeah, but that one *right* there is *us!*' Jake's face split in two.

'Us?'

'Yeah,' said Jake. 'They're *us*. These are *mason marks*.'

'So, what are they when they're at home?'

'They're like a signature. All masons have them. They carve them on buildings and walls. And this one, *this one* is ours – well, Granddad Stanley's.'

'Signatures?'

'Yeah.'

'Like graffiti tags?' said Elizabeth bluntly.

'No! I mean, yeah a bit – no, look, stop fregging about! This is important!'

'*Why* is it? I mean, yeah it's important that dad never told us anything about living here, but *this*? These marks? *They're* not important.'

Jake deflated and looked at the pages in his hands. Couldn't she see this was exciting and puzzling and important? That it *meant* something, even though he didn't know yet what it was? Couldn't she *tell* that with this, the holiday might not be quite so empty – without dad being here to show us around and take us out – and didn't she know that this – finding out about dad's childhood – is a mystery we can solve?

'I– I don't know why it's important,' he said, flatly. 'I just know that it is.'

Elizabeth, for all her eleven years of wisdom and need to torture her brother at every opportunity, knew when to stop. She finished her now cold coffee, took a bite out of what was left of Jake's muffin and looked at the pages.

'Okay, this one?' she said, an encouraging glimmer in her eyes. 'This is Granddad Stanley's, yeah?'

'Yeah. There's one on the library doorway,' said Jake. 'I saw it in a photo and went to check it out.'

'What's it meant to be?' Elizabeth peered closer, 'A circle with an arrow through it?' Her finger automatically traced and re-traced the lines of the mark. They felt warm on the cool, dry page.

'Yeah, it looks like it doesn't it?' said Jake. 'It's limestone. The archway. And he did marble too. Carving circles must have been hard – these other mason marks are mainly straight lines.'

'What for? Why an arrow on a circle?' said Elizabeth ignoring her brother. 'Why not a 'W'?'

'I dunno,' said Jake. 'I don't know *everything*. Maybe he was an archer.'

A sudden thought hit Elizabeth, 'Maybe his *name* was Archer!' she said excitedly.

'Are you taking the piss or just being stupid? He's Dad's dad. His name's Walker.'

'Oh, yeah,' said his sister, deflated, then, 'Aah, yeah but he might have changed his name!'

'Why? Why would he do that?' asked Jake, not really wanting an answer. Elizabeth gave him one anyway.

'Maybe he was wanted for murder or grand theft!' she said in a triumphant tone.

'Wha – what! Jeeez, Bett! He wasn't wanted for *murder*.'

'You don't know that!' she answered.

'Yes, I do! This is Granddad Stanley, not Jack the Ripper! He *wasn't* a murderer. I don't know about the arrow, but I do know about Granddad Stanley and his name's definitely Walker!' Jake said stabbing the name on the Parish records.

Elizabeth shrugged a little non-committal shrug, handed her

brother the pages of mason marks, and said, 'I s'pose so.'

'Yeah,' said Jake, firmly.

There was a long and awkward pause. Eventually Elizabeth, dabbing up crumbs from Jake's plate, said, 'Remember that birthday cake he made me with glitter on?'

'Yeah.'

He did remember it, it was the year their grandmother had died and their grandfather had wanted Elizabeth to have the cake his wife would have baked.

'I loved that cake. It was yellow,' said Elizabeth, lost in the birthday.

'I know.'

'The glitter was gold.'

'Yeah, and there were candles too...'

'D'you think it was proper edible glitter?'

'Doesn't matter, it din't kill us,' said Jake.

Elizabeth started to laugh. 'I was only four. I don't remember him much, 'cept he smelt like our First Aid kit. And fresh air.'

Jake remembered the smell, chemical like burnt-out fireworks, but sweet as well. 'Yeah, yeah he did...'

Elizabeth broke the long moment with a bright. 'Maybe Mam'll know something?'

Jake dragged himself back from memories of sitting with his grandfather in his Edinburgh garden. Stanley had told stories and pointed out birds on the feeder. Normal, grandparent things. Nothing sinister, nothing untoward. He even carried mints in his pocket. Murderer... hah!

'Maybe,' said Jake. 'But, I don't want to ask Mam. Not yet.'

'Why not?'

Jake glanced down at the Parish records. He caught his sister's eye and said, 'Dad... y'know?'

Elizabeth nodded. 'Yeah. Dad.' The last moments of her father's life sneaked into her mind like a burglar in the night. She shook her head, blinked back a sudden prickle of tears and swallowed.

'Yeah. Anyroad,' she said, a catch in her throat, 'What's brought all this up? Why go to the library? You're on holiday.'

Jake, packing up the papers, scratched his ear and said, 'Mam asked me that this morning. I don't know. I was reading this book back at the cottage and I thought I could learn a bit more about the place.'

'What book?'

'Just a book I found on a shelf. It said something in it about the masons that built the house and how the stone was some special limestone, and it had a rough drawing of granddad's mark. Really rough. It din't mean anything this morning...'

'...does now.'

'Yeah. But this mark, right...' Jake said, picking up the last of the muffin.

'Yeah?'

'I've seen it before.'

'Yeah at the library, you said.'

'No, I mean *before* then.'

'Where,' asked Elizabeth. There was something strange in Jake's voice, a worried yet fascinated tone she'd never heard before.

'Remember those letters in dad's box?'

'Not really. You never showed 'em me.'

'I think this mark has something to do with them.'

Elizabeth puffed out her cheeks. 'How?'

'I dunno.' Jake bit his lips and pulled a random photograph from the pile. It was the library archway. 'And I've seen it somewhere else...'

'Where?' asked Elizabeth.

'On the comb.'

'What *comb*?' she asked, mystified, then, '*That* comb?!'

'Yeah,' said Jake staring at the mason mark on the library photograph. 'Its handle's made from stone, y'know.'

⊗

Sitting on the newly moved bed, Jake thought about his grandfather's letters.

When they got back, he'd spent hours pawing through the photocopies and the old book and, while he'd learned a fair bit about geology, the mason mark still bothered him.

Stifling a yawn, he glanced over to the bookshelves where the box skulked. Inside it was the comb, and the letters.

Jake had flicked through them one Sunday months ago when he'd been bored. He was still bored when he'd finished, so he'd put them away.

They were neatly written, neatly folded and on the whole said neat things. They asked tidy questions about his father's studies, and later his work, and later still Jake's mother. They asked a lot about Jake and his sister.

They were ordinary letters.

But for all their tidiness, the earlier ones were badly punctuated with capital letters randomly placed. On the later ones, the lines were double-spaced – a massive waste of paper – especially when the letters had lots to say and ran into pages. And most of them had lots to say.

Jake drowsily remembered his grandfather: a big, broad man who lived in Scotland with his wife. He'd been a caretaker in the local school until he'd retired early to look after Granny May. Jake always remembered him as a grey and blue mountain that went fishing and grew vegetables. A mountain with a voice to match. He'd tell Jake wild stories about the animals at the bottom of his garden – badgers and rats, foxes and stoats.

Jake loved the stories – foxes eating jam sandwiches and badgers taking peanuts out of his grandfather's hands – but he didn't love them nearly as much as the ones about dragons, or vampires, or cannibals and ghosts roaming Edinburgh's dark streets. They'd huddle together, sipping hot cocoa while Jake peered nervously at the fragile garden gate – the only thing that protected them from the monsters in the city.

He would ask, more often than not, if they were real.

'Aaah,' his grandfather would say, 'As real as like. What do you call real, lad? What *feels* real to you?' And before Jake could ever answer, his father would come out. There'd be a look between the men – nothing said – and the boy would be sent to bed.

Lying there, he'd listen to the whispered argument on the porch below his window. His father was always angry and his grandfather would always end by saying, 'There are things that must be known, Billy, *must* be known.'

⊘

He could feel him.

The companion was close by. He could feel him through the stones.

It was time.

A generation had passed and he had slept. No, not slept exactly. Waited. Was not wanted. Needed, yes, yet denied.

Now he was needed more than ever. This time he would not be denied.

He circled the cave like a tiger in a cage. Water dripped down the stalactites and stalagmites. He crouched low and lapped from their puddles. It tasted good. Strong. Cool.

His throat burned.

For millennia it had burned.

The natural yearning of fire restrained is a dangerous thing.

It will out. It will burn.

It will burn fiercely.

⊘

It was raining again. The storm had come on suddenly against the night. Jake had finally given in to reading the letters, and anyway he couldn't sleep with all the noise.

He'd laid out the pages in date order as best he could. Some overlapped one another on the duvet, some were in danger of falling to the floor. He noticed with satisfaction that each one was signed

40

with the mason mark and his grandfather's squiggle. But what was he missing? He didn't *get* it. He knew there was *something* here, he could feel it buzz like the taste of batteries, but what was it?

Maybe he was trying to make a mystery where none was to be found.

There was a soft knock on the door. He hadn't even heard the creak of the attic stairs. Jake jumped off the bed looking for something to cover the letters with. Stupid! He'd put them *on top* of the duvet!

The door opened slowly enough for Jake to grab it. He tried to look calm.

'Jeeze Bett, I thought it was Mam!'

Elizabeth pushed passed him casually and sat on the bed where he'd been sitting. She heard a comic *boing* of a mattress spring beneath her and gave a sort of facial shrug.

'Why? What you doing?' she asked, innocently.

'Nothing.' Jake looked down at the scrambled piles. 'I just don't want to upset her. This holiday's supposed to stop her thinking about Dad.'

Elizabeth's look was older than mountains. 'No it isn't,' she said quietly. 'It's just a holiday. She's not gunna stop thinking about Dad coz we're on holiday. None of us are. Are these the letters?'

'Yeah, these are 'em. There's something here, but I don't know what.'

Elizabeth examined her brother like he was some newly discovered insect held up to a magnifying glass by a Victorian biologist.

'There's something different about you,' she said, eventually. 'Since this afternoon.'

Jake's hand involuntarily moved up to his face. 'There's nothing wrong with me,' he said.

'There is. Not *wrong*, though, just... different. Like you've woken up or something... you're sort of... fizzy.'

'Shuddup, I'm not. I'm just a bit knackered.'

Elizabeth shrugged and smiled warmly. 'Hmmm... Forget it then. I'm probably imagining it, anyway, my mind's all...' She shook her hands at the sides of her head to indicate something electrical, and laughed.

'Now, these letters?' She looked briefly at the pages and said, 'I don't know about these ones with the gaps in the lines, but these ones here are in code.'

'Code?' Jake said, amazed.

'Yeah, a simple one too. I'm surprised you din't see it, look...' Elizabeth picked up a letter and read it aloud:

'dear son,

your mam and i are well. auld reekie...

'What's Auld Reekie?' Elizabeth interrupted herself.

'Old Scottish for Edinburgh,' answered Jake.

'Yeah? Huh...

'...auld reekie is cold but beautiful. the new house is very different from hOME. the garden looks like a bombsite, STONEs and rubbish everywhere, but the snow has abated for now and may will plant her garlic tonight. let's hope for More snow for a good croP...'

'Eh?' said Jake, 'That doesn't make sense 'may will plant'... shouldn't that be 'may *well* plant' or summats?'

'Granny May, you spoon! She'll plant garlic.'

'Oh. There's no capital letter,' muttered Jake. Elizabeth stared at him.

'Jake, shuddup and look...

'...she has already set some onions and will extend the vegetable patch in spring. i had to DRAG four bags of compost in yesterday. ON a nicer note, how is lucy? she's a lovely girl. WHY do you have to live so far away. WON'T YOU come and visit again? hope sheffield finds you well. i walked to the top of cAlton hill this morning. not an exacting walk but braCing enough in the winter air. may stayed at home and made stew and dumPlings. a good sTew IT was as well. you'd have enjoyed it. she got the cuts off the butcher round the corner. HE'S good with beef he had some brawn which we'll eat for tea tomorrow. i LOST my glasses again – YOU CAN say that again - but your mam HELPed me find them in THE shed. she wants to get me one of thoSE string things but I'll look a nARnEr and i'm NOT that BAD am i? Anyroad, that's all for now, sweet DREAms, love maM and dad (Stan and may).'

It didn't sound any different to Jake read aloud as when he read it himself.

'I don't get it. How is that code?' he said, taking the letter from his sister's unresisting fingers. 'It just sounds like a normal letter to me, a bit batty and cheery, but so what, he's writing to his son.'

Elizabeth sighed and took the letter back.

'Yes, but look at this,' she said pointing here and there to something on the page. 'You can't always see it because it's handwritten but he puts capital letters in odd places.'

'I *know*! *I* said that!' said Jake.

'That's the code, you numpty!' She slapped the paper with the back of her hand. Jake looked down at the writing.

'Oh. Okay, what does it say?'

'Erm, have you got a pen and some paper?'

Jake fumbled about in his bag found his sketchbook and a pencil. 'Here.'

'Right, then,' Elizabeth's eyes scanned the page. She made small marks on the paper, rubbing a letter out every so often. She went over the letter twice, making odd, tutting noises and muttering to herself.

'Are you ready? This is about it: *LIMESTONE IS IMPORTANT. DRAGON. WHY WON'T YOU ACCEPT THIS? HE'S LOST. YOU CAN HELP HIM. THESE ARE NOT BAD DREAMS.*'

Elizabeth looked up into Jake's mystified face. She was good at codes, always had been. Jake had been given a spy kit when he was ten and Elizabeth had cracked the codes in a day. She was only eight. It was the guitar music, Jake had decided. After all that was just another code – black notes on a page becoming sounds. He looked up at Elizabeth.

'What the hell does that mean?'

'I don't know!' said Elizabeth. '*Who's* lost?'

Jake shrugged.

'Well,' Elizabeth added. 'He says limestone's important. He was a mason, maybe he wanted dad to be a mason.'

'Yeah, but it's a bit of a weird thing to tell somebody in code, innit? I don't like your career choices. And what about 'dragon'? What dragon?'

It was Elizabeth's turn to shrug. 'A nickname? For dad?'

'Stupid nickname to call your son.'

'It's a bit of a stupid message all round... *who's* lost? And why can dad help him?'

'I bet it's a location. I bet there's a dragon in town – like a pub or a statue – and dad used to meet someone there, an old mate or somebody.'

'He sent it from Scotland, Jake, not here.'

'It dun't matter, it dun't matter...' said Jake excitedly, caught up in his own theories. 'Did granddad carve a dragon statue? A tombstone?'

Elizabeth threw her arms into the air, upsetting some of the letters. '*I don't know*, you're the one with all the family history!'

'I am, yeah!...' Jake skittered through the files and pictures of Stanley's buildings on his bed-side table. Not one of them had a dragon statue, not even in the cemetery.

Jake, deflated, took a deep breath and let it out slowly. He felt like he, himself, were made of stone. He rubbed his eyes; gritty and sore under his palm heels.

'Maybe it *was* in Scotland,' he yawned. 'Don't they have a dragon on the flag?'

'That's Wales,' said Elizabeth. She watched her brother crumple up from tiredness. 'Look, it's getting late, Jake. We'll have a look around in the morning,' she said, gently, as she helped him tidy up the letters. She left him putting the box on the shelf, and she crept down the attic stairs, careful not to make them creak.

Jake lay in the bed, exhausted. Outside the thunderstorm raged. He tried to sleep but it wouldn't come. His thoughts kept being pulled back to the letters stashed away in the box. And their mysterious, confusing messages.

CHAPTER 3

The mattress was much better than the air-bed – more inclined to be the same shape when Jake awoke in the morning as when he went to bed. Yet, he was agitated. Everyone else was still in bed, but he'd woken up too early and couldn't get back to sleep. He needed to calm himself down.

In the pre-morning gloom, he pulled on his clothes and boots and snuck downstairs and out the back door. The rain had stopped and a warm haze already furred the daylight over the fields. He marked out his steady pace waiting for the calm to come.

But it didn't come.

While he walked he felt his skin itching, a restlessness in his bones, his teeth grinding in his skull. He couldn't shake the feeling – under his feet and across his back – of something *present* as if he were being watched. But he was the only person around. Not even the farmers were up yet.

He passed a dry-stone wall and with some satisfaction, noticed how each stone perfectly fitted one another. He'd taken a course once, years ago with his father, so he knew the wall in front of him was made up of two solid layers with a gap down the centre where the stones don't meet. It would be packed and strengthened with little stones called *hearting* because they were the very heart of the wall.

Jake steadied himself against the rough limestone as he fished a pebble out of his trainer, and was surprised by how warm the wall was this early in the morning. The thick moss that covered most of one side sprang back when he removed his hand, and the print that it left made the stone look darker. The feeling of being watched prickled his skin even more. He hurried on.

Anyone walking along the path at the same time as Jake would have seen shapes and shadows appear now and then across the drystone wall – shapes like an eye, an ear, the precise outline of a clawed hand. Shadows that seemed for all the world to be following the boy.

But there was no one around to see anything. Even the birds had better things to do.

Chapter 4

It really was a very simple code. Who was his grandfather trying to fool? Jake had spent the rest of the morning searching through the letters. Only about twenty of them had the code, and in each one the messages were pretty much the same – short telegraphic sentences: *He needs us. Listen to the dreams. Something is coming. Believe. Come home.* And later on, *He must know. Train him!*

What did it mean? What was in the dreams? Who was this *he*? And what had *he* got to do with Jake's father? A small thought ticked like a bomb: was he, Jake, the person his father had to train? The thought made him laugh out loud. His father? *Train* him! In what? Genetics? Photography!

Not for the first time that morning did Jake wish he had the letters his father must have written back. Maybe *he'd* used code too.

He poured himself a glass of water and tried to think. The dragon thing was bugging him. He tried to picture his father in his oversized fleece and jeans being nicknamed Dragon, and failed. No, he was never, in this universe, going to be nicknamed Dragon. Then, maybe it was something to do with his work: name of a project. But then why would his grandfather be writing to his son about genetics?

It *had* to be someone – someone cool like Bruce Lee in *Enter The Dragon.*

Jake sipped his drink and pawed through the letters and photocopies. His mother had a meeting in London with her editor and wouldn't be back until tea-time, so he was safe. She'd left

48

instructions for re-heating lunch and Jake was babysitting. Elizabeth was in her room playing her music as loud as she could. Jake let her get on with it. It wasn't bothering him.

Absently, he ran a finger over the rim of the glass and listened to it sing. It was something his father had taught him. It helped him concentrate sometimes.

He stared at the messages and thought about what he knew about his father. It wasn't much. He *knew* he was William Walker (Bill to his friends), a scientist who'd published papers on evolutionary processes under climate change – Jake had read them and understood only half of what he was saying. He also *knew* that every Christmas his father dressed up as Santa Claus and carefully placed presents under the huge tree because he'd liked the fun of it (even though his children no longer believed in Santa and neither did he). And Jake *knew* he loved walking and could identify hundreds of plants, animals and birds by sight alone. Also that he talked about his own father a lot and so he must have loved him (even though they didn't always get along).

Jake *knew* all of these things and more, but it wasn't enough, could never be enough now. He'd heard that children never really know their parents and maybe that was true.

He wished, now more than ever, that he'd sat down with him – just once – and asked him to tell *his* stories. He wished he'd made videos of him on his phone so that he could play them over and over. He'd *almost* forgotten what his laugh sounded like. He wanted to hear his voice again. All Jake had was photographs.

And they couldn't speak.

He turned a letter over in his hands. These could sort of speak. In a way. His family was here on these pages.

And something else...

Dragon... dragon...?

He bit his little fingernail and spat it out.

No, the dragon wasn't a man. He didn't know why but he could feel it in his bones. It was a statue. And it was somewhere around here. He *knew it*.

Jake rinsed his glass under the cold tap and watched the water flow down the stone plug-hole. Little pocks of fossils glinted back. He went to the bottom of the stairs and shouted, 'Bett!... Bett!' He heard the muffled annoyance of his sister open her bedroom door.

'What!'

'What's the password for the WiFi here?'

'There's WiFi here?' asked Elizabeth.

'Isn't there?'

'I dunno. You just said there was. Have you checked that booklet thingy?'

Jake looked up at her, bemused.

'In the kitchen drawer,' said his sister. 'Emergency numbers and how to use the boiler... that sort of thing. God, and *you're* meant to be babysitting *me*!'

Jake scratched the back of his head and said simply, 'I know what the dragon is. It's a statue.'

Elizabeth's interest picked up. 'How d'you know? What've you found?'

'It's just a feeling... in my bones.'

'Your bones? Well,' she said, disappearing in to her room. 'Tell me when you've got something more concrete...'

Like a ghost, he passed through the limestone of the cave wall. But he was solid – more than solid – he was as solid as the stone itself.

As he passed, he left behind nothing: no scar in the rock, no scorch marks or burnt smell. It was as if the wall was simply not there for him, gave no resistance.

The wall. Cold, damp, mossy and salty.

But solid and present. Incredibly present.

Lucy stepped off the train. She looked hot and harassed. The carriage had been full of tourists and football fans and she'd had to stand for half the journey until she could force her way down the aisle to the seat she'd reserved. They'd been delayed by ten minutes. She checked the time on the station clock, 3.35. Her gaze instinctively followed the length of the platform. At its end, walking towards her, were her children. She gave a surprised wave.

'Eyup,' said Jake as he reached her. 'Good trip?'

He took her bag of files and folders as Elizabeth fell in at Lucy's side and gave her a light kiss on her cheek. Lucy smiled, bewildered.

'It wasn't really a trip, Jake. Just a meeting.'

'Good though?' said Jake. 'Productive?'

'Well, yes. Yes it was. Thanks for asking,' she said.

'Cool.'

'I'm surprised to see you here.'

'Nice surprise, though in't it?'

'Yes, it's lovely.'

Lucy and her children walked up a concrete ramp and over a bridge that crossed the tracks. Between the gritted laths they could see the railway sleepers below. At one time the station would have had a ticket barrier but not anymore, tickets were checked on the trains nowadays. They left through an old stone archway like the one in the library. Jake clocked it as they passed – at the bottom was a circle bisected by an arrow. He smiled to himself.

Outside, the car park was half-full of baking cars. It was almost as big as the whole station. As they crossed it, they could smell the sickly stench of exhaust fumes and melting tarmac. Elizabeth squeezed her mother's arm affectionately.

'Okay, what're you two after?' asked Lucy, suspiciously.

'Nothing,' said Elizabeth pretending to be shocked. 'Mam! Can't we just want to meet you from a hard day's work?'

Lucy was even more suspicious now. She stopped in her tracks and Jake, who'd been trailing slightly behind, bumped into her.

Lucy laughed. 'Not usually you can't, no. What're you after?' she said. 'C'mon, I know you two. What're you scheming?'

Elizabeth pulled one of her many faces and Jake shrugged one of his famous shrugs. He pushed his sunglasses up his nose.

'Well,' said Jake. 'You've had a busy day, so we thought you'd like to have tea somewhere... somewhere nice. As a reward.'

'That's...' Lucy paused. '...very thoughtful of you.'

Then, holding her daughter's chin in her hands and looking into her eyes, she said, 'Are you really *my* children? They do say there are aliens in them thar hills!'

'Har har,' said Elizabeth, 'You try to do someone something nice and this is what you get. C'mon Jake,' she said, hooking his arm and feigning to leave.

'Ah, yes...' said Lucy, markedly. '...definitely *my* kids. Bett you're a mardy-bum.' Lucy laughed again and continued walking.

'Mam! I'm not three y'know!' said Elizabeth, this time actually shocked.

'Maaaaardy-bum, Maaaaardy-bum,' Lucy said in a sing-song as she walked. She needed to get out of this heat. It was the first truly hot day of summer.

'Oh my God...' muttered her daughter, storming off. Lucy ran up to her and hooked her daughter in a bear hug. She squeezed, laughing. Elizabeth tried to resist but couldn't help herself and hugged her back. Jake stood there, embarrassed.

'Mam. C'mon, this is *public*,' he said.

Lucy dropped her daughter and turned to her son. Jake backed away slightly.

'Come here you, you want some of this?' She grabbed him and kissed him noisily on the cheek leaving a copper pair of lips on his face.

'Oh, thanks, Mam,' Jake said, wiping his scrunched-up face with the flat of his hand and looking around. 'Yeah, thanks for that, in't nothing embarrassing about that then, is there?'

Lucy raised an eyebrow. 'Want another?'

'Woah, no! No, thanks.' he said smartly.

Lucy laughed again and fished in her handbag for her car keys.

'So, my little thoughtful cherubs, my little tea-fairies, where do you have in mind? Burgers? Pizza?' she said into her bag as she rummaged around.

'No,' said Elizabeth. 'Seriously Mam, we thought somewhere nice and posh.'

Lucy looked up and cocked her head to one side. 'Posh?'

'There's this place not far away,' said Jake. 'It looks nice. I found it on the internet.'

'O-kaay,' said Lucy. 'You found the WiFi then?'

'Yes. You're dressed perfectly for the place too, so don't worry,' said Elizabeth as they reached the car.

Lucy unlocked it and popped the boot for her bags and files.

'I wasn't worried, love. I was thinking *who's going to pay*?'

'Well we thought we'd pay for you...' said Elizabeth stoutly.

'...and I could pay for you two?' finished Lucy.

'Something like that yes,' said Jake grinning. Lucy slammed the boot and pointed to the back seats.

'Yep, *definitely* my kids,' she said. 'Go on, get in. Where is this place?'

'It's a few miles away–' said Elizabeth.

'Ah, of course...' nodded Lucy.

'–so you'll have to drive. It's part of an old ruined abbey. Lakes and grounds and things. Swans and carp. '

'Hmmm? Swans? I like swans.' Lucy walked round the car and entered the driver's seat. The sun was high enough in the sky and hot enough to squash your breath, but she'd parked under a copse of broad-leafed sycamore trees so the car inside was relatively cool.

'There you are then,' said Jake.

'Shotgun!' shouted Elizabeth. Jake grabbed his sister's shoulder and shepherded her into the back.

'No, I'll get in the front so's I can direct Mam...'

He could feel him through the stone. Moving over land.

Away. Away from this place but still detectable. Moving fast, as if he were flying.

The Companion. Yes.

He must be contacted.

He was running out of time.

'This is lovely,' said Lucy opening the plain white menu. On the front was a little embossed summerhouse and in fine, sky blue writing the words, '*Summer Pavilion*'. She smoothed her hand over the linen table cloths and said, 'Let's have a look what they've got.'

They were alone in the room, the lunch rush over and the tea crowd not yet in. A waitress in her late-fifties, wearing a white and black uniform, came over and smiled warmly.

'Hallo,' she said. Her voice rang of 'buttermints' and 'fairy cakes', but her eyes sparkled and said something more like 'salsa lessons' and 'long weekends abroad'.

'Hello,' said Lucy. The children smiled shyly and said 'hi'. It was posher than they'd expected and they weren't used to posh. Even the napkins were cloth and the menus had been given them by a young woman when they'd come in. Jake was nervous, until the waitress spoke.

'We've got some luvelly specials on today,' she said, tucking a rogue strand of silver hair behind her ear. 'Nice bit of haddock and proper chips – nothing frozen here – comes with peas and tartar sauce.'

She leaned over and, without looking, tapped the specials menu with her pen. 'There's also Cumberland sausage and mash, oh and *the gravy* – not even I make it this good and I make *good* gravy – and we also have a Warm Goats Cheese Salad with toasted triangles. I had that one for my lunch. *Deeelicious*. Comes with redcurrant jam. Perfect if you're watching your weight like me.' She smiled again and tapped her stomach.

Lucy stared at the woman. She was struck by the oddest sensation that she knew her. She stared a little too long.

'Are you alright, love? Shall I give you another minute?'

Jake reached over and nudged his mother's arm. 'Mam?' he hissed.

Lucy blinked. 'Yes, yes sorry. I was miles away.'

'You look a bit pale, love. Would you like some water?' The waitress put a hand on Lucy's shoulder. Lucy caught a waft of familiar smelling violets.

'Umm, no. I'm fine.' Lucy said and tried a weak smile. 'Those specials all sound delicious, but we thought we'd just come for tea. Do you do old fashioned proper teas?'

The strange moment passed and the woman beamed.

'Oh yes, love. We're famed for it. We have three different sorts: *Classic*, *Splendide* and *Luxurious*. The Luxurious one has chocolates and champagne as well as smoked salmon sandwiches and mini-cakes.'

The children's eyes lit up.

'Can I have *that* one?' Elizabeth jumped in.

'No!' said Lucy and the waitress together.

They looked at one another. There, *that* look. So familiar.

The waitress looked away and said, 'We can't serve alcohol to under-18's, lovey.'

Elizabeth visibly deflated. She'd liked the idea of smoked salmon, chocolate and champagne. She could easily get used to posh.

'What's the Classic like?' asked Lucy.

'Ooh, it's a good choice, that one. One of my favourites. A classic English Tea – sandwiches, small cakes, cream scone with a choice of jams and a big pot of tea, of course.'

'What's in the sandwiches, please?' asked Jake.

The waitress unclasped a pair of reading glasses from a black cord around her neck, slipped them on her face and pointed to the menu again with her pen.

'You can have any two of these: ham, cheese, cream cheese and cucumber or beef.' She looked up, pushing her glasses further up her nose and half-whispered in a conspiratorial tone. 'But if you fancy a nice bit of smoked salmon I'm sure I can manage that. The chef's a friend of mine.'

'Can *I*?' asked Elizabeth.

'Well, it was you I was thinking of, lovey' said the waitress and winked. 'And maybe a chocolate?'

Elizabeth beamed. Perhaps she could work on her for the champagne...

'Now, this is a lot of food,' the waitress said, turning to Jake. '*More* than enough to share between the two of you. So, young man, shall I bring you one Classic and two cups for the tea?' She winked theatrically. Jake laughed.

'That's very kind of you,' interjected Lucy.

'No problem. Now, *two* smoked salmon or...?' She looked at Jake, pen hovering.

'Can I have cucumber, please?' he asked.

'*Just* cucumber? No cream cheese.'

Jake nodded shyly. 'Yes – no – I mean *just* cucumber, please.'

'Ah, a traditionalist, I see. Crusts cut off?'

Jake shook his head.

'Good,' she said. 'Crusts put hairs on your chest.'

'Urgheuw,' said Elizabeth.

The woman laughed gently and patted Elizabeth on the arm.

'It's not the same for girls, crusts makes their hair curl.'

'Oh,' said Elizabeth caught off guard. 'Okay then. I'll have crusts on mine, please.'

'Good choice. And for you madam?'

Lucy scanned the menu quickly again. She'd not really been paying much attention – an odd thought was worming through her mind. She plucked her order out of thin air.

'Could I just have a ham sandwich and a pot of tea please? And a scone to follow.'

'Cream and jam with the scone?'

Jake noticed that she'd rhymed scone with bone. He liked it. It sounded full and tasty.

'Yes, please,' said Lucy. 'Raspberry if you've got it.'

The woman wrote it all down, nodding. 'And for you two? Raspberry?'

'Have you got cherry?' asked Elizabeth.

'We have. A whole orchard of fruit jams!'

'Cool,' said Elizabeth.

'So, that's one ham-off-the-bone sandwich, cream scone with raspberry jam – comes with butter – and one Classic Tea *à la Mary*, and a pot of tea for two with three cups? Anything else?'

'Chocolates!'

'Goes without saying, lovey,' said the waitress to Elizabeth.

'I think that might be enough, don't you? *Mary* is it?' said Lucy, reading off a white badge.

'Yes. They make us wear these.' She winced. 'I say if I'm going to wear name jewellery then it should at least be diamonds. If that's all I'll be back in a mo with the tea.'

Mary left and everyone watched her go. Lucy turned to Jake.

'Jake, d'you remember Granny May?'

'Erm...' he said, then faltered. He'd been young when May had died. A big woman with blue eyes and silver, hair, always with a sweet and a good hug.

'Yeah, just about,' said Jake.

At the far end of the room, Mary entered through a wide door carrying a small tray. She made for a counter filled with tea-pots and a giant Jackson urn at one end. She busied herself with jars and crockery.

'Does the waitress remind you of her?'

Jake watched Mary fuss over the caddies of leaf tea. *Granny May*. Same shape, almost. Same colour hair. Same fussiness, and her voice.

'Little bit,' he answered.

'Yeah? She *really* reminds me of her.'

Jake glanced over at his mother then back at Mary. She would have been about the same age as Granny May... He bit his bottom lip and said, 'Mam. Did *you* know they came from around here? Gran and Grandad..'

Lucy looked bemused. 'Sorry, what?'

Jake ploughed on. 'Yeah. In the town.'

'No, Jake, they lived in Scotland.'

'No, honest. Dad was born here. They moved when he was a boy. Didn't he say anything?'

'No. No, he didn't.'

'It's true, Mam,' interjected Elizabeth. 'We found some stuff, records and things.'

'Stuff? Where? What things?'

'Well, Jake found them. Not me.'

Lucy looked expectantly at Jake. 'What things? Jake, you can't take your dad's things without asking me...'

'No...not Dad's things,' he said, glaring at Elizabeth. 'I found them in the library in town. Parish records.'

'Oh.' Lucy was suddenly uncomfortable. 'Your dad was very... private... Jakey. He didn't talk much about growing up... It was a bit difficult for him. He didn't always see eye to eye with your granddad...'

She spread her napkin neatly over her lap, coughed and said, 'I don't understand what you've found, Jake, or what you were looking for, but I'm ninety-nine per cent sure your dad came from Scotland. He had an accent and everything...'

Jake started to speak but was shushed by a look from Lucy; the chink-chink of china said Mary was coming over with a tray of crockery.

'There you are. Lovely cup of tea.'

'Mary... Are you from around here' asked Lucy, out of the blue.

'Oh, yes, love, born and bred.'

Mary arranged the cups neatly and started to pour the tea through a silver-coloured strainer. Elizabeth looked on amazed – this *was* posh! Lucy continued, stumbling over the words.

'This might sound a bit, well, odd but you didn't know anyone called May Walker did you? Growing up?'

Mary held the tea pot and stared at Lucy. Her hand started to shake under its weight.

'May? May *Walker*?'

'Yes, Walker.'

Mary placed three fingers under the pot to steady it and said,

'Well, yes love. I did. She was my cousin. We went to school together.'

Lucy glanced at Jake, then back to Mary.

'So she was from around here, then?'she asked.

'Oh yes. But she was a Staniland back then. Not a Walker. She flitted not long after marrying her young man, Stan. Flitted with their little boy, what was his name now...?'

'William? Bill?'

'Yes, love. Bill. Billy we called him. But she's died, love, May has. Ooh a long time back now. I heard it was a lovely funeral service. Up in Scotland. Did you know her then?'

'Yes... it was a nice funeral,' said Lucy taking the teapot and setting it on the table. Red tea splashed onto the white cloth.

May's had been a simple funeral but filled with people. She was well loved by friends in the luncheon clubs, the School Boards, her sewing and gardening classes at the college. Bill had stood at the chapel door, head slightly bent, shaking people's hands sadly. His father stood next to him. Lucy had noticed how alike they'd looked.

She took in a deep breath and said to Mary, 'May was my husband's mother. These are her grandchildren, Jacob and Elizabeth; Jake and Bett.'

Elizabeth gave a warm little wave. Mary looked at the children then back at Lucy, amazed. She patted her apron absently.

'Little *Billy's* young 'uns?'

Lucy laughed. 'Yes. Bill's kids.'

Mary took hold of Jake's chin and scanned his face.

'Well look at *you*,' she said. 'You've your dad's eyes, haven't you?'

She turned to Elizabeth. Both of them beamed at one another.

'And look at you. By gum, you can see our May in you. Her eyes – cheeky as chocolate. Well, I'll stand locking up, I will!' She turned back to Lucy, and pulled up a chair.

'Our Little Billy's young 'uns! He'll be joining you will he?' She said, glancing at the door in case she caught a glimpse of Bill. She realized she'd said something wrong when Elizabeth's jaw tensed and Lucy's face clouded.

'Oh, no. No, Mary,' Lucy stammered. 'I'm afraid Bill passed away just over a year ago.' No matter how many times she said it, she still couldn't get used to it.

'Oh, love,' said Mary. 'I *am* sorry to hear that. Really. He was a lovely lad, Billy. Kind. I remember he loved animals.' Her eyes formed the question Lucy was so familiar with now – What happened?

'Car accident.'

'Oh, that's *terrible*. I always say there's too many cars on the roads. Oh, I am sorry,' she said, taking Lucy's hand. Then she leaned forward and said gently, 'My, it's a small world, isn't it? It really is!'

Behind them a brass bell pinged twice as their order was pushed through a hatch door at the far end of the counter.

⌖

He travelled fast, moving like a shark looking for its prey. He travelled through rock, deep underground, and saw everything through its fossils: how the world began, how the fuels formed, how life sprang forth then died, withering under the vast glacial freezes.

He saw the advent of man.

He saw it all, tasted it, smelled it...

And beneath it all... the destruction.

And pressing against everything, the other worlds.

He drove on as if stone had no substance.

⌖

Jake managed finally to get away. He'd left his mother and Elizabeth in the café chatting with Mary. They'd probably be there for hours and he had work to do. It was why he was here, after all.

He'd nearly choked when he'd found what he was looking for on a website of the old abbey: almost hidden in the corner of an old photo, a statue of a dragon.

And now, like a makeshift theodolite, he positioned his print-out map of the grounds at arms length with one hand and the photo with the other. His eyes flicked repeatedly from one to the other. A long, steep path led down to water. This was definitely the way to go – to the Great Lake. The statue was near the west wall.

In the distance a heavy cloud formed grey. Rain threatened. He could feel the electricity in the air, tinny and sharp. Beneath his feet he felt the heavy rumbling of distant thunder. So long as it stays distant, thought Jake as he set off down the stony path.

He had to admit he was lost. Very lost. It made no sense. He'd followed the path, followed the map, and it still didn't bring him out where he wanted to be.

He was hot, bothered and starting to get a headache. It felt like he'd been wandering around for hours. He wiped his eyes and looked out over a small lake. The sun blazed back from the still surface. A juvenile swan, not moving in the water, had his eye on him.

Where the hell had he gone wrong? thought Jake. At one point, the path had split into three and he'd continued in what he thought was a straight line.

He sighed and carried on until he came up against a temporary metal fence cordoning off some building works. A dead-end.

Is this it? Is *this* the abbey ruins? Jake snorted and tried to peek through the fence and the hedge behind it. All he could see was a field and a small Portacabin. No ruins. No statue. No people.

No *people?* There'd been people milling around when he set off, so where had they all gone to? Weird.

To one side of the fence, and hidden in the general architecture, Jake noticed a set of deep-cut limestone steps. As he took the first one, he caught sight of a small carving, barely noticeable: a circle bisected by an outlined arrow. His heart started to pound. His *grandfather* had made these steps! Jake bent down and touched the mark with his forefinger – the air almost crackled! Laughing, he jumped the stairs two at a time.

They opened out onto another world.

A Japanese garden.

Black and green bamboo, striped like tigers, bunched out of pale stubby shrubs as they cast their shadows over half a dozen stone shrines taller than Jake. A handful of tiny bridges crossed here and there over long, still ponds swimming with black and golden koi. It looked like something from *National Geographic* – too exotic for the midlands of England. Jake could hear the buzzing thrill of bees and the chirrup of crickets. He wandered from one shrine to another until he reached the centre.

He could see it was a heptagon with seven flagstoned paths radiating from its heart. And in its heart, a temple. Grey and red and so intricately carved it looked alive. It housed a stone Buddha: fat and happy, as if he'd eaten all the steamed dumplings and went back for the pies.

At his feet was a tiny statue carved from limestone.

A dragon.

Jake was stunned.

This was the statue?!

All that searching and this *lawn ornament* was the result?

Jake knelt down, careful not to disturb anything. On the dragon's scaly stomach he could see, clear as day and small as his little fingernail, a circle bisected by an arrow.

Well then, this *was* it.

Jake swore. He peered down and prodded the statue, daring it to move. He leaned in for a better look. It was as if the dragon and the Buddha had been carved up from the ground itself.

Good foundations then, he thought sarcastically as he sat back on his haunches and wiped his hands. He blew out an irritated sigh and stood up, swinging his camera around on to his chest.

Apart from the Buddha and the statue, the temple was empty of furniture. And surprisingly clean. As though it had been swept clean.

He sucked at his teeth, annoyed. There was nothing here to learn about his grandfather, *or* his father.

The thunder in the distance pulsed closer and the air around him started to push against his chest. Dark clouds were coming in. He took some photographs for the hell of it and pulled out his father's watch. In this light, the numerals on the face glowed golden. It was coming up to twenty to six.

He tried to phone Elizabeth to see if they were still in the café but the signal bars on his phone had drained to nothing. He swore again. How come nowhere around this place had a decent signal!

The thunder bawled and a dull pain set firmly behind his left eye. Too much sun and not enough water! He ignored the pain as best he could, and bent his ear to the sounds. The thunder was catching up with him. If he was lucky, he might make it back to the café before it started to rain.

He stood up, capped his camera, slipped it into his bag and set off down a random path.

The path was longer than it first seemed and wound like a discarded piece of string – here and there a knot formed into an opening with a bench or pond in it. Everything was bordered with bamboo, thick and leafy, as if Jake was working his way through a jungle. He had no idea if he was going in the right direction.

The air was hulking and electrified.

That was lightning!

He felt like his head was being squeezed. Sweat poured off him in rivers and his breathing caught in his throat. Jeeze, he thought, covering one eye with the palm of a hand, I feel sick. His stomach lurched. The dense foliage closed in. Then a wave of panic hit him like a fireball. He stumbled on, half-blind with pain, and retching with every step. Without warning, the path opened out and Jake staggered into a wide field. He started to shake. The rainstorm had arrived!

Thunder boomed and lightning skewered the sky like a pig on a spit. Jake's stomach reeled and pitched and he couldn't be sure that the flashes he could see were real or in his head. He retched again. When he managed to straighten up, he saw – not more than twenty yards away – the abbey ruins.

And towering thirty feet into the sky, greeting the lightning and the clouds, a stone dragon.

Jake laughed out loud.

Around him the sky blackened and the air buzzed like a fridge. There was only colour and light.

And the dragon.

He felt a soft splash of warm rain on his face as he started to run. Images flashed into his pounding head: scales, teeth, wings, a sharp whipping tail. And smells too: volcanoes, sulphur like rotten eggs, a seething, rank breath.

Finally, the rain came down like a wall of water. Where it hit the boy, it sizzled.

In front of him, the statue glowed yellow in the darkness. Jake slipped awkwardly, caught his balance, and kept on running.

He was almost there!

The dragon now glowed red as magma, as the setting sun. Red as blood.

The pain in Jake's head and guts was so solid he could practically *see* it inside him.

Almost there!

Then, a sudden shock of lightning seared his mind and with thunder bellowing in his throat, he fell down into the slick of the newly-formed mud.

As his body closed into unconsciousness, he could taste tin and rotten eggs. He felt heavy as sin, as if he were being dragged into the earth.

'No,' he grunted, 'no...'

The old sofa in the staff-room of the Summer Pavilion sagged underneath Jake's waking body. A groundsman had half-dragged, half-carried him through the deluge and the treacherous mud and dumped him there. He'd been concious at one point, the man said, delirious and jabbering on about some statue on fire.

Jake glanced around at all the people in the room. Too many for him to deal with right now. He felt sick and said so. His mother clucked and fussed and followed the groundsman as he went to fetch a bucket and a flannel. Mary looked Jake over, nodded at Elizabeth and fetched a glass of water. Elizabeth stood to one side, shocked.

Jake's clothes were caked in mud, his bone-white face filthy and snotty, his eyes red raw. He was still shivering. Elizabeth found an old blanket in a cupboard and wrapped it around him. He still looked terrified.

'What happened?' she whispered. Jake clamped his lips tightly together and shook his head in tiny movements.

'MmMMmm.' he tried, then stopped in case he really did throw up. He swallowed slowly. He felt the sharp twang of his jawbone.

'Tell me later,' said Elizabeth hurriedly, standing back.

Mary returned, followed closely by Lucy and the groundsman. The waitress eyed Jake warily as he took the glass from her. He drank it slowly.

'Just breathe slowly, lad,' said Mary. 'That's right, that's good.'

Jake was calming down. His head no longer pounded, his heartbeat slowed. He'd almost stopped shaking and colour was gradually coming back to his cheeks.

Lucy took the flannel and wiped down what she could of the mud. Jake let her.

It took him a few minutes before he was calm enough to speak. Everyone wanted to know what had happened.

Jake shrugged ineffectually. He couldn't really remember, except he got a headache and it started to rain and when he ran for cover he slipped in the mud. That was it. He must have passed out. He'd had a migraine attack, that's all. Too much sun and no hat. And the running made it worse. He'd been stupid.

Did he want to go to the hospital? No, he was okay. Lucy wasn't happy but she didn't see any point in arguing.

Mary sucked at her cheeks and clucked.

'I remember his dad used to get headaches like them when *he* were a babby,' she said to Lucy, hardly taking her eyes off Jake.

'I'm alright, honest,' stammered Jake, as his mother opened her mouth to speak. 'I just need paracetamols and a sleep. I'll be fine.'

He tried a little embarrassed laugh to show how fine he was.

He didn't look fine, he was still pallid and his throat was dry, but what could they do? He took a small sip of water and flicked the blanket off his shoulders. He noticed it had stopped raining. The day shining through the window was bright and sun-filled again.

'I'd like to go home, Mam, please,' Jake said trying not to sound whiny, and failing miserably.

'Okay, Jakey,' said his mother, helping him off the sofa. He winced. His steps, wobbly at first, quickly grew steady. Lucy left him leaning against his sister in the doorway of the tea rooms and went to fetch the car. Elizabeth wrapped an arm around her brother's waist securely.

'I'm alright,' he said.

'I know,' she replied, squeezing. Jake smiled weakly. He felt unbelievably tired. And very embarrassed.

'It *was* a migraine wasn't it? Nothing else?' asked Elizabeth quietly. Jake looked at her, then looked away.

The groundsman opened up the main gate and Lucy brought the car up to the door. On the drive home everyone was silent. Elizabeth watched her brother as he nodded off, her head filled with thoughts. In his sleepy state, Jake felt the cool of the air-conditioning shave the edge off the heat and he dreamed childish dreams about dragons and glitter-covered birthday cakes.

The sun was still very much in the sky when they reached the cottage. Jake was already feeling much better but this didn't stop his mother fussing. She chattered aimlessly as she went up stairs to run her son a bath.

Clean and dry, Jake came downstairs smelling of whatever Lucy had put in his bath. It was okay, a bit girly but with none of his friends around he could live with it. Just about. He could hear his mother pottering around her study, not working, not doing anything useful. Jake felt a fool. What had he been thinking?

There was a freshly made pan of soup on the stove and Elizabeth was making tea.

'Are you okay?' she asked quietly.

Jake nodded sleepily, ladled himself some soup, cut some bread and went into the living room to eat it while he watched telly.

Their mother came into the kitchen and nodded to Elizabeth.

'Is Jake okay?'

'Yeah Mam, he's okay. He's just a bit tired. He's eating soup and watching telly.'

'I'll just go and see how he is...' Lucy said heading to the living room.

'Mam, leave him,' said Elizabeth softly. 'He'll be alright, *really*. You know he doesn't like fuss. Let him watch telly.'

Lucy hesitated. Elizabeth stepped towards her and held onto the elbow of her mother's shirt, something she used to do to her father whenever she needed help.

'Really, he'll be fine, yeah. It was just a headache,' she said.

'He's *never* been that bad before, Bett. Never.' Tears welled in Lucy's eyes.

'It wa' a bit of sun-stroke, Mam,' said Elizabeth wrapping her arms around her mother and squeezing hard. 'You know what a pillock he can be. No hat, huh!'

She negotiated the hallway leading her mother into her study and said, 'God, it's been a weird day, hasn't it?' Lucy laughed under her daughter's charms. It always amazed her how grown up she was becoming; sometimes she wondered who was the daughter and who the mother.

'I liked that waitress,' Elizabeth chattered on, 'but God, she could talk couldn't she? And I thought *I* was gobby.'

There were two overstuffed armchairs in the study in front of an empty fireplace. Lucy sat on one of them, keeping an ear out for her son in the next room. On the mantelpiece, she'd arranged a selection of photographs: six weeks was a long time to be without memories.

Colourful faces smiled out at Elizabeth, and five black and white ones: Lucy's parents on a canal boat, and Bill's in front of a big stone wall. They were holding a baby in their arms.

'Is this gran and granddad, Mam?' Elizabeth picked it up and passed it down to Lucy. She peered at it.

'Yes, yes it is. And the little one's your dad.'

'How old was he?' Elizabeth asked, taking the photo again.

'I don't know. But your dad loved that photo. It made him happy.'

'They *look* happy,' said Elizabeth placing it back on the marble shelf.

'They do, don't they?'

There was a sad pause that neither wanted to fill. Eventually, Lucy said, 'You never really knew your gran, Bett, but you'd have loved her. She made her own ice-cream, you know?'

'Seriously?'

'Yes. Banana. She really liked bananas. She had a proper machine and everything. It was amazing ice-cream! I've never tasted anything like it.'

Elizabeth found herself laughing as she looked into the eyes of the hopeful young man and woman holding their son and staring out at the camera. One day they'd tasted their own home-made ice-cream and it had been amazing! She held the photo up to the light.

'Mam...' she asked curiously.

'Yes, love.'

'Where's this photo taken?'

'Erm... I don't know, why d'you ask?'

'I just looks familiar.'

Lucy stood up and looked over her daughter's shoulder. 'Bett, it's a wall. How can a *wall* look familiar?' she laughed.

'Hah, yeah,' said Elizabeth as if snapping out of a dream, 'Yeah. Dopey.'

She put the photograph down. 'I should go and see how Sunshine's getting on,' she said.

'Don't torment him, Bett,' said Lucy distractedly. She was standing by the fireplace, looking at the past displayed in front of her.

'I won't,' said Elizabeth, closing the door.

The grounds near the old shrine.

Weather against him. The companion too weak, too ill-prepared to receive him.

Retreat. Through soil and substrata. Return to his cave.

Too strong for this one. Too much fire.

He will calm himself. Then the companion will see.

They must communicate. Communicate.

He will return to the stone house.

Seek out the lad again.

Tonight.

Jake flicked off the ancient television. A tiny red dot flickered in the darkness. It reminded him of the statue. Red burning. He shuddered.

His head still hurt, though not badly. He'd felt better for the soup and bread. Good old vegetable soup. His mother had looked in on him and told him it was time for bed. It probably was.

He sat in the dark listening to the snuffle of hedgehogs in the garden. He'd been putting out cat food and water for them. They seemed happy enough. After a while he went upstairs and changed into sweats and a t-shirt. Give it ten minutes, maybe fifteen.

It was eight.

Eight minutes later his sister knocked on the door and poked her head around the jamb. 'Are you decent?' she said jokily.

'Half-decent,' came his reply. It was a ritual he'd shared with his father – 'Are you decent, Jake?' 'Half-decent.' It wasn't very funny but they always laughed anyway. He didn't laugh now.

Elizabeth slipped in and sat on the bed. Jake propped himself up against the headboard.

'How do you get up them stairs with making them creak?'

'Years of ninja training, oh ignorant one.'

Jake laughed. Elizabeth, pulled her feet up and said, trying to sound casual, 'So, what happened today, then?'

'I dunno,' shrugged Jake.

'Oh, well I'll go if you don't wanna talk about it,' Elizabeth made as if to leave. Jake grabbed her wrist, just a little too quickly to be comfortable.

'I found it, Bett.' He squeezed.

'Oi, that hurts!' Elizabeth pulled her hand away.

'Sorry.'

'Fine,' she said rubbing her wrist cautiously. 'Found what?'

'The dragon. It *is* a statue.' He smiled weakly.

'Cool! You were right then.'

'Yeah. There were two. There's this little garden thing with a tiny statue of a dragon in it. I thought that was *it* – the one from the photo – because it had granddad's mark on it. But it wasn't.' Jake's eyes gleamed with a golden sheen that was almost hypnotic.

'Your eyes look a bit weird, are you alright?'

'They're fine. Lissenlissenlissen to me. There was this other statue. It was massive. Massive!'

'Honest, Jake, your eyes are a bit–'

'My eyes are fine, Bett, stop fussing! You're worse than Mam! Anyroad, it started raining, din't it? I could see the statue – I must've been about twenty yards away. There was lightning and I thought it must've hit the statue because it was glowing. I started to run–'

'With a migraine! You pillock, no wonder you passed out!'

'– anyway,' said Jake stonily. 'I ran and then the rain got worse and then I fell over–'

'–Pillock.'

'But I saw it... before I went down,' said Jake.

'Well, ye-ah! Durrr!'

'...I mean I *saw* it, Bett. It wasn't just *glowing*. It was moving!'

It was a clear night. The moon, not quite full, bleached out the nearby stars. Everything was still. No wind. No traffic in the distant lanes. Anything in the garden – hedgehogs, mice, rats – had long since gone to ground. Nothing nocturnal could be heard.

At least, nothing *usual*.

A shadow blanketed the moonlit garden.

The cottage was quiet and everyone slept and so no one witnessed what drew up to the glass of the attic window. An eye, gold as lava, peered in and rested its gaze on the body of the sleeping boy. Behind it was half a face. If Jake had been awake, he might have described the face as muscular, and attributed a kind of fossilized, skeletal quality to it. He'd have called it mucky-yellow for sure, and he might even have thought that the eye was set in it like a gemstone in a magic sword. If he'd have been awake.

The eye watched the boy's chest rise and drop. An arm slipped out from under Jake's cover, his hand twitching as if he were trying to push something away, or, in fact, as if he were trying to *grasp* something, and each time he was just out of reach.

The boy's legs started to jerk in a running motion. Faster. *Faster.* His whole body spasmed! In his sleep, he was terrified!

The eye watched impassively, curious about the dreaming boy.

Then its golden fire flickered as it blinked, deep as landslides.

Jake's body shuddered and seized, and his eyes snapped open. For a second he didn't know where he was. And he could smell fire! His head whipped round to see an eye glaring like a sun at midnight.

He scrambled, balling himself up against the headboard, and opened his mouth to scream. But nothing came out. He tried to scream again and still there was no sound, not even the rustle of the bedclothes, the ticking of his watch. It was as if sound had been stripped from the air.

Jake swallowed the rising hysteria and tried to edge himself off the bed – *if he could make it to the door…*

But just like the sound, he was frozen.

The eye blinked again, slow as erosion.

Then, one sound. A rumble echoing through Jake's blood, tearing through his bones and muscle. Deeper than caves, darker than fathoms. It harnessed every soundwave in the room.

A voice.

'Jacob.'

Jake tried to explain much later to Elizabeth how his body had throbbed, how he'd felt sick and his head pounded while at the same time it was as if he'd been enrobed in calm. He even used the word 'enrobed' – which he wasn't really sure he knew the meaning of.

But right now in the middle of the night, Jake uncurled himself slowly from the bed.

'Jacob…'

The voice was strangely restful, like walking over hills. And Jake didn't hear it, he *felt* it pounding through his body.

He slid onto the edge of the bed, staring at the thing in the window. It *was* real. Maybe I'm dreaming, he thought, God, I hope so!

The room was alive in the flare from the creature's eye. Jake could see his own shaking hand in front of him. His bare feet sunk into the rug that had seen much better days. He wasn't sure his legs would support him.

Jake licked his lips and swallowed. His saliva tasted tinny – had he bitten his cheek? Was it blood? He swallowed again.

He should have been terrified but instead he felt *protected*. He stared into the sun of the eye and knew that if this creature had come to kill him, he'd already be dead.

He stood up and clutched his churning stomach. His legs were holding their own so he took a step towards the window. The moon bulged in at the top corner of the glass – he focused on the craters, grey against the white. Anything to avoid looking at the face.

The face. It too had craters. Above the eye was a line of tiny whorls – an eyebrow? The eye was bigger than Jake's fist.

The creature blinked again and Jake was hypnotised by its slow progression.

'Jacob.'

It sounded, and felt, as if all the air had been sucked from the room and released in an instant. The nausea and dizziness grew. Jake held his chest and wheezed.

'It will abate,' said the voice slowly. 'The discomfort. You will grow accustomed to it.'

What little Jake could see of the mouth didn't move. How was it speaking?

A surge of adrenaline – violent and unexpected – pushed through Jake's system. This time he really was going to be sick, he was sure of it. Sweat poured down his face and his hands shook.

Then, stars. Green and gold like burning photographs.

He collapsed against the blanket box at the foot of his bed and reached out in the same way he had in his dreams. The eye narrowed and flared orange as if the creature was smiling. Jake retched with another surge of force. He could smell sulphur and lime. He tried to breath through his mouth, his teeth gritted.

'Wha–' he managed. 'W-what are you?'

White noise filled Jake's head. He put his hands over ears but the noise grew worse.

'You are my companion,' said the voice. 'We must talk.'

Jake swallowed the bile burning his throat. Through his dizziness and nausea he could hear the creak of footsteps on the attic stairs.

The light changed as his mother opened his bedroom door. She saw her son slumped on an old wooden box. He was staring out of the window and shouting, 'No! Wait!'

Lucy rushed in as Jake folded up like a concertina.

'Jake?!' She tried to catch him but he dragged her down. He was heavier than a gravestone.

Tears streamed down his face as he raised his head and rasped, 'Where's... it gone...?'

Lucy struggled to heave Jake up and over to the bed. She lunged forward and fell with her son onto the mattress. He still trembled and sweat was already cooling on his skin, smelling stale and musky. The room was like a greenhouse in high summer.

She hoiked herself from the bed and examined her son. He hadn't moved. His eyes were closed, and he was breathing rapidly. Lucy lifted up his feet and placed her hand against his forehead. He felt warm, but not hot, not burning up. No fever, then.

But where was all the air?

She walked over to the window and opened it wide. A faint trace of steam from the night air breezed in. It was a familiar smell, a misplaced smell – sulphur and caves, and the old quarries she'd played in as a child. She glanced back at her son, found an old padded chair and slumped down.

Jake was breathing normally now and slept a sleep as quiet as graveyards. Occasionally he grunted. Lucy settled down.

So, she thought, he's dreaming again. And there's no Bill anymore to calm him down. No Bill to show him there are no monsters under the bed. She bit her thumb nail, thoughtfully, and watched her son sleeping until she too slipped into a troubled sleep.

CHAPTER 5

'Where is she...?' Jake whispered in case his mother heard him. Elizabeth pointed in exaggerated gestures to the thin wall that separated them from Lucy's study. Her brother rolled his eyes. He'd woken up that morning with his mother asleep in the corner of his room. She'd almost scared the life out of him. He'd almost scared the life out of her, she reasoned, which was why she was there in the first place.

She'd made him a bed downstairs on the sofa. Sun-stroke, she'd said. She didn't mention the dreams. Jake was grounded for the whole day for his own good. He'd tried the usual wheedling, swearing, sulking and bargaining but his mother was being stubborn.

'Just one day, then,' he'd agreed. Lucy nodded and went to her study.

That was an hour ago, now Elizabeth sat on a footstool leaning towards her brother.

'You look knackered,' she whispered.

Jake couldn't remember being put back to bed or his mother coming into the room, but he remembered the face and the eye as if they were in front of him still. He shuddered. To think he'd thought that the dragon might be a statue! Or even a man!

'Bett...' he began, warily. 'What I'm gunna say, yeah, you've got to promise not to laugh or anything...'

Elizabeth eyed her brother thoughtfully then asked, 'What is it?'

'Promise me.' Jake's voice was low and serious.

'Don't be lame, we're not little kids anymore.'

'Then, I'm not saying.'

It was an anxious but determined look, and it sat badly on her brother's face.

'Okay, then,' Elizabeth whispered. 'Promise.'

Jake cleared his throat then stopped; he could hear his mother shuffling to the door of her study. When the door didn't open, he continued.

'Last night, yeah, I woke up and there was something in my room.'

Elizabeth sighed. Was that all? She wasn't surprised.

'Was it a ghost?' she said knowingly. If Elizabeth believed in anything, it was ghosts, and if anywhere was going to be haunted it was a 500 year old stone cottage in the middle of nowhere.

'What?' Jake shook his head, irritably. 'No! It was – where did you get the idea of a ghost from? – no, forget I asked. It was a face. An eye.'

'Urgh,' said Elizabeth. 'Urgh... an eye?'

'Yeah. At the window.'

'Outside? That's not in your room.'

'Well, it's bloody close enough. Practically in my room!' Jake shuddered.

Elizabeth had just re-read Wuthering Heights for the fifth time and knew all about spirits at windows desperate to get in. She told Jake so.

'No,' he said slowly, 'It was nothing like that. Look, it wasn't a ghost – jeeze, you're obsessed! It was big – bigger than the whole window! And the eye was as big as... I dunno, a boulder or something.'

'What did it look like?'

'It was burning.'

'A fiery eye?'

'Yeah. And it kept blinking.'

'Blinking? A blinking eye? That doesn't sound scary.'

'No?! *No*?! You try it next time then! I'll tell it not today thanks but our Bett's in, *she'd* like to say hello!!'

Elizabeth took a sip from a glass she lifted off the coffee table. 'When did you last watch Lord of the Rings, Jake?'

'Yeah, yeah, you're so funny.' Jake bit his lip until it went white.

'You weren't... y'know, dreaming, were you?' Elizabeth asked.

Jake sighed. He really wished he had been. 'It was real,' he said stoutly. 'I could smell it. I could even taste it.'

'Taste it?'

'I could taste something in the air, like tin or whatever. And a bit rotten-eggy. I tasted it yesterday in the park when I saw that statue. It was real. You don't taste in dreams.'

'Not tin and rotten eggs anyway.'

'No.' Jake twisted a corner of the blanket his mother had wrapped around him. It was blue with small green flowers on it. He reached out and took his sister's glass with no resistance.

'What d'you think it was? This face-thingy?' asked Elizabeth

'You promised, remember?'

'Jake, do I look like I'm gunna laugh? God!'

'I think it was a dragon.'

There. Jake said it out straight and waited for the ridicule. His sister surprised him.

'A dragon? Like in fairy stories?' she whispered.

'Like in history,' answered Jake, relieved.

'What did it want?'

'I did say a dragon, y'know. Aren't you gunna take the piss?'

'Jake, you've dreamt about dragons all your life and who knows what's out there ...as well as us, I mean. Did it do anything?'

'It just stared and said I was a ...companion.'

'...a what?'

'Companion.'

'That's a bit lame, innit? Don't old ladies have companions?'

Jake shrugged. He supposed it was lame.

'It made me feel sick,' he said eventually. 'When it spoke.'

'That's nasty,' said Elizabeth.

'Yeah, nasty.'

Elizabeth pulled a face, trying to dislodge the image of Jake being sick. 'Is it the same thing? From the park? You saw it move, yeah?'

'Dunno. But this thing last night was real. *Really* real. Breathing real. And there was another thing,' Jake said nervously, his eyes flicking from the glass to his sister.

'What?' she prompted.

'It knew my name.'

'Jake?'

'No, that's what's *weird*. It called me by my full name.'

'Really? You think *that's* what's weird? That it called you, what, *Jacob*?'

Jake nodded, ignoring the sarcasm.

'How did it know?' asked Elizabeth.

There was a loud rap-rap on the wall, then a voice.

'Elizabeth! Leave your brother alone. Jake, rest!'

'I'm alright, Mam,' shouted Jake to the white-painted stone.

'Rest!'

Elizabeth stood up to leave. 'I'm off then,' she said loudly. 'I'll be back in an hour and we can watch telly,' and in a whisper she added, 'then you can tell me some more about your dragon.'

Jake's eyes followed his sister as she left the room. She closed the door behind her with a heavy click for her mother's ears.

From where he lay, he could see out into the back garden. Just about there... yeah. He stood up and crept over to the French windows. On the lawn, softened in the morning light, were two indentations, shallower than he'd expected but clearly there. Two footprints the size of flagstones.

⊘

Jake dreamt of his father again.

In his dream, Bill was not much older than Jake was now and they looked almost like twins. He was in a field and running. Away from his son.

Jake shouted but his voice belonged to someone else. It was the sound of earthquakes and the shifting of tectonic plates.

'William! William Jacob!'

His father ignored him.

Jake called again. This time his voice was his grandfather's.

'Son!'

Bill, still running, looked back once and firmly shook his young head.

The field became a path of cracked stones like the limestone pavements of the Giant's Causeway, and ahead of Bill was moorland and the dense heaths of the Peaks. Head down he ran on, unable to look up and unwilling to come back.

All of a sudden, a shadow, black and slick, seeped out of the stones behind him. Then, the shadow changed; now it was an oil slick, an ocean of black. It started to race Bill.

Jake screamed but his voice was ripped from his throat. The shadow was gaining on his father. He could outrun this, surely? Bill glanced back, and sped up.

Jake could see a cave ahead. Bill would be safe. He started to cheer as his father sprinted on.

Then the shadow began to rise into a wave over fifty feet high.

When it crashed down, it would ram his father's body into the crazed stones, smash his bones and crack his skull. Jake had to do something. He screamed. *Dad! Dad!*

The shadow-wave fell. A wall of blackness, fierce and fatal.

Bill had run out of time. He crouched, covered his head with his arms and waited for the blackness.

The path in front of him exploded.

A tail, thick as a linden tree and twenty feet long, coiled up and around his waist and dragged him, winded, into the earth.

When the black wave crashed down seconds later it was onto bare, unbroken land littered with boulders and fist-sized stones...

Jake awoke hot and sticky and desperate for the toilet. The arm of the sofa had forced his head into a crooked position so that his neck ached. He'd kicked the blanket to the floor. The air around him smelled greasy and his mouth tasted like something had slept in it.

The day had passed slowly and without incident. Jake had slept for most of it – his mother would be pleased – but he'd checked out the marks in the garden: close-up they looked more like the old indentations of plant pots than footprints from monsters.

Outside now the daylight was fading.

He could hear his mother in the kitchen finishing supper and Elizabeth upstairs playing her guitar. The pressure in his bladder forced him upstairs.

In the old-fashioned bathroom, he emptied his bladder then peeled off his t-shirt and filled the sink with cold water. He felt like he'd been dragged through a tropical greenhouse. He bent over and immersed his face. The water felt good. He stayed there for a count of ten, listening to the cooling bubbles rise up from his nose in tiny pops. He emerged dripping. He did it again. This time he stayed until his chest tightened, and emerged spraying water. It felt really good. Alive.

He washed himself then stood in front of the mirror, water

trickling down his skin. He fetched a new towel from the airing cupboard; white fluff stuck to his chin. He leaned in and tried to pick it off, then he saw out the corner of his eye his comb. He must have put it there this morning. He picked it up. It was warm.

He could have sworn it was vibrating.

He ran a thumb over the join and a small spark, snake-like, leapt up and bit him. He dropped the comb in the sink. It clattered against the porcelain, like pebbles tumbling on shale.

Gingerly he reached in and picked it up again. No spark this time. Jake laughed a nervous little chuckle.

'Static,' he said, his voice bouncing loudly around the bathroom's acoustics. 'Yeah, from the carpet downstairs,' he added and carefully ignored the small voice in his head that said, *but isn't it only something* metal *that earths static electricity?*

He looked in the mirror. He looked rough. He put the comb to his wet hair and pulled.

A crackle of sparks. His scalp tingled.

He laughed and pulled the comb through his hair again. Tingle. Pull. Tingle.

He felt dizzy. He closed his eyes.

He could see fire. And colour. And the edge of the horizon. He felt like he was flying; he felt... powerful. As if he knew things.

He laughed out loud and opened his eyes – in this light, in the mirror, he thought he saw a glimmer of orange in his eyes. In his fingers, unnoticable unless you were looking for it, the comb glowed.

A strange feeling of happiness overwhelmed him. He hadn't felt happy for a long time. He remembered the nightmare and felt a tinge of guilt. He shrugged it off, shoved the comb in his back pocket, grabbed a clean t-shirt from the towel rail and went downstairs, trailing happiness and a feeling of flying.

The cave grew warm.

He coiled himself around the map as if protecting it.

His body glowed. He was content. Almost. Fire burned in him.

Soon it would be released.

He closed his eyes and focused on the stones. He saw the companion eating. Laughing. Happy.

CHAPTER 6

And now it was night-time. Jake's eyes scanned the summer sky for the Plough. He loved it. He knew technically it was an asterism in Ursa Major, but that didn't stop it being his favourite constellation. It was a constant. Stable. You could always see the Plough. And he liked the name. It was a tool – much better than the Big Dipper. Stronger. Grounded. It even sounded heavy. *Plough*.

And there it was half-way between the heavens and the horizon.

Jake had persuaded his mother to let him stay up and stargaze. It was something he used to do with his father, when the nights were cold and clear. They'd bundle up in sleeping bags on deckchairs in the back garden with a flask of hot cocoa and the telescope Lucy had bought them one Christmas.

And tonight she'd tried to put up some kind of fight but, in the face of all the evidence, gave in. Her son was rested and feeling fine. Too rested, Jake had argued, he probably wouldn't sleep before midnight anyway.

That was over an hour ago and Lucy and Elizabeth were already in bed.

Stars bejeweled the darkness for miles around: the 'W' of Cassiopeia, Cygnus the swan, Andromeda and her galaxy. Jake looked for Ursa Minor but could never remember where it was so gave up. There was Pegasus somewhere too. But no shooting stars tonight – nothing to wish on.

The warm night welcomed the boy. He sat quietly on a deckchair he'd found in the shed. It was more comfortable than it looked, but not as comfortable as the ones back home. It felt like it had been a lifetime since he'd last done this. He took a sip of water from a bottle and popped two white tablets into his mouth. Travel-sickness tablets. You never knew.

He settled down and waited.

His watch glowed eleven-fifteen.

A troop of bats darted in and out of the trees feeding on late-night insects. Two hedgehogs came and ate separately, one big, one small. Moths flickered in the porch light. Some died. Jake relaxed to the sound of beetles chirruping in the grass. He turned over in his mind the odd events of the last few days, trying to make some sense of it all, so when all the noises suddenly stopped, he was half-expecting it.

He looked up and almost choked on his own breath.

Flying in front of the fat moon was a shape. Jake could make out the tip of a snout, more like a bird's bill, yellow in the moonlight, and a body, long and lithe, pointed from tip to tail.

Tail. Strong and thick as a linden tree.

He felt pinned down by the memory, his throat dry. He could taste the sting of the travel pills at the back of his throat. He tried to blink but his eyes were transfixed.

Framing the sky was the slow movement of the creature's wings. One beat. Two. Dragging the air.

Jake watched soundlessly.

The creature landed carefully on the lawn, and snorted – the only sound in the stifling night.

Whooomph.

The heat struck Jake like an airbag. He drew in a breath and couldn't hold it. What was he thinking – travel sickness tablets against this! That was like taking an aspirin for heart-surgery.

He squinted through the sudden sweat pouring down his face. If he could hold back the dizziness, he'd be fine.

The creature snorted again. It was huge. Standing upright it could easily reach the attic window. Jake wiped his face awkwardly on his t-shirt sleeve. He stood up and waited until the creature, eyeing him thoughtfully, settled down.

'Hello,' Jake said, his head already pounding like a bass guitar. The creature brought its face down and sniffed.

'Hello, Jacob.' It was the sound of slabs crashing against slabs. Jake's stomach lurched.

'H– how do you know my name?' he managed.

The monster snorted again. A small flame, blue and banked by steam, re-heated the air. Jake felt the ground beneath him shudder.

'I know your name, Jacob, because I have known you for a long time.'

'...?'

If the heat of the steam was bad, then the speed of the creature's face zooming in to barely an inch from Jake's was much worse. It was as if the world contained only it.

It snorted again. Jake winced against the smell; eggy and hot.

'Jacob. I have been waiting for you.'

'What do you mean, *waiting*?'

Jake steadied himself against the deck chair. It wobbled. Behind him the house was curiously silent. The only light in the garden came from the moon. Enough to see by.

The creature's body was sinewy. It moved carefully as though it needed time to think about where it should place itself. It raised its slender head into the air and, sniffing, twisted its neck, at least three times longer than a giraffe's, to face Jake squarely. It opened its mouth slightly. Jake could see row on row of ridged teeth.

The creature spoke without mouthing the words; they entered Jake through his skin and bones. As it spoke, the boy's nausea swelled again.

'I have waited a long time for you, Jacob.'

'H-how do you mean?' Jake's mouth was dry. He wished he could reach down for a sip of water but he was transfixed by the words. Even his gums throbbed.

'I have waited more than decades.'

Jake's gut wrenched painfully. He clenched his teeth and stared at the thing, trying to size it up.

There was something oddly familiar about it, but also wrong. *Was it a dragon?* It sort of looked like a dragon, but its head was too thin and bullet-shaped. And its colour, which in the bleached-out moonlight was difficult to judge, surely should have been greener. It had a belly that definitely should have been fatter. And forearms – did dragons even have forearms? And did they have such long necks? This one curved into an S.

Only its hind legs, muscular and sturdy, seemed about right in Jake's opinion. Those and its tail. Its long and dangerously barbed tail.

But Jake was forgetting the wings.

Folded onto the creatures back, the wings should have been impossible.

Jake stared with his mouth open. He could see tiny whorls tattooed onto the folds. As if able to read Jake's mind, the creature opened up its wings and stretched them out with deliberation. They were broader than the whole cottage and they looked solid – even bats' wings were translucent in flight. These were solid as rock.

Jake knew what he was looking at, but this thing in front of him was no where near lizardy enough to be a dragon: it had no scales, no horns. It hadn't even tried to burn him alive.

'Are you a–a dragon?' Jake stammered.

The dragon's eyes flared white.

'Close, lad. Close enough.' Again the words sank into Jake's head and body. 'It is merely a form.'

It blinked again and coiled its tail around its body. The voice, heavy as stone, continued. 'I am elemental.'

Jake pulled his gaze from the tail and looked at the creature's golden eyes. It blinked.

'What is?' he said, confused. 'What's elemental?'

'I am, lad. I am elemental.'

'What d'you mean?'

'I am of the elements, Jacob.'

The dragon's voice was as patient as mountains. Images formed in Jake's mind of oceans pressing down on layer after layer of settling rocks and stones, of glaciers carving the landscape. He saw fire, explosions. Mountains being born.

'Of...?' he managed.

'The elements. Limestone. My element is limestone.'

'Limestone?' asked Jake weakly. Then, the words rushed out of his mouth as if they had somewhere important to go.

'Limestone! You can't be made out of *stone*, you're *alive*!'

'I am, lad. Limestone. Believe your eyes.'

In the moonlight Jake could see a... stone-iness... to the creature's skin, and when it moved its tail, it sounded like the scraping of tombstones in a crypt. He rubbed his eyes with his palm heels. His head was trying explode.

'You're really real?' he asked, a nervous tremor in his voice.

'Yes. William Jacob knew this to be true,' said the dragon.

Jake shook his head from side to side. 'Who?'

'–your father–'

'–Dad?' asked Jake bewildered. *William Jacob!* Jake's fear was sudden. His nightmare! The creature, the wave, the tail dragging his father into the earth. This really was the thing from his dream. Jake leaned back, instinctively and scanned the area for somewhere to run.

The dragon took a step forward, and fixed Jake with a stare like concrete. After a long minute it asked, 'What do you know of me, lad?'

Jake shook his head. The word 'nothing' came out as a croak.

The dragon's eyes flared deep red.

'Your father told you nothing of me?'

Jake didn't know what to say, the last thing he wanted to do was anger the creature. But he realised it was too late for that when the ground beneath him growled as if thunder was forcing its way through. The dragon's tail swooped back and forth like an angry cat's and Jake could feel the hot slipstream of every swoop.

He edged back as far as he could until he almost fell into the deck chair. The dragon ignored him. It was thinking. When at last it spoke, the air shook.

'It is worse than I thought,' it said. 'At least you have the talisman.'

How far, thought Jake, would I get before I was toast? The porch? The backdoor? Inside the boot-hall?

'I an't got nothing,' he answered trying to keep his voice casual.

The dragon's eyes narrowed into white slits. It snorted.

'You are mistaken. I can feel it, lad. *Smell* it.'

'Look, I don't know what you can smell but it's not me...'

The dragon reared onto his haunches and cracked open his massive wings. It sounded like petrified bones breaking. It flexed its claws. A black shadow covered Jake as he screwed his eyes closed, hunkered down and screamed.

The dragon's voice was quiet and curious. 'Lad. Why do you scream?'

Jake opened his eyes and rasped, 'You're going to kill me!'

'Kill you?' The dragon was astounded. 'Kill you? You are my companion, I have waited a long time for you...'

'B-but the... claws?'

'I was... uncomfortable. I merely stretched. Live to be as old as I am, lad, and you'll know what stiffness means,' muttered the creature.

A river, a sea, an ocean of relief swept over Jake. He collapsed into the chair, trying to catch his breath. Above him, the reassuring Plough sparkled. He laughed nervously and tried to focus on the creature, which was difficult because it moved in an almost constant heat-haze of steam. He stopped laughing.

'How did you know my dad?' he asked, cautiously.

'I did not know him.'

'But you just said–'

'Your father and I never met. He would not believe in me.'

'I don't geddit – just now you said...'

'I said he knew I existed. Knowing I exist and believing in me are two different things.'

'No, they're not. That's stupid.'

The dragon twitched its shoulders in a shrug. 'Humans believe in things – the existence of which they have no proof – all the time, Jacob. Throughout history it has been the case.'

The dragon glanced up at the heavens and smiled.

'Do you believe in science, Jacob?'

It was a strange question, and the dragon said it as if it was asking Jake if he believed in God.

'Well, yeah!' said Jake, and to himself he added, *God, I'm talking to a dragon about science!*

'And if a scientist, such as your father, found something he could not explain, what do you surmise he would do?'

'He'd find out what it was.'

'Aah... this has not always been the case, lad. Let us take fossils. What if I told you that many scientists, very learned men, knew of the existence of fossils but did not believe in the truth of them?'

'Eh–'

'These men believed the world was created by a god. Fossils upset this idea. In their thinking, an accommodation was reached, and so they made up theories of a life force within rock that wanted so much to be like God's creatures that it emulated them. But just being rock, and not touched by God's grace, it failed in its attempt.'

'That's wrong,' said Jake. 'Scientists want to find out the truth! They need to know how the world works! They don't just make stuff up!'

'Ah, I see the acorn did not fall far from the tree,' the dragon said in a dismissive tone.

'What's that supposed to mean?!'

'What do you *see*, lad?' The dragon flexed its neck muscles and stretched its wings.

'Am I a dragon made of limestone? Or a figment of your

imagination? A thing, perhaps, from your dreams?'

Jake winced at the way the dragon said 'dreams' – there were far too many eeees in it for his liking.

'Maybe I am dreaming...' he said, stubbornly.

'Perhaps...' said the dragon, tossing its head back. 'Do you remember your grandfather?'

It threw the question to Jake like it was a ball in a simple game of catch.

'Granddad?'

'Yes, your grandfather. You have read his letters. He knew about dreams.'

'How do you know that?! What d'you know about my granddad?'

In this light, the dragon's eyes flared in such a way it might be mistaken for a smile.

'You have much to learn, lad,' it said, shortly. 'Tomorrow I will return. Sleep. Dream about the talisman...'

The dragon took a step towards Jake, then another and another. It was almost on top of him when it lifted off the ground and rose high and dangerously quick. Jake felt the rush of air as it passed. He could see the crazing of the dragon's stone underbelly, pale as marble. Then it was gone.

He slumped on the deck-chair bewildered and exhausted. He closed his eyes and saw the after-image of the dragon cutting through the night sky. When he opened them again all he wanted to see was stars. And they were all there was to see: Cygnus, Cassiopeia and, stable and bright, the Plough.

And now Jake was in his bed. He felt like he'd not slept for weeks. He lay on top of his duvet running the last half hour over and over in his mind.

So... a dragon. Made of limestone. In his garden. On his summer holidays.

What?!

Why hadn't anybody in the house woken up? They'd made enough noise between them.

A dragon!

Perhaps he'd imagined it. *Had he imagined it?* Sometimes travel sickness tablets made you drowsy, had he slept and dreamt it?

No. It was *real*.

A dragon.

Not like dragons in any book I know, thought Jake. Those things were like dinosaurs. And they ate people: knights and virgins. And they were flesh and blood. Jake was sure of that. Not *made of stone*.

Weirdo dragon!

Dream of the talisman... *Hah!* Knowing his luck he probably would!

Yawning, he pulled out his watch and held it up to the gloomy light, it read 12.15. His head spun with too many thoughts and his bones were heavy. His eyelids fought hard to stay open but it was a losing battle. The watch dropped quietly onto his pillow, and in minutes he was asleep.

CHAPTER 7

Sunlight didn't burst in through Jake's curtains because someone had been in during the night and drawn them closed.

It was now ten to eleven. He'd missed most of the morning but he didn't mind. He'd needed the sleep. He hadn't dreamt at all last night but he still felt tired.

He stumbled out of bed, down the creaking stairs, into the bathroom to shower. The water was just warm enough to keep him there for ten minutes. He dried, dressed and went down to the kitchen.

On the table was a note from his mother:

Gone into to town with Bett. Back about 2ish. On my mobile if you need me. Love Mam.

She'd drawn a little smiley face after 'Mam'.

Jake ate some cereal for breakfast and fetched his Macbook. The signal was pretty weak, but okay for what he wanted. It just took longer to upload that's all. He keyed in 'dragons'.

A hundred and seventy-two million websites. The usual suspects: George and the Dragon, Dragon myths, Dragon's Den, Here be Dragons, Komodo Dragons, Dragon Breath...

Jake learnt that dragons in China were generally considered good luck, and at one time were treated as gods. Hah! *Good luck!* Hah!

Jake keyed in 'elemental'. Almost as many sites. This gave him a hundred versions of the periodic table; shops to buy ingredients to cast spells; weather sites; horoscopes; events organizers; Scottish wedding photographers; even a badly punned site for fans of chemistry and Sherlock Holmes, 'Elemental, Dr Watson, elemental'. Jeeze, thought Jake.

'Talisman' was as bad: good luck charms; rings; board games; theatres; hexes; gemstones that were meant to make men better in bed; hundreds of dictionary definitions and a recipe for a Chinese casserole.

Jake sighed and tried them together:

I'm sorry your search for 'elemental dragons talisman' yielded no results. Did you mean 'Elementary school tales'? Try removing the quote marks and searching again.

Jake swore and tried 'elemental' + 'dragon'. It yielded a few hundred results selling pewter jewellery and video games, and a short article about how clouds could look like dragons. Not much help, there.

He rubbed his eyes and let out a long, frustrated sigh. This is ridiculous, he thought. I don't have any talisman. Charms, rings, gemstones... Where would I get something like that from?

And then a small thought crept into his brain... he tried not to think about it in case he jinxed it somehow. He rushed upstairs and fetched down his father's box. He emptied it on the kitchen table where the contents looked like props from a film: the jet marble, the small book of words, the dried flowers...

He picked up the marble and held it up to the window light. He rolled it along the table and a miraculous amount of nothing happened.

Not the marble, then.

He picked up the book and read the words aloud, starting at the beginning.

'Elephantine,' he said.

No dragon appeared. No thunderclap.

He read on. 'Board. Insubstantial. Egregious. Magnanimous. Them. Orange. Poinsettia. Established. World.'

It was a bizarre book. Just random words in a random order with not even definitions like in a dictionary. Maybe there was a special word that would trigger something mystical? Jake read page after page. When he reached the end and nothing had happened he stopped, feeling foolish.

Was he even on the right track? He flicked the remaining contents around. Maybe the flowers? He sniffed them and sneezed from the dust.

This was ridiculous. There was nothing here that was a talisman!

So what was it?

Another thought crept up on him, but this one was small and powerful and Jake knew, instinctively, it was right: Dad *did* know exactly what the talisman was. And so did Granddad.

So... was it in the letters?

Jake loped upstairs, fetched the bundle and spread the letters out, picking one up at random. He read aloud, carefully listening for anything that would hint at what the talisman might be. He took notes.

After half an hour or so he stopped reading and checked his notes.

So far, not so good.

Not one of the hidden messages mentioned a talisman, but the bits about the dragon started to make more sense. One message had said: *Dragon here. Help, son. Believe.*

Believe. That was the thing, Jake's father *hadn't* believed. Wouldn't believe.

But why not?

Granddad, now, he believed. It was here in blue and faded white. Granddad had believed, so why not Dad?

Jake scratched his head and rubbed his face in irritation. This was getting him nowhere. He needed to talk to someone. Maybe Mam, he thought. Dad must have said something to her, surely? A thirty foot dragon made of limestone wasn't the kind of thing you could exactly keep a secret from each other was it? Not for long anyway.

Jake folded the letters back into their envelopes and looked at his watch. About an hour to go before his mother and sister got home. That was enough time. Yes. Plenty of time to work out what to say.

When it came to the crunch, Jake couldn't bring himself to ask his mother about any of it: not the talisman, not his father's involvement and definitely not the dragon. By the time she and his sister had returned from shopping, arms straining with bags of vegetables, bread, tins and biscuits, it all seemed a bit childish to bring up. And anyway, she'd think he was still ill and ground him until he was better.

Elizabeth, though... he could talk to her. She already knew some of it. After tea, he invited her on a walk. She gave him a long, withering look and said, stoutly, 'No thanks.'

'Why not?' asked Jake, taken aback.

'Because I've got a life. I'm not a nature nerd.'

Jake let it pass. 'I need to, you know, show you that thing.'

Jake waggled his eyebrows and flared his eyes.

'What thing?' asked Elizabeth picking at the flaking polish on her nails.

At the end of the table Lucy was finishing a coffee and reading an old Sunday newspaper. She never managed to read them on the day, she was always a day or two behind. She glanced up but paid her children little mind. Jake was on a fool's errand, she thought, if he thought he could get Elizabeth to go for a ramble with him.

Jake sighed. 'That stone thing I wanted to show you, y'know, that stone... wall... *statue*... thing...'

It was like a new day slowly dawning on her face.

'Oh! Oh, *that* thing. Yeah, yeah. *That*. Okay. Hang on, let me get my cardie.'

'Right...' Jake turned to his mother. 'Mam, we're just off out...'

'Uh-huh, to see a thing...' said Lucy into her newspaper.

'Yeah... we won't be long...'

'Well, don't let this *thing* get you into any trouble. And don't forget to take your phone.' She turned the page slowly.

'Okay,' said Jake. Elizabeth appeared with a blue cardigan more fluff than fabric and tied it around her waist. She checked her reflection in the hall mirror and shouted 'see ya' to their mother. Lucy answered, her eyes not leaving her paper.

Jake and Elizabeth walked down to the lower fields. They could see the walkers on the bright peaks even from here. The few clouds in the sky, weren't large enough to dull the bright sun.

As they walked, Jake talked. Elizabeth didn't interrupt him once. She accepted everything he said as the truth. She had no reason not to.

Eventually they slumped down under a large ash tree on a small hill. They could see for miles and miles. Everything was peaceful, as if the world had been created for that moment.

Jake plucked a blade of grass and twiddled it in his fingers.

'It could be anything,' said Elizabeth. Jake nodded, 'I know.'

'What does it want you to do with it?'

'I dunno.'

'It'll be a precious object, Jake. That's what all the books say.'

'What books?'

'Y'know, the...books, the mythy books...'

'Oh. Them.' Jake dropped the grass-blade and plucked another.

'It'll be a necklace or a ring or summats. From Dad.'

'Yeah? I don't have anything like that.' He flicked the blade twice. 'Eyup, maybe you've got it,' he said, hopefully.

'Jewellery from Dad?'

'Yeah!'

Elizabeth shook her head. 'No, I never got that kind of stuff from Dad, only Mam. Anyway, it'd be old, wouldn't it? Antique?'

'Probably,' agreed Jake. 'Probably a necklace with a dragon on it, or a coiled dragon ring.'

'Nah. When did you ever see Granddad or dad or any of us with anything like that?'

Jake shrugged and sighed. 'What's if it's in disguise?'

'It's a bloody good disguise. No, it's got to be summats, Jake, that Dad gave you.'

'He never gave me anything special except my camera. And that box after he died. But I've been through it, and there's nothing in it.'

Elizabeth stood up straightening her cardigan. 'C'mon,' she said. 'There's *something* in that box. Let's both have a look. Hey, look!'

She pointed out to a far field. Brightly painted vans and lorries trundled up a winding road. 'It's a fair!' she squealed.

Jake peered into the distance. They'd not been to a fair in years. The last time had been with their father.

'Is it coming or going?' he asked.

'Coming. It's gotta be.' Elizabeth shielded her eyes against the sun's last blaze.

'I thought you wanted to check out this box?'

'Yeah, we will. But it's a *fair*, Jake.'

Jake nodded and held out a hand. 'Tomorrow. We'll go tomorrow. C'mon. Giz a hand up.'

Elizabeth grabbed Jake's wrist and yanked. He felt something fall from his pocket.

'Oh, my watch!' He bent down and picked it up. He put it automatically to his ear and said, laughing, 'It's alright, it's tough as boots this.'

'-'time is it?' asked Elizabeth, gazing at the lorries.

'Quart-past-six.'

'They'll be setting up then,' she added, wistfully. Jake followed his sister's gaze and said, 'There's meant to be rain tonight.'

They scanned the horizon. The summer sky, with its vivid reds and golds, already looked like it was on fire. There was no sign of rain. Elizabeth smiled, tugged on Jake's sleeve and said, 'C'mon, let's go have a look.'

'No! Tomorrow.'

Elizabeth scowled and swore under her breath.

Jake folded the strap behind the watch and slipped it back into his pocket. They set off down the hill with the sun behind them.

'Did the dragon say it was coming back?' asked Elizabeth, sulkily.

'Yeah, tonight.'

'Can I see it, then? If I can't go to the fair.'

'I don't think so. I think it might be dangerous. Maybe next time.'

Elizabeth sighed and said, 'Oh, go on.'

'No,' Jake replied.

'Go oooonnn.'

'No.'

'Go on.'

'No. Really! No!'

Elizabeth glared at her brother. The early midges were clustering along the grassy paths. 'Can we go and look at the fair, then?'

'Yes.'

'Cool!'

'Tomorrow!'

He reached out to the stones.

They sang to him. The boy was secure.

The map pulsated, its signature glowing crimson.

A fine spray of black oil covered the algae on the far cave wall. How it had managed to break through, even this ineffectually, the elemental had no idea. He reared up and breathed a white plume of fire. The oil, the algae, withered under its heat.

The elemental dragon growled angrily and left.

Tonight came. Jake sat on the old deckchair glancing nervously at the dragon. It seemed angry for some reason. Every so often it would raise its head and sniff like a tiger at a tree. Eventually it settled down. Above them, stars twinkled as if nothing was wrong.

'I would imagine you have questions, lad,' the creature said, gruffly.

'Erm... a few, yeah,' squeaked Jake.

'In good time I will answer them, but first I must know, what did your father tell you about me?'

'Tell me? I told ya, dad din't tell me anything about you. I din't even know you existed until the other night.'

The dragon's eyes burned orange.

'Do you mean to tell me he told you nothing, lad?! Nothing of your heritage?'

Jake shrugged. His bones felt heavy and his head throbbed. There had to be a better way to communicate.

'Is that telepathy?' he wheezed, holding his temples.

'No,' said the dragon. 'The words want to be heard, they will find a way to you. Your body forms them like waves in water.'

'What makes the words form?' Jake managed.

'My needs.'

'Is there an easier way to talk? Please?'

The dragon stepped closer and studied Jake's face. It came to a private conclusion. The pressure in Jake's body dropped.

'Is this better?' it said.

'Yes... thanks. A bit.' Jake swallowed. 'How did you do that?'

'It is of no importance, lad.' It flicked its tail again, as slowly as a cat watching a mouse, and flexed the muscles of his shoulders to the sound of slabs being dragged across sand. It stretched its fingers that were more like talons. Jake briefly noted one was missing.

The dragon raised an eyebrow and its eyes cooled to yellow, as if sighing. 'At least you have the comb, Jacob?'

'What comb?'

'You have a comb, half-bone half-stone?'

Jake thought about his comb. What did this dragon know about it?

'Well, yeah. I have,' said Jake cautiously. 'I've got this weird comb, yeah? But, what's it got to do with you?'

'Your father gave you the comb, but told you nothing of its powers?'

'Dad? No, I got it after he died. It was granddad's. What *powers*?'

But the dragon, too lost in its own reverie, wasn't really listening to Jake. It blinked slowly then said, as if thinking aloud,

'I knew he had forsaken us, but this is worse than I had thought.'

'What is? Who's forsaken us?'

The dragon looked at Jake and snapped, 'Your father!'

'What... *Dad*?'

'The comb, Jacob, is the talisman.'

'*That's* the talisman!'

'Yes. Your father owned it last. He was the only companion not to believe in me. The others – your grandfather, his father and so on – all respected their destinies. But your father...

'...and not even to acknowledge me to his bloodline!'

The creature snorted a short, angry flame and seared a patch of grass at Jake's feet.

'Hey!' Jake stomped the smoking patch away, ignoring the churning of the dragon's voice in his stomach.

'He was irresponsible, lad! He knew of the dangers...'

'Eyup, that's my dad you're talking about!' Without thinking, Jake struck out.

'Ow!' He pulled his stinging hand back and tried to shake some life into it. The dragon looked down as if noticing him for the first time.

'You should have been prepared, lad,' it said, quietly.

'Prepared for what?'

'There's little time, now.'

'Prepared for what? *What* dangers?' Jake insisted.

'Grave dangers, Jacob.'

'What *are* you? And don't give me any of that 'I am elemental' crap because I don't know that means!'

The dragon stepped back and eyed the boy. It was impressed.

'Well, it seems you have *something* about you, lad. Something your father did not possess.'

'You just watch it, mate,' snarled Jake.

The dragon relented. 'What is it you would like to know?'

'What *are* you. I mean, *really* what are elementals?'

'We were born of elements, Jacob,' said the dragon. 'Many of us are very ancient and some are much younger: as new elements have emerged so have we.'

'Like plutonium?' said Jake. The dragon chuckled.

'Why is it that human boys are obsessed with this metal? What is so special about plutonium except that it is named after a planet?'

'Not any more it's not,' slipped in Jake. 'They say Pluto's a sub-planet now. Or a satellite. I'm not sure.'

The dragon snorted and continued. 'You have a name, lad, for the shapes we adopted. You call us dragon after drakon, the serpent. It is entirely wrong, but as good a name as any.'

Jake felt a soft splash of water on his face. 'Why dragons, though?' he asked, wiping it away. It started to mizzle.

'The form has its efficiencies.'

'Dragons are *massive*,' said Jake, wishing he'd brought his coat. The rain was picking up weight.

'There are times when mass is useful,' the creature said. There was a sound like mountains splitting in two and Jake panicked as a canopy of wings opened out above him. The rain drummed a tattoo on the dragon's hide. It was the strangest umbrella he'd ever used.

'However,' the dragon continued. 'Some elementals will barely fill your hand while others, my lad, can take up the whole sky. And there are as many dragons as there are elements. But only a few now have companions.'

'Which ones?'

'Fire, Jet, Wood, some of the Flowers, Coal, Granite, Cloud, Water, Light, Word, Snow, Clay. And me, of course.'

'Words aren't an element,' said Jake knowingly. The dragon raised an eyebrow.

'Jacob, the element of speech, the element of *books*, is words. Just as the element of mountains, of caves, is stone... You have to broaden your ideas of what elements are: many are not pinned down by your periodic table, lad. Take thoughts, now. Thoughts are the element of great ideas.' Stone tapped Jake's head twice with a claw.

'There's a Thought dragon?'

'Yes.'

'You're having me on!'

The elemental looked confused. 'On what?'

'Show it me then! This Thought dragon.'

'That I cannot do, Jacob.'

'Hah! It doesn't exist!'

'He has no companion, and will not allow himself to be seen by mankind. It is his perogative. You see, *I* was the first elemental to take the dragon form and the first to have a companion. Not all of us have.'

'You're a king, then?'

'No, we have no hierarchy,' laughed Stone.

'What you're like Communism?'

The dragon laughed and Jake's stomach rumbled because of it. This time it wasn't unpleasant.

'No, lad, we have no politics. We are...' Stone struggled for a word, '...a *system*. You might call us an environment, a *biome* comes close. We connect as elements. As the planet works, so do we.'

'So, what, like, in harmony with nature?'

'Yes, Jacob. Very like that, yes.'

Jake sucked at his cheek and said, 'the stories say dragons were evil and knights killed them.'

The creature laughed, a rich, heavy laugh like treacle.

'Evil? Killed? No, lad, not dragons. No elemental dragon has been directly killed by man.'

'They have you know.'

'No. Some poor cave-bears who could barely defend themselves, perhaps, but no dragons. No elementals.'

It looked suddenly very sad.

'Jacob. The history of man and elemental is both simple and complex.

'There was a time when mankind *could* see us and, though many cherished us and understood our ways, some were afraid. These foolish ones tried to destroy us, and so your stories were born. But they succeeded only in killing half-starved animals.

'It requires much to kill an elemental dragon, Jacob. You must obliterate every single trace of the element before any one of us is destroyed.'

'You're immortal!?' gasped Jake.

The dragon shook his head.

'Nothing lasts forever, lad. It *is* possible to destroy an elemental. I have seen it happen. Thankfully only once.' He snorted a mixture of anger and sadness. 'But that is a story for another day.'

'What do you eat?' asked Jake apropos of nothing.

'We eat many different things. Water eats fish, Fire eats coal, wood...'

'Isn't that cannibalism?'

It looked puzzled and said, 'Only if eating pig's flesh is cannibalism to humans.'

'Noooo... it's not cannibalism,' Jake said, knowing he'd never eat a bacon sandwich again. Ever.

The creature shrugged, and its whole body rippled like a landslide.

'What do *you* eat?' asked Jake.

It brought its face close to Jake. Its whole head was taller than the boy entirely. It blinked slowly, a small inferno flaring in each eye.

'What do I eat?' it snarled, gleefully. 'Well... young men by the name of Jacob.'

CHAPTER 8

It was the next day, and so far Jake hadn't been eaten. In the clear light of morning, over wheatpuffs for breakfast, it had felt like none of it was real.

But it was.

Right now Jake was staring at exactly how real it was.

In broad daylight, swooping like a swallow over the waters, the dragon was enjoying itself.

Behind Jake, trees rustled quietly with a summer breeze and he could hear blue tits chirping in the branches. In front of him fields spanned for miles; sheep and cows were white and brown blobs in the distance. The Peak mountains rose and dipped against the horizon. If he squinted, he could just about see the fishermen on the riverbank and the empty cars of walkers lined up by the roadside. They were as small as toy soldiers. What was wrong with these people, he thought, the dragon was as big as a house, and no one seemed to notice it!

It skimmed along the tops of the trees.

What was it like to fly?

Jake stared. He could make out simple shapes on the creature's hide of what looked like ammonites and other fossils. Where the boy expected to see scales, he saw smooth limestone. It came in to land. Its neck arced into an S.

Once again all the everyday sounds had stopped.

'Good afternoon, Jacob.'

The words filled Jake's head with images of landslides. Already the nausea was rising.

'Hello,' said Jake, his throat suddenly dry.

The dragon seemed to be in a good mood. It flexed its shoulders and Jake saw the tight muscles at the base of its wings. Small joints. How on earth did they support such a huge animal? They reminded him of swan's wings. His father had told him once how swans could break a man's arm with one wing. He wondered what damage these could do.

The wings flexed, ready to unfold. Jake stepped back.

'An itch,' said the dragon, casually, as they settled down again. 'How are you today, Jacob? Well rested, I hope.'

Jake watched the dragon with a wary eye as sweat trickled down his face. It promised to be a blistering day.

'Uh, yeah... I slept okay. Why?'

The dragon brought its face up to Jake's and said, 'We have much to do, lad.'

He could smell the creature's sulphurous breath, could map out the striations in its skin.

'About that,' he said in a nervous tone of voice. 'Look, I'm not sure I'm right for this.'

The dragon turned gently and stared into the boy's eyes. Jake tried to stare back but it was like staring into a furnace. A core of molten rock. It bore into his soul.

And in that instant, Jake *knew*.

He knew the creature in front of him was not a dragon, but something deeper, something fundamental.

It was old as time. It had seen worlds form, stars die.

It had lived through the beginnings of life and through mass extinctions. And through it all it had protected. Protected everything.

The knowledge was suddenly a part of Jake, floating to the surface of his consciousness like fat in a stew. And like lumps of fat in a stew, it made him dizzy and sick.

He closed his eyes and immediately wished he hadn't; on the

screen of his eyelids he saw millions of layers of strata, all the way down to the molten core.

The dragon was there, in the centre of it all. Eyes burning.

Jake opened his eyes, gasping for breath.

What the hell just happened?

He took a step back, his hands flailing in front of him. The dragon watched him with curiosity, its eyes now the colour of yellow marble. But in his mind's eye Jake had *seen them burn*.

He came to a decision.

'No,' he said firmly. 'I know you're an elemental and everything, but I need to know what I'm getting into. This could be dangerous y'know!'

The dragon's eyes flared red.

'It is dangerous, Jacob,' it growled. 'And will be more so if we do not set to work.'

'What do you mean, dangerous!? I didn't ask for any of this weirdness, and definitely not danger, mate. Not without knowing what it's about, it's not–'

'–fair?' sighed the dragon wearily.

Jake barely paused. 'I was going to say *right*.'

The dragon looked at him thoughtfully as if it was measuring him up for a coffin. With some effort, it sat down next to the boy. Jake didn't dare move – it was like standing next to a cottage that could walk about.

The creature flicked its tail slowly back and forth. Flick. Flack. Flick... Flack.

'Okay...?' said Jake, quietly.

Sharply, the dragon jerked its head up, making Jake jump.

'Nervous?' it said. Flick.

Jake felt a rumble in his muscles.

The creature was laughing. Flack.

'No!' Jake said, hotly.

'Hmm... a hero, then... Well, lad, where would you like me to start?'

Jake filed away the hero comment for later. There was something about this dragon that he didn't like. It was too cocky by far.

He shrugged and said, 'Anywhere. Beginning?'

'Ah, predictably conventional too.'

'That's it,' thought Jake. 'Sod curiosity! Sarcastic bugger!' Annoyance flared like a struck match.

'Well, alright then, let's not start at the beginning. Let's start somewhere else...'

The dragon stood up suddenly a blur. Was anything *really* that quick?

It towered over Jake, eyes glowing.

'Yeah,' continued the boy, trying to conceal his nerves. 'Let's, erm, let's start with how this is all meant to work, then.'

The dragon remained still, and Jake had an uncomfortable feeling that the words 'control' and 'anger' were important to him right now.

'So, then,' the boy croaked, 'I mean, I've got your talisman thingy, am I your master or what?'

The dragon opened its mouth to speak then stopped. Its teeth were long but not especially sharp. 'Strange that', Jake thought, 'the teeth should be like flint knives or diamonds'. Behind the first set, was a row of smaller teeth waiting their turn. Like a shark's. The mouth stretched slowly into a grin.

It said, 'You could try, lad.'

The already familiar pressure in Jake's stomach now felt volatile.

'What d'you mean?' he asked.

'Would you like to be my master?' asked the dragon, casually.

'Well, what would I have to do?' Jake could feel a prickling heat on his forehead. He had a feeling that he'd dug a deep hole and he was at the bottom of it looking up at daylight. His mouth couldn't stop talking. 'Well... in the films and things the boy always has to... Look, you said something about preparing. Don't I have to *train* you or something?' he splurted.

'Films and things?' said the dragon, curiously. It ran its ancient gaze over the boy (with his hands in jean-pockets and his bag ripped at the strap) standing in front of it. Its ears twtiched.

Jake carried on. 'Yeah, there's always some sort of dragon training. In the films...'

'Tell me, lad, what does it mean to be a master?' the elemental asked calmly.

Deeper and deeper Jake dug his hole, not knowing he should have stopped at the first spadeful.

'Sort of... I have to tell you what to do and stuff.'

He could feel the heavy rumble of the dragon's soft laughter in his stomach and chest. No outbursts. No anger. Just laughter.

It grew louder.

'Now then, lad,' said the dragon, gleefully. 'This will be good. Tell me what it is I should *do*.'

'...'

Jake stumbled over his thoughts. He laughed nervously.

'I am here,' the dragon said. 'To do as you *bid*. Tell me what to do.' It paused and added, with a theatricality Jake had only ever seen in terrible school plays, 'Young *Master*.'

And that was it, right *there*. That *tone*!

Right, thought Jake. You cocky bastard. He stood up, gripped his backpack and looked the dragon squarely in the eyes.

'Okay,' he said firmly, his eyes narrowed, his features set in defiance. 'You're a dragon, right?'

'I believe we can say that is roughly correct, lad,' said the creature, impressed by Jake's small acts of strength.

'Then, I want to fly.'

The dragon's eyes flared like tiny supernovae.

'Fly?' it whispered.

'Yes,' answered the boy, braver than he actually felt. 'I saw you, just now. I want to fly – with you.'

Without pause, the dragon said simply, 'As you wish.'

Jake couldn't believe his ears. It was *that* easy?

'What, *really*?'

'If that is your wish, young *Master*. It is achievable. However it takes some preparation.'

Jake grinned. Yes, he imagined there *would* be some preparation. How would he get on for a start? And how would he stay on? (probably by some sort of magic.) When he was riding it, how would he steer or would he just be a passenger for the first flight?

Being a dragon-master was going to be great!

And because he was amazed and astounded he forgot all the rules everyone knows about wishes. About what you might get.

He was going to fly.

'What do I do?' he asked eagerly.

'You must stand there. Be very still.'

The dragon shuffled its back to the boy and scanned the fields. It held up its slender head, testing the wind, and squinted into the distance. It took one step, then another, then more until its wings unfolded to the complicated sounds of stone scraping against stone. It took off. The surrounding trees and hedgerows bent so low they almost broke. Jake watched him and laughed, gleefully.

The dragon soared. It swept across the sky until Jake lost sight of it in the sun's glare. It disappeared over the hills on the horizon.

Long minutes passed.

And passed.

And passed some more.

Jake stood on the hill feeling foolish.

That bastard! he thought. *Master* my foot!

Alone, humiliated and angry, the boy started to walk down the field. 'Well', he muttered, '*it's* the one that needs me, I don't need it, just wait, just wait until–'

–he felt the sound in his bones and gut: a low sickening throb like a swarm of angry bees. He looked up. The sky was empty.

Then a pain in his shoulders like nothing he'd felt before. He'd once skewered his hand on a rusty clout sticking out of an old plank, but this was nothing like that. It was as if his shoulders had been filled with molten lava.

A wash of crimson flooded his eyes.

And that scream; it hadn't belonged to him, surely?

Then he felt his body lifted one, five, ten feet – up and up until he was dangling over the tree-line and heading for the mountains.

If he could breathe, he didn't know it.

The pain steadied to a dull throb, never lessening, never worsening.

And the soft laughing voice filled his wracked body once more.

'How do you like it so far, *Master?*'

Jake landed stumbling until he slumped over, shaking with cold and anger. Ice particles defrosted on his eyebrows and lashes. The ground felt good. Firm. His breath caught in his throat.

The dragon swept up and flew in circles above him, marking small contrails though the clouds. It alighted a few feet from the boy and snorted. It was no longer laughing.

'That was NOT funny!' screamed Jake. He dug up sods of rough turf with his fingers and flung them at the dragon.

'Not fregging funny at all! I could have been killed!'

'No,' said the dragon quietly, firmly.

'Yes I could of!' said Jake trying to stand.

'No.' The dragon watched as the boy's knees buckled under him. 'You were safe. You would not have fallen.'

Jake remembered the lurching of his stomach as he was lifted. He had no idea how fast they'd travelled but the ground had been a blur. Tears from the cold had streamed down his face. The fishermen and walkers from earlier on had been tiny dots in the patchwork of fields and hills.

He'd felt his breath ripped from his lungs as they soared above the clouds.

'I could have froze to death,' he hissed. With some effort, he held back reluctant tears and wiped his suddenly sweating face on the back of his hands. His chest heaved under his damp jacket.

'No,' said the dragon. 'You were only cold, perhaps also a little shocked, but nothing more. I would not have let you fall. I would not have let you freeze. You could breathe. The pain in your shoulders will abate, the wounds lessen. They are, in any case, insignificant.'

'Insignificant?! You nearly ripped my shoulders off—'

'What is it about you, lad, that you are so given over to exaggeration?' The dragon said calmly. 'You wished to fly. This I enabled you to do. You should be careful for what you wish.'

This time Jake managed to stand. He stared at the dragon.

'You're a bastard, you know?' he said, icily. His spat, his mouth dry and gritty, and picked up his backpack ready to leave.

'Be aware, lad,' the dragon began, 'that no elemental has a master save him or herself. It is your own arrogance that makes you suffer today.'

Unbelievable, said Jake under his breath. I get the crap scared out of me and it's *my* fault. He spat again and shook his head.

'Sod off,' he said and turned. As he passed the dragon, he felt its steady, marble gaze follow him.

His heart pounded. He ignored the jelly in his knees and forced himself to walk straight and assured down to the lower field and the path back up to the cottage.

'Jacob...' said the dragon.

And really how does it know my name? thought Jake.

The voice, as if reading Jake's mind, continued, gentler this time. 'Jacob, I *know* you as you – in your very *essence* – know me.'

The boy lumbered on, not responding.

'We are companions, Jacob,' continued the voice. 'You know it to be true.'

Jake gritted his teeth and walked quickly, ramming his hands deep into his jacket pockets. He tried to ignore the pain in his shoulders; dull and unrelenting. He swallowed hard – the taste of bile at the back of his throat, but he *definitely* wasn't going to be sick! He wasn't going to give that bastard the satisfaction!

He was almost at the stile when he glanced back. The dragon stood at the top of the hill, a line of conifers measuring its height.

Jake's glance lasted only seconds and because of this he didn't see the dragon watching him; its long grey head shaking slowly in frustration and regret. Then it moved: a step, another, one more, and it was airborne again.

At some primal prey-level Jake, without looking, registered the creature's flight – he tensed his shoulders and crouched ready to be lifted again. The agony of his wounds wrenched his spine and he dropped his bag.

But the vice-grip didn't come.

There were no more nasty lessons for him today.

He waited, shoulders hunched, until the sound of the dragon dissolved into the air and the everyday sounds of nature flooded in. If he'd have looked back, he would have seen the shape of the creature's wings unfolding and opening out, carrying the dragon away.

☞

Jake slipped deeper into the bath. It steamed around his ears. At least Elizabeth had left some hot water tonight; he didn't know what he would have done if she hadn't.

Probably nothing.

That was the problem, he never did anything. Not really. He avoided confrontations and sidestepped arguments as best he could. He and his sister fought, yes, but not for long, and he always gave in at the end. It was the same with everyone. He had a quick temper but it never lasted. He could always find a way to calm down. Tonight for instance; he wasn't even halfway home before the anger subsided, and by the time he'd stepped through the door it was something else, some different feeling between embarrassment and resignation.

The heat of the bath soothed his bones and the water stung where the wounds sunk deep into his shoulders. Jake noticed they were smaller than they should have been. He *had* felt the dragon's claws skewer his skin, then his muscles; he'd felt them *crush* his bones, so the wounds should have been at least an inch in diameter and deep as a finger-length, but when he'd undressed, slowly and painfully in front of the bathroom mirror, he saw among the bruises four or five gashes, no bigger than dog bites, already congealed and scabby.

Hot water swirled his drying blood around the bath making the liquid an ugly yellow-brown. Jake held his nose and sank under. He lay there in the quiet and warmth until his lungs could no longer hold out and he emerged, gasping.

What the hell was happening to him? Was he losing it? Dragons don't exist! And definitely not smart-arsed ones made from stone! God, he said to no one, I've gone nuts!

Then a small voice at the back of his mind said, *Yeah but it is real, Jakey. I've got the scars to prove it. They're real. And I flew. I mean, I actually flew. It scared the crap out of me but I flew. Sort of. I was in the air anyway. I dangled.*

He chuckled and let himself remember the feeling: the rush of cold air stinging his eyes, his stomach flipping as he'd soared over the tops of trees. The rush! And he remembered the leaden, steady whomp of the dragon's beating wings, the acrid stench of its body.

No, it was weird, but it was real alright. But why now? Why did it turn up now?

He lay back in the water and tried to relax.

Then, suddenly, he felt cold. Feverishly cold.

He tried to turn on the old brass tap with his toes but he slipped and banged his foot on the enamel tub. Aching and swearing, he sat up and leaned forward. The tap was stuck fast. He felt a rumble throb through the house. He watched the water's surface like a storm at sea.

The dragon?!

Then a loud thud.

And another.

Glass bottles and seashells fell from the window ledge and smashed onto the tiled floor.

Jake heard his sister on the landing shouting to his mother, panic rising in her voice, and his mother downstairs, quieter, calmer – but there was worry there. Fear.

Then, all of a sudden, it stopped.

The trembling, thumping, the falling bottles, all just stopped. The hot tap gave way and poured blistering water into Jake's bath. He turned it off.

He slipped a little as he stepped out of the tub, careful to avoid the broken glass and shells, and wrapped a towel around his waist. He stepped out onto the landing. His sister stood there, nervously holding on to the bannister.

'What happened?' she asked, holding an empty CD case in her hands.

'Did you feel it?' said Jake.

'Yeah, like the ground was shaking.'

'The ground?' said Jake. 'What like an *earthquake*?'

'What here?' Elizabeth looked around at the fallen pictures and books from the landing shelves, her mouth a small 'o'. 'We don't have earthquakes.' She looked up at Jake. 'Do we?'

'I dunno.' He realized that for some reason he was whispering.

Lucy appeared at the bottom of the stairs. In the gloom from a window, Jake could see the dark worry on her face.

'Are you two okay?' she called, uneasily.

'Yeah,' they answered together.

'We're fine,' said Jake. 'What was it, Mam?'

'I think maybe it was an earthquake,' she said. 'It felt like one, didn't it?'

Jake and Elizabeth shrugged, they didn't know what an earthquake felt like. They waited unsure of what, if anything, might happen next. Weren't there usually aftershocks with earthquakes? Weren't you supposed to stay inside a door frame?

Minutes passed that felt like hours.

'I think that's it.' said Lucy eventually. 'We don't get big earthquakes in England.'

'I din't know we got them at all!' said Elizabeth.

'All the time, love, there was one in Birmingham last year. Now, let's get things tidied up.' She started to climb the stairs, then stopped.

'Jake! What's that on your shoulders? Are they bruises? Have you been fighting?' she said, accusingly.

Jake had forgotten about the bruises and the claw marks on his shoulders. He'd forgotten because the pain was mostly gone. He looked down instinctively. The bruises, although still there, were yellowing as if they were days old. The claw-marks had completely healed.

'No! I mean, yeah they're bruises. Not fighting. Sorry. I fell out of a tree–'

'A what?! When?!'

'Uh, the other day. I was trying to get a good view. Y'know, of the valley. Photos...'

His sister stared at him suspiciously but Jake avoided her face.

Lucy sighed. 'Be careful, Jake. You could have broken something. I don't even know where the hospital here is. Honestly, *you're* meant to be the *sensible* one!'

'Hey, I'm right here, you know!' said Elizabeth.

Her mother laughed. The moment had passed. From earthquake-terror to everyday family life in 0–60 seconds.

'I know you are, love. Now, Jake, go put some clothes on.'

Jake slipped into the bathroom as Lucy turned to her daughter.

'C'mon, we'll sort these shelves out, Bett.' She called through the door to her son, 'Jake, you do the bathroom!' She tapped twice on the wooden panel, 'Did I hear glass breaking? Jake? Was it the mirror?'

'No, Mam,' said Jake through the closed door. 'Just some bottles.'

'My smellies?!' squealed Elizabeth rushing forward.

'No, you don't,' said her mother, grabbing her daughter's arm and pointing to a rough pile of open books. 'Don't worry about the smellies, we'll go shopping tomorrow. There, *that's* your job!' She pointed again to the books and then said quietly, 'Just so long as it wasn't the mirror.'

'Why,' asked Elizabeth, reluctantly picking up books.

'Because it's seven years bad luck if you break a mirror. And we've had enough bad luck in our family. Now, pass me those books, love, please. Yes, those ones...'

⊘

There was a mirror in Jake's room – an old, gilt-framed mirror with liver spots and crazing in the glass. He stripped off his t-shirt to check on the damage. The bruises were almost gone. He prodded them and winced, but there were no gashes, no scabs. No scars.

That was impossible!

He slumped over to his bed, accidentally knocking a packet off the bedside table; the photographs his mother had picked up from the chemist. He opened the paper wallet and flicked through them. There was nothing but disappointment: a grey blur, green reeds, water...

Then the little voice in his head said quietly, *Hey, why don't I take a proper photo? That'll prove if it's real or not.*

He lay back in the bed, flicked off the light, and smiled. Yeah, he thought. Good idea.

Chapter 9

Jake sat on a grassy verge in an old cemetery, leaning forward and resting his elbows on his knees. The pain in his shoulders had almost gone and there were no bruises left, but he was still wary...

And he'd already put his foot in it.

'Lame?' The dragon asked as it circled Jake, moving its head slowly from side to side. 'I do not understand lad. It has no legs, no feet, it cannot walk, how can it be made lame?'

'No, no, not *made* lame, just, y'know, *lame*,' said Jake weakly. He gestured with his hands and pulled a face but the dragon looked bewildered.

'Y'know?... *lame*?' Jake continued. 'I thought you were meant to be clever and stuff!'

He looked around him for some kind of support, but all he found were grassy stubs and headstones.

'Look, okay, 'lame' is like 'a little bit rubbish'.'

The dragon stopped moving. 'Ah, I think I understand, Jacob,' it said, eventually.

'Okay,' said Jake, relieved.

'You believe the talisman to be a worthless thing. I do not know why you should think this, yet you do.'

'Not worthless, just lame. It is a comb–' Jake started to say.

'I can only tell you, lad, that it is the talisman of the first elemental and his companion.'

The dragon leaned in. It was hypnotic, the way its eyes changed colour. It looked like it was trying to decide on something, then it took Jake's chin in its tail and said, quietly,

'Jacob, attend...'

The companion's son stood beside the embers of the pyre watching the remaining flames flicker and dance like tiny demons. He was wrapped in skins and furs but he was still cold; not even the fire's heat could warm his heart, today. The limestone elemental stood by his side and matched his gaze. Neither spoke.

The sky was as still as a winter lake.

No birds, no animals.

This was a sacred place, here among the ridges and clefts of rock. Mountains sheltered them.

The boy made a thick clicking noise in the back of his throat and held up a hand. Tiny chips of marble, not much bigger than grains of sand, sprung from the ground and swirled in the air around him. He clicked his tongue again and the stones coated his fingers and worked their way over the wrist and up to the elbow in a fine gauntlet. A tear rolled down his filthy cheek as he looked up into the mournful face of the limestone dragon, who nodded once.

The boy stepped forward and thrust his hand into the dying fire; right through the burnt shreds of shroud that now barely covered the companion's body. There was only a little resistance; tough and gristly. When he pulled out his arm, the stone gauntlet was blackened and hot, but his skin was unscathed.

In his hand he held a rib that until today had protected his father's heart. He wanted to sob, but he didn't. It was not the action of one with his responsibilities. His inheritance.

The rib was white as snow when it should have been charred, but that didn't surprise him. The smell of his father's burning corpse still filled his throat. It mingled with the smell of sulphur. He swallowed hard and held the bone up to the elemental. Solemnly, the elemental regarded the rib and brought its tail round and up. If the boy had been born in another time he would have described the movement as slow motion; but instead he thought it reminded him of the way the great cats stalk their prey.

And after they stalk, they strike.

The tail ripped across his face almost knocking him to the ground. Then it caught the rib as it fell from the boy's grasp.

He stood, wounded and grieving.

The tail came up gently and took the new companion by the chin.

He was bleeding beneath his left eye and his blood ran freely down his face. When he looked up he saw the other bone, the stone talon. He glanced up at the elemental, amazed, and when he looked down again the bones, bloodied and cold, were conjoined as if they had never been apart.

And in the centre was a mark like a circle dissected by an arrow.

'He was the first,' said the limestone dragon to the boy in a language so old it lived in the throat and heart.

'What he learned as my companion is held within this talisman and passed on to you. It holds the lore. You must make of it a tool, as he desired. Carve it with care. He was the first. You are the legacy.'

Already the wound on the boy's face had healed.

Jake blinked as if he'd been staring at the sun, and swallowed hard. The dragon was still there.

'That was you?' he managed.

'Yes.'

'Who was the boy?'

'A child who loved his father and learned from him.'

Jake looked away. All around him, headstones marked out the sum of people's lives telling little or nothing of their history. He thought about his own father's plaque back home: a rough marble slab with the usual things: the dates, *A loving father and husband who will be deeply missed...*

'Why did he make it into a comb? Not a sword or a proper weapon?' asked Jake.

The dragon cocked its head to one side. 'You saw the boy and thought 'primitive', yes?'

Jake nodded.

'My first companion knew the value of fighting, and also the greater value of *not* fighting. And this he taught his son. A comb is a tool for preparing skins, for seed drills, it can also be used to clear the hair and beard of lice and fleas that carry contagion.'

'Eugh.'

'And it is unlikely to be taken away as a weapon if, for example, you are captured. Is this primitive?'

Jake didn't know how to answer, so he said. 'Why did you hit him?'

'His blood sealed the talisman.'

'I thought that mark was Granddad Stanley's...'

'It is mine.'

'Oh.'

Jake's eye was drawn to the space where the talon was missing.

'It's never grown back?'

'Do yours?'

'Ha.'

'In any case, I prefer my tail.' The dragon flicked its tail up into the branches of a tree and brought down a cherry. It handed it delicately to Jake. He ate it. It was sour.

The moment was broken, to the relief of both of them.

'D'y'know,' said Jake. 'I don't know what to call you! What's your name?'

The dragon held its head onto one side, surprised.

'None of my companions have made such a request. I think, it would be appropriate to call me by my element. In your words it is Liiiimestonnnne.'

The dragon dragged out the word as if it had never said it before.

Jake almost laughed. 'Limestone?' he said. 'That's a bit— a bit of a mouthful in't it?'

'In my own language it fills the mouth, Jacob, in yours it is perhaps – what were you going to say – *lame*?'

'No, no, no, Limestone's... nice,' Jake lied. 'Limestone. Limestone. What about Limey, though? Good, short name?'

The elemental dragon flicked its tail.

'Limestone is appropriate,' it said.

'Okay. Okay.'

Jake sat quietly thinking.

'There is much you will learn as a companion, Jacob,' said the elemental.

'I can't. Sorry. I just *can't* call you Limestone.'

The dragon stopped short and sighed. 'Why not?'

'It's too long. Names should be short. Like Jake.'

The dragon grunted. '*I* call you *Jacob*.'

'I know. I prefer Jake.'

The dragon sniffed. 'I will call you Jacob.'

'Whatever, but I'm *not* calling you Limestone. What did granddad call you?'

'I was referred to as Elemental. Sometimes Dragon.'

'Oh.'

The dragon saw the disappointment on Jake's face.

'I will call you Jacob, and you, if you dislike my name so much, may call me 'Stone'.'

Jake tried the word in his mouth, '*Stone*. Stone. Yeah, *Stone's* good. I like it. Ta.'

'You are welcome. Though it does not make me happy.'

'You'll be fine.'

'And with names, Jacob, come *pronouns*. From now on it would be fitting to refer to me as 'he' rather than 'it'. When, for instance, you converse with your sibling…'

'Oh, you know about that?'

'I know a good many things, lad.'

'How.'

'I have told you, you are my companion.'

'Why do you need a companion? What are you here for? *Really*?'

Stone answered with a question. 'Why does mankind exist, Jacob?'

'I don't know, why does anything? To live, I s'pose.' Jake gave an embarrassed little chuckle.

'And do you live well?'

'*Me?* Oh, *mankind* you mean? Well, yeah! We've developed loads of stuff. Planes and computers, plumbing, electricity, gas. We built houses and cities. People are safe nowadays.'

There was something in the tone of the question that Jake wasn't picking up on and it troubled him.

'When you say 'people', do you mean 'man', Jacob?' asked Stone.

'Well, yeah. Humans. We're the only people.'

'So, humans are safe?' said the dragon quietly, and now the tone was just a little bit menacing.

Jake nodded.

The air around them flared like a kettle in an oven in a furnace. Jake's stomach pitched. Stone exploded with anger.

'*This* is man's arrogance!' he snarled.

'Eh?' stammered Jake. 'What've *we* done?'

'There was so much he could do for this world, to help all of it! And yet he worked only for himself. He developed intelligence, learned tooling, how to harness the fire elemental, and for what? His own selfish improvements. And so the world weeps at the hands of man.' The dragon growled and snapped at the air.

Jake stood up sharply. 'Woah! Hang on a minute, that's not true. We've done loads for animals and things.'

'Yes,' said the dragon, carefully pronouncing every word. 'Your kind has done much for *animals and things.*'

He let the sentence hang in the air. It had barbs in it.

'Is this what all this companion stuff's about?' Jake snapped. 'Alright some of us do some crappy things, but so *what*? I can't do anything about it? I'm just a kid! I can't stop oil-drilling and killing rainforests and stuff!'

Jake's whole body was shaking and, if his own eyes could have flared like Stone's, they would have.

Stone stopped short and backed down. Slowly, Jake's cramps subsided.

'I am sorry, Jacob. You are right,' said the dragon.

'Yeah. Well, I'm sorry too...' said Jake, rubbing his stomack.

'But, y'know, I *really* am just a kid. I can't even vote yet. Maybe I'm not really your companion.'

'You are... what you are, Jacob,' said the dragon steadily. Then he curled his heavy tail around Jake's shoulders and pulled him down to a sitting position.

'Now, do you remember the vision, Jacob? The marble gauntlet?'

'Ye-ah. That was cool. How did he do that?'

'It is a simple trick, Jacob. Hold out your hand...'

Jake held his hand at arm's length. He *felt* the rumble coming through the air. The space around his head thrummed and glittered like snow in an antique snowglobe. He thought he could hear the very particles in the air singing to him, and when he looked down, his hand was covered in tiny shards of marble. He rubbed it with his other hand but it didn't come off. He knew in that moment it could break through walls.

'It's amazing!' he said, turning it over and over. Little after-sparks danced in the light in front of his eyes. He laughed.

Stone turned and said, 'Jacob, you will learn how to do this, in time.'

'Cool. When?'

'That is up to you. You must train first.'

'Can we start now?!'

The dragon laughed, and the marble shards fell to the floor.

Elizabeth crunched a chocolate-chip cookie and stared at the letters. Jake had said find out what she could, and so here she was. Apart from the ones she'd already deciphered – the easy ones Jake had had a go at – she had a handful that were giving her a headache.

She sat on the bed ignoring the crumbs the biscuit was making and twirled her pencil. Codes. She'd tried simple alpha-numerics but they'd ended in gibberish. A shuffled alphabetical code had provided even more gibberish. And she'd achieved the most gibberish with a tie between a Caesar and a tri code.

She pulled out a letter at random, the dry paper crackling against her thumb as she read:

Dear Son,

Not much news to tell you about today. Your Mam

caught a bad cold and we had to take her to the doctors

for some antibiotics. She's a lot better now, but has to

have an inhaler now and again...

The letter continued for two and a half double-sided pages. Elizabeth skipped none of it, even the bits about vegetables and things his grandfather had seen in the classified ads.

But it was useless!

She sighed and took another biscuit.

'You're not gonna beat me,' she said to the paper. 'No way.'

She wished she'd brought her book of cyphers and codes with her, but who knew she'd need it in the wilds of Derbyshire? She tried to picture it in her head: all the different cyphers, all the different keys.

Not one picture tied in to what she had here.

The letters just looked weird with their over-large handwriting and the big gaps between the lines. She'd even, with some embarrassment, tried lemon juice, but it hadn't worked.

She rubbed her eyes and stared out at the window. Where was Jake anyhow? She glanced at her clock: 9.15. God knows how he'd persuaded Mam to let him stay out all day. If she'd tried it, she'd have stood no chance. But that was the thing about Jake; people trusted him.

Elizabeth finished her last biscuit and slumped over to the window to look at the moon. She liked moonlight. It was romantic and comforting. This one was an overly fat not-quite-full waxing moon and it made the pale night sky paler. A bank of clouds threatened it occasionally. There was no sign of Jake.

She sat on the wide window ledge and pulled out the letter again. One eye on the paper and one on the garden waiting for Jake. Then she noticed it, in the broad spaces between the scribbled lines: faint red marks that hadn't been there before.

She held the letter up to the gloomy light. On cue, the clouds that had covered the moon drifted slowly across the sky and released it.

In the moonlight, she saw deep red words scrawled beneath each neatly scripted line of blue biro. It was amazing! Occasionally the ink blotched as if it had been written with a fountain pen.

The words huddled on the line like children in a bunker. No millimetre of space was wasted.

There was a lot to be said.

Dear Son,

Not much news to tell you about today. Your Mam
I had another dream from the elemental. This is NOT
caught a bad cold and we had to take her to the doctors
something to ignore, lad, no matter who you think you're
for some antibiotics. She's a lot better now, but has to
protecting. No one's safe. Billy. You MUST train the lad
have an inhaler now and again. I've bought a new hot
before it's too late, or at least get him prepared! By God,
water bottle, so she'll be warm at least – it can get very
you're a scientist, so open your eyes! Tidalwaves, floods,
chilly here, especially in spring when you least expect it.
earthquakes, hurricanes – if I was religious I'd say this is
The doctor says she is very healthy for her age, but
Armageddon coming! Tell him! Tell Jake about the dragon!

Elizabeth stared at the paper as if it were a smoking gun. A cloud drifted across the moon and the red ink disappeared again.

'Jeez, this ink really does react to moonlight,' she said out loud. 'What's it made of? And what's all this about Jake? And does he *know*?'

Her heart pounded as she read on, greedily.

I don't think sixty-eight is especially old, do you? I also
He needs the talisman, Billy, it's his only weapon. Show
bought a new lawnmower for the lawn. It's an electric one
him how to ~~sum~~ summon the elemental & if you can't
and easier to push than that old petrol thing we had. You
remember then send him to us! It didn't take me long to
and Jake will have to have a go on it when you're next up.
teach you! If you don't do this, Bill, then when the time
How's wee Elizabeth? The photographs Lucy sent us were
comes your own son will be defenceless. We ALL will!
just bonny, lad. She's done well there. You both have.
Even the elemental. For God's sake, Bill, Be sensible.

The writing worsened until Elizabeth could barely read it. What she could make out talked about the family's responsibilities to the elemental; it appealed to his father's humanity, pleaded with him to help. There was some kind of animal – some beast – something really dangerous by the look of it.

Elizabeth went to the bed and pulled out one letter after another. All of them hid the small, secret scribble. The same message.

Jake needed to see them. He needed to know what they said. What their father had, or *hadn't* done.

She stared out of the window praying for her brother to turn up soon. The moon shone down: bright now, and slightly menacing.

Stone's voice came deep and low. He pointed with his tail to the open sky.

'Those stars, Jacob, you call them Cygnus.'

Jake looked up. Because of the moonlight, he could barely see the outstretched, wonky wings and the long neck of the constellation, but it was there. The Swan. Somehow, it always reminded him of a cross-bow – much more dangerous than a swan.

'Yeah,' said Jake.

'Why Cygnus?'

'Because it's s'posed to look like a swan. It's old-Greek for 'swan'. It's meant to have a black hole inside it y'know,' Jake chattered on.

'No, not a swan, Jacob. An elemental. It looks like me.'

The dragon took off without warning. For a second he was spread against the starry sky, wings outstretched.

Moonlight glittered on his back.

A dragon.

More dangerous than a swan. More dangerous even than a crossbow.

Yes! *That's* what he'd reminded Jake of, what he couldn't put his finger on! At home, he had a screensaver of a swan's skeleton in Groningen museum – stone-like and sculptural. Stone looked like that!

'Do you come from outerspace?' he shouted into the air. 'Is that where you're from? Are you an alien!'

The dragon swooped and tipped, his body dancing in the night air.

'Jacob, do you see that star?' The dragon's voice was quiet and soft and suddenly in Jake's head. 'The bright one?'

Jake's eyes sought it out. 'Yeah,' he said.

Stone swooped low and landed gently beside the boy. He wasn't even panting.

'Her name is Vega,' he said. Jake stared, his head tilted back on his aching neck.

'Now, Jacob, do you see that other star, almost as bright? His name is Deneb.'

Jake's head flipped around.

'And that one? Do you see that one? We will call him Altair.'

'Does this have something to do with you being an alien?' asked Jake, mystified.

'Together, lad, they make The Summer Triangle. Can you see it, there, bisecting your Milky Way?'

The boy could make out the clear outline of a triangle against the scattered mass of the Milky Way. He was amazed, he'd never seen it before but it was there, bright and clear as crystal.

'I can. Yeah.'

'Deneb is the furthest star from you Jake, Altair the closest. Between the three are millions of years and light years and yet we see them clearly as a triangle: bright and full and alive in the summer sky.'

'They are a triangle. It's a matter of perspective.'

'Yes, lad, they are,' chuckled the dragon. 'You and I are like that triangle: there are millions of years between us and yet I am here, bright and full and alive for you to see.'

Stone's tail curled over Jake's shoulder as he sat down. Jake leaned back, the stone hide cool and soothing on his neck. The dragon smelled of the night sky. Stars twinkled.

In all their billions, Jake thought, and all their brilliance, why do they need to cluster together? Why do they seem lonely?

'It is not the stars that are lonely,' said the dragon, as if reading the boy's mind. 'Man needed heroes and gods and gave them a home in the sky.' Stone continued quietly, 'Perhaps it is you who are lonely.'

'Us?'

'*You*, Jacob.'

A moment, awkward and raw, passed between them and Jake reached into his pocket to cover his embarrassment. Out of habit he brought out his father's watch. Nearly five past ten. He looked at the face and said, quietly, 'I'm alright,' then much louder, 'What now?'

'Now, you must go home.'

Jake opened his mouth to protest but thought better of it, he could barely keep his eyes open.

'I will walk with you, Jacob.'

Above them, the stars of Cygnus and the summer triangle glittered as bright as the marble in an ancient gauntlet.

Stone and Jake walked slowly past the woods and ascended the path that led to the cottage.

'Do you know, lad, that all life comes from the stars? One of your scientists put it well: we are made of star stuff,' said the dragon, casually.

'What like light beams and things?' said Jake doubtfully.

'When the universe began, stars exploded, Jacob. They threw out into the cosmos particles of water, gases, proteins, minerals. Some became planets – became Earth – some settled in the atmosphere, others developed into plant and animal life.

'In those first stars, everything was defined. lad. The *potential* of life. The essence of limestone existed long before the moon and Earth crashed into one another. To trace mankind's origins, the origins of all life, is to look to those stars.

The dragon stopped walking for a moment and waited for the boy's imagination to catch up with him.

'We are made of those particles, Jacob, and when eventually we die, we will be reduced to particles again.'

Jake's head started to swim. 'So I'm a star?' he said uncertainly.

Stone nodded. 'Yes, lad. In a way you are.'

Jake grinned, 'Hey, I'm a star!'

'Well done!' said Stone, pleased he'd gotten through to the boy.

'I'm a star! I'm a star!' Jake, in a sudden surge of giddiness, jumped up and down, laughing and shouting, his arms and legs pointed out in star-shapes.

'I'm made of star!'

He jumped once more and tumbled to the ground, rolling and laughing until he met the dragon's feet.

The elemental blinked and said stonily, 'I see you are not taking this quite as seriously as I intended.'

'I am,' laughed Jake. 'I'm just messing.'

The dragon sniffed.

'I know it's important,' said Jake, stifling his laughter. 'It's just too much to take in. What you mean is that *everything's* made of the same stuff. You and me, we're the same. Me and that fence. That tree. We come from stardust. It's just mad! Unreal. I mean, *you're* a dragon!'

'I assure you,' said Stone. 'It is very real.' The dragon turned his back to the field and flexed his wings.

'These, Jacob, are as real as your bones and your flesh.' He folded them away and turned back to the boy.

Jake giggled, drunk with exhaustion. He stared at the dragon and held his breath to calm himself down.

They'd reached the cottage gate.

'What we must worry about, Jacob, is not the stuff we are made of, but the stuff we cannot easily see. Dangers lie in the things we cannot see,' said Stone.

'I don't understand,' said Jake, suddenly sober.

'You will, lad. Soon enough.'

'Psst, Jake.'

Elizabeth poked her head out of her bedroom door.

'Jeez, Bett, don't sneak up on people!'

'Come in her!' She glanced down the stairwell in case her mother heard them.

'What for?' Jake stifled a yawn.

'I need to show you this. I've got to tell you something.'

Elizabeth grabbed her brother's wrist and pulled him through the door.

'Show me what? What you on about?'

She pointed to the pile of papers on her bed, her eyes darting with worried excitement.

'It's them letters, Jake. You won't believe it!'

CHAPTER 10

'Yes,' said Stone. 'There is a beast.'

The sun ached in the boiling sky, its heat already overpowering.

'What beast?' said Jake. He hadn't told the dragon much about the letters, and he didn't intend to. He didn't want to get his sister any more involved than she was. She'd kept him up for an hour telling him how dangerous it was and that he might get killed. Right now, he couldn't argue with that.

'You didn't say anything about a beast.'

Stone sighed. '*Beast* is only a word, Jacob. The beast is an entity. It... as you would say *feeds* off people.'

Jake narrowed his eyes, put his hands on his hips and said, 'I'm sorry but there's not some big monster running around eating people. We'd notice.'

'It does not eat people, it feeds off them. I called it *beast* because I believed *beast* to be a word that conveys an image to humans. Concrete, not numinous. In this, Jake, you should find an anchor that will help you understand.'

Jake's face was blank. 'What does *numinous* mean?'

'However, I see I was incorrect in my assumption.'

Stone sighed and continued.

'Jacob, the beast feeds off the apathy, selfishness and ignorance of mankind. It is the rainbow slick of oil in a street puddle, the balloon choking a seagull to death. It is the steady heating of the world's surface.'

'You mean pollution? Global warming?'

The dragon spoke on, staring at a point somewhere in both the past and the future. He sighed with sadness.

'It is only a part of it, Jacob. The universe is filled with many worlds like your own. Almost *exactly* like your own. In every one of them, *you* exist, as does your sister, your mother and so on. But not the beast. The potential of the beast, yes, *traces* of it, but not the whole beast itself.'

'Potential...?' asked Jake bemused.

'Yes. It travels from one world to the next searching for one that will let it in. Its trace is everywhere. And some of the worlds are less... protected than this one.'

The dragon coiled his tail around his feet and continued.

'Imagine a life force born even before the elementals, and made almost entirely of raw energy. If it had a colour it would be beyond black. If it finds a form it will destroy.'

Jake tried to concentrate. 'What do you mean 'a form'? Like a dinosaur?'

'Like the meteor that killed the dinosaurs.'

'But that came from out of space!'

Stone stared hard at the boy. 'I can tell you only, Jacob, that the crater at Chicxolub still to this day carries the memory of the beast.'

'But that had nothing to do with us. There were no men on earth back then. Not with the dinosaurs. Even I know that!'

'True, but anger and selfishness hide in the heart of most living things. The beast had broken through, and then learnt to adapt.'

'Evolved?'

'Almost, but evolution comes from mutation, development. The beast merely changes to suit its needs. Nowadays it control nature – or more correctly, certain *states* of nature.'

'What like?'

'Hurricanes. Acid Rain. Other things that mankind has polluted, decayed. There are many it can choose from. It works well using earthquakes.'

'Why din't the elementals stop it!?'

'We did. It has killed many species, but many more have survived–'

'How? How did you stop it?'

The dragon's nostrils flared and Jake's stomach churned.

'Jacob, must you always interrupt? Over millennia, the elementals have been called upon to intervene.'

'By humans?'

'By the Earth, Jacob.'

'What, *muck*?'

'The Earth, lad. Your planet. She speaks to all of us, you have only to listen.'

Jake cocked his head to one side and watched the dragon out of the corner of his eye. With one ear he tried to listen to the sounds coming from the ground. He couldn't hear anything.

Stone continued. 'I have waited in readiness, lad. At times intervention has been necessary – although I am less willing than others just to step in regardless.' He glanced up at a dark cloud passing over his face.

Jake following his glance, thinking, *o-kay*.

'In these last two centuries I have intervened more and more, I am sad to say,' said Stone.

'Why?'

'Your wars, lad. Until recently they have been small games to mark out boundaries and control people. In the middle of the 20th century you created a weapon. It destroys. Not just man, but *everything*. Like the meteorite.'

Images of mushroom clouds from videos in his history class filled Jake's head.

'The atom bomb?'

The dragon blinked and nodded.

'But it *was* dropped... on Hiroshima and Naga... erm...'

'Nagasaki. Localised activity, Jacob.'

'That's a bit cold innit?' Jake said in a spikey tone of voice.

'Cold? No, the heat of such a bomb...'

'I mean the way you said 'localised activity' like it was, I dunno...
acceptable or summats.'

'No, lad. Not acceptable. It caused much damage that still echoes
today. But the *world* was not destroyed. A trace of the beast was in
the weapon. Humanity thought that by splitting the atom it could
understand the world better, give mankind more of what it wanted.'

'But that's right. We do understand more now. Nuclear power and
microwaves and things?'

'Some of what was learned was good for humanity and some was
not. Little of it was good for the Earth. The beast is able to control
the detritus mankind has made of the planet.'

'Can we control the beast?'

'We have so far managed to contain its traces in this world, but
the beast strengthens daily.'

'It's coming in't it?' asked Jake, suspiciously. Hairs prickled on his
neck and arms.

The dragon nodded.

'How do you know?'

'I can sense its presence.'

'Well, *I* can't do anything,' said Jake.

'*Only* you can.'

'No. I *can't*! And anyway I still don't know if this is real – it's *just*
like my dreams – scary and freaky!'

Stone's tail came up quickly and smashed into Jake's side lifting
him off his feet and almost sending him to the floor.

'Jesus! What the *hell* did you do that for?' shouted Jake, rubbing
his side.

'Did you feel that?' snarled Stone.

'Of course I did. It bloody hurt!'

'Was it a *dream*?' The dragon spat the word at Jake. His head
swerved in the air, snake-like and hypnotic.

'You're not funny y'know,' said Jake, angry tears pricking his eyes.

For the first time, the dragon saw in front of him a young boy.

By God, he thought, he is small. Were all his other companions this small? Surely not?

But he was certain none of them were this scared. Stone's eyes calmed down to their usual golden glow. His voice was measured but firm.

'I am not trying to be funny, lad. I am never funny. This is gravely serious business. Gravely.'

'Gravely serious,' sneered Jake. 'You talk so stupidly, y'know. Can't you talk normal like me?'

Stone stifled a laugh. 'I prefer English, lad. You should try it one day.'

Jake stared at the dragon with a face like steel cooling in a foundry. The dragon stared back, unblinking. It was like trying to stare down a desert storm.

'Jacob, what you *know* of this world, what you feel is *safe*, is not. Your ancestors knew this.'

'And Dad!?' spat Jake, testily.

Stone stopped in his tracks. 'No... not your father.'

'Did you hit *him*?' snapped Jake.

'No, lad. He never gave me the chance to,' said the dragon dolefully. 'And for this, Jacob, I am grateful to you. For the chance.'

'You trained him, though!' barked Jake.

'Trained him... ah? I see. Your grandfather's correspondence. Your father and I never met. Your grandfather trained him. He was, I am led to understand, quite talented.'

A small pang of pride stabbed Jake's chest, pushing his anger to one side.

'He could have been a powerful companion,' said Stone, as if reading the boy's mind.

'But he wasn't,' Jake muttered.

He stood chewing his thumbnail and holding his sore arm. He'd thought it was going to be fun, like in the movies, but so far training had just been a lot of talk and bringing up memories. His father had lied to them all. He'd had responsibilities which he'd never faced.

It was written across Jake's face like... well, like his grandfather's letters. He was scared and angry and disappointed.

'There is something I must show you, lad,' said Stone.

His wings cracked open and then closed around the boy like a venus fly trap.

'Close your mouth. Do not scream,' he said.

'Scream? Why would I scr–'

The earth opened up. And dragon and boy were dragged down.

Jake screamed.

⊕

Now imagine this: a map, twenty feet by fifteen, centred in a cave, is carved into the floor (although its texture's more organic than the word carved suggests), and small puddles of water, collecting here and there, reflect the phosphorescent glow of algae along the walls. Next to the algae are scorch marks.

At the top end is a pillar of stone formed from centuries of limestone deposits, and it casts a shadow to bisect the map in equal parts.

On one side of the map is a cluster of circles and semi-circles like tiny moons, and on the other is a grid of squares and rectangles, and a wavy line snaking through the shadow cast by the pillar.

Each square has a pattern of dots or V's (some squares almost entirely covered) and in the very centre of the map is a rectangle, solid and divided in two like a domino, and, very much like a domino, it has three dots on one side and three on the other.

Sometimes it glows.

'It's incredible,' said Jake, crouching down to see better.

Stone prowled the perimeter. Every so often he snorted. Something was unsettling him, and to have the companion here made him uncomfortable.

Jake had eventually calmed down after the shock of the journey, and was amazed to find he could see impossibly well. He didn't even need his phone's torch app.

'It's stone,' he said, running a hand over the map's surface. The dragon snorted. There was a warning edge to it.

Jake pulled his hand back quickly.

'What's it a map of?' he asked.

Another snort, this time sharper. Jake flicked a glance at the dragon.

'I wish I could take a photo of it,' he mused. '–Hey! I can use my phone!'

He started to dig into his pockets.

'No!' A sharp, painful bark. 'Make no copy of the map whole.'

The dragon's rumble filled Jake's body. And beneath him Jake was sure that just for a second the ground trembled.

The domino glowed yellow, like the dragon's eyes, then faded as if it had never happened.

'It is dangerous having you here for any length of time, lad,' growled Stone.

'Oh, oh. Right. Well, let's go then,' Jake stammered.

'Not yet. You must memorize it.'

Jake's eyes flicked between the dragon and the map.

'*Memorize* it?'

'All of it.'

'I can't memorize *that*. It's too complicated.'

'You can. It is in your blood. *Study* it.'

'But–'

'Quickly. We must leave soon.'

Jake concentrated. He could see it as clearly as if the cave was full of sunlight. He glanced around; the rest of the cave was dark and creepy. He shuddered.

He studied: vertical rectangle, horizontal rectangle, three vertical lines – wait – that rectangle, wasn't it vertical a second ago? And that circle, wasn't it a crescent? It was as if the map was trying not to be memorized.

'It's moving!' shouted Jake.

'Concentrate, lad!'

This time the whole cave shuddered.

Jake focused solely on the map. The shapes stopped moving. By breaking it down into a proper grid he could remember what went where.

It was hard work, and hot too. Was that right? Weren't caves meant to be a constant 7 or 8 degrees Celsius?

'We must leave, lad! It is protecting itself!'

The domino carving glowed white. The tremble around them heaved into a rumble. Jake tried to zone-out the new sounds of rocks falling in the distance. He lost his balance, tumbling from his crouching position.

'Gimme a minute!'

'Now!'

'Just a–'

'–Now, lad!'

The dragon's tail coiled around the boy, as he cocooned his wings and they melted into the cave's wall.

On the cave floor the map sank until it was immersed totally in water. All that remained was the faint glow of the already fading domino. Even the dragon's footsteps marking the map's borders disappeared as if they'd never been there. The map was trying to hide.

The rumbling deep inside the cave subsided.

On the walls, the glow from the algae dimmed as something dark and oily passed over it once more.

Jake was shaking when the dragon set him on the ground.

He couldn't believe it. They had *passed* through stone. And he wasn't dead! He'd seen layers of strata filled with fossils. It had been as if he were moving through a very thick, dense wall of treacle. He could breathe and his lungs *hadn't* filled with limestone and grit. It was astounding!

He turned to the dragon and said, 'What on earth was that place!'

The dragon looked agitated. 'That is my home.'

'You live there? In that cave?'

Stone nodded. Through the haze of excitement, Jake's radar picked up on the worried undertones.

'Are you okay?' he asked.

'I... *felt* something, lad. In my cave. The beast is trying to get in...'

'G-get in?' Jake's excitement drained out of him like dishwater down a plug-hole. 'Hang on, what *is* that map? Why did you want me to memorize it?' he added, his eyes narrowing.

'The map is both simple and complex. It is a plan of this world,' said the dragon, shaking grass and rubble off his back.

'It looks nothing like this world!'

'It is not meant to *look* like it, Jacob. The closest I can describe it as is a *mind atlas* of this world and the doorways to other worlds. Some maps mark cartography, others power. This one maps ideas.'

'What!? What ideas?'

'The idea that other worlds exist, for one. This map shows the entrances to them. If you know how to read it and have the key. Complete, the map enables ingress to *every* world. Therefore you must *never* reproduce it in its entirety.'

Jake looked blankly at the elemental. 'Yeah, that *is* complex,' he said, flatly.

'No, Jacob, the *complexity* comes from the map's presence. It is *everywhere*. What you see in the cave is the *original* map, however, an echo – a partial *projection* as it were – can be seen in locations all over the world. They are protected by us.'

'Us?'

'Elementals. Each elemental has a version of the key – limited in its powers. While I can open all doors, they each can open only one.'

'So, how come you've got the whole map then?'

'I created it. Assisted to an extent by Fire.' Stone snorted, a strange dismissive snort, then seemed to realize he wasn't alone.

'We needed to ensure the doorways' security,' he said thoughtfully. 'If a doorway is somehow opened, I can find it on the map and close it.'

'How?'

'It is a complex procedure and difficult.' He paused then added, 'Do you believe in magic, lad?'

'No! Don't be stupid.'

'Science, then?'

'Well... yeah.'

'Science is a kind of magic... The cave protects the map in ways that your scientists have not yet discovered.'

'What ways?' Jake persisted.

The dragon leaned down and whispered, 'Can you keep a secret, Jacob?'

'Yes,' said Jake firmly.

'So can I.' The dragon's eyes flared and he winked.

'I *knew* you were going to say that.'

Jake sat down on the grass and looked at his clothes. They were clean of earth and rubble. The odd broken stems of grass poked out here and there. He shook them off him and turned to the dragon.

'Okay, so why memorize it?' said Jake.

'I can control the map from the cave but to activate the key *there* will cause all the doors to open simultaneously. In the cave the map is at its most powerful, and therefore most dangerous.

'I took you there for two reasons: to show you what we must fight for and because you have the memory for it.'

'You don't know anything about my memory!'

'You have a good memory, Jacob. It is in your bloodline.'

'Tell my history teacher that, then,' muttered Jake under his breath.

'Jacob, we must open a doorway. We must anticipate the beast.'

'What? *What*! You just said it was dangerous to open doorways.'

'The doorways here are weakening because the beast is gaining in strength, and there are fault lines too...' The dragon stretched his neck and brought his head in line with Jake's.

'The beast can control nature to a degree – the recent earthquakes here for example–'

'It did *that*?'

'Earthquakes are natural, Jacob. However, as humanity alters the balance of nature, earthquakes become more frequent, in this respect, yes, the beast caused that earthquake.'

Jake shook his head stubbornly. 'I still can't believe it.'

'Take my word for it, lad.'

Jake sagged and looked down at his dusty trainers with their frayed laces.

'What do I have to do?' he sighed.

'I need your assistance to open a door. The ingress is in a cave called The Devil's Arse.'

Jake started laughing. It might have been the inevitable shock of travelling through stone or the realization he was up to his eyeballs in trouble, but this was the funniest thing he'd ever heard.

'Seriously?' he said, wiping tears from his eyes.

The elemental dragon looked at the bent over boy who was now wheezing like a steam train going up hill.

'I am always serious, Jacob,' he said.

'How? What've I got to do?'

'We will go to the cave and you will draw part, and *only* part, of the map. The doorway will open.'

'From a drawing, I don't think so!'

'From a *companion's* drawing. And of course, you have a key, and I have the words.'

'Me, I an't got nothing.'

'Your talisman. It is rare in that it is the only key that can open all the doorways. It is why the map was so upset. But in this instance, we will open only one, one doorway that is.' The dragon smiled.

'What does it look like, this doorway?'

'You will recognise it. It should sing to you.'

'Sing?'

'Yes, sing.'

'What, like la-la-la-lahh?'

'Not quite.'

'This is just too much.' Jake said, shaking his head.

'It is better to swim well in deep water than paddle badly in shallow,' said Stone, briskly.

'Not if you can't swim!'

'You will soon learn, lad.'

Stone looked up at the sky. A dark cloud had formed over the mountain peaks, its steady fall of rain slanting down in grey streaks.

'We must go before the weather worsens. You have everything you need: pencil? paper?'

Jake tapped his rucksack where his camera, sketchbook and pens lived and asked, almost innocently,

'So, this cave, where is it again?'

Stone turned on him eyes flat and grey as slate.

'Don't make me repeat its name, lad.'

Jake grinned. 'The Devil's Arse?'

The dragon sighed, meaningfully.

'Yes,' he said. 'The Devil's Arse.'

The path was narrow and led down from a new car-park to a small village built of stone houses and old-fashioned shops, none of which were open. A river ran alongside them thinning out until eventually it disappeared into underground, its bank crazed and barren beneath the July heat.

It was a difficult path to walk on in trainers: part cobbles, part grit, mainly moss and always damp in the humid temperature. Small lichen and alpine flowers sprung up here and there. Jake slipped twice before he got the sense of how to stay upright; an odd, almost lurching step when the path wound down hill, and a reaching stride when it started to ascend.

Above him, the dragon flew close by unnoticed by anyone. It still amazed Jake how no one noticed the dragon. It was one of those things you think your eye would be drawn to.

He slipped again and righted himself. More thunder growled not far away.

The village gave way to a wooded copse and a bank of grass as the river reappeared. Bog-stars, rock-roses and Devil's-bit scabious sprang up in a swell of colour. A brown and white cat perched itself on a rotting stump and watched the bees and butterflies until something bigger came along to entertain it. Jackdaws called and swooped, hunting for food.

Then the cobbled path swept out to a vista so impressive Jake stopped and gasped.

He'd heard the word 'dale' many times; a small, soft word, which in no way described the sight in front of him. 'Gorge' was closer: sheer walls of ragged limestone as if something had *eaten* straight through a mountain to make a path.

Sparsely covered in ivy, grass and moss, the sides were scattered through with birds' nests and tree saplings. Jake's head spun trying to work out the hundreds of colours in the rock, the shapes of faces and animals, and the dizzying sense that here was something that went much, much deeper than anything he could imagine.

Then the path rose and Jake saw where the river, now fifteen or so feet below him, was swallowed whole by the mountain.

But that was nothing compared to the cavern mouth. From where he stood, it was a black hole in the face of the rock, about a hundred feet high and almost as wide. It ate Jake's path.

Almost on cue, thunder bellowed.

Jake shivered in the peak's cold shadow. The day's heat had stayed in the village, aware it wasn't welcome here. He slipped his thin hoodie from his waist, put it on and held the iron railing that was all that stood between him and the depths of the gorge. Flakes of rust, like dried blood, coloured his palm.

High in the sky, the elemental curved back on the summer therms and readied himself to land.

Then the skies opened.

He was freezing and saturated, and struggling to draw. The dragon stood beside Jake in the gloomy cavern, keeping watch. Curiously no one was around; not even the guide who'd sold Jake his ticket or the four other tourists who'd followed him in.

'Couldn't I have done this earlier?' he whined.

'No!' thundered the dragon, then, in a more reasonable voice, he added, 'The power is at its strongest when freshly drawn.'

'I still don't see why you couldn't use the stone map.'

'The doorways are geographical realities, Jacob. Even if I could section off just one doorway, it would be impossible to reach it in in its *actual location* in order to close it before something came through. And *anything* could come through.'

The sentence hung in the air like a day-old corpse. Jake shuddered and said, 'Where's the doorway then?'

'You tell me.'

Jake looked around. All he could see was a large advertising poster and a chocolate-vending machine.

'I can't see any doorway. And anyway, I thought you said it'd sing.'

'Oh! My! God! A dragon!'

She was a large woman in a yellow raincoat with curly black hair. Behind her was a gaggle of tourists. Jake shoved his sketchbook in his bag and searched in vain for somewhere to hide. The woman waddled over to them. He held his breath and closed his eyes in the time honoured tradition of 'if I can't see you, you can't see me'. Astonishingly, it seemed to work.

'This is amazing!' she squealed, ignoring Jake. 'It's gar-gan-tu-an! Do you think it's natch-ural?'

Jake opened his mouth to speak just as a bespectacled man in a green oilskin coat trotted over to her. The man stared at Stone like he was a a dead rat.

'Dear me, no hmmmm. Not natural, not from *here* by any means.' The man spoke begrudgingly, as if the world didn't deserve his wisdom. His voice was reedy and came out of his nose.

'I daresay it's a new marketing feature hmmmm.' He wiped rainwater from his glasses and went on.

'Indeed, yes. It's said there were dragons here, y'know? In these parts.' — he said, *in these parts* as if he was swearing— 'Centuries ago of course. In mythology, that is.'

The curly-haired woman nodded appreciatively, her eyes sparkling under the artificial lights of the vending machine.

'It's so con-vin-cing. I thought maybe it was a foss-sil or skel-lin-ton, or something.'

Hope shone off her like a beacon in the night.

'It looks rather good though, doesn't it hmmmm?' The dragon-expert continued. 'But my dear lady, dragons *never really existed*. And after all, its neck is rather too long, excuse me young man.' He pushed Jake roughly out of the way so that the rest of the party could crowd around.

'I believe... yes... it's fibreglass. Here, look, you can see the seam.'

He prodded and scraped Stone's sides with a penknife. The blade skittered across the surface. Undeterred the man forged on.

'And look, someone's already vandalised it; a claw's missing.' He tapped the knife on the dragon's fingers. Jake saw them flex slightly. He took a deep breath, *ohgod ohgod ohgod...*

The woman with the curly hair looked disappointed. 'Oh,' she said. 'Maybe it's, like, a natch-ural sculpture?'

'I'm afraid not,' said the man, with a touch of smugness.

'No, it's not stone at all– but wouldn't it be *wonderful* if it was hmmmm! See? Fibreglass.' He laughed and tried to push it.

'Oh,' he said. 'It's quite heavy hmmmm. They must have filled it with concrete. To make it stable. That would be apt, of course. Concrete is, after all, made from limestone and this is *meant* to be a limestone statue.'

He tapped Stone with the penknife again. 'I must say they *have* got the colouring spot on, hmmmm. And look,' (tap, tap) 'Ammonites. *Wonderful* attention to detail!'

The group leaned forward and peered at the dragon's elbows. The small man clicked his camera and filled the room with flash.

'Wonderful!' repeated the dragon expert before adding, 'However, hmmmm it's about as *stone* as I am. Ha ha. And,' just in case any of his party hadn't realized he was joking, 'I am not *stone!* Ha ha ha.'

'Ha ha ha'

'Ha ha ha'

'Shall we go hmmmmm?'

And they were gone.

Jake stood astonished. He hadn't met anyone before who thought they were so clever while being thicker than pudding batter.

Stone growled, angrily. 'That *human*,' he spat the word as if it was rotten, 'prodded me with his puny knife!'

'Yeah,' said Jake laughing.

'Repeatedly!' The dragon's eyes flared red.

'I know, I was there. Don't worry. He *pushed* me. I nearly fell over.'

'*As* stone *as he is!* The man is a fool!' Stone's eyes flared once more. Jake's stomach lurched.

'Don't worry about it,' Jake grunted.

'An imbecile who can't tell glass fibres from sedimentary limestone! *And* who feels at liberty to assault bystanders!' Stone trembled, his whole body aching to follow the man into the cave. He could show him what dragons *really* were!

'Let it go,' urged Jake, clutching at his heaving gut.

'Hah! I should let *him* go,' muttered Stone. Jake's could feel the dragon's temper raging in his own bones.

'Look, when you get upset, I end up feeling sick, so just come on!'

The dragon snorted and his whole body heaved. The air warmed with his out breath. Jake's sickness stopped as quickly as it had arrived.

'You are right, Jacob. There is work to be done,' Stone said firmly, and under his breath he muttered, 'yes work to save these *idiot* humans.'

'Eyup! *I'm* human.'

'Yes, lad, but you are not an idiot. Foolhardy perhaps, impulsive, impatient...'

'Well, thanks,' said Jake sarcastically. 'It answers me one thing, though.'

'And that is?'

'So far no one's noticed you – not even when you fly over their heads – but *they* did because they thought you were a statue. It made sense to them. The tour guide didn't see you when we came in because it didn't make sense to him. I don't know how it works, but I'm glad it did.'

'Yes, lad. That is very astute. You are learning well. And, these idiots – humans – did not notice you because...?'

'They *did* notice me,' said Jake, puzzled.

'No, I am afraid not lad. And this was because...?'

'Hang on, they pushed me!'

'*One* of them pushed you, Jacob, the others *ignored* you. And the reason for this is that you were not *important* to them,' said the elemental, happy in the knowledge his student was learning.

Jake sagged, 'Oh, great. Thanks for that. Makes me feel right good, that does.'

The dragon turned to Jake, his head cocked to one side and said, 'But you are important to me, lad. Now, let us continue.'

Jake sketched, rapidly.

'Here. That's what I remember of the map.'

So far he hadn't heard any singing.

The dragon looked down and positioned his tail an inch above the drawing. He mumbled something Jake could barely hear: sounds from a time before language had been tamed.

Power surged through his body. He fought hard to stay upright against the pressure building in the air.

The cave was suddenly stifling.

Stone's body glowed golden and his eyes turned a white that was almost blue.

When Jake turned around, half-expecting to see a swirling vortex, he saw the posters on the wall blister and the chocolate bars in the vending machine melt.

But there was no doorway.

Suddenly Stone slumped to the floor, his body heaving up and down with a ragged breath. All of a sudden, the elemental looked ancient.

It hadn't worked.

'What happened?' Jake managed through gritted teeth.

Stone looked at him with rheumy eyes and half-closed lids.

'I do not... know... It... should... have... succeeded.'

The words were pulled from the dragon's mouth like a barber-dentist wrenching teeth.

Stone coughed and Jake felt the pit of his own stomach boil. He could hear the ping, ping of cooling stone.

'Was it my fault?' he asked. Stone tried to smile and shake his head.

'No, Jacob. It... should have... opened. The map... I am confident... was correct.'

'As best as I could remember. I didn't hear any songs, though.'

Jake looked around helplessly. The limestone elemental slumped to the floor, exhausted. Jake reached out to touch him but whipped his hand straight back. The creature's skin was a furnace.

'Can I help?' Jake said, sucking his blistered fingers.

'Must rest, lad... Rest and think...' Stone's eyes closed and his breathing deepened.

'You can't rest *here!*' Jake hissed, looking frantically around. 'Some people are coming!'

The dragon smiled faintly then sank into the floor as if he was sinking into quicksand.

Like the dragon, the instant heat of the cavern vanished. It was replaced with the cold, biting air of shock. And then came a sudden strange calm. A calm that said in a familiar, stony voice:

Everything is fine now Jacob. Go home.

CHAPTER 11

Jake did go home. Straight home. The storm had raged around him and, saturated, he'd walked for miles. How he knew the way, he couldn't be sure. He was cold, frustrated and tired, and beyond disappointed. He needed to get a handle on this. What had gone wrong?

He sank into his second bath that week and tried to concentrate. He held a cluster of soap bubbles in his hand and watched them popping in the warm air.

When he was small he used to blow bubbles with a plastic wand. He could blow three or four from just one dip of the liquid and, if he was quick, he could catch one on the wand and then catch all the other bubbles on that first bubble so that if he blew on it he could make it rotate like a carousel.

Our world, Stone had said, was like one of these bubbles.

With no one holding the wand.

And there were other bubbles, other worlds. And sometimes things, and occasionally people, could move from one to the other.

Jake dipped his hand into the bathwater and brought it up covered in bubbles. It glistened like a rainbow. Bubble worlds. Well, in Jake's experience, bubbles always went *pop!*

He pulled up the memory of Stone's exhausted body sinking into the rocky ground. It scared him. He'd looked so old.

Then there was that strange sudden feeling of calm. Jake felt it was meant to tell him something, but he wasn't sure what.

He leaned forward for the soap and knocked a plastic duck into the bath. It wobbled unsteadily for a moment then followed the waves of the water up and over Jake's knees. It reminded him of the game he used to play with his father where they flicked a small stick into a river and watched it carried along on the current. Jake felt like that stick: small, detached and not knowing where he would end up.

The duck wobbled and grinned at him with duckish ignorance.

This is *stupid*, Jake said aloud. This is me feeling sorry for myself because the doorway didn't open.

This trip was meant to be simple: a holiday where Jake could take photos and enjoy the sun and the quiet. But now, not even a week later, it seemed he was a companion – from a long line of companions – to a dragon made of limestone.

A long line broken by his father.

Why had Dad been so stubborn? He'd believed in science, in empirical evidence, so why couldn't he believe in this dragon – if he could see it, and surely he *had* seen it, then he should have believed in it.

Jake quickly scrubbed his face, stepped out and towelled himself down, all the while running the recent events of his life over in his mind. He wrapped a grey towel around him and crept up to his room, one aching step at a time.

He'd travelled through rock! Cool!

He dressed quickly in his sweats and threw himself on his bed. The map floated to his mind. He took a pencil from his desk drawer and his good drawing pad from the bookshelf, and started to sketch a section at random.

Sections were okay to draw: that was the rule, wasn't it?

He pulled the image of the map to the front of his mind. It was partly submerged in water (as if it was hiding even from his memory). Ignore the water. Concentrate on the corner: Four squares. Two circles three centimetres apart. Five parallel lines. Simple.

He couldn't see any signs of doorways but Stone knew where they were. What had he called them? 'ingresses' – what a weird word.

Jake closed the sketchbook and emptied his sportsbag. There on the bed was the page from this afternoon. It was still damp from the rain.

Why hadn't it worked? He'd copied it exactly as he remembered it: square, rectangle, semi-circle in a triangle – that could easily mean the cave inside the mountain – three wavy lines (was that the river?) And these four lines– No, wait! Not four. *Five*.

Five lines!

Jake's sketch *had* been wrong.

Cautiously, he picked up his pencil and drew in the fifth line. The drawing throbbed and the air suddenly tasted like tin. The sketch glowed.

He needed to find Stone, right now! But how to summon him? His eyes fell involuntarily on the spilled contents of his sportsbag.

There was the talisman.

He snatched it up and stood in front of the crackly mirror. Clutching it to his chest, he flung out his arms and said in his best, deepest tones, 'Limestone dragon COME TO ME!'

The air felt as if it was being sucked through a sieve with a vaccum cleaner. The sky outside Jake's window opened and the growling dragon appeared out of thin air like a genie from a lamp!

Except he didn't.

The only living thing in Jake's room was a teenage boy standing, arms and legs wide open, in front of a long mirror. Looking embarrassed.

He brought his hands down limply and looked at his sad self. He reminded him of a character in a cheesy graphic novel, but rougher, as if he'd been dragged though a field of hedges.

'God, I look a state,' he thought. He straightened his t-shirt and, without thinking, tugged the comb through his short hair.

Static crackled and fizzed around his head like a Van de Graaff generator. He laughed, loudly.

He was still laughing when behind him, the dragon's eye appeared at his window.

'You *needed* me, lad?'

'What, so when I comb my hair you just appear?'

'No. That would be... inefficient. I am generally receptive to your thoughts, Jacob. More so when you use the talisman. I sensed that you needed me, therefore I came.'

'Oh.' Jake opened the windows as widely as possible and stared at Stone. He felt, once more, the familiar rumble of the dragon's voice in his gut and bones.

'*Do* you need me, Jacob?'

'I was wrong,' said Jake flatly.

'Wrong?' The dragon looked puzzled.

'This afternoon. I missed off a line. From the map. I'm sorry.'

'The drawing was wrong?' Stone's eyes flared red.

'Yes! Yes, but don't get angry. I've fixed it, look!'

Jake held the sketch up to the dragon. Stone peered and sniffed, angrily.

'We can go *now* if you want? To the cave.' Jake said, his knees suddenly weak. 'I'm not too tired,' he lied.

'No!' said Stone. 'We should not go looking for the beast while it is dark.'

Jake sensed a nervousness in the creature, was it... *fear*? 'Why not?' he asked carefully.

'We should not.' That was, as far as Stone was concerned, the end of the matter. Not Jake.

'Are you chicken?' he asked.

'A chicken? You have a strange imagination, Jacob. I am not a chicken. Simply, I am *afraid*.'

'Oh.' He hadn't expected that. 'Afraid of what, the beast?'

'In the dark people are afraid...'

'You're scared of the dark!?'

'No, Jacob, *humans* are. They are afraid, frustrated, selfish, anxious. All of these things feed the beast. It is *much* stronger by night.'

'Like a vampire?' Jake said eventually.

The dragon opened his mouth to snap at the boy but stopped.

'Yes,' he said. 'Quite like a vampire. At night it will be too strong. We will go in the morning, Jacob.'

'What are we going to do when we get there?'

'There is someone we must talk to, Jacob.'

'Who?'

'You will find out in the morning.'

It was barely morning when Stone returned. Dark shadows crept across the landscape making him uneasy.

Jake knuckled his gritty eyes and shook some life into his body. His dreams had been full of oil-slicks seeping out of stone walls and smothering everything. In the dreams Stone had watched on, helpless. Jake was really starting to hate his dreams.

'Look lively, lad,' came the rich, warm, voice of the dragon.

'I am,' Jake yawned struggling in the gloom with his jeans. 'I need to wake up a bit. I had a rough night. Bad dreams.'

The dragon's ears twitched and his eyes flared. 'Dreams?'

Jake sat on the warm bed as he finished dressing and tried his best to recall his nightmares. From the corner of his eye he saw Stone's gaze scour the shadows of the room.

'These dreams, Jacob, could you... taste anything in them?'

Unconsciously, Jake smacked his lips together. There was a strange taste on the back of his tongue. He nodded, nervously.

'Was it a chemical taste? Oily? Was it rotten?'

'Yeah, like... exhaust fumes. And rotten bananas. Why, what does it mean? What's wrong?' Jake asked.

Stone took a short breath and released it slowly.

'Jacob, as you know, all elementals have a connection with their companions,' he said eventually. 'Our... introductions... are made often through dreams. You yourself have dreamed for many years of dragons. In these dreams my *presence* was being felt by you.'

'*You* sent me all those nightmares? Of dragons and monsters?' fumed Jake.

The dragon looked thoughtful. 'We manipulate the energy that exists across the world – some see it as electricity, others a life force. In truth it is the energy that keeps this planet alive. I sent you an echo of myself, showed you scenarios that have been and that might be.'

'All my life!'

'It was necessary!'

'I hardly slept at all last night!'

The dragon spoke simply and honestly. 'That was not me, Jacob. I fear it has found your dreams.'

'What has?' snapped Jake.

'The beast.'

Jake recoiled. 'What do you mean!?'

'Your analogy of the vampire stands: the beast, I fear, can enter the minds of humans through their dreams. Have you ever heard of dreams of power and wealth? Success and fame?...'

Jake felt itchy and grubby. The taste of the dreams was bitter.

'Urgh, I need to brush my teeth,' he said, his voice rising with panic. 'I need a shower.'

'No. There is not time. You will be fine. We have much training to do to build up your defences against these dreams.' The dragon pushed his snout into the room and sniffed.

'You said it's in my mind!' said Jake. 'What does it do in there?! Can it *kill* me?'

'In your dreams it can do you no harm. It seeks a way in, Jacob; a weakness in your resolve, a chink in your moral armour. It will find nothing, lad. You are safe.'

He sniffed again, satisfied they were safe, and said, 'Now, come. We must go.'

And if Stone had not been too careful to allay Jake's fears, he might not have omitted one small but vital fact: the beast can also *influence* humans through their dreams. And if Jake had known this fact, he might have mentioned to the elemental that hiding under his bed were two drawings – quite innocent on their own – of sections of the dragon's stone map.

⊘

Already it was proving to be a hot day. Sweat trickled down Jake's t-shirt and face. His bag hung heavily on his back. The gnats and midges were already biting.

They followed the track beside the river, the dragon walking clumsily next to the boy. They hadn't spoken since they'd left the house. Jake was worrying about the dreams and what Stone said about being safe. He didn't feel safe. He felt like he was being watched. He said as much.

'The beast is not yet here, Jacob,' said the dragon matter-of-factly. 'And you must remember that *I* know where you are, lad, at all times.'

Jake stopped in his tracks; the dragon continued walking, oblivious.

'What do you mean?' Jake said coldly.

Stone turned and shuffled back. He cocked his head to one side, and spoke as if he were reading from a script.

'Three days ago, you walked down to the wall that edges the field next to your cottage. You followed it to the small road. You boarded some sort of omnibus that took you along the old routes to the village. It took a long time. You stopped often. You alighted. Then you ran over the main road, stumbling once, and used the small path that circumnavigated the old Priory until you reached the library. You stayed there a good long time. The sun was high when you left the library to find a place to eat some greasy strips of fried potato–'

'A-a-are you following me?' snapped Jake, the rhythm of his step now matching his sudden anger.

The dragon flicked a fly in front of his face with his tail.

'These flying beasts bother me,' he said, casually.

'Oi! I said, *are you following me*?'

'I know always where you are, lad.'

'So, you are following me?'

'No.'

'You just said you are!'

'I did not. I am not. There are things, Jacob, that prevent me from being with you at all times,' said Stone, as if this was a grave and unfortunate character flaw.

'However, I am *connected* to you. I am aware, at any given time, of *where* you are.'

'How?'

'I track you.'

'What?! Like an animal?!' growled Jake. And it *was* a growl, like an angry dog.

'You *are* an animal, Jacob.'

'I am not!'

'Then, lad, what are you?' The dragon was puzzled and curious. A fly landed under his eye. He shook his head twice and it flew off.

'I'm a boy!' Jake fizzed. 'A human being!'

'Yes,' said Stone. 'A human animal. You are a creature high on the food chain. You fight and hunt and conquer, as does the tiger, the elephant, the eagle: *all* of them animals, Jacob.'

'Yes...' Jake faltered, '...but, *they're* different.'

'They eat, do they not? Sleep, respire, defecate.'

'Shuddup!'

'I do not understand. Do you no longer wish to talk about this, lad?'

'Not if you're going to say things like 'defecate'!'

The dragon paused, then said, 'You are an odd being, Jacob Walker. Sensitive, I think.'

'Shuddup!'

Jake shoved his hands deep into his pockets and wallowed in the awkward silence that followed. Flies buzzed around his face as he stomped along. Stone swatted the air indiscriminately.

Jake knew the dragon was right: human beings *were* just animals. But he didn't like hearing it. Especially from an impossible thing made of stone.

Human animal – hah! *Like the tiger and elephant!* Hah! *Top of the food chain* – Hah! No, wait...

'What did you mean 'high on the food chain'? We're at the top.'

The dragon stopped, flicked one more fly from his snout and answered in a low, rumbling sound.

'You wish to speak now?'

'Yes.'

'Hmm... I think you have a word, it means feeling regret or penitence.'

'What's that got to do with owt?'

The dragon stared at Jake. 'It has *some* connection, yes, Jacob.'

Jake opened his mouth to snap once more, then closed it.

'I'm sorry for telling you to shuddup... I was... rude.'

'Yes,' said the dragon. 'You were unconscionably rude.' Then he smiled briskly and walked on.

'Hey!'called Jake.

Stone turned back, still walking, and sniffed. 'To answer your question, Jacob, I will ask one.'

'Why do you always do that?' said Jake, a little sarcastically.

'*What* eats man?' asked the dragon

For a moment the boy was puzzled then said, 'Sharks? Grizzly bears?'

Stone sighed, 'What, lad, *feeds* off man?'

'*Feeds*? Nothing feeds off us. Except your beast thing, mebbe.'

The dragon closed his eyes in the slow way that Jake suspected meant *I am being very patient with your ignorance, Jacob*. All of a sudden, he flicked his tail in irritation.

'What are these creatures that bother me so?!'

'They're mozzies. Just ignore them.' Jake batted at a small fly on his own cheek.

'Mozzies?'

'Mosquitoes. Midges too probably. My mam's allergic to them – when she's bitten she gets these massive lumps.'

'Bitten?'

'Yeah, they bite. In Africa the females carry malaria. Not here though.'

'Malaria?'

'Malaria – it's a disease! It gets into your blood.' Jake snorted. 'Huh, I thought you knew all about everything! Malaria can kill you.'

'Humans?'

'Yeah! Well... *and* animals. Not *you*. I mean, you're limestone.'

The dragon nodded a steady rhythm as he shuffled along.

'I see, this creature bites man and sometimes man dies. The disease kills him...?'

Jake could see where he was going with this. It wasn't the same.

'A disease isn't top of the food chain. It's not really alive. It doesn't work like we do, it doesn't have arms and legs and organs like we do.'

'...like humans. Creatures made of cells that divide, multiply and survive by eating other things?'

'Exactly,' said Jake, smugly. The small triumphs were often the best.

'Like bacteria?' said Stone with a firm but quiet voice.

'What?'

'Bacteria – creatures made of cells that divide, multiply and survive by eating other things. Bacteria. The thing higher on the food chain than man.'

'That's just... that's got to be wrong,' stammered Jake. 'Bacteria's like... like...'

'You seem lost for words, lad.' The dragon said, chuckling to himself. He flicked his tail viciously at the flying bugs. Jake felt the updraft as it whipped past his face.

'Oi watchit!'

'I am afraid I must go a little higher, lad. The buzzing of these *mozzies*...' the word was like glue in Stone's mouth '...is incessant. I cannot concentrate.'

He took off, leaving Jake to walk the river alone.

The boy's mind was full of flies, viruses and bacteria. As he trundled along, his train of thought pulled into the unhappy station in Jake's memory of his father's hospital bed. He remembered the smell of disinfectant; the small bottles of green antibacterial gel, the curtains pulled across during visiting times when the patients needed privacy.

These memories mixed quite happily with the friendly smell of soap on his father's neck as his hugged him, and his smile, broad and safe, telling him everything was fine, that he was okay and anyway what could happen here in a hospital?

And he did look fine, considering. He was broken but mending.

And then he was gone.

Jake walked on, ignoring the midges and gnats, lost in those memories. The day before his father had been taken back to ICU, Jake had given him a drawing of a hawkmoth. Bill had smiled and said, 'Jakey, look at the detail. It's great!' and he'd propped it up on his bedside table next to a bottle of orange squash.

He'd stared at it thoughtfully, then said, out of the blue, 'By God, Jake, can you imagine what it must be like, eh? What it's like to *fly*? Really fly.'

Jake swallowed back the memory and looked up. Stone soared beneath the early wisps of cloud and over the tree-tops. 'Yeah, Dad', he thought, sadly, 'yeah, I can'.

The Devil's Arse looked no different in this early light than it had in the previous day's stormy afternoon. Jake saw Stone land by the cave mouth and ran to catch up with him.

The tour-guide at the ticket counter recognized him. He didn't even acknowledge the dragon.

'Back again? You're an early bird. We're only just open.'

'Uh, yeah. I missed some of it yesterday.'

'Most of it I think. It's still t'same price unless you want a season ticket.'

'No, no just one for today, ta.'

'Right you are. 'Ere you go, then. I hope you've had breakfast coz there's no chocolate – the machine's broke.'

The man passed over the ticket. Jake smiled and walked over to the now familiar poster. It wasn't burned. It was not even scorched. On it, happy tourists in a coal train smiled out at Jake. He checked the vending machine. It was dead, but the chocolate inside looked perfectly fine.

'How come? It was all melted yesterday,' said Jake, flicking a glance at Stone.

'Maybe it's magic, lad.' The dragon winked his slow wink and smiled. 'Do you have the map in your mind?'

'Uh-huh'

'And it is now *correct.*'

'I think so,' Jake said.

'Think so?' growled the dragon.

'Yeah! It's correct, yeah.'

'Then let us try once more.'

Stone nodded and crooned gently, and the limestone around them throbbed to his welcome presence.

Jake swore he could hear a faint, tremulous sound, beautiful and deep. It sounded as if the air was singing...

It looked the same except for a few small differences: the poster was on the other wall, the vending machine had drinks in it instead of chocolate (though when it had last served a drink was anyone's guess), and everything looked old and abandoned.

Jake was disappointed. He'd expected strange silver deserts. Or purple mountains. Or green skies. This other world was far too much like his own for him to get too excited about it.

The journey had been a non-starter too. It was very lo-fi. Where he'd expected to enter a spiralling, holographic vortex, all that happened was that they stepped through a weird shift in the light –

as if they were walking through an invisible mirror – and then they stepped out here. In Shabbyville.

Jake sighed and turned back: the picture in the poster looked odd: the D of Devils's Arse was cut in two and one edge of the train was doubled up so it looked like it had been made by an over-excited Meccano fan. It looked a little fuzzy too.

Right, thought Jake, so *that's* the doorway.

It wasn't much taller than Jake's head and no wider than his shoulders. He had no idea how the dragon had fitted through.

'Hey! Hey you!' shouted a man from behind a wood and glass counter. 'Where did you come from!' he said, striding over.

Shitshitshitshitshitshit, thought Jake desperately trying to find somewhere to hide.

The man was a few feet in front of him now, looking annoyed and not afraid of giving Jake a clip round the ear. He looked just like the tour-guide back home. Only older, greyer and a little sadder.

'I've got a ticket!' yelled Jake thrusting the old-fashioned paper stub at the man's face. The man stopped short and stared at the ticket.

'Where'd you get this from?' he snarled, suspiciously.

'I bought it this morning,' said Jake with as much confidence as he could muster. The tour-guide studied the stub and handed it back to Jake. It was the right colour at least. He looked at Jake as if he had been scraped from the bottom of his shoe.

'Who sold it ya? A woman?'

Jake shook his head and felt the adrenaline rising in him – *don'tstartshaking don'tstartshaking now!*

'Bloke,' he blurted.

The man sniffed, scratched his nose and stood aside.

'Right answer, lad. It woulda been Fred. We an't 'ad a woman workin here for donkeys years. You after a tour? You're a bit early.'

'No, no I'm alright thanks. Been here before.' Jake tried a weak smile. The man stared at him for an uncomfortable minute then sidled back to his little cubby hole.

In front of the poster, seemingly oblivious, Stone made low rumbling sounds.

'What are you doing?' hissed Jake.

'I am protecting the doorway. We do not want anything to enter through it by accident. Or leave by it...'

'What if that man sees you!'

'You know he will not.'

'You never *said* there'd be people here! You never said we could get caught!'

'It is the same as it is in your world, Jacob. Populated. And anyhow, you handled the situation very well.'

The dragon stepped back and admired his own handiwork.

'That should do it,' he said, satisfied.

Distracted by the compliment and the strange haze blurring the doorway Jake asked, 'How did you get through it? That's a pretty small door.'

'The doorways calculate shape and form, and so adjust. If I had been a mouse, the doorway would have been much, much smaller.'

'That's just weird.'

'Economical. It saves energy.'

'Weird,' said Jake.

The limestone elemental shrugged his heavy shoulders and scanned the cave. He sniffed. It was as if he was searching for something.

'Hmmmm. We must go. This way.'

They left the cave, walking past the tour-guide who nodded stiffly at Jake. Jake stopped at the counter. Why not, he thought.

'Excuse me? Sorry? Erm, I need to go and get some dinner - erm lunch – but can I use this ticket to come back after?' He smiled an angelic smile. The man grunted and nodded again.

'It's good all day. There's not much in there anymore, y'know,' he grumbled, indicating the cave. 'They mined it out years ago. There's only stalactites and a few fossils now. I don't know why they keep it open to be honest.'

'Thanks,' said Jake. 'I'll be back later.'

The guide grunted again, took a slurp of tea from a flask-cup and went back to his book.

Even in the daylight everything looked shabby: the gift shop, the rolling hills, the sudden cliffs onto the roads, even the sheep looked grubby. Litter was everywhere. The surrounding grass was scorched to a stub, and the trees suffered in the heat.

The sun ached in the sky.

Jake turned to the elemental and asked, 'Why's it all so... manky?'

'I am unfamiliar with this synonym, Jacob. However,' Stone's tail took in their surroundings, '...this is the effect of pollution, overworking the land and undermining it. You are seeing the effects of climate change, lad. And of the beast.'

'So where do we go now?' asked Jake, eager to get out of the greasy air. He didn't like the smell. It reminded him of his dream. Stone stood high on his back legs and scoured the view. He sniffed again.

'I am not sure yet, lad,' he said

'Not sure? You've dragged us here to find some evil beast and you don't know where we've got to go.'

The elemental sighed and said, 'The beast is not evil, Jacob. It does not know *good* from *bad*. That is a human construct. All it knows is *hunger*. It will feed until it is sated. And as it feeds, it grows.'

'Eh? You couldn't have said this ten minutes ago? Before I went through that doorway?'

'Yes, I could easily have.'

'...!'

'Would you have come, Jacob?'

Stone sniffed the air again and set off in the direction of a huddle of old buildings. Jake ran after him.

'Selfishness, apathy, ignorance – these... *emotional states*... all give off energy, Jacob, in the same way that rotting fish do when they glow. And energy attracts energy. The beast consumes this energy and grows in strength. What it leaves of a world is little more than a husk.'

'Urgh!' Jake fought against the images rising in his imagination. 'H-how does it feed?'

'In many ways. I have mentioned some. Pollution is a favourite. And fire.'

'Fire?' asked Jake.

'Yes, fire – Fire gives off its own energy...'

'You said Fire's an elemental.'

'And so he is... Ah here we are.'

They stopped in front of a boarded-up pub. The once-white paint now peeled off in scabby flakes and the stainless steel window-guards had been wrenched off. The frame was splintered and the glass broken. Jake peered in. It smelled of dead flies, hutches and urine – animal and human.

'We're not going in there?' Jake grimaced. 'It stinks.'

Stone's tail ploughed through the pub's door like a ball on a chain. Splinters showered the half-crouching boy.

'Yes, I am afraid it does smell,' said the dragon. 'Come. It is as good a place to start as any. And I believe there will be someone there to meet us,' he said, stepping into the gloom.

'Who?' asked Jake, reluctantly.

The dragon sniffed again, not catching his gaze.

'You will see soon enough, Jacob. Although I fear you may not like it.'

⊘

And now Jake was angry.

He hadn't been prepared for this.

This was sick... a sick joke. He was still shaking from the shock, and angry tears welled in his eyes.

The pub had been dark and covered in dust and rubbish. Animals clearly nested in it, leaving their smell and the bones of prey decaying in dark corners. The bar was covered in guano from the pigeons roosting on the open ceiling beams. The stink was overpowering.

Light skewered the darkness, not so much illuminating it as emphasizing the shadows. At the far end, concealed in the gloom,

164

stood the form of a man. At least Jake *hoped* it was a man.

The dragon cautiously flicked his tail and shuffled forward. When he spoke, his voice was steady and rich.

'Lad,' he said. Jake looked up at him to answer, but Stone hadn't been speaking to him; he was speaking to the man.

'I knew you would come,' the shadow said holding his own stomach. (So he could feel the pressure of the dragon's voice too, thought Jake). The man continued, his voice vaguely familiar but gruff as though it hurt to speak. 'I saw the signs. It's time.'

'Nearly time,' Stone replied.

From where Jake stood, partly hidden behind Stone, he could see the slouching stoop of a tall, lean man. He couldn't get a clear look at the stranger's face but he looked normal enough, hair longish and greying at the sides, two eyes, a mouth...

'Is the companion with you?' The man craned his neck to see better. Jake edged behind the dragon. There was a feeling here... a sense that something wasn't quite right... Jake's skin itched.

'He is with me. Do you know the whereabouts of the beast?'

The man fumbled in his pockets and brought out a notebook. He held it at arm's-length.

'I think so. I've kept a record. All the disturbances. Disasters. I don't know what form it'll take yet.'

Stone grunted and sniffed. 'You must tell me all that you know, lad. Not yet–' he added as the man opened his mouth to speak. '–we must move out into the light. It is not safe here.'

The shadow nodded. 'It's not safe anywhere... but I know what you mean,' he said.

The dragon shuffled over to a barred door and, like a fist through newspaper, put his tail straight through it. The gloom of the pub melted under the ferocity of daylight. Jake squinted against the pain. It took him a few seconds to become accustomed to the light but once he did he could see the beady-eyed pigeons in the rafters and the pub's filth in all its glory.

And the man was no longer a shadow.

'D- *Dad?!*'
'Son?!'

In the rafters, other shadows moved like black oil. Pigeon eggs addled as the shades passed over them. Woodlice curled into plated balls. And then died.

Chapter 12

Jake was trying not to cry. This was wrong. The dragon had said nothing, *nothing* about who they were going to meet.

Dad! It *really* was him!

Stone stepped out of the foetid pub's gloom into the old beer garden. The man and boy followed him, eyeing each other cautiously.

One or two surviving benches cowered on the yellowing lawn; crisp packets, plastic bottles, papers and rusting tin cans huddled around their bases. The dragon squatted nearby as the man and boy sat down at a small distance from one another.

Jake stared. Everything about him was his father, except he looked older and tired – as if he'd seen things he shouldn't have and knew things he didn't want to know. Jake, unaware he was doing so, leaned in. The man's face was covered in greying stubble and his left eye was slightly lazy. Above his nose was a v-shaped scar.

As if on automatic Jake's mouth silently repeated a single, unassuming word: *dad*.

The elemental broke the awkward silence.

'William James,' he growled. 'This is Jacob.' Stone pointed his tail at Jake. Jake, startled, glanced at the dragon.

'Jacob?' whispered the man.

Stone nodded imperceptibly, then said, '*Jacob*.'

But as far as Jake was concerned, Stone could be saying the world was on fire because he couldn't hear him; he was still trying to make sense of it the man in front of him.

The dragon growled again. 'Jacob, *Jacob*! This is William James.'

Jake looked at Stone, then the man.

'*Dad*?' he managed.

'Yes?' choked the man, leaning forward, his arms outstretched.

The dragon's tail swept up between them.

'No!' he said as gently as he could. 'I am sorry. No.'

He swayed his head to keep both of them in his sight and turned his great, sad eyes on Jake. They looked like lava cooling on a glacial plain.

'Jacob, this man is William James. He is a narrator. He is not your father.' He held the boy's gaze for half a minute before turning to the stranger.

'William,' he said, his slow tail turning to Jake, 'this boy is not your son. He is *not* James.'

'But–' stammered the man. He looked like he was living through a small and personal hell. He stared at Jake. Jake stared back.

Stone continued, but his voice sounded to Jake as though he were speaking through treacle.

'Your family William, are gone. You know this to be true. I am so very sorry.'

The dragon let out a long-drawn breath and settled back on his haunches. He watched the man and boy for a few seconds, then said to William, 'You asked me about my companion?'

William twisted his gaze from Jake to the dragon. 'Y-yes.'

The elemental's tail came around and nudged Jake gently along the bench. 'Here is the companion.'

The man glared at Stone. 'He's just a *boy*!'

'He is. They always are,' said Stone, quietly.

'Does he know...?' he glanced at Jake. *I hope he knows,* he thought, *because if he doesn't, he's going to get killed.*

'He is not yet fully prepared and there is much to do,' sniffed Stone. 'You have read the signs.'

'It's impossible! If he's not ready! He's a boy!'

Jake head spun and he felt like he was invisible. What was

impossible? And what was his father doing here? Alive.

'Shuddup!' he shouted, suddenly, then, grabbing William's sleeve, 'Dad! You're *alive*?'

William froze. Slowly he reached out and held Jake's arm. His voice had the same gravelly texture as Jake's father.

'No,' he said softly. He couldn't hold Jake's gaze. 'The elemental's right, Jame– Jacob–'

'Jake! You call me *Jake*!' shouted Jake, ripping his arm out of William's grasp.

'Er... *Jake*? Jake, I'm not your father.' William took a breath. 'My son, he – God you look so much like him – but he died, you see. In hospital. A car accident. With his mother and sister. Over a year ago now.'

'NO!' snapped Jake. His head felt like it was being crushed. '*You* died! You died in that hospital! You were getting better then you just died. Not *us*! We never got in the car because you were late. You hit a patch of oil on the road!' Tears streamed down the boy's face. 'But now you're *here*. You're alive, dad!'

William slid up the bench, reached around Jake's waist, and pulled him towards him. He was stronger than he looked. Jake resisted but William kept a hold of him. The boy sagged in his arms, sobbing.

'Think about what you're saying... Jake,' William's voice was soft and soothing. He shot an angry look at the dragon.

'I feel sick,' Jake mumbled from the folds of William's jacket. It smelled slightly of sweat and familiar aftershave.

Stone lowered his face towards the boy.

'Jacob,' he said, quietly but firmly. 'Jacob. I understand this is difficult for you to absorb right now, but you must try. William James is a narrator. If *you* had lived in *this world*, your father would have been a narrator: a keeper of chronicles. As would you. In *your world* you are the companion. Perhaps in other worlds, Jakob or Jamie or Jack Walker might not even know about the elementals...'

'Hah! Jake rasped, pulling away. 'Good! Can I go there!'

He wiped his snotty face on the sleeve of his jacket. He was hot and grubby and ashamed of crying. He glared at the dragon. Stone met him with eyes of amber.

'We have work to do, lad...' his tail curled around and took the boy's chin, '...and I cannot do this without a companion.'

Jake clenched his jaw and pursed his lips. Yeah, right. Well, they'd come here for a reason. He bit back his spiky response and simply said, 'You should have warned me.'

'Yes. I told you that you existed in these worlds, but I should have been more explicit. I sought to protect you from distress. I failed. I am sorry, Jacob.'

'Yeah,' said Jake dully. He looked up at William who smiled. The same eyes, the same shaped face. The same smile.

'What do I have to do?' Jake asked, quietly.

'We should go to my cottage,' said William, glancing over his shoulder again. 'It's safer.'

'What from?' asked Jake, narrowing his eyes.

'You'll find out,' mumbled William, then louder. 'Come on. This way.'

They set off down a stony path.

In the gloomy pub, the darkness was heavy and sticky. Alive. What it sensed was the primal emotions: anger, pain, guilt, disappointment, envy, heartbreak.

And it drank them in.

'It is secure here?' Stone's head poked through the open kitchen window. William slung his keys on the table and his coat on a hook on the door.

'Yes,' he said. 'The building's limestone, the mortar's limestone-based. It should be fine.'

Jake looked around the room. The whole place was made of stone. Even the table, covered in papers and books, was stone and the kitchen counters were marble. It looked familiar.

'How's it safe?' he asked.

William James fussed around the kitchen, moving piles of paper from chairs, and opening cupboards until he found a tea caddy and a spare cup.

'I don't really now how it works, but the limestone somehow stops the beast getting in. Even when things seemed to be at their worst – when the fault lines were compromised and enough of the beast had come into our world to feed – only the minutest traces got in to this cottage. That's all I know... We've lived here for centuries, my family.'

Jake leant against the counter and surveyed the room, scanning the details. *There's something special about this place, Jake...*

'This is the cottage we're staying in!' Jake said bluntly.

William looked up from piling spoons of tea leaves into an old teapot (he likes his tea from a pot as well, thought Jake, just like Dad!). The narrator followed the boy's gaze around the room. He tried a thin smile.

'In your world?'

'Er, yeah,' said Jake. 'It's the same. But different.'

'How so?'

Jake looked around and pointed here and there. 'Well, there are beams running all over the ceiling, and the wall over there is much bigger and made of brick.'

'Brick?' asked William, glancing nervously at the dragon.

Jake noticed and said, 'It's the boot hall. And what did you look at him for?'

Stone shook his head, a small gesture committing to nothing.

William shrugged. 'Nothing. You'll be fine. Brick's are clay. Anyway,' he added just a little too brightly, 'fancy a cuppa tea?'

'I think,' interjected Stone, 'we must press on, William James.'

William stared down at the teapot.

'Ah, of course, maybe later, then.'

He reached over the table and picked up his large, leather-backed book. Written in meticulous handwriting, was a log of dates and notes: some entries covered pages, others only a sentence or two.

Jake looked over William's shoulder to try and read it, but the writing was too compact. He caught the odd phrase such as 'positive feedback', and 'hearts of many'. It was an uncomfortable mixture of poetry and science.

He noticed, at the bottom of one page a small line-chart, its fine zigzag running up and down then up again until it levelled out.

'What's that?' he asked.

'It's quite old, this,' said William.' Not as old as when records began, but, still, quite old. It charts the beast's activities in the last two centuries.'

'Here,' he said, pointing to a peak in the chart, 'was when it was the most active. A lot of earthquakes at the time, and tsunami, volcanoes. The world was heating up and no one believed us. People just carried on: wasting fuel, using plastic, flying over short distances, driving over even shorter ones. It mounts up. Adds to the heat. Uses a lot of carbon.

'We used to have penguins but we don't anymore. We've lost hundreds of species of bees. No more dolphins, polar bears...' William's voice trailed off and his jaw tightened. 'We've lost almost half our *ant* species. I mean, ants for God's sake!'

Jake was horrified. He looked accusingly from William to Stone.

'Didn't anyone do anything to stop it?' meaning *didn't* you *do anything to stop it?*

'Oh yes,' said William pointing to the chart once more. 'Here, look, you can see is where the activity dips. We all tried to help, once the politicians finally believed the scientists - that's what I do for my day-job. Did, I mean.' He looked up at Jake, then carried on.

'Anyway, billions of people – normal people like you and me – back-tracked and worked hard at not wasting things, not using so many plastic bags, not driving everywhere. But we were very selfish by then. Very *developed*. We expected a certain standard of living. And the business men!' William paused to wipe a piece of invisible dirt from the chart, then carried on.

'Some of them did believe what was happening and what *would* happen if we kept on wasting resources, but most of them just jumped on the green bandwagon to make more money out of us. The green-pound they called it. They set up *projects…*' He coughed awkwardly.

'So,' Jake began, 'so they did *something*, right? That's *good* right? Even if they *did* make money from it. Money's important, too. People need money. For food and stuff. And you can't go back and *undevelop* things!'

'Yes, yes, but most of it was too little too late. Take pesticides. They're inexpensive, quick to use, they kill all the bugs off the plants – bang! dead! Yes?'

'Yeah?' said Jake carefully.

'This meant more crops so that billions of people could be fed, which is great, yes? I mean, we needed food because people were starving.'

'That's what I mean. It's a *good* thing.'

'Yes, making sure people have food *that's* important. But we over-used the pesticides and most of us turned a blind eye to it all. There were other ways to deal with crop disease and infestations but they were time-consuming and, to some minds, expensive. And people don't like spending money. It's how rich people stay rich.'

William drove on like a snow-plough in the Yukon.

'It all comes down to monoculture, Jake.'

'What's that?'

'It's a way of farming that grows only one crop, over and over again. That's a bit simple, but that's basically it. When the land's nutrients are depleted the farmer has to feed it with chemical fertilizers or, if we're lucky, manure.

'But if you keep growing the same crops, the land gets infections and infestations that stick around and get passed on to the next crop and so on. So okay, we say, let's blast them with pesticides!'

Jake stared at William, bemused.

William was on a roll. 'But pesticides kill *all* insects, Jake, not just the ones eating the crops. And *they* get eaten by birds and animals, and, if they don't die first from second-hand poisoning, *they* get eaten by *other* animals and birds. Then they die. Erm, have you ever seen a hedgehog that's eaten a slug after its eaten slug pellets?'

Jake pulled a face and shook his head.

'It's horrible,' said William, grimly. 'But, like I said, most people turned a blind eye... Apathy and ignorance. See this blip on the chart, just before it levels off?'

'Yeah?' Jake's eyes flittered between the narrator and the diagram.

'It fed well then. The beast, I mean.'

William stroked his lips and tapped his pencil thoughtfully on the page. 'Sad isn't it?' he added.

Jake looked at him trying to make sense of it. *We do this*, he thought, bewildered, *we do this stuff on our world.*

'There's no point, is there?' he said numbly. 'We can't stop it.'

William was about to speak when Stone interrupted. 'No, Jacob, we cannot stop the evolution and nature of man, nor should we, but we can *control* the beast.'

'How?' snapped Jake, angrily. 'We're as badly burned as scalded!'

'I do not understand this phrase...'

'He means we're damned if we do and damned if we don't,' added William, trying to be helpful.

'To be damned is a religious concept. I have been to the centre of the world and there is certainly no hell for damned souls.'

'I don't think it's meant to be taken quite like that–'

The sentence withered under Stone's glare. William tapped his pencil once more and shut up. Stone sniffed.

'Jacob, imagine the beast as an arachnid,' he said.

'What, so it's a spider *and* a vampire?' said Jake sarcastically.

'If you will. It first incapacitates its prey with poison, and over time feeds off it until it is completely dead. The poison here is in the *idea* that in order for man to develop it must protect *only* itself; this breeds selfishness, greed, anger, which gives rise to apathy and lack of responsibility.'

'So, it *is* the beast's fault, not ours! We can't help it if we're poisoned.'

'It is not so simple, I'm afraid, lad.'

Jake tried to avoid the dragon's gaze. Whatever he was going to say, Jake didn't want to hear it.

'No, it wouldn't be,' he muttered.

William put his hand on Jake's shoulder. It felt warm and paternal.

'Jake, what Stone means is that the poison isn't made by the beast – it's only a sort of life force after all. No, the poison – the idea – came from us in the first place. The beast just latched on to it – a bit like a parasite. When we first used fire, to cook food and to keep warm, we caused some of the first pollutants. It sort of went on from there. And who knows how it evolves? It learns from us, this much we know.'

Jake stood up, sharply. This was too much for him to think about. He thought they'd come to find out how to kill some monster and instead he finds out that humans were killing themselves and nothing could be done to stop it.

He stepped up to the table and riffled nastily though the books and papers.

'It existed before we did!' he spat.

'Yes,' said William quietly tidying up the papers. 'The stories say it lived off primal fear. It was weak. When we came along we sort of expanded its diet: fear and greed, with a side-dish or two of apathy and selfishness.'

'It's not funny, you know!' Jake snapped.

William coughed. 'No, Jake, it's not. And it's a lot to take in, I can see.'

Jake went to slap at the papers again: he was angry and overwhelmed and someone else was going to have to deal with it. He'd had enough.

He wasn't the only one.

Stone stopped the boy in his tracks.

'Jacob, enough!' said the dragon. 'There is much to do and tantrums will avail us of nothing! This is a cycle and while it can never be fully destroyed it can be diminished. The beast found in man a receptivity that no other creature afforded it.'

Jake opened his mouth but was cut off with a sudden wave of nausea. The dragon's eyes flared.

'However,' Stone continued, 'the humans on your world can be *educated*. It is not yet too late. The beast is *still* in this world, but if it breaks through to your world, Jacob, there will be more destruction. And our task will be that much *more* difficult. There will be more earthquakes, tornadoes, tidal waves, more land fires and rising seas. More *deaths*.'

The boy leaned against the marble counter, arms crossed tightly over his chest. His face was red. The dragon stared at him for a minute then turned to William.

'You must show us where it has been most active. If we can contain it here, then Jacob's world should be fine for a while.'

'Huh!' grumbled Jake. The dragon glared at him and Jake felt a pain in his head that sunk like a stone into his gut.

'Jacob, come here. I need for you to concentrate. You will see things that I cannot.'

'Such as?' said Jake, a residual mixture of petulance and curiosity.

'Look, lad!'

Jake stared at the map William James spread out in front of him. It was filled with a legion of tiny coloured pins: blue to mark either a fault line or a doorway between the worlds, black a spate of activity from the beast. Each pin recorded a number that correlated to another chart in the red-leather book: a list of columns describing exactly what had occurred and when.

Jake looked hard at the map. The pins seemed to dance.

'This one's wrong,' he said and moved it to another spot. 'And this one.' He fixed a dozen pins, moving some only millimetres and others fifteen or twenty centimetres from their original positions. Two he removed entirely. William tried to stop him, complaining about the centuries spent calculating the fault lines, until Stone grumbled deeply and the man (stomach churning) gave up.

'I don't know how I know, but they just didn't want to be where they were,' said Jake apologetically. 'They were jiggling about – couldn't you see 'em?'

He looked into William's blank face. 'They've stopped now,' he added. 'They're right now.'

'So, we have the weak spots,' rumbled the dragon. 'Do you see activity around them?'

'Activity?' asked Jake. The dragon nodded.

Jake bit his lip and honed in on the pins. On the map's surface he could make out dark smudges spreading out like sump oil on a newly laid driveway.

The more he focused, the darker the smudges became.

'There. There. There. There. There and there too.'

William looked worried. That was a lot of activity.

'Anymore?' he asked, trying to control the concern in his voice.

'No,' said Jake. 'No wait! *There*. But that one's small. Fresh, maybe? New? Or maybe really, really old?'

'No, Jacob. It would not be old. The beast, like a vampire bat, finds a source and returns time and time again, cauterizing before it leaves. It is why some areas are larger than others.'

'They look like ink blobs,' said Jake. 'Really, can't you see 'em?' William and Stone shook their heads.

'*They* will be the oldest fault lines,' said Stone. 'Or perhaps they are doorways. The beast is trying to weaken them.' The dragon chewed over the thought.

'But what is here,' he wondered aloud, 'that would make a fresh fault line? It is merely a field.'

It was merely a field. Or had been when it started. The traffic to and from the fair had been heavy, so now it was half an acre of mud, sawdust and wooden planks.

It was an old fashioned Fair with a capital F: part-circus, part-fun-fair, part-casino. All the stall holders were dressed in clothes from two centuries ago – brightly striped trousers and oversized moustaches.

Custom had been quiet at first, but news had got out that they were giving away free sweets and toys and people soon flooded in.

Jake and Elizabeth had gone on the second night, when the field still had grass. It should have been really lame. But it wasn't. The talents included a half-naked man who would eat anything from light bulbs to nails to spiders, and a woman almost totally covered in tattoos who if you could come up with something new would get it tattooed there and then. There was a firewalker. And a magician who could read minds.

As much as Jake wanted *not* to like these corny things he found he loved them. Elizabeth complained they were exploitative but she still watched in gleeful horror as a woman made out of rubber twisted her legs over her neck, tucked them under her backside and walked off stage on her hands.

Everything was cheap to buy, not like at the usual fairs. Even the rides were half the price of the fairs back home. Jake had watched a group of children ride the Meteor, throw up in a corner, then go back, laughing and screaming for more.

It was excessive and garish and wonderful. No one went home with money left in their pockets, but everyone *loved* it. Elizabeth and Jake had left full of hotdogs and candy-floss, and happiness.

That was almost a week ago. People were *still* loving the Fair and it was set to stay for two more weeks. But no one noticed the small changes that were happening every day: the slightly smaller candyfloss; the chances of winning a little prize now more like one in fifty (when before they seemed to be giving them away). And the rides were just that little bit shorter...

No one noticed these things, just as no one noticed the small dark shadows gliding over the stalls and rides, and the oily sheen on the mud beneath their feet.

'What is a fair?' asked the dragon in a slow, inquisitive tone.

'A fun-fair?' asked William amazed. 'You've been around forever and you've never been to a fair?'

The dragon snorted.

'I have never had reason to visit one,' Stone said. 'What is its purpose?'

William looked to Jake, who rolled his eyes and said, 'It's like a travelling show-thingy that people go to. To go on rides. For fun. Usually they're lame, but this one was quite good.'

'You have *been* to this fair?' asked Stone.

'Yeah, me and Bett went. She was bored, and I'd promised. There's not *that* much to do around here.' Jake checked himself and added, 'Well, y'know, 'around here' in *my* world.'

Stone snorted again and flicked his tail. Jake could hear it outside on the dried-out lawn. Thud. Thud. Thud.

'Hmmm, perhaps I should visit this fair?' Stone said.

Jake laughed and folded his arms. 'Yee-eah... no. I can't see that working,' he said.

The dragon gave him a withered look that meant, *tell me why this should not be, companion?* Jake answered as if reading the dragon's mind: 'Loads of people around and you're the size of a house.'

Stone was about to say something sharp when Jake added, 'Anyway. People enjoy themselves at fairs. They're happy: nothing for the beast to eat there.'

'You tell us there is a fault line here, Jacob. No doubt there is selfishness and greed, pollution and filth at these fairs.'

Jake thought about the exhausts spewing out of the generators and the mountains of litter piled up beside the few bins in the once grassy fairground.

Stone continued, 'It is has the attention of the beast. Now, lad,' he said, turning their attention back to the map – 'Are there more distrubances? Weak spots?'

Jake stared. If he moved his head slightly he could see a small patch of black out the corner of his eye.

'There... there's something there. I can't see it clearly, it's like its hiding.'

The dragon drew a sharp breath. '*There*? You are certain, lad?'

'Yeah. Why? What's wrong?'

It was a bare patch of land, down by the mountains.

The dragon growled angrily. In a quiet rumble he said, 'Jacob, the beast is certainly trying to break through. And it is looking for the map.'

'The map?' asked William. 'What's it want *my* map for?'

'No,' said the dragon sadly. 'The *limestone* map.'

'It really *exists*?' William asked, astonished.

'Yes, William it does. What you saw, Jacob... *that* is my cave.'

Chapter 13

It had been a long day and Jake wasn't an easy student. He'd tried to listen to the instructions but the elemental spoke too fast, and had too high expectations of him. Stone had been worried by the news from yesterday and had started Jake's training first thing.

The day was baking: they were calling it the hottest summer on record and the T.V. news was full of it: in France eighty people had died from heatstroke, in England train tracks had buckled. It was not a good day for training.

And now, Stone was tired. It was the kind of dull tiredness you got from concentrating too hard.

Jake sat down and tried not to stare. Stone was panting like a terrier. He opened his wings to let some air in and cocked out a foot. He left it there barely touching the ground. Jake had seen swans in the park do this kind of thing when they were hot. He'd never been able to work out how they kept their balance. And in any case, swans' bones were hollow and weighed hardly anything, but Stone...?

'Stone, can I ask you a question?'

'I am sure you can,' said the dragon, wearily. His voice felt heavy as mountains. He turned to face the boy. His eyes were small, rheumy marbles.

'I mean, would it be alright if I did? It's a bit personal?'

The dragon's ears twitched and his eyes narrowed but he nodded yes.

'How come you're *alive*?' asked Jake.

'All elements are alive, Jacob. You just have to modify your understanding of the definition.'

Jake knew he wouldn't get a straight answer, not outright.

'Okay, but what do you eat? Seriously? I *know* you don't eat people. And how do you breathe? Do you *sweat*? I- I mean because you were panting and...' Jake trailed off.

Stone paused for a minute, thinking. 'You want to know how I function?' he said, eventually.

'Well, that's a bit, y'know, *geeky* I s'pose, but yeah. Yeah.'

The dragon's head twitched with curiosity and his tired eyes blinked.

'Very well. Limestone is a sedimentary rock – it is not the porous rock of pumice that is riddled with holes and can retain very little moisture, neither is it the impenetrable rock of grit-stone that traps liquids inside yet prevents their absorption from the outside. Does this answer your question about the perspiring?'

'No,' Jake said flatly. 'Not really. Not at all, in fact.'

'I perspire, but only a little,' sighed the dragon. 'If I draw air in quickly through my mouth it cools me faster. In this heat, I become weary.'

'Oh.'

'Heat is a transformative process for stone. Metamorphic. I find power in extreme heat, but heat can also be enervating. It drains me. Especially if I must work so hard.' In his tiredness, he didn't notice the pained look flash across the boy's face.

'Oh,' said Jake.

'Is this all, Jacob?'

'Erm... how do you *breathe*?'

The dragon sighed. 'I have a similar respiratory system to you. Lungs of a sort, air-ways in, air-ways out.'

'You breathe *oxygen*?'

'Carbon dioxide.'

'Like trees?'

'Yes, a little like trees,' the elemental laughed softly. 'I extract the carbon dioxide from the air and release the waste gases.

Nitrogen and oxygen – although I retain traces of these – and carbon monoxide.'

'Carbon monoxide, that's a poison! That's pollution!' said Jake, suddenly very awake.

'It is the most efficient way for me to have developed my body. And in any case, I produce much, *much* less CO than even one of your cars.'

'Oh,' Jake relented. 'What do you use the other gases for?'

'You *truly* need to know this?' Stone asked, yawning. When Jake nodded, he continued.

'I retain a little oxygen to maintain my central combustion system and nitrogen to regulate its temperature.'

'Eh?'

'Jacob, do they teach you nothing of chemistry in your school?'

'I'm just rubbish at it.'

The dragon grumbled. Jake felt his stomach flip.

'In *simple* terms I mean this: my blood is a form of molten rock – as the core of this planet is magma. Oxygen provides the fuel to maintain the furnace that is my heart. The nitrogen I use is a coolant and prevents the furnace becoming so hot that I explode.'

'Are you *nuclear*?' said Jake, both shocked and fascinated.

'Ah, you understand a little of physics, then?'

'Not really. I saw a programme on Chernobyl. It was horrible.'

A dark look of memory passed across the dragon's face, then he shook his head and said, 'No. I am not nuclear. I am... more like a volcano. The difference is that I *control* myself. Volcanoes do not. Now, have you finished your interrogation, lad?'

Stone's head was almost touching the ground. 'I am tired. I must sleep. For a while.'

'What, *here*?'

'Just... a... while...'

The dragon closed his eyes, nodding slowly. A minute later, Jake could feel the soft throbbing of his snoring. He watched as the stone head, tucked into the dragon's chest, rose and fell with every breath, and he imagined the great cavern of the creature's heart: the pressure, the intense heat. The burning centre.

William James stood at the cavernous mouth of The Devil's Arse on his world and peered into the gloom. He felt edgy. This is where they'd left him yesterday.

The limestone dragon.

The elementals.

The stories had been passed down through generations and William knew them all, could recite them by heart. But he'd never expected them to be true... not *actually* true.

The stories charted the end of worlds: to anyone who knew how to properly read them. For most people they were legends, fairy stories, but to the narrators... Even his son had known three quarters of them before he'd— He tried to put any thoughts about the accident to the back of his mind. His wife, his daughter. His *son*.

And now William was the last. The last of the narrators and the last of his family.

It was astounding how much Jake looked like James: he even *dressed* like him. For God's sake, he had the same voice, the same bad habit of biting his thumbnails. William wanted to know what he was like. What were his hobbies, his favourite subjects in school?

The dragon was fine enough as a guardian but the boy needed guidance: real, human, guidance. A boy needs a father. A father needs a son.

William walked to the nearest wall and placed a hand on it. Light filtering in from outside turned the rock a gloomy yellow. He sighed. A woman in overalls called over.

'You all right, love?'

William James smiled generously and said, 'I'm fine thanks.'

'They don't do tours here, anymore. And you need a ticket to go into the caves.'

'I just wanted to study the rocks, thanks,' said William patting the walls with the flat of his hands.

The woman nodded curtly and unlocked the ticket booth. William waited until he could hear the rattle of a cleaner's bucket and pressed his hands to the rock. It was cold.

He closed his eyes and pictured the boy that looked like his dead son.

Come and fetch me. Come and fetch me, Jake, he whispered over and over until eventually he heard the click of the key in the ticket-booth and the footfall of the woman coming to tell him it was closing time.

Rain had soaked the night sky as well as Jake's dreams. He couldn't remember any details when he woke up that morning, but he had the taste of rotten bananas in his throat again.

'Out again?'

Elizabeth sat on the last stair as he edged past.

'Yeah,' said Jake.

'You're never in,' she muttered.

'I'm a bit busy.' Jake shrugged his bag on his back and smiled sheepishly. Elizabeth glared at him.

'I don't know what you're up to but it's dangerous Jake, and if you don't give over I'm gunna tell Mam.'

'Bett, look, I can't explain but it's important. Don't tell Mam. It'll be alright, honest.'

'Yeah, whateva,' said Elizabeth, snapping upright and marching stiffly into the kitchen. Jake knew she was upset with him but there was nothing he could do about it. He had training to do, and anyway he had enough to worry about without adding his sister to his list. He pulled his key off a hook and went looking for the elemental.

'Die, Jacob? Not even *humans* can eliminate every trace of *limestone* from this world.'

Jake flapped his t-shirt against the heat, and sighed. His head was still spinning from the Lore.

'Yeah right. But you are old, though,' he said.

'I am billions of years old, lad,' replied Stone, happily. He chuckled. For some reason, he was in a good mood today.

'In this form, Jacob, I am more than 500 million years old. However my core, what you would call my *heart*, is always new. Always regenerating.'

'You looked tired the other day.' Jake twiddled with the tie on his sports bag; it was frayed where he'd lost the toggle.

'I have not had to work so hard with a companion for a very long time...' Stone began. Jake looked anywhere but at him. The dragon nodded and continued, '...I find it *exhilarating*...'

Jake allowed himself a small smile, then added for reassurance, 'So you can't die, then?'

'Not really. Not until the end of this world. However, I am not invulnerable.'

'You just said...!'

'This is not a fairy tale, lad. I *will* survive the beast's attacks, but I might well be damaged. And if I am damaged badly then it may well take me centuries, to recover.'

'What? I'll be dead by then!'

The dragon looked squarely into the boy's eyes and found, for the first time in his long, long life, he could not hold the stare. He swallowed.

'There is only one thing I could do to speed any recovery and that is as dangerous as battling the beast itself.'

'What is it?'

'Find my centre.'

'What's that mean?' asked Jake.

Stone chuckled again. 'By coincidence it is what we will be

considering today. Now,' he said, briskly. 'We have a great battle ahead of us and if we do not prepare, it will be a very short battle indeed. So, what is the first tenet of lore?'

'Elementals are each made of an element,' Jake said, brooding.

'And this is significant because?'

'Because the element is connected all over the world.'

'Well done,' said Stone.

'What does that mean though?' whined Jake. '*Why* is it important?'

'The third tenet?'

'Elementals and companions are joined by a talisman,' said Jake, sulkily.

'And...?'

Jake bit his lip and carried on as if he was reading a script. 'The talisman binds them in a bond that cannot be broken.'

...yadder, yadder, yadder... The lore. Boring and repetitive: a list of pointless commandments.

Stone listened to the boy churn out one maxim after another. It was clear his heart wasn't in it.

'Jacob,' said Stone in reflective tone. 'Do you have the talisman?'

Jake fumbled in his bag, pulling out sandwiches, juice, notebooks and binoculars.

And the comb. It felt warm in his hand.

'Can it really be a *weapon*?' he asked. He didn't take his eyes off the talisman.

'*Anything* can be a weapon, Jacob,' answered the dragon. 'Even your empty bag might one day save your life.'

'What can it do?'

'It can act as a blade, yes. A very powerful blade.'

'It's blunt.'

'Looks are not everything, lad. Now, place it on the ground. Over there is perfect.'

Jake placed the comb on the ground about four feet away from him. 'Now, come back here.'

The boy came back to the dragon who said, 'I want you to concentrate only on the talisman. The limestone. Ignore everything else. Is it in your mind?'

'Uh-huh.'

'Good, now bring it to you.'

Jake faltered, looked around, shrugged and walked back to pick up the comb.

'No!' said the dragon impatiently. 'Come back here! *I said concentrate*. Close your eyes. Focus on the comb. *Centre* yourself. Make limestone the *only* thing you can see, Jacob.'

Jake concentrated hard.

The comb was there, in his blind vision: a tiny speck.

He focused, watching it grow until his whole mind was filled with the heavy, solid *feeling* of limestone. He could taste its gritty, sourness, smell the alkaline damp of caves. He could feel the damp stone in his hands.

He looked down. He was holding the comb like a dagger, its bone teeth digging into his palm. He hadn't moved an inch.

'How?' he gasped.

'You *know* how, Jacob.'

'No! I – I really don't!'

'Then you will work it out and tell me tomorrow,' laughed the elemental.

'What?' said Jake, incredulously.

'Yes, consider it an extra curricular task. Today we will finish early.'

'Homework!? You're giving me homework, now?'

The dragon chuckled once more, this time louder, deeper and longer. 'Yes,' he said. 'I believe I am.'

CHAPTER 14

Dreams... dreams were always the key. The life force that was known to Jake as the beast had no mind, no heart, no morality to talk of, but it had a hunger. A need to live. This world barely nourished it now. It needed fresh food. All the worlds over, humanity had an idea – a dream – that it was the most important species in the universe. And not only did humanity dream, but it remembered its dreams...

Already enough sections of the map existed. If the beast had a mind, it would have thought to itself: yes *there* is a way in. Through a child's dreams. And when the child has finished his drawings, a doorway will be opened. And the elemental's map will be secured...

And then, the beast will enter the new world in its myriad parts and be made whole.

The world of the companion was a feast.

The beast's nebulous mass stripped the last sap from the dying fibres of an ash tree. It ached from hunger.

But first, the key would be needed. And to find the key, the beast would need to use a vessel: a form that breathed and moved freely in the world of humans...

The beast reared on the air and without ears it listened... It listened to the hunger of a desperate, lonely soul.

Elizabeth opened her window, not sure whether she was letting the warm air of the room out or the hot air of the day in. The storms of the last few nights had done nothing to clear the air, only to make it sticky and unbearable.

She sighed a long, drawn out sigh and watched a bluebottle bang against the window pane. It bounced twice then flew off towards the direction of the oak trees.

She could hear a cacophony of buzzes, whirrs and twittering, and Elizabeth realized how much she missed her city sounds. Every now and then she heard a car on the distant road but it wasn't the same. There were no frequent sirens: police cars chasing villains, or ambulances coming to people's rescue. No fire engines racing against time and the rapid spread of fire. She liked fire engines.

Elizabeth had thought it would be good to be away for the whole summer; they'd not had a proper holiday in ages and it would be *so rock 'n' roll* just to spend time on her music, inspired by the isolation.

She watched another fly bang into the glass and thought, isolation's all well and good just so long as you have someone you can talk to about it. Jake was too busy doing God knows what – he came home some nights hardly able to get up the stairs. He never mentioned the dragon anymore, but she knew it had something to do with what he was doing.

She picked up a glossy magazine and fanned herself. She flipped open her phone. NO SIGNAL. The only place she could get a signal was out in the fields amongst the stench of sheep and the buzz of flies. Downstairs, she could hear her mother swearing away at her old laptop.

She leaned further out the window to see if her brother was back yet. If you squinted you could just about make out the road in the distant shadow of the great peaks. Elizabeth squinted now.

On the horizon, a grey cloud shaped like a dragon crawled over the expanse of sky.

Hah! Dragons.

Elizabeth sighed again. She looked like she felt: hot, bothered and bored. Her red shorts stuck to her legs. Her plastic sandals dug into her toes because the heels were too high. Her black and white striped top was the coolest thing on her, and that was only because it was baggy and split wide on the neck-line.

She needed to get out. She needed a chocolate muffin and a frozen mango smoothie in a building with *air-conditioning*. She needed civilization!

She flicked off her sandals and fetched her flip-flops out from under the bed. Good, comfortable. Now, bag? Bag? Ahhh... she grabbed a small blue handbag, threw her phone, purse and a zillion other essentials into it and checked her lipgloss in the mirror. Then she said to a world not quite ready for a bored Elizabeth, *Right! Where's my bloody brother?*

Jake stood in the baking heat in the centre of the low field. He was trying to listen. To what he had no idea. *You must listen*, the dragon had said, then disappeared.

Tied around his eyes was one of Elizabeth's old scarfs. As he stood, one foot planted firmly in front of the other, both arms outstretched, he moved his hands very slowly in large, arcing circles as if he was dousing for water.

A hot and uncomfortable churning started in his stomach. Stone was back. Jake moved his hand to lift up the blindfold and felt a violent rush of air almost knock him off his feet.

'Eyup!!' he shouted blindly to the sky.

There was no reply. He paused and tried to remove the blindfold again. And again came the pounding of air. This time Jake stumbled.

'Give over!'

'Then do not cheat.'

'I thought you'd buggered off!' shouted Jake.

There was no reply.

Jake stood up slowly. 'This isn't fighting! We were meant to be doing fighting! I know what fighting is, you know.'

The dragon pounded the air above Jake's head. The boy crouched and swore under his breath.

'Find your balance, lad, then be quiet and listen.'

'I look like a pillock!'

Jake sucked in a breath and positioned himself again. He'd seen things like this in lots of movies: the ignorant but incredibly bright young boy is taught how to find his centre and tune in to the world around him by the wise but curmudgeonly old master. Only then would he be able to distinguish a field cricket from a grasshopper just by *listening to it*.

In the movies, this usually only took about ten minutes. Jake had been there for an hour and a half. And he already knew the difference between a field cricket and a grasshopper.

'So...' he muttered to himself. 'Find my centre? ...no, sorry, no centre here...' He let out a deep breath. He could feel the steady thrum of the dragon nearby. *That's not what he said, was it? He just said* listen.

Jake straightened his back and concentrated.

'Okay, I'm listening,' he said. 'I'm *listening* to the blackbirds, and there's a car in the distance. That's a buzzard over there.'

The sounds were clear and bright.

'I can hear bees buzzing and there's something in the bushes there, probably a dunnock or a field vole – better watch out for that buzzard. I can hear–' Jake tensed his body, 'What's *that*? Something's moving in the ground. Worms? Bloody hell, I can hear worms churning up the soil! And beetles too, crawling over pebbles. I can hear...'

A picture formed in Jake's mind. Yellow and grey. He saw the fossilized remnants of swamps and meadows. It *felt* like a billion years pushing down on him; *sounded* like a billion voices.

'...*stone*?' he gasped. 'I can hear the stones moving in the soil...'

The stones were *calling*... calling to one another.

Calling to him.

A symphony of words. A statement. Clear, decisive. Terrified.

IT IS COMING.

Jake rushed back into the normal songs of the blistering day.

'The s-stones...' he murmered, trying to catch his breath. 'How?'

'Remember, on some level *everything* is alive, lad. With practice, you will be able to distinguish one stone from another. They know much. Listening to them could be the difference between you coming through this adventure alive or dead.'

'I'm gunna get creamed, aren't I?' Jake said, flatly.

'Creamed?' asked Stone.

'Y'know... killed. *Really* killed.'

'Ah, I see. *Creamed*? Your vocabulary, Jacob, is very distinctive. No, it is not my belief that you will be,' Stone sniffed, '*creamed*. I believe that you will succeed. You are my companion...' He cocked his head to the sky. 'Ah, your sister is coming.'

Jake glanced back over at the field. 'I can't see anything,' he said turning back.

The dragon sank quickly into the earth.

Jake couldn't see Elizabeth anywhere. He picked up his bag and slung it over his shoulder, its weight banging against him as he headed off down to the path. A heavy grey cloud drifted overhead. It was going to rain later.

'Jake!'

He heard the voice in the distance: small, shrill and frustrated.

'Oi, Jake!'

Elizabeth was a dot on the long path, waving her arms frantically. Jake waved back.

Below his feet he knew the stones were listening.

And waiting.

The coffee shop was full of people desperate to get out of the heat. The welcome air conditioning poured out its cold air as Elizabeth stirred the crushed ice of her raspberry smoothie with her straw and scooped some up. It made her teeth zing.

'How can they run out of mango?'

She scooped up some more flavoured ice and piled it onto her tongue. God, it felt good. Through the window she could see a rancid heat-haze rising off the pavements while people kept to the shade of the awnings. A storm-cloud loomed menacingly.

Outside smelled of petrol and baked tarmac, sweaty people and sticky sun-block, and inside smelled of muffins and cookies and coffee being poured over ice. For the first time in days, Elizabeth felt comfortable, and said so.

Jake slurped his juice and shrugged.

'Are you gunna be mardy all day?' she snapped.

'I'm tired.'

'You're always tired.'

'Shuddup,' said Jake firmly.

Elizabeth leaned in and lowered her voice. 'Is it that thing?' she said, waggling her eyebrows. 'Y'know... grrrr.'

And there it was.

The perfect opportunity to tell his sister everything. To get it all off his chest. It was dangerous, but he was going to explode if he didn't tell someone. And so, relief welling in his tired bones, he surprised himself and took it.

'It'sinsaneBett!!Iwalkedthroughrock!annaflew!annaknowwhatthe talismanisit'sthecomb...!'

Jake talked and talked and talked as his sister listened. Every now and again she asked a question, but mainly she nodded, astonished, and slurped her smoothie, feeling a strange déjà vu and not sure what to believe.

It started to rain.

It had rained all day. Jake scribbled like a madman in the gloom of his bedroom. Occasionally he paused and pushed a palm heel against the pain behind his eyes.

A frozen image of the stone map faded from his mind. Maybe he needed to go back. Have another look?

He cocked his ear to the sounds of what he thought were footsteps on the attic stairs but was mistaken. Then, the door swung open sharply and his sister poked her head in.

'Jeeze!' said Jake hotly, as he scrabbled to hide the pages. 'Why don't you ever knock! I could have been nekkid you know!'

'Yeeeeuuuwww,' said Elizabeth, screwing up her face in disgust. Her head-phones dangled round her neck so that Jake could hear the tinny, scratchy sound of music. He paused then laughed. Some sort of spell had been broken by his sister's presence, but he couldn't work out what.

'Anyway, what's up?' he asked, casually.

'Mam wants to know if you want to come and play a board game with us.'

'A *board* game? Seriously?'

Elizabeth nodded with mock-pity. 'Yeah. She fancied it.'

'I've got a headache,' said Jake flatly, but curiously the pain behind his eyes didn't seem so bad now.

Elizabeth stared at her brother and folded her arms. 'She's not seen you for days, Jake. You come in late go out early. You've got a headache, take a pill!'

Jake sighed, 'What game?'

'Not Scrabble coz you cheat.'

'I don't *cheat*!'

Elizabeth narrowed her eyes and said, 'No? All I'm gunna say is *squalene*.'

'That's a *word*!'

'Not in my dictionary.'

'Your dictionary's this big!' Jake indicated something not much bigger than a matchbox.

'If it's good enough for school, it's good enough for Scrabble.'

'It's not even got *directional* in it!'

'No? Well it's not got *squark* in either coz no dictionary has!'

'That is *definitely* a word!'

'Yeah, spelt s-q-u-a-w-k,' said his sister as she slipped out of the room.

'Do you want me to come and play or not?!'

'You can if you want,' said Elizabeth sweetly, poking her head back through the door. 'Operation?' she added, reading his mind. She knew him better than he thought. He stood up.

'I thought we'd lost the tweezers.' Jake said, holding onto his sister's shoulders as he followed her downstairs.

'Mam found them.'

'Okay,' said Jake. 'But no crying when I beat you,' he joked. His headache was almost gone.

They reached the bottom of the stairs and Elizabeth paused listening to the rain drumming on the windows.

'God this rain's rubbish, isn't it?' she said to no one in particular. 'It just makes everything hotter.'

'Yeah,' said Jake quietly. 'Rubbish.' They stood in the hallway for ten long seconds, not saying another word.

'C'mon,' said Jake. 'Operation.'

Stone arched his back, and prowled around his cave. The map was trying to sink deep into the ground.

He turned his mind to the cottage. He could see Jake's room and his bed; he could feel the boy's body heat, but try as he might, he couldn't see him. Something was blocking his sight.

Anger bubbled inside him like a geyser. It could only be the beast, but how? He thought about what the narrator had said about its evolution. What if, over the years, the beast had *learned* from the elementals. Had *befriended*. What if it also had a companion?

Someone who could influence the boy, maybe even hide him from the dragon.

It would be someone close to him.

Someone he would trust.

CHAPTER 15

'**N**ow, I will teach you connectivity, lad.' The dragon looked closely at Jake as if weighing something up. The day had been going well.

'Really?' Jake asked excitedly.

'Yes,' he sniffed. 'You are ready.'

'Tracking and stuff?'

'Tracking is part of it, yes. And travelling.'

Stone scoured the sky with his golden eyes and brought his gaze back round to Jake.

'I am aware,' he said, 'that you have worked hard and have learnt much over the last weeks. I am aware also that these lessons are difficult for you.'

'Well, I'm getting better I think.' Jake said in a solid tone.

'I am aware, Jacob, that *everyday* you question your necessity to be here: you are, after all, just a boy and this is work for a hero.'

'– er hang on a minute...' said Jake, his pride rising. The dragon cut him off.

'To be connected to the world, lad, is to *know* it. To be a *part* of it.'

'O-kaay.'

Stone spoke in a voice that made the boy's hair stand on end, his skin tingle.

'Close your eyes, Jacob.'

'Why do I always have to close my eyes? I look stupid.'

'Trust me, lad. Close them. Both of them. *Both*. Good. Now, hold out your hands. Palms facing me, lad.'

Stone stepped up to Jake so that he was gently touching the boy's palms. Jake pulled back, startled.

'Do not be alarmed, lad,' said Stone, moving forward again. 'Imagine you are pushing against a heavy door. There. Perfect.'

Jake's hands rested on the rough hide. He felt uncomfortable.

'What do you feel, Jacob?'

'Like a pillock!'

'We do not have to continue!' warned the dragon.

'No! Erm, I can feel *you*. You're warm.'

'Good. Now, describe what you can feel. Eyes closed!'

'Well... as I said, you're warm.' He moved his hands up and down, his fingers finding the shapes of fossils and crags. 'You're rough here, and smooth too like glass that's been melted. This feels like a shell – a pencil crab.'

'What colour is it, Jacob – keep your eyes closed, I said!'

Jake grasped for a colour. 'Umm, sorry. I dunno, *yellow*?'

'Don't try to *remember*, lad. *Feel* it. *See* it.'

Jake could feel the shell firmly imbedded in the dragon's skin. It was long and thin, tapering to a blunt point. It was a centimetre wide at the base. He could feel the cartilage of the crab that had lived inside it. He could feel the memory of the crab, could picture its skittering travels along the sea bed. It was blue like a summer sky, with pink blotches the colour of piglets.

Jake told the dragon.

'Good. Now, tell me more.'

Jake could see and feel everything through his *hands*. The colour-changes in Stone's skin from golden to white to grey. Textures and shapes. A small damp patch just below the dragon's heart.

Jake talked. And talked.

He talked about the places the dragon had visited. He could *see* history: the ancient landscape around them, once covered in great ash trees. He could see the things the elemental had done: a meteor re-directed on its course, an earthquake stripped of its power.

Power. Jake could feel incredible power rising from the ground up into the dragon. With his eyes closed he could see *everything* – even the words that the dragon was about to say. They said:

'Do you feel connected?'

Jake nodded, mutely. His mind buzzed.

'If I was to move away from you, would you still feel connected?'

Jake thought, then shook his head.

'Open your eyes, lad.'

The dragon stood two feet away, smiling. Jake looked at his hands as if he'd never seen them before. He could still feel the stone skin on his fingers, the furnace of Stone's heart warming them.

'You moved?' Jake gasped. 'When?'

'Remember when I asked you to tell me the colour of the shell?'

'Back then?'

Stone nodded.

'B-but I can still feel you!'

'Good, that is good. Now, turn your hands over.'

Jake, his arms still outstretched, did as he was instructed. He could still feel the dragon's skin.

'What you feel, Jacob, is *limestone*. It covers much of this land. When it is closest to the surface, the connection will be stronger.'

'Like a mobile phone mast?'

The dragon paused and said, 'Yes. You can feel the limestone because you have learned its energy – its *signal* – from me.'

'Cool.' Jake's eyes gleamed. 'What can I do with it?'

'I know you are keen to learn tracking–'

'Yeah!'

'Then you must choose a subject to track.'

Jake knew exactly who to choose, and grinned evilly.

'You have chosen your sister.'

'How did you *know*?'

'Because to be connected, is to *know*. This is the lesson, Jacob,' said Stone firmly. 'Now then, close your eyes and picture her?'

'Good. The image must be clear. Think of the clothes she wears, how she moves. Make her as real in your mind as possible, Jacob.'

Jake turned a picture of Elizabeth around in his mind like a CGI model on a computer screen: red top, green jeans, black sandals, her hair tied back in a scrunchie. She floated in front of him, motionless and unreal.

Then the image in his head was sucked out of him until it became a tiny point of nothingness, and came twanging back, dragging with it a real-life picture of his sister, lying on her bed, playing her guitar to something on her iPod. She stopped and scratched her face.

'I can't believe it,' Jake breathed. 'How?'

'You are connected to the limestone. In the walls of the building and in the concrete foundations.'

'In the *walls*? Is it real? Why is it so sort of greasy looking?'

'What you see, is happening *now*, lad. With time it gets clearer. You will be able to monitor anyone.'

'Anyone?'

'Anyone,' said Stone. As an afterthought he added, 'Do not use it for spying, Jacob.'

'Cool!' Jake turned his head and the image turned with him. He could see the bed, the window, the floor. He laughed.

'It is a great responsibility, Jacob,' said Stone.

'Yeah, I know. How do I make it stop?'

Stone gave up and rolled his eyes. 'You shake your head.'

'It's that easy?' Jake shook his head and the image of his sister vanished completely. 'Cool!'

Elizabeth sat on her bed listening to her iPod. She was playing her guitar badly, her fingers half asleep because of the heat. She stopped, closed her eyes and held the guitar gently on her lap. She was tired too. The rain-storms had kept her awake again and she'd had bad dreams for most of the night. She half-wished Jake hadn't told her about the dragon. She'd dreamt she was trapped in a burning house and no one could hear her shouting.

She shuddered at the memory and opened her eyes. Suddenly, she had the creepiest feeling that someone was watching her. She shuddered again and, as quickly as it came, the sensation went. It left behind a greasy feeling and the taste in the air of petrol stations and refuse trucks.

Outside the sun shone brilliantly and the heat pressed down. She pushed her guitar from her lap and quickly made for the door. That's what she wanted, she thought, *sunshine*.

In the corners of her room, dark shadows slid into the plasterwork like oil on a sandy beach.

'Jacob?'

Jake lay on the ground wheezing. His ribs ached and his chest burned. He was bleeding from his nose and one eye was blackened.

'Your manoeuvres are improving, lad,' said Stone, cheerfully.

Ten minutes into training and the dragon had picked him up with a flick of his tail and hurled him into a nearby tree. Jake was sure he'd heard something crack and he wouldn't have been surprised if it had been his neck.

'Are they?' he gasped, dabbing at the blood with his hand. 'Tell my ribs that.'

'Ahh but you avoided at least three swipes before I made contact and you placed one good punch to my stomach.'

'I nearly broke my fist!'

'In retrospect, you might think more strategically about the weapons you choose to employ.'

Jake opened his swollen eye and peered at the dragon. 'Thanks, you might have mentioned that before.'

The dragon chuckled. 'You have a game, Jacob? Rock-Paper-Scissors?'

'Uh-huh,' grunted Jake.

'Rock wins more times than you may think.'

Stone chuckled again. 'I am impressed, Jacob, by your improvements. Do you think you can continue without me for a day or two?'

'What? Why?' Jake wiped his face on his t-shirt.

'I have... an errand I must embark upon.' Stone's great eyes were calm as the sun on a spring day.

'What kind of errand?'

'I have called a Colloquium: a gathering of the elementals. A parliament, if you will.'

'What for?'

'We have things to discuss.'

'Me?'

'The world does not centre around you, Jacob.' Stone flicked his tail absently, then added, 'But yes, you will be a topic.'

'When're you coming back?'

'Three days at the most. The journey is far, even travelling underground.'

'Can I come?'

'I am afraid not. The Colloquium is – for want of a better word – sacred to the elementals. And in any case, it would be cold, even this time of year. I fear you would not enjoy it.'

'Where is it?'

'Iceland.'

'Iceland!'

'Yes.'

'Cool!'

'Indeed it is. Very cool.'

Chapter 16

Jake stood, hands on hips, fifteen feet away. It was a dry-stone wall built by prisoners of war over a century before. Limestone through and through, covered in lichen and moss.

He bit his lip and considered what he was about to do. He thought he'd worked out the trick to it: it wasn't just about convincing *himself* he could walk through stone, he had to somehow convince the *stone* that he could.

He had to *become* stone, not just tap into it.

There was no way the dragon would have let him try it so soon, but he wasn't here. And Jake was.

How hard could it be?

He stared at the wall.

He could feel it staring back.

Okay, he thought, standing legs apart, now *focus*. He closed his eyes and pictured the stone in front of him. *Okay, you're stone, I'm stone.* The wall moved slightly under his mind's gaze like a rain beetle under a magnifying glass. Jake reached out invisible fingers to touch it. It was warm. *On some level all things are alive, Jacob.*

He grinned.

His fingers stiffened, his breathing started to slow. His thoughts became as solid as mountains. He lifted his left leg and it weighed more than a ton. A feeling of stone spread through him. A small landslide tumbled down his face as his grin widened.

Hah! Nothing to it!

The wall seemed to squirm, unsure of what it was facing: was it a boy standing in front of it, or was it stone?

Jake laughed again and pinned his sights on a patch of mossy stone. He forced his legs into a run; slow at first, then picking up speed until he was charging onwards, carried along by the momentum of the hill.

The wall loomed.

Jake laughed like an avalanche. He'd *cracked* it! *Who needs the lore!*

He ran on.

The wall was upon him...

He smashed into the stonework, then bounced off, blood streaming down his face.

'Ohbhygod!'

He slumped down, wiped his snotty nose on the back of his hand then pinched his nostrils together. Bubbles of red squeezed out over his lips. He stood up on shaking legs and wobbled over to the wall. It was as solid as...well, rock. He kicked it and swore.

But, he *had* become *stone*! The wall *knew* he had!

It should have let him through!

He turned around and slid down, feeling dizzy and annoyed. When he breathed in, one nostril whistled a cracked tune.

Why didn't it work?

He sighed and started to compose himself. The coolth of the stones seeped into his angry body. It felt good. Safe.

The blood stopped flowing as Jake's breathing slowed to a cloud of calm. He listened to it and felt the pain slipping away. He thought about the wall: its two layers, its solid endurance of winter, its stone shell shielding an ancient centre – all connected implicitly to the elemental dragon. He forgot about the blood drying on his face; his mind was filled with the sedentary nature of the stone wall. Cool. Calm.

And it could have gone very badly for him if, at the point he'd realised he was sinking deep into the wall, he'd allowed his brain to panic. Instead he anchored his thoughts to the calm coolness of the stone, to how similar its carbon atoms were to his own. And he sat forward until he was clear.

When he was sure he was safe, he turned back and reached out. The wall was solid.

Eyeless, it looked back at him, and some recognition passed between them. Some calm, quiet, simple recognition.

The midnight sun, low on the horizon, glinted off the basalt slab that marked the Lorestone. Its surface, blacker than universes, reflected the shapes of the gathered elementals: Water, Paper, Coal, Word, Granite, Silver, Wood, Bone, Iron, Fire and Cloud. Around them the broken rock of the rift plain dragged the sounds of the valley into itself as the dragons waited for the limestone elemental to arrive.

There was power, here. You could feel it in the air. It felt like history dammed up against a wall of time. The history of the elementals, recorded in stone.

The first Colloquium had been convened when the Earth was still sticky with new life. Hundreds of elementals had travelled thousands of miles to help write the lore that would protect the world. To find and seal the doorways.

Already, they had foreseen the world's destruction.

The Lorestone had listened. And remembered.

And now, the dragons made themselves comfortable, and waited.

Stone alighted, rosy sunlight haloing his body. He nodded a greeting to the assembly and spoke. His voice was careful in tone, and articulate.

'I have come with concerns. The lad, who is training even as we speak, is I believe... vulnerable.'

Cloud stepped forward, her nebulous mass full in the summer air. She nodded once.

'Vulnerable from what? The beast or himself?' she said.

The two elementals eyed each other like animals. There was some past there, some history…

Stone snorted, a hot plume in the cold air.

'It is true he is… green in his knowledge, however, he is evergreen in his passion to succeed.'

'Is he his father's son?!' snapped a dragon at the front. A grey bulk belying patches of rusty red, snorted and growled. When he moved, the sounds of girders creaking in a gale echoed out across the rocky plain. Stone fixed him with a steely eye.

'He has his father's stubbornness, and his will to protect those he loves.'

'What about the rest of us, does he want to protect us too!'

'Iron, I see your patience has grown acute,' growled Stone sarcastically. 'And your tolerance abounds. The lad *cares*. His father did not. Jacob is bewildered perhaps and, I would say, a little afraid, but this is understandable. He wants to help.'

'Is he capable? Has he skill? Is there talent? Do we have an adept?'

This dragon pushed himself to the front of the group by stepping painlessly *through* the dragons in his way. He was almost invisible but for the delicate silver outline of words said and unsaid. When he spoke, it was as if a chorus of every possible synonym spoke at once.

'Of all my companions, Word, I have never encountered a lad with such potential,' answered Stone. 'He is quick, very clever if he allows himself to be, and his stamina is exemplary for one with so little training. But most significantly the limestone *listens* to him. It welcomes him as if it is welcoming a lost child.'

'But this is not enough.' This was a new voice.

Stone looked up. At the back of the gathering stood a dragon who was one moment twice, the next half, the size of Stone; his body swelling and flickering like flames in a hearth. Even from here, Stone could feel the searing heat of the dragon's volcanic heart. Fire smiled. It was a graceful smile, and it reminded Stone of a cat strolling away from an empty nest.

Cloud's gaze flicked nervously between the two dragons.

Stone clenched his jaw and said, 'Your meaning?'

'That he is committed to his destiny is a given, also that he has strength; there is a bloodline here that dictates as much. Word asked you not of his *potential*, but of his *capability*. When *it* comes, will the boy be ready?'

'He has had no training, save these last weeks, he knew nothing of his abilities until now–'

'I assume he has the talisman!?' interrupted Iron.

Stone's head snapped towards him, never once taking his eyes off Fire.

'Yes!' he growled. 'He has my talisman. He is a child thrown into a whirlwind hoping he will survive with only bruises! And *yet*, when the time comes, I believe he will *do well*.'

'Will he defeat the beast?' snarled Iron, thrusting himself forward.

'He will do that which he is able to do,' said Stone, simply.

'Doing his best is not good enough!'

'It is all any of our companions can do!'

The two elementals were now inches from one another. Stone's eyes flared crimson. Iron looked like a bomb about to explode.

'*Our* companions,' Iron shouted, 'are not DESCENDED FROM THE *FIRST*!!'

'My companion will do what needs TO BE DONE!!'

B o o o o m !

It shook the air and blew the dragons apart.

Cloud stood on the Lorestone shimmering in a rosy light.

'You know better than this,' she said quietly, ruffling the misty feathers of her vast wings. 'Bickering like human children. *Really*!'

Stone picked himself up from the edge of the stone circle. Iron sat, looking sheepish. Fire laughed, rich and crackly like a forest fire. Cloud glared at him.

'Now,' she said. 'You called us together, elskan...' she flicked another glare at Fire, daring him to criticise her endearment, '...your concerns?'

Elskan? Stone met Cloud's look with a puzzled tenderness; perhaps she had forgiven him… it was such a long time ago.

'I am here to ask you to be prepared,' he said. 'The fault lines weaken daily and the lad is, as Iron has so eloquently pointed out, very green. If something should happen to me, then I will need time to recover.'

'The doorways are protected. The portals are secured. The ingresses are guarded,' said Word.

'Yes, but for how long?' asked Stone.

None of the elementals caught one another's eyes.

'Is this all?' asked Fire, eventually.

'It is enough,' said Stone. 'Except… I said the lad was vulnerable. It has been suggested to me that the beast might have adapted. Learned from us. My worry is that it could groom a child to be its own companion.'

'Impossible!' growled Iron.

'*Why* is it impossible?' asked Fire, turning towards Iron.

'It would need a form!'

'It has taken on forms in the past. Humans. Animals.'

'No! No, no, no! I will not believe it has a companion!'

'It might be dangerous to do so,' sighed Fire.

'I think,' said Cloud opening her wings in an undisguised threat. 'That we must agree to keep a vigil. If it has a companion, it might be stronger than we think. We might consider the possibility of a vessel. This is more the beasts way.'

The elementals tried not to think of what the beast could do with a human vessel.

Cloud spoke again. 'Is this all, Limestone, or do you have more surprises to delight us with?'

Stone shook his head. 'That is all,' he said.

'Good, then we should go.'

One by one the dragons took to the sky, filling the now gloomy light with their dark shadows. As Stone stepped forward he felt the familiar curl of the cloud elemental's tail around his neck. She drew him closer and said, 'You are worried. There is something you have not told us.'

Stone blinked slowly.

'The lad is dreaming. And the stones are... nervous.'

'Nervous? How can you tell?'

'Tremors. There are more of them than usual. And the map... it keeps trying to hide.'

'These dreams are nothing to do with you?'

'Nothing. I have a feeling, Cloud... I might be too late.'

'Nonsense, and in any case the boy came to you. But I will tell you one thing, elskan, I too have a sense of something strange. Water also is concerned...'

Stone leaned in close, he could feel her cold breath on his face.

'He has family, does he not?' she asked. He nodded.

'I fear his family will be his undoing,' she added.

'In what way?'

'I am unsure.' She gave a nervous chuckle and straightened up. 'It is probably nothing... just a feeling.'

'Hmmm,' said Stone. 'Cloud?' he added, looking uncomfortable

'Yes?'

'You call me elskan, does this mean you have forgiven me?'

Cloud fixed Stone with a stare, her eyes like thunderstorms.

'No, elskan,' she said with quiet menace. 'I have not.'

Chapter 17

Jake swung round the door and poked his head into the living room. His mother sat in the dark watching the end of a film; the flickering light from the old television set casting yellow and blue shadows across her face. She looked withdrawn, ghost-like.

'Weepy?' he said in his gentlest voice. He noticed the edge of the photo album pushed quickly down the side of the sofa so that he couldn't see it. It was blue with gold edging. They'd made it together just after his father's funeral. He knew his mother took it out whenever she was feeling lonely.

'A bit of a weepy, yes,' she said thankfully.

Jake slid onto the sofa and kicked off his shoes. Drying mud littered the floor. He pulled up his feet just like his mother had and tucked them under his thighs. He wriggled a little and nestled into her side. They hadn't done this for years because he'd grown out of it, but some nights it was the kind of thing you needed. You needed to know you were safe.

'Any chockies left?' he asked, casually flicking through a small box of chocolates. He could see by the ever-changing T.V. light that there weren't very many left and even then probably only the white ones. He fished one out and popped it in his mouth. It tasted of cream and vanilla and would have been much too sweet on a normal day, but tonight sugar was good. He licked his lips and looked for another.

Lucy wrapped her arms around her unresisting son and rubbed his sleeve up and down like she used to when he was very little.

'You're in late,' she said.

'Barn owls,' lied Jake. He couldn't believe how easily the lies came to him, now. He'd never lied to his mother before. Not really, not even when he was caught skipping school. He'd been *acting out*. Everyone said it: teachers, doctors, the counsellor from school that he was forced to go and talk to. His mother. Acting out because his father had died.

His father. Hah! The man had lied *all the time*.

But Jake had loved him. Everything about him – even if it was all a lie.

God, Mam, he thought, *if only you knew*. He bit the thought down and welcomed his mother's warmth. The day had been hot but tonight, for some reason, he felt cold.

They sat listening to the comforting drone of the television. It felt right. He sank deeper into the sofa and let the sounds wash over him.

'Jake,' said his mother eventually, keeping her eyes on the screen. 'Is everything okay?'

Jake looked up and said, careful not to let anything in his voice give him away, 'What d'you mean?'

'With you. Is everything alright?' Lucy turned to her son. 'I know it's probably not what you'd wanted in a holiday, and you don't have any of your friends here, but you're *okay* aren't you? Not getting into... y'know, trouble or anything?'

Jake pulled stiffly away and stared at his mother.

'Yes, yes I *am* in trouble. Things are *not* okay. Really not okay. Look, Mam, Dad lied to you for years. To *all* of us. He was meant to be this amazing man who could see and speak to a dragon. A stone dragon! Seriously! And he was meant to be this dragon's companion and help him look after us. But he *never* did. He was ashamed or too scientific or whatever. He had this amazing gift and he wasted it. And he was meant to tell *me* all about it but he didn't! So now I have to learn it all from the dragon before some...some *thing* comes and kills us all. And I'm *useless*. I don't even know if I can do it. But I *do* know it's not safe. And I'm bricking myself. So, yeah I *am* in trouble, Mam!'

He wanted to say all of this and more, but he didn't. Instead he said, 'No everything's fine. Why?'

The look he gave her was just a fraction too short before he looked away. She squeezed his arm.

'It's just, you're out all day, you get in late, and the other day when I was doing the washing... there was... on your blue t-shirt... well it looked like *blood*. You're not getting into fights are you? In town?'

His t-shirt!

'Mam, honest. Everything's fine. I don't even know anyone here. I'm not getting into fights with the locals, honest. I was in a tree and I just slipped, that's all.'

'Another tree? You seem to be up a lot of them lately.'

'Hah, yeah.'

'What were you doing in *this* tree?' Lucy asked stoutly.

'Trying to get a better shot of a... woodpecker.'

'Mmmm... Okay,' said his mother, suspiciously. 'You'll have to show me these photos when they've been developed,' she added. Jake looked uncomfortable.

Lucy squeezed his arm again. 'You do know you can tell me anything don't you?'

Jake smiled and nodded. 'Yeah, Mam, I know,' he said. 'But I'm fine. Honest.'

Lucy smiled back. 'Good,' she said knowing when to let it lie.

'Did you get it out?' asked Jake casually.

'What?'

'The blood?'

'Oh, God, no. It was trashed, Jake. Ripped to shreds. No I binned it. You'll need to get some more t-shirts.'

Jake's shoulders sagged. 'That was my *favourite* shirt,' he said.

'Never mind,' said Lucy, briskly. 'Next time you're photographing dangerous woodpeckers you'll remember to wear something you're not so bothered about, won't you?'

Jake slumped back, suddenly very tired. 'Yeah,' he said. He liked that t-shirt. It was an original 1970s. Blue with a white surfer on it.

He wondered if he could retrieve it from the bin, then thought better of it.

'What's on the telly?' he asked, and picked up the remote control.

'I don't know, have a look. I'm going to make a cup of tea. Fancy one?' Lucy squeezed herself out of the space between the chair-arm and her bean-bag son and made for the door.

'God, Jake, look at all this mud!'

'I'll clean it later. I'll have tea please. Got any biscuits?'

'You'd better! Rich Tea?'

Jake pulled a face.

'They'll do,' he said as he flicked from one channel to the next. Nothing but soap operas and some talent show his sister was obsessed with – she was probably watching on the small T.V. upstairs. Jake flicked some more. Ah...

It was a film, half-way through. In it a young, blonde boy in a mediaeval smock was trying to ride a dragon and failing miserably.

Jake started to laugh out loud. He was still laughing when the blonde boy fell off for the fifth time, and Lucy entered the room with two mugs of tea and a packet of biscuits.

'What is it?' she asked sitting. 'A comedy?'

'No,' said Jake between breaths. 'I don't think so but it's just funny. *Really* funny!' Tears streamed down Jake's face. His voice was high and broken. 'Look, look at him! He's gone *again*! Ha ha ha...'

Lucy put the mugs down and glanced from her son to the T.V. It wasn't *that* funny, *was* it? She watched the dragon grow more and more frustrated with the boy as he fell off, time after time. It *was* funny: it shouldn't have been but it was. And Jake's laugh was contagious.

The dragon sent a small flame searing across the boy's backside and Lucy burst out laughing. She sat down and wrapped an arm around her son. Both of them laughed, trying hard to catch their breaths. On screen the furious dragon shot up into the sky, and the boy was left alone in the forest: frustrated, angry and deeply disappointed with himself.

As soon as his head hit the pillow, Jake was asleep. It was a restless, choleric sleep filled with more dreams, each worse than the last. He felt as if he would wake up in one and never escape.

His last was the worst. In it, he dreamed of his father as a small wax man, blackened by the shadows of Jake's bedroom and the sooty smears of the melted candle he was made from. Jake held him safely in one hand as he knelt on the floor drawing the limestone map with the other. With the map, he could bring his father back. He *knew* it, as sure as night follows day, because his father had told him so.

But time was running short.

He could hear the whoosh of the elemental's stone wings and the roar of his fiery breath.

One small section of the map was left, that was all. But what did it look like? Remember, Jakey, came his father's voice, remember...

But he couldn't remember and as the dragon smashed through the limestone walls of his room, fire spewing from his mouth, the wax man was suddenly alive in Jake's hands, wriggling and screeching. The flash of fire struck him and he melted.

And Jake, staring at what the elemental had done, woke up screaming.

'Jake, ssshh, don't worry.' Lucy sat on the edge of Jake's bed, holding her son. She'd heard the scream even from her room. Something about fire and stones and a dragon. What was it about this place and his deams? They hadn't been this bad in years, and now they were every other day.

Jake coughed, he still had the taste of soot in his throat. When he brought his hand to his mouth his mother gasped. It was blistered and red.

'Jake, what's happened to your hand?' Lucy turned it over so she could see the damage. Jake pulled it away.

'I- I must have burnt it on the lamp or summats,' he managed, shivering from shock.

'Jakey, you need some tea. Sweet tea.'

Jake nodded and looked up to see his sister's face in the doorway, small and concerned.

'Bett, you go back to bed,' said Lucy. 'Jake's just had a nightmare that's all.' Some nightmare, she thought... the scalding, the shock...

'She's alright, Mam,' said Jake. 'She can stay.'

'Okay, then. I'll make some tea?'

Elizabeth nodded. When Lucy was safely on the landing, Elizabeth turned to Jake and said, simply, 'Dragon?'

Jake nodded, then shook his head frantically.

'I don't know what it was, but it looked like Stone only he was a *bastard*, Bett... *Evil*. He... he tried to *kill* me. In the dream he killed *dad*. Burned him alive.'

'*Killed* Dad!?'

'Well, no, it was this doll that looked like dad. It could bring dad back, I mean. Like a spell.'

The shadows in the room seemed darker to Elizabeth just then, and the look on Jake's face had been just that little bit too certain that he could bring their father back...

'Jake, that's just... just a dream... you know you can't, yeah? bring him back, I mean.'

'I know, I know...'

They heard Lucy padding up the stairs. She brought an ice-bag, a bandage, some burn cream and three cups of cocoa on a tray.

'I thought cocoa would be nicer than tea,' she said. She placed the tray down, put the ice-bag and cream on Jake's hand then fixed the bandage, all the while soothing and chattering.

When they'd drained their mugs Lucy ushered her daughter out the room and went turn to out the light.

'Leave it on, Mam, please,' said Jake sleepily.

Stone surged on. Something was wrong, he could sense it. The companion's dreams. He should not have left him unprotected for this long. Foolish! *Foolish!*

Beneath him the ground swirled and swept by as one long beat of his stone wings followed another. A mid-summer breeze buffered him, playing over his calcified hide. On any other night he would have played back, but tonight he soared with the certainty that the boy was in danger.

What was it Cloud had said at the Colloquium? *His family would be his undoing.* And now with the cries of the stones ringing in his ears, the limestone elemental was sure he knew exactly what she'd meant.

He banked over the training field keeping the small cottage firmly in his sights. The upstairs lights were on. He landed silently on the lawn and concentrated. The image was blurred: he could see Jake sitting on his bed whispering to his sister.

What was she saying in reply? Stone's eyes narrowed and his vast jaw set like concrete.

The sister leaned in, a strange look on her face. Stone felt the fire rising in him and he fought to keep it down – he would need it soon, but if he showed his hand too early...

He blinked the image of Elizabeth out of his head and focused on her brother, straining to hear him... *Stone... he was a bastard... evil... tried to kill me... he killed dad. Burned him.*

Stone cocked his head to one side, thinking. So that is the way of it, then? Corrupted dreams. He snorted an angry plume of grey smoke and took grim pleasure in the fact that he'd been right to seek advice. *Stone ...evil... tried to kill me...*

Instead of making his way to Jake's room, the dragon sank slowly into the earth. If he tried to visit Jake tonight, he would only scare him more. The boy looked safe enough for now. Stone wasn't happy about it but the best thing he could do was wait until tomorrow.

Tomorrow came. Clouds trammelled the sultry sky, dark and bruised. Jake sat on a boulder edged by spiky grasses with spent flower heads. He picked one and twirled it aimlessly between finger and thumb.

Stone was back. Jake wasn't sure how he felt about it.

It had been a clumsy and unproductive morning and there had been a very awkward moment when Stone had asked his companion about his dreams. Jake had brushed him off; he couldn't tell him about the fire and the wax man, he just couldn't. But it was telling that every time the dragon moved too quickly or lost his composure, Jake flinched.

Then, Stone had asked after Elizabeth and Jake wasn't sure why. Maybe he thought she could help – well he could think again! There was no way Jake was going to let his little sister get caught up in all *this*!

In the end, Stone had told Jake to go home before someone got hurt. They could resume training tomorrow.

Jake didn't argue.

And now, he sat twiddling grasses and staring out into the fields. He heard a buzzard call out and wondered what it was doing. Probably waiting for its mate to bring food. Or hunting, itself. It called again. He couldn't see it.

The wind was picking up: another storm coming. The days were getting hotter and the storms at night even fiercer. Last night was the first in days when it hadn't actually rained.

None of it made sense to him... why *here*? Why *now*? Why not America or China or India – places with data on proper geological fault lines. Places with *serious* weather. Not here in a small, rural area in the middle of England. He'd asked the dragon about it and the only answer he'd got was 'why not', which, as far as Jake was concerned, was just a cop out.

He sighed, feeling a little bit sorry for himself, and caught a movement out of the corner of his eye. It was the buzzard, hovering over a patch of scrub, waiting patiently for its prey. It dipped and scooped up a small brown scrap of something hiding in the grass. It struck Jake how incredibly tiny the field mouse was, and how massive the buzzard.

Thirsty, he rummaged in his bag for a bottle of water and came across the comb.

It had all started with this, hadn't it?

For some reason, he'd taken to carrying the talisman everywhere with him. If he spent time away from it he worried more, but when he had it with him the world seemed a slightly safer place.

He lifted it out, placed it on his knee, and found his water at the bottom of his bag. He unscrewed it slowly, and noticed the buzzard had gone.

The water was cold when it should have at least been warm in all this heat, and it tasted clean and sweet. He'd filled the bottle from one of the natural springs. It was a good discovery and even thinking about it made him smile. Free spring water!

His eyes fell on the comb. He was sure it kept his drinks cold *and* his food hot – he'd put a fried egg sandwich in his bag this morning and it burned his lip when he came to eat it. It was one of those new elemental mysteries that confounded him.

He turned the talisman over in his palm and felt its energy throbbing through his bones: it felt like Stone when he laughed. He slipped it into his pocket and shifted awkwardly on his rock. The seat was smooth but uncomfortable so he stood up, shook some life back into his legs, and set off across the scrubby field. If he was lucky, he'd make it back to the cottage before it rained.

Halfway across the field, he felt the first heavy blob of water fall onto his face. It was unusually hot. Then came another. And another. Then the skies opened and sheets of water poured down.

The buzzard was already on its killing post (a dead branch in a sheltering tree) and occupied with shredding up the mouse. If it had looked up, it might have seen in its hunting fields the rapid movements of a human boy trying to out-run the rain. Trying to find cover along the hedgerows. Trying to get back to his own hidey-hole.

⊘

The companion was hiding something from him, Stone knew. The dragon sat on the cliff of Dark Peak and stared out over the land. Even when he'd asked Jake outright about the dreams he'd mumbled some incoherent rubbish. And he was evasive when it came to the sister. In the end he'd let him go home because he wasn't concentrating and sooner or later he'd end up hurting himself.

And besides Stone had to prepare. The beast was coming, the other elementals had been very clear about that.

He needed to think.

He needed the vast expanse of sky, cradled in cloud, not the close protection of rock and earth. In the sky he could think as clear as glacial water.

He stretched his wings, braced his spine and leapt up, scrabbling for leverage on the mountain top. It felt good. He always forgot how good it felt *just to fly*. As he glided above the wispy clouds he opened his mind, and the sky and all its elements poured in.

CHAPTER 18

'Jacob, I would very much like to meet your sister,' said the dragon, casually. They were shading themselves under the canopy of the small wood by the training field.

'Why?' asked Jake, suspiciously. He'd woken up that morning with another headache after another night filled with nightmares, and he was feeling peevish.

'You have much responsibility to shoulder, lad, and your family could be an asset to you.'

'I don't want Bett getting involved. She'll get hurt!'

'It might be beneficial to meet her.'

'Scare the crap out of her, you mean!'

'...?'

If Stone's look had been something like anger Jake would have stood firm, but instead it was an odd mixture of hurt and puzzlement. He gave in.

'Okay. I'll ask her. She'll say yes, anyway. So when?' A small beetle crawled laboriously up his jean leg. It was black and yellow and shone like a star against a denim night-sky. He picked up a leaf, guided the beetle onto it and held it in his hands for a few seconds before lowering it to the fallen tree trunk he was sitting on.

'This afternoon would be acceptable.' Stone flicked his tail at the passing flies, missing.

'It's a bit short notice.'

'We should strike while the iron is hot!'

Jake shrugged. 'I don't think she likes you much.'

'Why should this be the case? She does not know me.' The dragon ruffled his stone wings.

'Have you *seen* my bruises? Well she has!'

Jake sighed deeply, 'I'll go and see if she's around, shall I?.'

'You do that.'

Jake set off then paused, turning back, 'I don't have a good feeling about this.' he said, pulling a face.

'I am sure she is a very charming young lass.' Stone smiled as he swatted the flies. His head moved in a figure of eight as he tried to follow the insects and failed. He swatted again, growling.

'Why do they bug you so much?'

The dragon sighed. 'It is my belief that if a creature can *fly*, it should at least be able to deport itself with grace. These, these, *flies* merely make irritating noises, appear out of nowhere and are legion. Where is the *grace* in that, I ask you.'

'They're flies. It's what they do. They buzz, annoy and live off crap. It's all about the cycle of life, my friend,' said Jake, laughing. 'You *have* to protect them.'

Stone snorted and grumbled, 'I am aware of the 'cycle of life', Jacob. And my responsibilities to protect. However, it does not mean I have to like it!'

Jake had been right on both counts: Elizabeth had practically given her right arm to meet the dragon, but she'd also declared she didn't trust him to save her life and she was going to give him a piece of her mind. It was a decision filled with body-parts.

'So when's it getting here, then?' asked Elizabeth, looking around the garden more out of curiosity than anything else. It was full of flowers. The seat beneath her was sticky with the heat and its paint peeled off in dull grey flakes.

'Werrrl, it should be about now,' said Jake nervously. He scratched the back of his head. 'And he's a *he*, not an *it*?'

'Whateva.' Elizabeth untied her hair and retied it, pulling every last tacky strand off her face.

'God, it's hot today in't it?' she said in a flat tone, then she sighed and added, 'Anyway, won't Mam see him?'

'She's not here,' Jake said, looking up. 'She went into town an hour ago. You were in the bath.'

'Oh.' Elizabeth wafted her hand in front of her face creating a small and ineffectual breeze against the burgeoning heat. Secretly she was excited but she wasn't going to admit it. She sidled casually along the garden bench until she was partly shaded by a sycamore tree.

'What's she gone in town for?' she asked casually.

'Remember that waitress from the tea-rooms?' Mam's gone to meet her. She's got some photos or summats.'

'She was nice, wasn't she?'

'Yeah,' Jake replied.

It had been a lifetime ago, that trip to the abbey.

Elizabeth puffed out her cheeks and let them go, a little bored. She leaned forward, her elbows resting on her bare knees, and steepled her fingers in front of her. Then she leaned back and flicked a large red ant off her arm. Then another, and another. She stood up abruptly and batted off five or six more. At the foot of the bench a small anthill leaned at an angle, the soil disturbed where Elizabeth had caught it. Angry ants busied round it.

'Urgh!' she said slapping her legs, hysterically, 'Urghhh!!' She shot to the other side of the garden away from the bench and the biting ants.

'They're more scared of you than you are of them,' called Jake after her, stifling a laugh.

'Wanna bet?' she shouted back, rubbing her legs in a spiky little dance.

'You're hundreds of times bigger than they are!'

'Doesn't mean anything! Black Widows are small but they can still *kill* a man.' She scratched at her arms, shuddering. She didn't like spiders either.

'What is it about you and insects?'

'I just don't like them. They creep and crawl and they're everywhere.' She slapped at an imaginary insect on her arm. Jake stifled a laugh.

'So are we,' he shouted.

Elizabeth stopped dancing like a chicken and stood hands on hips. '*What?*'

'Humans. We're everywhere,' Jake repeated.

'You gone wappy?' Elizabeth asked. Momentarily forgetting about the ants, she strode back.

'Think about it.' said Jake, calmly. 'We go everywhere and colonise every bit of land we can. Even the frozen bits.'

'Oh, here we go. We *look after things*, Jakey. We're not like insects: they just sting and bite and annoy people. We *nurture* and take care of everything. Insects too!'

Elizabeth gave Jake a no-nonsense look. He was about to respond when the ground began to shake. *Another earthquake?* their looks said. The rumble was deep and sonorous. Then it stopped.

Elizabeth looked down at the bench. All the ants had gone to ground. She cocked an ear to the trees: no bird song.

Then the lawn cracked open in front of her.

First a head emerged, yellow and grey, its huge eyes smouldering embers; then a neck, prehensile; then shoulders, until, released with a sharp snap, two massive wings opened and instantly shaded the garden. The temperature dropped like hail. Elizabeth started to shiver. A body followed and a brawny tail whipped around in a cascade of grass and earth. When Elizabeth looked down, the ground was no more disturbed than the anthill.

'Good morning, young lady,' said a gut-churning voice that entered her whole body. Elizabeth's head travelled upwards taking in the size and width of the thing standing in front of her. It gently pulled in its wings. The temperature rose again.

'Err,' she gibbered. 'I- I prefer Bett. Or Elizabeth. But not Betty. And not Young Lady.' She swallowed, her throat dry and tight. At her side, Jake was secretly laughing.

'As you wish. Elizabeth it is.'

'Yeah,' said Jake, casually slipping his hands into his jean pockets, 'Stone's into long names.'

Elizabeth turned and registered her brother as if for the first time.

'Stone this is Elizabeth,' he said. 'Bett, this is Stone. He prefers Limestone though, so you'd best ask him.'

The dragon's tail came around to hang over his shoulder. Elizabeth's eyes were glued to it.

'*Stone* will suffice, lad,' checked the dragon. 'I have grown accustomed to it.'

'Fine,' laughed Jake

Elizabeth couldn't believe it. She knew when Jake had said it existed that she'd *said* she believed him, but a large part of her hadn't really. Not *really*.

But it was true.

She reached out and touched Stone. He felt like the wall of a cave. Cool but not cold, and damp.

'You're made from *stone*,' she whispered.

'Yes, yes I am,' he said, with a glint in his eyes.

'From stone?'

The dragon cast his eyes over the girl. She looked like any young female human to him: not overly skinny but not fat, two legs, two arms, eyes, ears, a nose, mouth, hair. He sniffed the air. She smelled normal: nothing *oily* about her. She'd very recently bathed. And she was afraid of something. Ah, *insects*. Ah, *ants*. And, something else... the talisman. She'd *used* the talisman. *Why?* Stone looked at Elizabeth for a few very long seconds.

'Yes, I am made of limestone,' he answered eventually. 'And I understood you to be the bright one,' he joked. His voice rumbled deep in the young girl's bones.

'I feel sick.' Elizabeth wavered and held her head. 'Why do I feel sick?'

'It is resonance. Tectonic. It will abate.'

She folded her arms over her stomach. 'I need to sit down.' she said, her voice hollow and gloopy.

'Jacob, help your sister.' The dragon motioned to the bench, then saw the panicked look on Elizabeth's face. 'I can assure you, lass, there are no ants there now?'

'How?' said Elizabeth weakly as Jake led her across the grass.

'They are afraid of the vibrations.'

'I mean, how did you *know*? About the ants.'

'Ah. Resonance. Your emotions leave traces.'

Elizabeth sat on the bench and gulped a deep breath. Her world was spinning.

'Jacob,' said Stone. 'You need to get your sister a drink of cold water. I would also suggest ice if you have it.'

Jake nipped into the house and ran the tap until it went cold. *Ice. Do we have any ice?*

Outside in the garden, the sinewy neck of the dragon curved around, bringing his head in line with the stricken girl's.

'Now,' he said with almost a hint of threat (*almost* and only if you were listening for it). 'Tell me *all* about yourself, lass. Leave nothing out.'

'I believe that if you think about it, Elizabeth you *do* know.'

Elizabeth bit her bottom lip. She could taste the sticky bubble-gum flavour of her lip gloss. After half a minute she said flatly, 'It's because it's none of your business, isn't it? We could all blow each other to bits and you wouldn't care.'

The dragon smiled. There was no humour in it. 'Is that what you think?'

'Yeah!'

'Then you must be correct,' he replied matter of factly. 'Or you could think about it another way: you could ask yourself why I am here now? How have I intervened in the past?'

'Why *are* you here now?' Deep down in her blood Elizabeth thought her father had been right not to trust this creature.

The dragon was thinking something similar: how much did this girl actually know about the beast, the elementals? How much could his companion trust her?

'I am here to protect you,' he said eventually.

'Me?' asked Elizabeth, centre of the world.

'All of you.'

'Why didn't you protect dad?'

It was a question so big it filled the space between them and spread out into the garden.

'He did not want my protection,' came Stone's answer.

'Not very good at policing then, are you?' she snapped.

'There are, *young lady*, more important things in this world to police than a reluctant companion.'

'I don't think so!' Elizabeth snapped. She leaned forward, still dizzy, splinters stabbing into her thighs. This thing wasn't going to bully her.

'What about Jake? Is he important enough?'

'Jacob has nothing to fear.'

'I don't believe you.'

'That is not my concern,' growled the elemental. 'Believe your brother.'

Elizabeth thought of her brother coming home night after night covered in bruises. She thought of the wax man.

'I don't like you. And I don't trust you,' she said bluntly.

Stone laughed, hollow as graves. 'There is some mutual ground covered here,' he said.

'What's that s'posed to mean?'

'It means that I will keep vigil over your brother and no harm will come to him. From *anyone*.' The barb in 'anyone' was as sharp as razorblades.

'He's *already* been half-killed!'

'No! He's already been *half-trained*.'

'If you hurt him – I mean *really* hurt him – I'll kill you.'

The air crackled between the two of them. Black and gold flashes filled their eyes. Stone smiled grimly, then snorted. A small, controlled jet of fire scorched the air in front of Elizabeth's face.

'Do you think you will be capable?' he asked, his voice cool as marble.

Elizabeth leaned forward again, her eyes stinging in the smoke.

'I'd find a way.'

The elemental dragon leaned back, slightly impressed. He might have misjudged her.

'Good. Hold on to that thought. You might need it. There are those that would try to destroy your brother, as they would try to destroy me.'

'What!? There are actual people who'd actually try to kill Jake?'

'I said nothing about *people*. And I will say nothing more. Ah, Jacob...'

And that was the end of that.

Jake scurried over the grass carrying a glass of pale pink liquid. As he reached them, he said, 'We didn't have any ice-cubes, so I put an ice-pop in instead.'

The air was as thick and nasty as razor-blades in custard. His sister took the glass and thanked him, quietly. She didn't look quite as ill as she had at first. Just angry. She took a sip, then another. She drained the glass. It tasted sweet and sherbetty. As she drank, she glared at the dragon. The dragon glared back.

Well, thought Jake, bitterly, this is going well!

'So, what've you been talking about?' he asked, as nonchalantly as he could muster. Stone was about to speak when he was interrupted by Elizabeth.

'Nothing much,' she said, forcing a thin smile. 'Your *friend* here was telling me how evil he thinks we all are.'

The dragon snorted and Jake could hear the soft repeated thud of his tail on the ground behind him.

'Not evil lass, ignorant. Morality is a form of regulation manufactured by man for man, it is of no concern to the elementals.'

'A lot of people think that morality is important–' Elizabeth began.

The dragon cut her dead. '*I* am not what you would consider *people*. What concerns me is balance. I will say no more of it.'

But Elizabeth was like a terrier with a bone. 'No, hang on–'

'Jacob,' said the dragon, ignoring the girl. 'I must leave. There are things to which I must attend.'

He turned and unsheathed his wings. The back-draft almost knocked Elizabeth sideways. Stone took off to the sound of buzzing, low like a swarm of angry bees. Then he was gone.

'Well, you two got on like a house on fire,' said Jake.

'Eh?' Elizabeth felt a tickling on her leg. She flicked at it, stunned.

'Yeah, y'know: burning and dangerous and you can only hope for survivors.'

'Har-har!' said Elizabeth sarcastically, and flicked her leg again. The ants were back. 'I'll tell you one thing, Jakey, he doesn't like me. He doesn't *trust* me.'

Jake sat down next to his sister. He'd expected her to be frightened, not angry.

Elizabeth, his floral smelling, music-obsessed, sherbet lip-glossed sister was angry at a thirty-foot stone dragon. What was happening to his world?! He stared at her and let out a sigh disguised as a laugh.

'I don't think he trusts anyone to be honest. I think he only trusts me because he has to...'

'Hah! I don't like him. He's, what's that word Mam uses about her editor? *Sanctimonious*. Yeah, he's sanctimonious.' She slapped at her leg and, without hysterics, moved along the bench.

'He's alright,' said Jake.

'*Sanctimonious*!' snapped the reply. Elizabeth looked small and hot like an angry tomato in shorts and a t-shirt. Jake tried not to laugh.

'Do you even *know* what that means?' he asked.

'Yes!'

Jake folded his arms and leaned back, smiling. 'What then?'

Standing, his sister turned her angry tomato glare on him. 'Shut up!' she barked.

Jake stood up too and took a hold of her shoulder. The tension seemed to flow out of her like milk from a jug. He started to give her a half-hug, but she held him just a little bit too long. Was she shaking?

'Don't worry about him, Bett. He's alright. And don't worry about me either.'

Elizabeth pulled a face and pushed her brother away.

'C'mon, let's get some ice-cream,' Jake said. 'Chunky Monkey.' He wiggled his arms around in a silly apish fashion. Elizabeth raised an eyebrow, and said, thoughtfully, 'I'll be in, in a bit.'

Jake gave a sort of full-body shrug and left her standing in the garden, looking up at the empty sky.

CHAPTER 19

Days passed in the way they do. These ones were filled with busyness.

Stone watched Jake from the shade of a tree. He was impressed with the boy; he was learning quicker than any other companion had done before. He had the feel of it. He could make it rain stones.

Watch Jake now at the base of the hill, drawing cobbles from an old stone wall and making them dance in the sky above his head. His movements are graceful and considered; he knows what he's doing. The stones jump in tiny circles as his hands measure the air. He makes it look effortless the way he moves them over the path, then layers them one-by-one and rebuilds the wall on the other side. He doesn't even have to think about it anymore.

Stone called in his bass rumble, 'Jacob!'

Jake looked over, waved briskly and started up the hill. At the top he said, 'Yeah?'

'You have worked hard today, lad.'

It sounded more like a question than a statement.

'Yeah?'

Jake stood with his hands in his back pockets, looking up. Despite himself, he was enjoying the training and he got the distinct feeling that the stones enjoyed it too: they seemed to want to please him. He grinned and squinted in the sunlight. The elemental grinned back.

'Yes,' Stone said, flexing his wings. 'I think we should celebrate.'

'There's still work to do, though,' said Jake, desperately hoping there wasn't.

The dragon's mouth turned up at the corners into a smile.

'There are so few *real* achievements in life, Jacob, that even the smallest ones are worth celebrating. What I am offering you will not take long. And might well be... enjoyable.'

But Jake was getting used to Stone now.

'That means there's a chance it might *not* be enjoyable,' he said.

The dragon chuckled. 'It depends on perspective, Jacob. Now, do you trust me?'

Jake nodded very slowly and said, 'Uh-huh.' It had taken him some time, but he'd found the best way to handle Stone was to do what he said and deal with the bruises afterwards.

The elemental shuffled forward and bent low, his throat touching the ground, his swan-like neck stretched against the hillside. He smiled a wide and impressive smile and the fire in his eyes was golden.

'Climb up,' he said, gently.

'Seriously?' Jake whispered hoarsely. Stone nodded.

Jake reached over the dragon's neck and grabbed the stone meat of his shoulder.

'It's not a joke is it?' he asked, leg half-cocked.

'It is not a joke, Jacob.'

Jake grinned, put his other hand on the base of Stone's neck and hoisted over his leg like he was mounting a horse. With some effort, he pulled himself up and nestled in where the neck and shoulders met. He could feel stone muscles bunching beneath him. He clasped his thighs as best he could and wrapped his arms tightly around Stone's throat.

'Jacob,' said the dragon gruffly. 'You must lean back. Place your hands behind you. Do not worry, you will not fall but if you insist on grabbing my throat so firmly while we are in flight, then we might both be in trouble.'

Jake leaned back. There was nothing to hold on to but his trust in the dragon.

He clasped his legs tighter.

Stone's low chuckle started in the pit of Jake's gut and rose into his chest as the dragon started to run. He took off with a sudden and polished thrust and, as the ground fell away, Jake heard a high-pitched *whoop! whoop!* that he was amazed to find was coming from his own mouth.

A thrusting wind ripped the sounds out of the sky. Jake's eyes streamed but he could still see for miles and blurry miles: the reservoir, the valley, the town, their cottage.

The higher they rose the thinner the air became, and when they swooped down, Jake could feel his heart leaping into his throat. He wasn't even a little cold and he put it down to some sort of elemental force field, the same one that kept him safely in place.

It was fantastic!

Stone flipped a slow sideward somersault against a bank of low clouds and Jake roared hysterically. The dragon roared too. A gaggle of confused geese had to break out of their V as the boy and dragon dipped and swerved.

'Soooorrrryyyyy...' called Jake, still laughing.

They came to land all too quickly and Jake slid off reluctant but happy.

'That was amazing!' he gasped, fighting to control his jelly legs.

Stone nodded his head demurely and said, 'I thought you might enjoy it, Jacob. Flying is a gift that I wanted to share with you.'

'*Amazing*! I mean, when you did that swooping thing,' (whooosh, went his hands) 'and that back-flip thing, that was cool! And when you scared the crap out of that bull in the end field...'

Stone coughed, embarrassed. 'Yes, that was regretable. But I did not see him between the trees.'

'The trees! *That* was *fantastic!*... Ssssyeeeewww straight through 'em! Not even a leaf fell!'

The dragon chuckled. It had been, he had to admit it, a tidy bit of manoeuvring.

'But I thought no one could ride elementals,' gabbled Jake.

'I thought it was... I dunno... banned or summats.'

'No. What I said, Jacob, was that no elemental has a master save him or herself.'

'Isn't that the same thing?'

'It is not. Many elementals will ride with their companions. Cloud, Fire, Word...all have.'

'Did granddad?' asked Jake, still giddy.

'Your grandfather, Jacob? Ride *me*?'

'Yeah? Did he?'

'Jacob, no companion has ridden on the back of the limestone elemental. Until now, that is.'

Stone stepped back and eyed Jake. If realisation was a lock, then the dragon watched a heavy tumbler had fall into place.

'Never?' gulped Jake. 'No one's never ridden you? Really?'

'Jacob, there is a first time for everything and if you do not cease this incessant babbling *this* first time will definitely be a last!'

The boy stood in front of the dragon grinning like a pumpkin.

He was the *first*.

'Fantastic,' he hissed, his legs finally giving way and smacking him down onto the baking hillside. He looked up, his eyes gleaming.

'Thanks. Thank you, Stone.'

'For this, lad, you are welcome. Now then, eat something,' he said plucking the lunch box from Jake's bag and tossing it to him.

'And when you have rested, prepare yourself. There is *much* more training to be done.'

Much more. And it seemed to go on forever.

The dragon watched as Jake melted into the stony ground or walked through walls. He taught him the different metamorphic states of limestone and how to manipulate them all, even marble. By the time the sun had melted onto the horizon Jake had a map of the solar system in neatly jig-sawed pebbles spinning in the air:

each perfectly-formed planet orbiting a marble sun.

Stone was pleased.

He'd say this for the boy, he knew in his bones how to control the lifecore; he *understood* it: the energy that made up the world. Years ago humans had divided it by names, and called it *vis plastica*, the force in the earth that could imitate living creatures and *vis viva*, the force that could bring them to life.

If it was anything, thought Stone, it was *vis prima;* the First lifeforce: the stuff of stars.

Stone was made of *vis prima*.

The beast was almost pure *vis viva*.

The limestone solar system spun and played in the light.

'Jacob?' Stone called to him quietly.

'Yeah?' Jake looked up.

'Time to go, now.' The dragon waddled over to the boy, smiling. 'It is getting dark.'

'Yeah.' The stones broke apart like the beginning of the universe, and fell to the ground soundlessly. 'It'll be here soon, won't it?' Jake didn't even need to say the word 'beast' now.

'Ah, now who reads minds?'

'You look worried.'

'It is what we are preparing for,' said Stone, thoughtfully.

'Am I ready?' Jake asked. He didn't like the answer.

'No. There is much to learn yet, Jacob.'

'Oh.' The word was thick in Jake's tired mouth.

'But you *will* be. The beast will try to manipulate you. You must remember that. It is what it does to survive. It will get into your head if you so allow it. It is already in your dreams.'

Stone shuffled another step then said, 'Jacob, do you trust me?'

This time it was he who didn't like the answer.

'...mainly,' said Jake.

'Mainly?' asked the dragon, surprised.

'I don't think you're telling me everything. Something's bugging you. You've been distracted since you came back from that thing.'

'Ah. The Colloquium.'

Jake shrugged. *Whatever*, his body said. He was tired and didn't really want this conversation. He'd enjoyed himself today. What did Stone have to go and spoil it for?

'The others believe you to be susceptible to the beast,' said Stone.

Jake swallowed. Did they know about the sketches under his bed? If *they* did, then Stone certainly did.

'What did you say?' he croaked.

'I said that you are young, that all companions are susceptible to the beast and that you will do your best. You work hard. This...' his tail swept in a vast curve to encompass the field, himself and the whole concept of being a companion, '...is all *new* to you. And it has been a few short weeks. They cannot expect too much of you.'

'Oh. What did they say?'

'Aahh, the usual huff and puff. They said that when I go up against the beast I had better be sure of my companion.'

'And *are* you?' said Jake.

Stone fixed Jake with his stare. His eyes burned.

'I have never been more sure of my companion. Given time you will be formidable, Jacob.'

'Oh.' Jake smiled, embarrassed and tired (and just a little bit proud). The elemental broke the pause with a gentle laugh, and patted Jake on the shoulder with his tail.

'But this is too solemn talk for this evening, lad. Today you *flew*!'

'Yeah!' said Jake. 'Yeah, I *did*.'

'Now, home!' Stone gave Jake a gentle shove down the hillside.

'Stone...?' he began in a wheedling tone.

'No.'

'No what?'

'I will not give you a lift.'

'I never asked!' Jake said dragging his feet across the grass.

'You did not need to. I could see it in your face.'

'I'm knackered!'

'The walk will build stamina,' laughed the dragon.

'Stamina?' said Jake, weakly.

'Yes,' said Stone, smiling to himself. 'Stamina.'

'Stamina...' muttered Jake as, sleepily, he followed the elemental dragon across the field.

⊘

Jake walked through the front door of the cottage and Stone watched the small windows of the landing, then the bathroom, fill with electric light until, eventually, Jake's bedroom light flicked on then five minutes later, flicked off again.

Every night since he'd returned, Stone had kept vigil while Jake slept restlessly.

He settled down beside the sycamore tree and let the night roll on, calm and quiet. Rainless. A shooting star streaked across the sky as he listened to the stones singing to him. It was comforting: a stream of chatter and gossip as if he was surfing old radio channels. Tonight, he asked a question he was avoiding.

The beast has found him?

YES, said the stones

It is the dreams, then?

YES

Danger?

SOME

Has it insinuated itself, yet?

WE DO NOT KNOW

Why not?

WE HAVE SEEN NOTHING... BUT THERE ARE NIGHTS WHEN YOUR COMPANION ACTS ODDLY

Oddly how?

HIS ACTIONS ARE METICULOUSLY CAREFUL. AND THERE IS SOMETHING BLOCKING WHAT WE SEE

Yes. I understand. Thank you

Stone stirred from his hiding place and glided up to the window.

Oddly, eh?

He nuzzled the window open and squeezed his snout in as far as possible. The boy was turning in the bed, frantically in pursuit of something in his dreams. His breathing was shallow, his forehead spiked with feverish droplets of sweat.

The dragon scoured the room for signs of the beast but found nothing. He concentrated on the boy. He found himself humming a low lullaby he'd heard somewhere in Europe centuries before. Jake's breathing grew deep, his fever broke. He turned, muttered something and dragged the thin bedsheet up to his chest.

Stone stared for a moment, deep in thought, then wrapped the lullaby around the boy's blood and bones. Jake slept then: a healthy, sound sleep. Stone smiled and, still humming, watched over him until the sun crept up the pale blue morning sky.

Sunlight streaked through the room like a red-hot poker. Jake rubbed his eyes. He felt... refreshed. He'd slept better than he had for weeks. He could remember snippets of some old tune but he'd hardly dreamed at all. He felt good. Happy.

So why was there left one dark abiding thought? *You need to go back, Jake. To Stone's cave. Do it today. And you can't tell Stone.*

The idea skulked at the back of Jake's mind all through training. How to get back to the cave without Stone knowing?

And now he had his chance.

The elemental slept beneath the trees, the thick-set sun beating down on him. He looked as if he hadn't slept all night. He'd just closed his eyes for a minute, and now he snored peacefully like a dog in a basket full of cotton wool.

Jake prodded him roughly. Stone didn't move. Satisfied, he walked half-way down the hill, the dragon's snoring throbbing in his gut, and stood with his back to the sun.

He focused: stone and flesh... stone... and flesh...

He held his breath and sank down into the ground.

The cave was cool and welcoming after the heat of training.

Jake stepped up to the map and jumped slightly as it shrank quickly into the murky water of the cave. He scooped some of the thin mud away and fixed the map under a stare like an iron weight. He had it. Pinned like blue and black flags.

The last piece of Stone's map slotted neatly into place in Jake's mind. Smiling, he drew in a long breath and focused.

Stone and flesh...

⊘

Stone opened his eyes. A murky film of water glistened over them. They glowed red.

He shook the sounds of stony voices from his head and grunted. His own voice was heavy as granite pulling at Jake's gut as the boy flicked a mossy pebble into the air and let it sit there.

'I slept,' Stone growled.

Jake nodded and shrugged, a lie already forming in his mind.

'And while I slept...?' The dragon left the question in the air between them. Jake cleared his throat and nodded to the pebble.

'I was practising.'

'Practising?'

'Yeah. Training.'

Jake met the dragon's gaze but broke away just a fraction too soon. Stone sniffed the air.

'Can you smell something? Petroleum?'

Jake sniffed too, shook his head then pointed to the road in the distance. 'A tractor went past...'

'Hmmmm? A tractor? Perhaps... Show me what you have done, Jacob.'

Stone clocked the small flash of panic in Jake's eyes. The boy swallowed nervously and said,'What do you mean?'

'Show me how you travel.'

'I don't know how to. Not properly.' A storm was brewing in Jake's head and sweat ran down his back.

'Hmmm... I see. You do not look well, lad,' said the dragon without sympathy.

'It's the heat.'

'Is it? Then you should go home.'

'No, I'll be alright,' said Jake, dropping the moss-covered pebble to the ground.

'Go home!' snarled Stone. He nodded once and started to sink into the ground.

'I'll see you in the morning,' said Jake, with a slightly cocky tone.

Stone's eyes flared like a volcano then he slipped into the yielding earth.

Go home! Jake kicked a pebble from one angry foot to another. He noticed it was a nub of flint and laughed peevishly. *Go home*. Like he was some kid!

Elizabeth had been right, the dragon could be really *sanctimonious*. And mardy. Jake was almost *sure* Stone knew he'd been to the cave, so why didn't he say anything instead of sulking. A proper, good old fashioned argument would have been better than sulking.

By the time he reached the cottage he was covered in sweat and his head felt like his brain was being pulled out through his ears. His mother was out again – was she *ever* in? – and Elizabeth had gone with her. He slammed the door and stormed up the stairs making as much noise as he could. He threw himself on the bed, stretched out and pulled the thin card folder from beneath it.

His hand smoothed over the papers, and in a curious way they seemed to calm him down. When he'd started drawing the sections of the map, he'd found the shapes came easier if he didn't try to think too much about them. Semi-circle, square. A wavy line.

And now he had a bundle of torn out pages. He laid them on the bed and noticed how seamlessly the ripped edges fitted one another.

The pounding in his head was building to a crescendo. Soon Lucy would notice the drop in paracetamols in the medicine cupboard and then there'd be trouble. It was all that dragon's fault!

He stood back and admired the incomplete map. It was beautiful, much better than the one drowning in muddy water on the floor of that cave.

He was doing a great job. No one could do a job *this* well. Not even that dragon. *Especially* not him, and anyway he can't do anything without Jake's help; that's why he'd slept for all those years.

Jake was important. Probably one of the *most* important people around here. His ancestors had *literally* built this place by hand! It was his blood that ran through the streets.

He should *do* something. *Tell* someone.

But first...

He picked up his sketch pad and closed his eyes. His hand moved scratchily across the paper until the final piece was complete.

He fitted it in place. It would be nice to think that thunder bellowed and lightning lit up the sky, but it didn't. Jake found some Sellotape in the kitchen drawer and finished the job of sticking it together.

The patchwork map looked good. Complete. And the world hadn't ended, no matter *what* that dragon had said.

He needed to show it to someone; but who?

Ah, yes, he thought, his blood pounding in his skull.

Him.

CHAPTER 20

Jake set the stone in the middle of the road. It was about the size of his own head. William James watched from the road-side with interest as Jake took four steps back from the boulder and, hands on hips, glared at it.

The sun baked down and the small shade from the over-hanging lime trees did little to stop the sweat sobbing down his face.

Nothing happened.

William stood up and beat some life back into his legs, then said in a rough whisper, 'Jake. Jake what's meant to happen?'

The boy's concentration broke, his gaze pulled back to the man.

'I can make it move,' he said simply.

'Move?'

'Yes. By thinking about it.'

'*Move*? Telekinesis?'

Jake sighed. His head still throbbed. He thought the pain might have stopped by now, but if anything it was worse.

'I picture it moving and it moves. All the molecules.'

William was impressed. He walked over to the boulder and lifted it. It was heavy, even for him, and he'd watched the boy struggle to carry it over to the middle of the road.

'Why put it here?' he asked.

Jake looked down, then up. 'So you didn't think I was cheating. So there's space around it.'

'Ah, nothing up your sleeve?' said William, dropping the stone and straightening up.

'Yeah. Something like that.'

William scratched his face and asked, 'How does it work?'

'I don't really know. I can see the carbon moving and it does. It's mainly colours; golds and greys and browns. It sort of knows where it should go.'

'And now?'

'It's not working. I don't understand it. Maybe I can't do it here, maybe I can only do it at home.'

Jake walked towards the man, hands in his pockets.

'Does it work on everything?' asked William.

'No, only stones. Limestone.'

William flicked a thumb towards the dark grey stone. 'That's granite, Jake.'

Jake looked down. 'Oh,' he said blankly.

'Didn't you know?'

Jake, still staring at the stone said, 'I've not been doing it for long.'

William said nothing but watched the boy bend down and roll the stone to the road's edge. It fell into a side ditch and splashed into the gloopy run-off from the hills. They watched it sink into the drying mud. Not for the first time since he'd met Jake did William see a clueless boy trying to do something that was clearly way over his head. He was going to get himself killed.

'Jake, why did you come here? Today? And where's the elemental,' he asked curiously.

'I don't know,' lied Jake. When he'd set off for the doorway, he'd been fired up with showing the map to William James, but once through he'd changed his mind. He had the awful sudden feeling that if he showed William the map it would put him in danger.

'How did you open the doorway, Jake?' the narrator asked quietly.

Jake thought about the talisman in his pocket. It had opened the doorway on its own; as though it remembered.

'I just can.'

'Oh. So where did you say Stone was?'

Jake looked away and bit his lip. 'We had a sort of falling out.'

William folded his arms. 'Over what?'

'I don't know–'

'Oh, come on!'

'No, seriously. He got all weird and told me to go home.'

William sucked at the back of his teeth, then came to a decision.

'Look Jake, I've been thinking...' he began. Jake looked up and shielded his eyes so he could see better.

'Hmmm?'

William stepped further into the road. 'Why don't I come with you? To your world? There's nothing for me here and I can talk to Stone–'

Jake stepped back. 'W-what d'you mean?'

'Well... I could help. Find the beast. I could show you things – the difference between stones, for instance.' He tried a small laugh and opened out his hands, palms up. *Nothing up my sleeves...*

'What, to *stay*?' asked Jake, aghast.

'Well, maybe. Perhaps. If it were possible.'

'Where?'

'I don't know. I thought at first I could stay with you...'

Jake stiffened and shook his head in small movements.

'No!' he said. 'No, no that'd be no good, no!' His lips puckered and tightened. 'It's my mam, my mam, y'see, and Bett. No, no that's no good.'

He knew he was gibbering but he didn't know how to stop.

'That's okay,' William said, kindly. 'But... just have a think about it...'

'Me? *I'm* alright with it,' Jake lied, 'I'm thinking about *them*.'

And he *was* thinking about his family, about how he would explain about this man (who looked so much like his father). The nerve of him. What was he trying to pull?

A shiver ran through Jake's spine.

William gave up, smiled thinly and said, 'Well, if you change your mind you know how to get me. Anyhow, I can show you the difference between granite and limestone wherever I am, can't I?'

Jake nodded and sagged with relief. He looked up and down the road; it was empty but for a few straggly weeds fighting one another for the smoggy light. The last time he'd been there was with Stone. Suddenly he felt vulnerable and alone. William stood three feet away with a look on his face that, in the right light was concern, but in the wrong light easily looked predatory.

Jake suddenly wanted to go home.

He shouldn't have come back, and not without the elemental. And where *was* Stone anyway? Why hadn't he followed him? He knew *exactly* where he was always, so he should have followed him.

He knew exactly where he was, always!

Jake could feel the map weighing down his bag and the realisation of what he'd done hit him like a fist. Why had he been so stupid!

He looked up at the bare sky. 'I've got to go,' he said firmly.

William faltered and took Jake's arm, 'You just got here.'

Jake pulled away. 'It's – it's getting late and I've got this headache. I need to get home.'

'Let me help you...'

'I'll be fine,' said Jake, and he loped off so fast William had to run to catch him up.

They followed the road towards the Devil's Arse. Behind them the dappled shade from the lime trees merged into a sleek of black shadow oiling across the road and into the ditch.

Stone sat in his cave and sniffed. Something had been here but he couldn't get a clear enough picture. Damn it! Had it been the boy? The beast? A dozen images flicked across his mind, and showed nothing but a blur, until – yes! A hand. A human hand. With a bitten thumb nail.

Stone drew in a chest full of anger and released it in one blue-white searing flame.

William James watched as the boy disappeared.

So, the map was complete. The dreams, then, had worked.

Good.

He dipped his hand into his pocket and drew out the folded paper. The child would have the key, how else could he have opened the doorway? He would have find a way to get him to use it. More dreams.

He blinked a slow, gecko-like blink. His eyes oiled black. Then, a second, shorter blink, and he was once again the man who looked like Jake's late father.

Stone was waiting outside the Devil's Arse.

He snapped his wings open as soon as he saw the boy.

Jake stopped in his tracks and stood there, puffing out his chest in defiance, and doing a bad job of it.

'Get on,' said the elemental, calmly lowering his body to the ground.

'Where are we going?' Jake asked, trying not to sound nervous.

'Somewhere safe.'

'Who for? Me?'

The dragon snorted and spat out, *'For everyone else!'*

Jake stepped sideways as if to run but his legs were jelly under of the dragon's thumping voice.

'No, you will not run! Get on!'

'I'm not going to!' stammered Jake.

'Jacob!'

Reluctantly the boy scrambled onto the dragon's back. He could feel the heat of his furnace heart burning through the stone skin. Stone, in a fury of fire and smoke, took off.

They flew in terrifying silence until the dragon alighted on an overgrown airfield built for the second World War. A concrete and metal hangar skulked solidly in the corner. A stone wall gave it a boundary.

Jake slid off, his legs stiff and his backside numb. It had been nothing like the flight he'd had – when? Was it only the day before? He leaned against the wall for support and breathed deeply.

Stone raised his huge head. A ball of flame rolled out and, as the dragon's neck muscles contracted, its colour faded from yellow to white to the palest of blues. Where it touched the hangar door the steel melted, spat and ran. Then it exploded in a shower of hot droplets.

Jake jumped behind the brick wall. He watched through a small hole in the decaying mortar. He couldn't see much, but he heard a lot.

'Enter, lad!'

'No way!'

'You want to be *clever*! To replicate the map! You think this is some *adventure* in a *story book*! Then enter!'

'You must think I'm stupid! I'm not going in *there*!'

'NO, boy! I do not *think* you are stupid, I KNOW YOU ARE! You will learn the power of anger, the power of fear! You will *learn*, – once and for all – what the beast feeds on, boy!'

'I KNOW what it feeds on! And stop calling me boy! *You're* the stupid one! *You* asked me to draw that map! I din't do nothing you din't tell me to!'

Adrenaline pounded through Jake's body. He could feel his anger lifting him up, telling him he could do *anything*. He could easily take on this dragon! What right, what *right* had he – hah! *it* – to challenge him?!

He *owned* this land!

Jake felt energy – raw and livid – rise from the ground and enter his skin. He pulled life from the stones around him. He was invincible!

'I told you NEVER to reproduce it whole. You have given the beast a doorway into this world!' growled Stone.

'I've not given it anything. *I've* got the map!' Jake shouted back.

'Foolish boy! I was wrong to believe you could be ready. You understand nothing.'

'Oh yes, I *understand*!' snapped Jake. 'I understand that for thousands of years you've *enslaved* my family until the only one that stood up to you was my dad! Well now it's *my* turn! Dad thought you could be ignored but he was wrong. *My* way's better! Come on then. You and me! Now! Let's get this sorted!'

Jakes eyes raged a blue so dark it was almost black; foam specked the corners of his mouth.

The melted frame of the steel door ping-pinged as it cooled. A storm of dust and light cascaded around Jake as he entered the building.

Stone followed.

The boy looked tiny in the limitless dark.

Tiny against the mountainous hulk of the limestone elemental.

Whoooomph!

Stone's tail crashed into the wall inches from Jake's face. Bricks and weak cement jerked and crumbled as the solid muscle pulled away and struck once more. Whoooomph!

Jake, so fatigued he could barely hold his head up, sank to the floor. His stomach heaved and he was dizzy from the blood pounding through him. He was riddled with adrenaline, useful enough when he'd started the fight, all fizzing and cocky as a summer storm. Now it only made him shake, rapid and uncontrollable.

But, even in this state, he knew the dragon was pulling his punches.

The tail paused, pulled away, and was replaced by the soft padding of heavy feet over debris.

Above him, Jake heard the wet snort he'd grown used to. He wiped his face with a bloodied hand and stared up. He had nothing left to give. The power that had driven him hard not more than fifteen minutes ago now drained from him like water through a sieve.

Through the gaps in the derelict roof he could see the comfort of the early evening sky: plums and oranges. And, in the distance, the moon already rising. Then nothing but solid shadow. Then the gloomy light picked out Stone's features; thin and grey, and longer than the whole of Jake's body. It was covered in dust and smoke and he leaned down until his eyes were level with the crumpled boy. They reminded Jake of the colour of mountains in winter. But they were still filled with fire.

Fire and disappointment.

Stone spoke. His voice went beyond deep; it was every sound he had ever made: the clacking of pebbles eroding on a beach, the wreck of valleys in a landslide, the tearing asunder of the earth's core. Jake felt it in his bones, his brain, his blood. His heart.

'There, lad,' the voice said. 'Now do you *understand*?'

And Jake did understand. He understood he'd been in a place filled with rage. Rage at everything: his father's death, the secrets, the daily humiliation of training, the fact that he was just a boy...

'I was so *angry*,' he sobbed.

Stone stood in the broken shell of the hangar. A lesson had been learned here. He stepped forward, and Jake flinched.

'Jacob,' he said as gently as he could. 'There is no need to fear me. No need for anger in your bones. *This* is how the beast found its way in. I did not protect you well enough and I underestimated it. I *overestimated* you.'

It had been a quick fight. Jake's first mistake had been to call on the limestone in the concrete of the hangar walls. It came in ragged chunks hurtling towards the dragon; and if he'd have been an ordinary animal, it would have crushed him, instead he reared up on his hind legs and drew the limestone into his body.

Jake stared on amazed as Stone doubled in size. It was his second mistake: never take your eye off the ball. Stone's tail came up from behind and lifted him into the rafters before it dropped him on a pile of gypsum. He felt a rib crack.

Things went downhill from there.

Jake now slumped against the wall while the dragon's tail curled over him, the tip resting like a finger on his forehead.

The fear had filled him for days. Fear and anger and guilt.

'Yes, said Stone. 'For days,'

'I thought you couldn't read minds,' Jake managed, his throat like sandpaper.

'I cannot, but emotions leave a trace of themselves, they linger for a long time until they fade.' He was right about that, thought Jake numbly; after his father had died it had taken months to stop feeling guilty: not guilty for any reason, just random guilt.

The dragon continued. 'There have been times, very recently Jacob, when I have been unable to track you. The beast concealed you. But yesterday in my cave I saw a glimpse of something human. It could only be you.'

''M 's'rry,' said Jake. A high wave of fatigue crashed against the shore of his brain.

'Do you have the simulacrum?' asked Stone, sternly.

'The wha'?'

'Your drawing. Of the map.'

'Yeah. S'in m'bag.' He pointed over to the hangar door.

'We must destroy it.' The dragon loped over to the wall. Jake dragged himself to his feet and followed, limping.

'Ahh...' said Stone.

The sports bag was a shredded and melted mess of plastic and metal. Jake could just about make out the remnants of a pencil case and his mobile phone. He swore, but without much effort. Did his mother's insurance have a category for 'Act of Dragon'?

'It is for the best,' Stone said.

The talisman sat on top of it all, unscathed. Stone picked it up and passed it to Jake.

'It is getting dark, Jacob. Tonight, you will sleep in my cave. It is not safe for you in the cottage, in this state you are too vulnerable.'

'No,' Jake's voice was slippery, tired and slurred. 'W't 'bout Mam 'n' Bett? Ow!' His lip was split livid and purple.

'They must not be your concern, tonight.'

Jake rallied a little. 'No! Wha' if somethin' happens to 'em. 'M goin' ome!'

'Jacob, *must* we fight once more? I am afraid you will not come off so well this time.'

Jake stumbled forward and took a deep breath.

'They won' b' safe.'

'I will keep sentry over your family. You *will* sleep in the cave.'

Jake tried to focus on the blurred dragon in front of him.

'O-Kay,' Jake said and slumped to the ground. Stone caught him soundlessly.

'– map won't like it,' mumbled Jake.

'The map will understand, lad. We must go now,' Stone said, then added, 'Jacob, *why* are you holding your breath?'

Jake looked up through swollen eyes. 'So's don't suffocate,' he said.

'Jacob,' sighed the dragon. 'You know you will not suffocate.'

'–but don' like it,' slurred Jake. ''m holdin' breath...'

Jake drew in a deep and painful breath while Stone, muttering to himself, wrapped his wings around the boy and took them down into the ground.

The body was a prison of tissue, hair and nerves. It had been a fierce but short-lived struggle to take over the man and now the beast looked at its reflection in a puddle and saw the narrator's face. It smiled and looked as if it had never smiled before.

It tried again.

Better.

The vessel walked over to the centre of the empty field. A memory of a black flag danced across his host mind as he looked down at Jake's sellotaped map.

A barn owl flew over and dropped out of the night sky, suddenly. The beast in the vessel's body watched the bird twitch and die. It held one newly aquired hand over the small corpse. Oil seeped from the vessel's pores and covered the wrangled feathers and bones. With disturbing interest he, for it was a he now, watched the bird's flesh melt away leaving only a frail skeleton. He smiled again: he liked the sensation of this twisting of the face. He was getting the hang of it.

He flexed his new fingers and paused, uncomfortable: deep inside him some small, human desperation (like a hard-to-reach itch) tried to make itself known. He ignored it.

He closed his black eyes and concentrated. Now, where was the child filled with anger and pain, and the selfish guilt of his father's death? Where was he?

Stone lifted his head up to Elizabeth's window and nudged his head into the room. The girl stood in front of an old mirror brushing her hair.

'Elizabeth,' he hissed, 'I am in need of your assistance.'

'What the freg!' She jumped back, brush held like a hammer, her heart pounding against her ribs.

'Where's Jake? What've you done with him?'

Stone blinked and said, carefully, 'Your brother has had a... trying day. He will sleep in my cave tonight.'

'No way,' said Elizabeth, narrowing her eyes. It was a command, not a statement. Stone met her glare with a look of confusion.

'I do not understand. There *is* a way. He is in my cave already. Resting.'

Elizabeth paused, also confused.

'No, I mean... Mam'll go *mental*,' she said

'I am at a loss as to your meaning, lass. What is this 'mental'?'

'Is Jake alright?' she asked, ignoring the question.

The dragon nodded, giving nothing away. 'He has been a little foolish. And he is tired.'

Elizabeth was about to ask what he'd done when the dragon interjected. 'You must find some explanation for your brother's absence that is plausible to your mother.'

'*Me?* You mean *I've* got to tell Mam?' *Was he coming to her for help?*

'Your brother would appreciate it greatly.' The dragon smiled and snorted a gentle puff of white smoke.

'What am I supposed to say?' Elizabeth asked.

Stone shrugged. Elizabeth chewed on her lip for a while, then said, 'He's gonna get into trouble, you know.'

Stone gave her a look that said *he already is*, then pulled back out of the room. The air smelled of sulphur and anxiety.

'I'm doing this for Jake. I don't actually like you!' she yelled at the window, knowing it was no longer quite so true. *He'd come to her for help.*

'Ah? Well, that is acceptable,' smiled the dragon. Then he was gone.

Elizabeth heard the dull thwack of stone wings as she slipped on her flip-flops to go downstairs and lie to her mother.

Chapter 21

Jake awoke on a bed of flagstones covered in thick, green moss. It was much softer than his bed back at the cottage. He stretched and yawned and smacked his lips. His mouth was dry and his stomach rumbled noisily about its emptiness. God, he could really murder an egg sandwich! But other than that, he felt invigorated. Alive. *Elated.* There wasn't a single bruise on his body, his cracked lips and broken rib were healed.

He kicked his legs off the bed and sat up. His whole body buzzed as though the Earth's fire coursed through his veins. He took in his surroundings. He was in Stone's cave. The map, wary of his presence now, shrunk further into the murky water. A small stab of guilt jabbed his stomach.

He closed his eyes and tried to gather his thoughts, but his head was filled with whispering. Easy, comforting whispering, and a low sonorous chant. It sounded like pebbles tumbling over a river-bed.

'They sing to you, Jacob,' came Stone's voice from the darkness. The swan-like shape of the dragon materialized in front of him. 'You slept well?'

'How's Mam? And Bett?' asked Jake, anxiously, the memories of yesterday flooding in.

The dragon cocked his head to one side. 'They are well. And good morning to you.'

'Oh, yeah. G'morning.' Jake looked sheepish.

'How do you feel?'

'Starving! And a bit *weird*.'

'As if the world is suddenly *very* real?'

Jake nodded suspiciously and said, 'What did you do to me?'

'I gave you a... tonic, yes a tonic.' It was the dragon's turn to look sheepish.

'What? Like an energy drink?'

'Yes,' Stone said, remembering the bottles of blue liquid Jake drank in training. The whispering and chattering buzzed loudly.

'What *is* that noise?' asked Jake.

'What you hear, Jacob, is the stones singing. They do it all the time. Humans call it electricity.'

'I've heard it before.'

'Yes. Have you ever felt the stones were happy, or perhaps wanting to please you?'

'Yeah, yeah I have,' laughed Jake, his eyes wide.

'My tonic sharpens the senses. From this moment on the singing of the stones will be as clear as a glacial lake.'

'Cool!'

'The songs are always beautiful, Jacob,' Stone paused, 'even when they are a lament.'

Jake tried to put yesterday out of his head. He failed.

'I'm sorry, Stone...yesterday.'

'I know you are lad.'

'It's here isn't it?' asked Jake matter-of-factly. 'I've let it in.'

'No. It is not here,' came the elemental's simple answer.

Jake bit his lip and listened to the low song of the stones. It's not here yet, they sang, but it's coming.

Jake was met in the garden by his sister dangling out of her bedroom window. The story was that he'd gone to bed early because he was getting up at dawn to photograph otters in the river.

His mother had bought it hook, line, sinker and the small boat the fisherman was standing in. It was the kind of thing Jake would do.

When he walked through the door and into the kitchen, Lucy was already frying eggs and flicking bread into the toaster.

'Any luck?' she asked over her shoulder. 'Did you get what you wanted?'

'Nah. All quiet,' he lied. *But I got what I deserved.* He watched his mother flipping eggs and humming 'Summertime'. Jake wanted to hug her tightly and ask her what he should do about the mess he was in. Instead he sat down, feeling edgy and anxious.

'Egg? I'd like to see some of these photos. I bet they're great.' Lucy said as she flicked a crispy egg onto a plate and nudged it along the kitchen counter. Jake leaned over and took it.

'Thanks,' he said, and to change the subject, 'D'you need a hand? Shall I make some tea?'

Lucy said yes and cracked another egg – a double-yolker – into the pan while Jake busied himself with tea-making, and avoided conversations about otters. After breakfast he showered, spent an hour thanking his sister until he nearly exploded, then went out to find Stone.

The day was hot, but undemanding and training went well. Stone focused on a critique of Jake's fighting techniques of the day before, much to the boy's embarrassment. Occasionally he turned his stony head to some movement in the trees or rumbling in the distance but he didn't dwell on it. In fact he reminded Jake of an old saying that he'd never understood until now: *A watched pot never boils.*

Stone put the pot to the back of their minds and they carried on training knowing that when it *did* boil they'd be ready for it.

It's funny how expectations change. They were wrong about the unwatched pot: when the beast came, they were far from ready.

The storm had come on suddenly. Jake lay in bed happy that he wasn't out in it. He settled down and listened to the choir of the stones in the cottage walls. Every so often he could make out simple words like 'training,' and 'father' and 'elemental'. The harder he listened the more words he could make out, like 'war' and 'beast'.

Look at me, he laughed. I'm *listening* to the walls. I know what the ground *thinks*! I must be mad!

It was simple, easy jabbering that stopped him thinking two things: one: Stone was out in the storm, and two: he had a serious fight on his hands and he wasn't ready. Nowhere near ready.

The night sky lit up with the rising storm. Eventually, listening to the chatter of the stones, Jake slipped into sleep.

Lightning raged around him as Stone scoured the landscape for signs. It had been a calm day and Stone mistrusted it immensely.

He covered the fields, towns and mountains, lingering over the field that still held the fun-fair. He hovered above the clouds, out of sight and let his mind out to the stones in the ground.

There *was* activity here: selfishness, greed, apathy, dishonesty... all of the things the beast fed on, and yes, there was a faint trace of its presence, but it was like background noise – practically harmless.

He flew on oblivious to the mistakes he'd made. The first came from believing that the beast was powerful enough to come through *by itself*; the second was that Jake, protected by the singing stones and the tonic surging through his body, was safe.

The vessel was back in the field. *This* was the fault line. The way in. This was the spot the companion had identified that day when he'd first come to this world.

A bright moon shone down on this small, despicable act as the beast concentrated on the boy's dream. It liked dreams. Dreams were so... malleable... It had learned the trick from the elementals. They knew what they were doing with dreams.

And so, as the companion dreamed, the beast watched from its field and the edge of Jake's sleep, and stretched out a pale hand. It pictured itself oozing out of the floorboards and the beams above the companion's head. In what passed for its mind, its image kept away from the stone walls of the Jake's bedroom and slinked up and over the boy's matress, squirming towards the pillow.

Orifices. The beast *liked* orifices.

Its oily form covered Jake's face and sank into eye-holes, nostrils, ear-holes.

From the depths of his sleep, Jake convulsed, snapped open his mouth and tried to scream. He could taste oil, stinking black oil... But it was just a nightmare. A bad dream...

And standing in a darkened field on another world, a passing observer might have seen a tall man in a green jacket move his arms spasmodically over what looked like a half-folded map. The observer might have been fascinated then astounded by the weird lightshow and the halo of black light outlining the man's body until a moment later it and the man vanished completely.

...As the fear fell from his body, and the black taste faded, Jake slipped back into sleep, hopeful of a night with no more dreams. But they came, none the less.

It was Jake's favourite lesson, art. But this was boring. At the front of the class the teacher stood with his back to everyone and wrote dull things on the board. Yawning, Jake stared out of the window. Outside black clouds coated the sky. It could almost be night.

The teacher was listing the names of unfamiliar artists. Jake turned to the seat next to him. A woman with long black hair looked at him and smiled. She was familiar, but the hair was wrong and she was much, much too old.

'Bett?'

'Jake, you've got to go up now. Take the drawing.' Jake's sister nodded her head towards the front of the class and winkled him out of his chair. She thrust a piece of paper into his hands.

He looked down at the rough drawing of a skeletal finger. It wasn't right though, it wasn't quite finished. He leaned over and sketched again. *Now* it was finished.

A finger and a rib.

Joined together.

Elizabeth looked over his shoulder. 'I don't get it,' she said. 'What is it?'

'It's this!' He said, taking the talisman out of his pocket.

'It looks like a map.'

'No it–' he looked down. There *was* a map. Divided into a familiar patchwork of torn squares. And beside it on a separate slip of paper the drawing of his talisman.

Jake felt the confusion swell up in him. 'This is a dream in't it?' he asked the air. Bett looked at him with blank eyes.

'Go on, Jakey,' she said, pushing him forward.

The teacher at the foot of the classroom turned, and Jake saw it was his father. *This is wrong,* he thought, *Dad never taught art.* The man nodded to the piece of paper in Jake's hand and smiled as if he was still learning how to.

'Here,' Jake said, nervously.

Over his father's left eye was a livid wound oozing black. Jake had seen it once before, back in the hospital when it had been stitched and bandaged and made presentable. He could smell the sour smell of detergents and antiseptics.

The man looked down at the drawing of the talisman.

'This is the key, child?' he hissed pointing to the drawing. His voice was thick and greasy. Oil oozed beneath his fingers. He blinked. His eyes were black as coal.

Suddenly Jake was terrified. He thrust his own talisman, the real thing, deep into his pocket and grabbed at the sketches.

'No!' he gasped.

'Yesss,' grinned his father. He tapped Jake once, sharply, on his forehead.

The limestone companion fell down among the smells of turpentine and oil paints.

Jake awoke just after 2 a.m. feeling sick. His head throbbed and his hand was cramped. All he could remember was a scrap of the dream. He reached quickly under his pillow and his hand found the reassuring shape of his talisman, the comb. He let out a controlled sigh of relief.

He badly needed a drink. He pulled back the covers and jumped up, skidding on the wooden floor. Urgh! His skin was covered in a film of oil. He padded and slid his way to the bathroom and ran the water as quietly as he could. He managed to scrape off the oil with two old flannels and a lot of soap.

He needed to speak to Stone. He didn't like this at all.

The beast loved this. It had forgotten what it felt like to use a human vessel. At first there was the discomfort of adjustments – the remembering to breathe, to focus the eyes etcetera – but now it enjoyed the smugness, the satisfaction of a bad job well done: the little delicacies that made the human form a bearable host.

It watched the child's dream playing out in front of it as if it were watching a silent movie. It particularly liked the scene of the artclass, it was the perfect touch (it was learning many things from this human shape; things attached to emotions and glands).

The beast reached into the dream and took the study of the talisman. This was enough of a key to take the vessel through to the other world and once there...

Then it tapped the child's forehead, not bothering to watch him fall.

The image flickered and was gone.

The beast held up a hand and laughed. There was something poetic about its choice of the narrator as its vessel, but up until that moment it had never thought of the word 'poetic', so it was at a loss to truly understand the feeling.

But it felt... apt.

It looked down and tried the smile again.

The map lay an inch above the ground on a puddle of black oil. Now, to the job at hand. The beast drew a breath and whispered low, incoherent words.

A shaft of red light shot out from the dragon's mark in the centre of the sketched-in map.

The beast held the drawing of the talisman over the mark and the light flared, turning red to green. Green for go.

Jake wouldn't know until it was too late what damage he'd done. How in a dream he'd handed over the memory of the elemental's essence – the drawing of the key by which the beast could open a brief gap in this small faultline and enter Jake's world.

Grinning and haloed in black the beast, wrapped up in a fleshy vessel, stepped into the light.

CHAPTER 22

Jake stepped into the shadow of the dragon's wing where he felt safe. Not even his beloved Plough was a comfort tonight. He glanced over at the dark cottage and shuddered.

'Do you remember the dream, Jacob?' asked Stone.

'No. Not really. I think it's the beast taking the piss.'

Stone translated in his head and said, 'Taunting you? No, that is a human action. The beast seeks only to feed.'

'Yeah? What about the oil?' Jake shivered at the memory. 'That's taking the piss if you ask me.'

'It is likely the oil was purged from your body by the tonic I gave you earlier.'

Jake looked at him wearily, not quite convinced.

The elemental was at a loss. He'd come as soon as Jake had called him, but once at the cottage all he'd found was a boy distressed by his dreams.

'You are welcome to stay in the cave, Jacob,' he said, eventually.

Jake shook his head. 'You're sure it's not come through yet? The beast, I mean?'

'I searched far tonight, lad. It is not yet here.'

'Famous last words?' said Jake.

The dragon shrugged and his wings folded back into his body. He rested his tail on Jake's shoulder. 'I will stay here tonight, Jacob. Until dawn.'

It's odd, thought the boy, the things you find reassuring (like the weight of the dragon's tail on his shoulder).

'I don't need you to,' he lied.

The dragon gave him a measured look and said, 'I am sure it would put *my* mind at rest. If you do not mind...'

'I don't mind,' said Jake much too hastily.

The elemental smiled and pushed the boy towards the house.

'Goodnight, Jacob,' he said. 'Sleep... better.'

''Night, then' said Jake.

'It was as if the bloke just came out of thin air, yeah, out of the mirror, right!'

The sounds of the fairground were gearing up around him as a man in his twenties stood in the shell of the house of mirrors and pointed to the glass shards on the floor.

'And he looked mad, mate, I'm tellin' yer, totally nuts!'

His best friend adjusted the angle of the mirrors so that they reflected back a million young men: images bouncing from one mirror to the next. In the centre was a frame empty except for a cheap plywood backboard. Someone *had* broken the mirror last night, but a magic man coming out of it at two in the morning wasn't high on the friend's list of suspects; beer bottle shards were mixed in with the mirror pieces.

'What did he look like then, this bloke?'

'Tall! He had a green jacket on, and a scar over one eye. And he walked funny.'

'Funny?'

'Yeah.'

'Ri-ight. Then what did he do, yer magic man.'

'He just smiled at me – bit creepy, like. I din't say he was magic.'

'Ri-ight. Well, unless he's coming back to clean this up, you'd better get started.' He passed his friend a stern look and an old yard brush and nodded to the floor before he left.

'Magic my eye,' muttered the first young man as he started to sweep up. 'What the...?' he bent down to see why the mirror splinters stuck to the floor. The shards were coated in a film of grease.

He fetched his friend over to have a look.

'Yeah,' the friend grunted, then disappeared again. He came back a moment later with a stiffer brush and left his friend to it.

The young man swore and swept harder. Then he saw, screwed up in a corner, a scrap of white paper covered in pencil lines. The picture they made looked a little bit like the teeth of a comb. The man shrugged and carried on sweeping.

Around him the Fair was waking up for its final days. People busied themselves with their stalls and rides, preparing for the final feature shows. It was the slow fuse for what would be a spectacular night full of fireworks and thunder.

Chapter 23

The morning was once again a quiet one. Beastless. Jake found it annoying, like waiting for the man to come and fix the boiler.

After the dream last night (because of it?) Stone had worked Jake even harder as if by picking up the pace he could force the boy to be ready. Jake wasn't convinced but he trained as hard as his body could take and as a reward, he was allowed home for lunch.

The kitchen was full of laughter. Jake could hear it from the garden path because the windows were flung open to the summer heat.

He walked across the back lawn and, leaning over a half-baked lavender bed, poked his head through the open casement. At the table sat Lucy, Elizabeth and Mary, the waitress from the tea-shop. She was telling stories of the tricks Jake's father used to get up to with her own daughter.

'He got her with a spider once! It scared the life out of her, without a word of a lie it did. Put it in her hair. You've never heard our Libbie scream so much.'

'What, *dad*?' squealed Elizabeth.

'Oh ah, lass, *your dad*, when he was oh about... seven, eight,' said Mary, laughing.

'A real spider?'

'No, that's what was so funny, it was a plastic 'un he'd brought from the post-office. Oh no, he wouldn't have used a *real* spider. Not your dad. Not even then. He did like his beasties.'

Elizabeth's eyes were as big as a bush-baby's and her ears as large as a hare's. This was a father she never knew; a father who hadn't been much younger than Elizabeth when he was scouring the toy shops for rubber frogs and plastic flies in ice-cubes. Once, apparantly, he'd even saved up bubble gum wrappers so that he could order a pair of X-ray specs.

'Did he?' asked Jake from the window. Everyone turned to the sound of his voice.

Mary beamed as if the sun lived in her smile.

'Eyup, lad, how long you been there? I thought I'd missed you. I bumped into your mam in town and she brought me 'ome, bless her, for a cuppa.'

She beckoned him over with quick movements of her hands.

'Are you coming through that winda or what, then?' she joked.

Jake glanced up at the long, square frame.

'Yeah, alright then,' he laughed, and hoisted himself up, holding tightly to the wood as flakes of paint crumbled under his fingers.

'Jake!' said his mother. 'Go round!' But Jake was half-way through already, and even though his laces snagged on the lavender he heaved himself onto the window-ledge then the draining board. He ended up with one foot in the sink but at least it was empty and dry. He sat, his free foot dangling over the kitchen counter and nodded a greeting to Mary.

'Alright?'

Mary laughed. 'You're your dad's lad, you are.' Lucy laughed too. Elizabeth hadn't stopped laughing since he'd started to climb on to the ledge,

'Did they work?' Jake asked Mary.

'Did what work, love?'

'The X-ray specs?'

'No, love, but it didn't stop him tormenting our Libbie. He said he could see her intestines and her skellington. He even said she had an apple tree in her belly from eating an apple core!' Mary laughed harder, and took a long gulp of tea.

'He knew how to wind my daughter up, that lad did. But she got him back, y'know?'

'How?' asked Jake.

'With a lizard,' said Mary, mysteriously.

'Eh? A lizard?' chipped in Elizabeth.

'I know, odd in't it? He couldn't abide lizards. It was rubber. Very life-like and it sort of moved if you held it right. Our Libbie went and put it on one of his wellies. It scared the wits out of him. He said they reminded him of dragons.'

'Dragons?' laughed Lucy. 'St George and all that?'

'Dragons, love. He hated them. They gave him bad dreams.'

'Dragons? But, they aren't real,' said Lucy, trying not to think about her son's sleepless nights.

'No?' said Mary, innocently. 'Well no, no o'course not. They're just stories. But he was a young lad and everyone has something they're scared of...' For a second she fixed Jake with a stare, Jake broke it off but there had been something there, in her deep eyes..

She drained her cup, and added, 'Oh, thanks Lucy love, I'd love another cuppa.'

'Oh,' said Lucy, unaware she'd offered. 'I'll warm up the pot shall I? Jake, pop the kettle on for me.' Jake did as she asked and leaned back, waiting for it to boil.

'I'm alright for cake, love,' Mary said as Lucy gestured with a cake-slice. 'Isn't it nice having someone else to wait on me instead of t'other way round, eh?' She smiled brightly at the children and added, casually,'Din't you notice the dragon in the Abbey grounds?'

A glance passed between Jake and Elizabeth. Jake tried to sound casual as well.

'Yeah, I think I did.'

'They say it protects us, that stone dragon.'

Mary wasn't half as simple as she let people believe. Then she broke the spell saying, 'But folk'll say anything, won't they? Anyroad, this isn't getting my pots washed. I'll have my tea and be off, love. It was lovely to see you again. You've got a lovely family.'

'Oh, they're alright at a push,' said Lucy putting the steaming cup in front of the old woman. 'You can have them if you want them... going cheap.'

'Ooh, I think you might miss them, eh lass...?' she winked at Elizabeth who smiled and nodded.

'Oh,' said Lucy, almost forgetting. 'Mary, did Bill have any other relatives? A cousin perhaps? A boy?!'

'No, love. Why do you ask?'

'Well, I know this sounds a bit daft, but before I bumped into you this morning, I saw this man crossing the road and I promise you he was practically Bill's *twin*. I thought I was seeing a ghost.'

Mary's face drained white. Jake exploded.

'What?! What man?!'

Lucy could have kicked herself – their father's death was all still too fresh.

'It's nothing to worry about, Jake.'

'I'm not worried,' lied Jake. 'Did he say anything? What did he say?'

'Well, it looked like he waved to me,' she said, trying to shake it off. 'But it was probably to the woman behind me.'

He *had* waved, a small, shy gesture so like Bill that it had made Lucy stop in her tracks. She missed that wave.

Then she'd bumped into Mary and when she'd turned back, the man had gone.

'Where did he go?' asked Elizabeth.

'He just disappeared.' Lucy saw the look on their faces. 'I don't mean he vanished into thin air,' she laughed nervously. 'He went into Boots I think.'

Mary came to her rescue.

'To be honest people do look alike round these parts. But it was funny you said twin though because... well... he was one.'

'No he wasn't,' said Lucy. This was all getting out of hand. She'd have known if her husband had a twin brother.

'He was love. But they were born on different days because Bill was born this side of midnight his brother an hour later. It was a very difficult hour...'

Lucy held on to the kitchen table – when you're drowning, you need something to reach for. What had started as a pleasant visit from an elderly woman was becoming something altogether too disturbing. Mary's voice droned on.

'There was a bad storm and tremors – earthquakes,' she explained catching Jake's eye. 'And the baby was born very small.'

'He died?' murmured Lucy.

'He hardly lived, love,' said Mary, her voice soothing and low.

Tears stung Lucy's eyes. She took in a deep breath. Why was she so upset, she never knew the baby? But it did upset her, it upset her deeply.

She looked at her own children, their faces suddenly pale.

'Billy wouldn't of known,' said Mary. 'Folks were different back then, they never spoke much about these things. And anyroad what could you say?'

Lucy clenched her jaw, and swallowed. Two brothers, twins. Both dead. Lucy always got the feeling there was something missing from Bill's life; maybe this was it.

Mary rubbed Lucy's shoulder. 'Perhaps you two should go and play or summats, eh?' she said to Jake and Elizabeth. As if waking from a trance, they stirred and stumbled out of the room into the hallway. Elizabeth stopped just by the door.

'What was all that about?' she whispered. 'Dad was a *twin*?'

Jake bit his lip and shrugged silently. He gestured to the door and they opened it as quietly as possible. They heard Mary close the window, her voice muffled now against the glass. Jake took one look at the sky, reached into the hallway and pulled a couple of plastic rain-coats off the coat pegs.

'I'm not wearing that!' hissed Elizabeth indignantly.

'Get wet then coz it's gunna rain later. C'mon. We're going into town.'

Jake set off down the path in a blaze of fury with his sister trailing behind.

'What's wrong? What's in town? What about Mam?'

'Mam'll be fine. Mary's with her. I wanna see this bloke.'

'What bloke?...*That* bloke? Why?'

'Because he shouldn't be here. It's not his place. And I want to know *how* he got here.'

'I don't geddit? Is he really dad's brother?'

'No. Don't be daft.'

'But Mary said...'

'...that he's dead. All she's gone and done is upset Mam.'

Elizabeth walked and thought for a while. Eventually she said,

'D'you you remember the Accident?' The word had a well-earned capital letter. Jake stormed on as she ran to keep up.

'A van ran into him,' he said.

'No. It was a lorry.'

'So? What difference does it make?' asked Jake darkly.

'The lorry was one of those oil truck things. It had a leak. Dad hit the oil on the road and skidded into the lorry. The driver didn't even get a scratch on him.'

'Not a scratch?' Jake's anger swelled. 'But that's... that's crap!'

'Yeah,' said Elizabeth. 'Jake, this bloke? The one Mam saw?'

Jake stopped dead in the middle of the path and sagged. He looked a little pathetic in his oversized mac, chewing on his lip.

'Look, there's something I need to tell you. And I should of told you before but I din't. This man. It's... sort of... Dad,' stammered Jake.

Elizabeth froze. 'What do you mean, *Dad?* Dad's dead!'

'Yeah. And no.'

Elizabeth's mouth was a little angry 'o'. 'You're not funny Jake.'

'I know,' he said bluntly. 'I'm not trying to be.'

William James basked like a lizard in the daylight. Between clouds, the sun beat down on his sweating face and the beast inside him realized there was something enjoyable about the sensation.

The mother *had* seen him, and so surely the child companion would come soon. Make contact.

He held his hand against his stomach and felt an unpleasant sluicing and gurgling in his gut. He had an uncontrollable urge to fill his mouth with liquids and sweet edibles. Ahh. Of course, this body needed sustenance different from its own.

He pulled a thin leather envelope out of his back pocket and opened it. It was filled with old, printed notes. The beast inside the man held one up. Yes. This paper, it reasoned (quite correctly as it turned out) could be swapped for food, and then the churning would stop. It needed an eatery.

Elizabeth sat in the coffee shop drinking an extra-grande cappuccino with cinnamon and two sugars and daring Jake to say something.

They'd been lucky with the bus, in fact they'd had to run for it.

Jake had told Elizabeth as much as he could about William James as they sat in a fug of exhaust fumes and her blinding silence. It didn't end when they got to the coffee shop. She was furious.

Jake opened his mouth to speak then thought better of it as Elizabeth blew on her coffee and took a long slurp. Quietly, controlling every syllable, she said,

'Why din't you tell me this before?'

Before he could answer she continued in the same, calm-but-angry whisper. 'I thought you'd told me everything, Jake, but this *bloke* you say is Dad...'

'He's not Dad,' Jake said, bluntly. 'Bett, he's not. Not *our* Dad. He's a different Jake's, a different Elizabeth's dad–'

'They're dead, Jake.' She spoke as if it didn't matter. In embarrassment, she looked down at the congealing mess of cinnamon, chocolate and milk in her cup. When she took in a deep breath, her chest hurt.

'Yeah they are,' said Jake, numbly.

'What's he doing here?'

'I don't know!'

'Why not?' She glared at Jake, wanting answers. 'How did he get here?'

'I don't know that either.'

'Why not?'

Jake sagged, 'Because I don't know everything,' he said. 'I know he *shouldn't* be here, this isn't his world. I don't know how he opened the doorway to get in. Stone–'

'Where do you think he'll be?' interrupted Elizabeth, she didn't want to hear anything about the dragon right now.

'I don't know. He knows where we're staying coz it's where he lives–'

'What!' Elizabeth raised her voice.

'In his world,' said Jake as gently as he could. 'Look, I know I should have told you, but I didn't. I'm sorry. William could be anywhere, but he's nice really, just a bit lonely and desperate I think.'

'He'll come to see Mam, won't he?'

'No, not Mam, I'm the one he's here to help,' said Jake nervously. Elizabeth scowled.

'We should start looking for him. Let's try the library,' Jake said.

'What do we say if we find him?'

'Oh, I've got a few questions for him. Have you finished that?'

Elizabeth pushed the congealed mess to one side.

'Yeah, it tastes horrible.'

For the first time since they'd got on the bus, Jake laughed. Elizabeth laughed too, a clumsy floundering kind of laugh.

At the far end of the coffee-shop the man for whom Jake was looking sat behind a large newspaper smiling to himself. He stirred his coffee and listened to the solid whispers of the two children. After they left he took a sip, careful not to burn his tongue. The coffee was thick, sweet and black. It looked like oil.

Chapter 24

'We're never gunna find him,' whined Elizabeth, following her brother over the road.

'Yeah, we will. It's not like he's going to be hiding from me, he's come here for a reason. He must have some news.'

Jake wiped the sweat out of his eyes. He'd tried everywhere except back at the cottage. The hotels were a dead-end – two had told him they didn't have anyone by that name and the rest wouldn't give him anything. *But he's my dad*, he'd snivelled at the receptionists. So why hadn't he checked in with him, then?

Elizabeth and Jake sat on a bench overlooking the bus station. Maybe it wasn't Jake who William had come to see, maybe it was Stone. He sighed and scratched his chin. All this legwork was getting him nowhere. He knew of a much better way to find William.

'Bett, you should go home. I've got something to do.'

'What like?'

'Just go home. It'll freak you out if you stay.'

'Well I'm staying now, aren't I? What'll freak me out?' she asked, curiously. 'You're not gunna, like, turn into a frog are you?'

'Don't be stupid. C'mon, if you're staying. I need somewhere quiet.'

He stood up, dragged his sister by the arm and crossed the road to the bus station. This time they weren't so lucky with the bus, but when it did arrive, they convinced the driver to drop them off at the field where Jake trained, even though it wasn't a designated stop.

Jake climbed up the hill with his sister panting behind him. He sat down beneath the trees.

'God, you can see everything from up here,' said Elizabeth scanning the fields, the town and the reservoir. In the distance she could see black clouds. 'You were right, it is gunna rain.'

'Yeah, I know,' said Jake. 'Now shush, I need to concentrate.'

He didn't need the field to track William James, but he felt safer for it. He closed his eyes and stretched out his mind to the stones beneath the grasses and the bridal-ways; then he stretched it further to the stones in the streets, the walls of the towns.

He opened his eyes quickly. 'I can't find him. He's shielding himself.'

Elizabeth stared at her brother. 'What d'you mean? What are you doing? I thought you'd nodded off.'

'I'm tracking him. I'll tell you about it later, don't ask now.'

Elizabeth bit her question in half and swallowed it. Jake tried again. Still no joy.

'Where is he?' he sighed.

'Maybe he's gone home,' said Elizabeth hopefully.

'No, lass, he is still here.'

Elizabeth swore loudly. Behind her the swan-like shape of the dragon materialized out of thin air.

'How long have you been here?!' she snapped.

'I have been waiting.'

'You weren't here when we came just now!'

Stone flicked his tail and stared into the eyes of the girl. 'Did you *expect* to see me?'

'No! Don't be daft!' The anger she felt for Jake and the man pretending to be her father now had its focus in Stone.

'Aah... this will be your explanation, then,' Stone said, placidly.

'What, so you can make yourself invisible now?'

'Look, Bett, it's just something he does,' said Jake wearily. He'd been so centred on trying to track William, he'd not even sensed Stone was there.

'I think the narrator's here,' he said turning to the dragon

'You are correct, lad.'

'Do you know why? Or how?'

'Neither. It should be impossible for a human to pass between the worlds unless he has a map, and the only *copy* was destroyed.' The air crackled between Jake and Stone. 'No, we must ask William about his journey.'

'Could it be something to do with the beast?' asked Jake bluntly. And equally bluntly, the dragon answered.

'The narrator is mindful of the beast. Travelling here is a dangerous task. Even then, he would need a key...' Stone looked suspiciously at Elizabeth, she wasn't entirely off the hook no matter what the elemental's gut told him. She glared back.

'He must have a good reason to come, Jacob,' Stone added.

'Where is he, then? I can't track him,' said Jake.

'Mmmm. Perhaps the beast is aware of his presence and is interfering.' –again, a glance at Elizabeth– 'We must wait until he makes contact. Now, go home. You are too agitated to train.'

'You expected him to train, after all this!?' Elizabeth glared at the dragon, who snorted loudly and said,

'He has much work still to do.' He turned to Jake. 'But not today. Go. Wait for contact. And Jacob...'

'Yeah?'

'Take your sister with you.'

It was a small hand-written note sitting on the doormat inside the boot hall. Elizabeth brought it to Jake. He was in the kitchen, a place that only a few hours ago had been filled with stories of their father. His mother was asleep, in bed with a headache. Jake flicked the note open. Elizabeth gasped over his shoulder. Even the handwriting was the same.

(Had his father ever called him 'son'? But this wasn't his father, it was William James: he must remember that.)

'I could,' said Elizabeth flatly.

'Could what?'

'Stay angry with him. What're you gunna do?'

Jake ran the words over in his head; *lifeforce* (why not call it the beast?), *evolved as humans have*. It all sounded weirdly formal.

'I need to know what info he's got. Where's the... Peakheights Hotel?'

Elizabeth took the letter out of Jake's unresisting hands and re-read it. 'I'll look online.'

'Yeah, or use the phonebook,' Jake said distractedly.

'Oh, yeah.' Elizabeth reached over for the yellow book. 'Shouldn't you go back to see the dragon?'

'Eh? Do you think I should?'

'*I* don't know. I'm new to all this.' She waved her hand at the world in general.

'No,' Jake said, firmly. 'Stone said to wait for contact. Well, this is contact. He'll know where I am if he needs me.'

Elizabeth turned her attention back to the thin pages and sucked at her cheeks. 'Oh, it's here look. 01773...'

CHAPTER 25

William sat in the foyer of the small hotel. It had seen better days. A range of purple flowers badly in need of dead-heading squatted in window-boxes outside the open window. The low chairs and sofas were filled with horse-hair, and smelled like it. He sipped a cup of black tea and waited. Beneath his skin, the beast simmered.

Jake was on time. He'd come through the rocks. William stood up when he saw him and smiled. It was a broad, generous smile, not right for the occasion. Jake didn't smile.

'Jake. Son. How are you?' He spoke like an uncle forced to have his nephew for a long weekend.

'What are you doing here? I told you not to come.' Jake glowered. Speckles of neglected dust glinted in the sunlight between them.

'Would you like some tea?' asked William. 'There's plenty.'

'No.'

William sighed and said, softly, 'Sit down, Jake. So that we can talk.'

Jake sidled onto the nearest sofa, his nose wrinkling in the gloom and must.

'What do you want?' he asked.

'The lifeforce has changed. It has evolved,' said William lifting his cup again.

'Yeah, your note said. Evolved how?'

'It has learned from the elementals. From mankind. It has, or will have, its own *companion*. To help it. *She* or he, will bring it over. Into your world.'

Jake bit his lip. 'How long has it had him? Does he fight?'

'I'm sure she does, but she – or he of course – may not even be here yet, which is why there has been no sign of the lifeforce.'

'Whaddya mean no signs? What about the weather? The earthquakes?'

'Weather, Jake? That's just Nature.'

'But you said it was coming here, now. You *calculated* it. I've been training.'

'I believe I might have been a little premature.' William sipped his tea, glancing at Jake over the rim of the cup.

'I need to tell Stone,' said Jake.

'Yes. However, if the lifeforce has a companion it will have to train her I suspect.'

'Why do you keep saying 'her'?'

'I deal in stories and legends. It is traditional that a boy goes up against a girl in these situations.'

'Do they?' asked Jake, unconvinced. William James nodded.

'Stone says the beast will come when it knows it can win.'

'I daresay the elemental's right.' William sipped his tea again.

The dust made Jake's eyes sting. He pinched his nose and clenched his jaw, thinking of what to say next.

'How did you get here?' Jake asked, eventually.

'I called in a favour,' lied William.

'Who from? Only elementals can travel between worlds. And even they need a key.'

William James raised an eyebrow like a villain in a b-movie and put down his tea. The cup chinked against the saucer in the awkward silence.

'Who was it?' asked Jake plainly.

'I cannot tell you,' said William, which was, in a twisted kind of way, strictly true.

'Was it Fire?'

'Jake, don't–' William reached out to Jake's arm. Jake pulled away.

'How are you getting back?'

William looked down at his hands. 'I can't Jake. It was a one-way trip.'

'Stone can get you back.'

'I would rather...'

'No! You can't stay. I said you can't stay and you can't. Go home!' And that was final.

Shaking, Jake stood up and left William James sitting in a stinking chair, staring sadly at his stewed tea.

Beneath the man's skin, the beast grinned.

Jake didn't go home. Instead he went to the top field he'd come to think of as his training ground and sat under the copse of trees.

He couldn't have been more angry if he tried. What is it about people that they just can't leave well alone? Coming here upsetting things!

Jake forced himself to calm down. If there *was* some other kind of companion, he'd need all his strength to deal with her (already he was thinking of the companion as a girl).

He concentrated on a small pebble hidden in the grass. It rose and shot towards him, missing his face by millimetres. A bit too much juice, he thought. Calm. Another stone. This one rose and floated towards him. He let it hover in front of his face. He noticed a small fossil glinting in the sunlight; he found it strangely reassuring. The stone turned on its own axis. He hardly had to think about it now.

'That is very nicely controlled, Jacob,' said Stone behind him.

Jake turned to face the dragon and the stone remained aloft.

He sighed softly. 'Sometimes it might be nice if you made a noise, you know. You can't just creep up on people.'

'What is ailing you, lad?'

'I don't know why *he's* here.' Jake skimmed the stone over the field like a pebble over water. He pulled up another.

'The narrator made contact this afternoon,' said the dragon. It was a statement not a question.

'Yeah. I went to see him. I thought you'd, y'know, be around,' said Jake.

Stone leaned in and said quietly, 'Jacob, this meeting was something between you and he. I had no place in it.'

'He had news about the beast.'

'Of which you will tell me in good time, however, I think you know what I mean, Jacob,' said the dragon kindly.

Jake shrugged. 'He said he'd called in a favour from another elemental to get here.'

'It is... possible. I will make enquiries. Did he say whom?'

'No,' muttered Jake. 'But I think it was Fire.'

'Aah. Fire.' The elemental brought his head up and scoured the sky. Grey clouds huddled and merged. He edged closer to the boy.

'I asked him not to come here,' mumbled Jake. He plucked up small handfuls of dried grass and flicked them off his palm; all the while the little stone spun in front of him.

'Jacob, he is lonely,' said the dragon matter-of-factly, then his eyes glowed a soft orange. 'Your own loss was great and your grief deep. You lost your father. But consider this: William James lost his wife, and his daughter. *And* he lost his son.'

'I'm not his son,' choked Jake.

'No, and neither is he your father. However, you do not have to be angry with him, Jacob. He has done you no harm.'

'He still shouldn't of come.'

'To be able to see his family again? Even if they are not his family, but only look like them? It would be a great temptation for anyone.'

'Would you do it?'

'No, not me, lad.'

Yeah, thought Jake, but you don't have any family. 'I'd not do it neither!' he said out loud. Stone paused the spinning pebble, startling the boy.

'Truly, Jacob? Can you *truly* say that the moment you learnt of the other worlds your heart didn't *yearn* to visit them? In case your father was alive?'

Jake clenched his jaw, his chin puckering. He took a breath and let it out in a slow, continuous sigh. 'But he wants to *stay*. I never wanted to stay!'

'Jacob, the narrator's presence here is an asset, of which we must take advantage. There is great danger. I am afraid that something has followed him through.'

'What thing? The beast?'

'I believe a part of it, yes. What did William James tell you?

'Not much really. He said it had evolved. He said it wasn't strong, though, and not ready to come through yet. Oh, and he thinks it's got a companion.'

Stone snorted. 'No, not a companion – the idea is too humane – it is most likely to be a vessel.'

'A whattle?'

'No, Jacob, not a wattle, a *vessel*. A creature, subdued and occupied by the beast. It can be man or animal. It is said to die slowly as the beast gains power. I have never encountered one before.'

'William thinks it might be a girl. Because of legends or something.'

'A girl,' said Stone thoughtfully. *His family would be his undoing...*

'If the vessel gains access to my cave and opens the doorways, Jacob, then we *will* have a fight on our hands!'

'Can it do that?'

'Well, I am not sure. Let us not underestimate it,' said Stone, and under his breath he said *again*. 'The beast will need the stone map to open all the doorways. That and the key.'

'My talisman?'

'Yes. It is safe?'

'Yeah, it's safe.'

'Good. Now, the vessel if it is indeed in human form, will try to blend in. But there will be oddities – unusual habits. Strange moods.'

Stone let the sentence hang in the air in case Jake recognised anything (about his sister perhaps). When Jake said nothing the elemental added,

'I will go and find the narrator, now. You should rest. Tomorrow there will be much work to do.' He offered his tail to the boy who used it to pull himself up from the grass.

'Sometimes it feels like all you ever do is send me off to rest,' said Jake, gruffly.

'Rest is good for you,' said the dragon without any trace of humour.'

'Stone. When you see William can you tell him I'm sorry for being... y'know?'

'No,' said the elemental straightening his back to the shifting crack of tectonic plates.

'No?' asked Jake, puzzled.

'You will do that yourself.'

'Oh. Right.' Jake picked up his new bag. Rainclouds thickened overhead as he set off. Stone's tail stopped him in his tracks.

'Are you not forgetting something?' he asked.

Jake looked around him and shrugged.

'I don't think so.'

Stone wiggled his eyebrows at the hovering pebble.

'You called on it...'

'Oh, right.' Jake shook his head once, and the stone fell.

Jake slipped in through the back door, grabbed some bread and cheese slices from the fridge. He definitely couldn't face his mother after everything that had happened today. He could hear her tapping away on her computer; every so often an email alert tinkled in more spam. He pulled his tired body upstairs, flung himself down on his bed and leaned on his elbow to wolf down the food. He felt better for it.

He emptied his bag on the quilt and sorted through his things, placing his father's watch carefully on the table. He noticed a new scratch on the glass. The talisman must have done it. Chuntering, he trawled through the bag's recesses, he still hadn't got the hang of all its pockets.

Was the key safe?

Hah! Jake laughed hollowly. He carried it everywhere with him, of course it was safe! He remembered putting it in his coat pocket just that morning. Honestly, you'd think by now the dragon would have more faith.

He lay in bed, listening to the low rumbles of thunder miles away. He was feeling anxious, as if he'd lost something.

A small tinkly bell sounded the arrival of new email in Lucy's inbox. Above her head the heavy thud of Jake's trainers on the landing stairs indicated he was back. Where he got to, she'd probably never know. At least he didn't seem to be getting into trouble.

She sat down, took a sip of coffee and adjusted the cushion on the old dining chair she used as an office chair. She clicked on the envelope icon, wary in case it was spam or, worse still, carrying a virus.

From:	James_vestel@notmail.co.uk
Subject:	Personal
Date:	28 July 2011 19:37:09 GMT
To:	lucy_j_walker@jeeemail.com

Dear Lucy

Forgive my forwardness. I understand you were married to my brother, William Jacob Walker. I'm not sure if you know much about me. I was sent down for adoption as a baby. I discovered this just over a year ago when my adopted parents died suddenly. I contacted William but received no reply from him. I later read that he was killed in a horrific car accident – I am very sorry about this, it must have been a tremendously difficult time for you and your children. Very sad. I wonder if

we could meet? I live in a small town in the East Midlands where William and I were born. I could come to your house or, if you are ever in the area, we could meet up nearby. This must be quite a shock to you, but it would be good to speak to someone who knew members of my biological family.
I look forward to hearing from you soon,

Sincerely,
James Vestle-Walker

⊘

The vessel leaned back in the plastic chair and smiled to himself as the sounds of the internet café buzzed around him. The woman staffing the till watched nervously, all the while thinking about deserts and things that hide under rocks. Even from here, the strange man smelled faintly of sweat. She caught his eye and he turned on her a slow, steady blink and a wide, deliberate smile. She shivered and stepped back from the counter, eager to get as much space between them as possible. He laughed softly and looked back to the screen.

Finding the email address he'd needed had been easy enough – it was surpising how many social network sites existed for academic translators. And the beast retained many of the skills the body of William had possessed. He waited a moment and when no bounce-back came, shut down the computer.

The companion's mother would respond quickly enough...

He rose and left the café, smiling greasily at the cashier as he did so.

⊘

Lucy sat back from the screen trying to take it in.

This was the *baby*!

Bill's twin!

It was unbelievable! He hadn't died at all but had been put up for adoption. But why? And why did Mary and Stanley tell everyone he'd died. People put babies up for adoption all the time, there was no shame in it, just circumstance.

Had Mary lied too or did she just not know?

Lucy read the email again, slowly this time. *Sent down*, what an odd way to describe it. Was he an ex-convict? You can never be too careful; she was forever warning Elizabeth about the dangers of chat rooms.

But it was an incredible coincidence!

Bill hadn't believed in coincidence, only the facts of one thing happening after another. He hadn't believed in lots of things: luck, astrology, fate... Lucy *did* believe in fate. And coincidence.

There were so many coincidences on this trip, thought Lucy. Firstly, meeting Mary in the café, then all that stuff Jake had learned about his Granddad. And now this?

Bill had always said we were made out of the same stuff as stars, so maybe the stars *could* control us afterall! Maybe we were *meant* to come here and *this* – meeting Bill's twin – was the reason why!

Lucy bit her bottom lip unsure whether she should ignore the email or meet up with the man. The sensible thing would be to talk to the children but if he was an *identical* twin, then meeting him might just upset them.

And anyway, what harm would it do to meet him if it was in a public place? She clicked the reply button and typed:

Dear James

It was a big surprise to receive your message. You're right, I don't know very much about you, but it might be a good idea to meet up. Coincidentally, I am here in the Peak District for a holiday with my children. We could meet up in the local coffee shop. I don't know if you know the town but I've added directions to this email. I'll be away all day tomorrow but back in the evening, so please do get in touch and we can arrange a time to meet.

Kind wishes
Lucy Walker.

She hovered the mouse over the send button and glanced over his email again not giving a second thought to how he'd got her address. She clicked send.

Chapter 26

It was a sort of fragile truce. Jake had phoned William after breakfast and arranged to meet up.

This café was stifling and small, its open kitchen a blast-furnace.

Jake explained Stone's theories about a vessel but William dismissed them outright. He'd seen nothing to indicate any kind of... what?... possession? No, what they were looking for was a companion, someone very much like Jake, he said. The way William James talked about the likelyhood of a vessel made the whole thing seem ridiculous.

The pauses in conversation were frequent and awkward. William talked a lot, but if Jake were asked to give a run down of the details of the conversation, he'd be hard pressed to. Eventually the man left for the bathroom. When he came back he saw Jake raking through his own sportsbag.

'Are you alright? You look worried?' William asked.

Jake looked up. He'd checked his bag and coat pockets a dozen times already but he couldn't help checking again. He gave William a strained, but hungry look.

'Yesterday, when I came to see you, did anything drop out of my pockets?'

William James shook his head. 'No, why?' he asked, placidly.

Jake bit his lip and answered the man in careful tones.

'I think I've lost my talisman.'

An almost-smile cracked at the corners of William's mouth,

but to Jake it came out looking like a picture of concern.

'The comb the elemental gave you?'

'Yeah.'

'My God, Jake, you can't have lost *that*! It's the lore. The key!'

'I know, I know. But I can't find it!' moaned Jake. 'I traced all my steps. I thought it was in my pocket but it wasn't.'

'Here, let me look.'

Jake nodded absently and emptied the contents of his bag onto the table: his camera, his sketch-book, pencils, juice bottle, a small first aid kit, his father's watch.

'Now, let me see. Oh, this is a nice watch,' said William, picking it up and turning it over.

'Yeah, it was my dad's,' said Jake looking up.

'Is it all you have left of him?'

Jake shrugged. 'I've got a few things. He gave me the talisman.'

William cocked his head to one side, '*Gave* it to you?'

'Well, sort of left it in a box of odds and sods.'

'Ah, so he didn't *really* give it you then. More like he didn't even want you to know it existed.'

'That's not helping me find it you know?' snapped Jake.

William James apologized and poured himself some more tea. He blew on it before each sip.

'It's not here, Jake. You know... (blow) ...yesterday when you were... (blow) ... in the coffee shop with your sister...'

'You were there? You never said anything!' said Jake, shocked.

'You never gave me a chance. I didn't want to come over in case it alarmed your sister. But I watched you. Both of you. She looked so... alive...'

William ran his hand over his face and sighed, stiffly. Jake remembered what Stone had said about the narrator's grief and looked away, ashamed at being so angry. It was a minute or two before William could speak.

'When you went to the bathroom,' he said. 'Elizabeth went into your bag and took something out. I thought it was a pen – I couldn't really see – but maybe it was the comb and she, well... *borrowed* it.'

Jake didn't even think before saying, 'No. She wouldn't just take it. We've already had that argument.'

'It *could* have been a pen,' William conceded. 'But she didn't write anything down. Maybe it wasn't anything. As I said, I wasn't really looking...'

Jake sat back and folded his arms. Maybe Elizabeth *had* borrowed it. But she'd have said – especially now. William must have been mistaken. (*There will be oddities – unusual habits, perhaps. Strange moods*).

Jake sat uncomfortably in the dense heat while William finished his tea. Blow-sip-blow-sip. Small chunks of ice melted in the bottom of Jake's juice glass; he siphoned the cold liquid through his straw, then said,

'William, I have to go to the bus station now. What are you going to do?'

William took a bite out of a small ginger biscuit and said, 'I thought I'd look into the status of the beast. See if it's still safe and secure... back home.'

Jake nodded. Good. 'Have you seen Stone, yet?' he asked.

'No, not yet. I'll walk with you to the bus-stop,' said William in a swift deflection.

'You don't need to,' said Jake, gruffly.

'I'm going in that direction,' smiled the narrator, crunching down on the ginger crisp.

On the way to the station, sun beating down on them without mercy, William James casually turned to Jake and said,

'I thought I would get in touch with your mother.'

Jake stopped in his tracks forcing a young woman with a pushchair to swerve around him, swearing.

'No! *Din't* you listen to me yesterday!? *Why* would you do that? Leave her alone. You'll freak her out.'

William looked as calm as a summers day. He seemed to be enjoying this.

'If it's because I look like your father, I could say I was a distant cous–'

'Don't! Jeez.'

'Don't what, Jake?'

'Don't *anything*! Right? Just, just *don't*!'

'Alright, I won't,' said William with an odd half-smile.

Jake made the bus just in time, but agitated and angry. William, his energy charged up on the back of Jake's fury, didn't wait to wave him off, instead he turned sharpish and set off down the street.

Right, he said to himself, smiling, *what I need now is to check my emails.*

A loud clanging bell, like a dirge, sounded the arrival of new email in the vessel's inbox. The morning was already hot and the air conditioners churned out used cold air. The newspapers were getting bored with the heat-wave and the nightly storms. It was unrelenting.

William's face split into a grin as he thought about the word *heat-wave*. It seemed such a friendly word that humans should wave back and welcome it: *hellloooo*. Instead they complained about it. Already three of them in a retirement home had died because of it. At least *they* no longer complained.

William chuckled and read his mail with interest. So, the mother was away until this evening. All the better. His face felt tight and hot, his eyes darkened.

Now, *where* is the sister?

'Look, I'm not angry this time, Elizabeth, I just want it back. It's important.'

Jake stood in the kitchen holding onto the door and barring the way. He *was* angry, but trying hard not to show it. Why wouldn't she just admit she took and give it back? It's not like she could do anything with it, *he* had all the power.

Elizabeth tried to push her way under his arm, but he grabbed her by the shoulders and pushed her back. His face radiated fake calm.

If Jake was angry it was nothing compared with his sister. And she had no problem showing it.

'I haven't got the fregging thing!' she shouted. Her face was white and her hands were fists. This was ridiculous. Why on Earth did he think she'd taken his stupid comb again?

Well, they'd started off the holiday arguing about it and it looked like they were going to end it the same way.

'You've probably dropped it during all that useless training you've been doing,' she snapped. 'What makes you think *I've* got it?'

In the bright sunlit kitchen, Jake could see what he thought was a dark ring around each of his sister's irises. Had they always been there?

He tensed up and felt the stones in the walls heat up, ready to dislodge. Anger rose in him. He pushed it down.

'Bett, just give it back,' he said slowly. 'I know you took it because someone saw you.'

Elizabeth opened her mouth to speak, then snapped it shut.

Hah! thought Jake, *got ya!*

She lunged forward and pushed Jake as hard as she could, which for an eleven year old girl was surprisingly hard. Jake felt the aftershocks in his spine.

'What...' she shouted. '... do you mean *someone saw me*? Who, Jake! Your dragon? You *trust* him over me?!'

'Right now I do, yeah!' snapped Jake.

'What!?' hissed Elizabeth. She shook with anger.

'It wasn't the dragon,' said Jake steadily. '*You're* the only one that could have taken it.'

He knew it was a mistake as soon as he'd said it.

His sister paused for only a second and her fury drew in a sharp breath.

'Really?! Maybe *he's* got it. Have you thought of that? Maybe he's taken the stupid thing back because you're SO USELESS!'

It was Jake's turn to open and close his mouth like a pelican stranded on an oil-slicked beach. Elizabeth seized the chance to barge her way past her brother. At the last minute he caught her arm and pulled her back.

'I want it back before Mam gets home, alright!' he hissed.

'Sod off!' She pulled herself away and stormed out.

She slammed the door just in time as a handful of fist-sized stones wrenched themselves from the wall and smashed into the ancient wood.

Jake steadied himself against the table, listening to his heart pounding like hailstones, and tried to slow down his breath.

He needed to calm down. Needed to talk to someone. *Where* was Stone?

He grabbed his bag, set off out the front door and marched down the path towards the field and the hills. Yes, he needed desperately to calm down.

He needed the talisman.

How could he get it back if she kept on lying to him?

Jake couldn't find Stone. So much for coming when he was needed.

Who he did find, in one of the marshy fields, was William James. He smiled as Jake approached.

'Hallo!'

'What are *you* doing here?'

'Walking. It's good for you.'

Jake looked at him carefully. He looked shiny. Probably sun-cream. There was a strange smell, like bacon on the turn. Probably sun-cream, again.

'You alright? You don't look too good,' he asked.

'Never better,' smiled William. 'You?'

'I'll be alright. Just had an argument with Bett.'

William cocked his head to one side. 'Was it bad? Would you like to talk about it?' He smiled a broad smile and subconsciously Jake took a step back.

'Err, yeah. Alright.' He stood, hands in pockets, feeling uncomfortable and gangly. He cleared his throat.

'Go on,' urged William.

'It was about the talisman–'

'Oh, Jake, that must have been difficult.' William reached out and patted him on his arm. Jake continued, but he couldn't quite shake the greasy, grubby feeling.

'Er, yeah. She tried to say she didn't hav–' he began again.

'Jake?'

Jake's sentence dried up in his mouth. 'Yeah?'

'Look, I know I said I'd be able to listen to you, but, I just realized that I don't have the time. I wanted to finish this walk.'

'Oh.' Jake deflated.

'I must go. We'll meet up later.' William said it as though it was a warning rather than a hope. Jake merely nodded and said 'Bye' to the narrator's retreating back.

At that moment, if he could have seen William's face, Jake would have been able to answer three troubling questions: *who'd taken the talisman? who was the vessel?* and, *why had the narrator come here?*

William James walked casually and noiselessly down the garden path towards the bench that Elizabeth sat on. It was clear, even from this distance, she'd been crying. She was quite attractive for such a small child. And being attractive, thought the beast inside the man, quite vain. Vanity was the most succulent of human emotions. William smiled warmly and stepped up to her. The girl was also... *yes...* angry, spiteful, hurt, humiliated...

Delicious.

He stood behind her drinking the energy in until, very brightly, he said in her ear. 'Hello young girl. Is your mother home?'

Elizabeth jumped. 'Jeez!'

She'd had enough of today, what with Jake and the unbearable heat and now this, this creepy man. He was cast as a black silhouette, the sun behind him.

'Where did you come from?' she asked.

William pointed vaguely behind him. 'Just over there. Your mother's expecting me.'

Elizabeth shielded her eyes and moved her hair out of her face. She started to say her mother wasn't in, when she got a clear look at the man's face.

Her heart nearly stopped. She felt the heavy tremble of the ground giving away. 'Dad?!' she stammered.

The man smiled. He made it look painful.

'No,' he said cheerfully. 'I'm a relative, Elizabeth. That's why your mother's expecting me.'

His eyes shone, his face glistened and his voice was far too bright and brittle to be him, but he *did* look like her father.

'Is your brother around?' the man asked. The ground shifted again.

'No,' said Elizabeth suddenly very afraid. The skin on her face wanted to creep around to the back of her head. A small part of her brain said, *whatever you do, don't tell this man anything about Jake.*

There was an underlying smell of raw bacon left on a sunny shelf. It made Elizabeth retch.

'Are you alright, child? You look quite pale.' He wiped at his face with a greasy hand. 'It's warm isn't it? I would like you to get me some water, please. With ice.'

Elizabeth stood up slowly. He reminded her of a children's book she used to have full of animals that could talk. He was the snake. Everything it said was a lie. As if reading her mind, he flicked out his tongue and licked his lips.

'No,' she said. 'I won't.'

The ground shuddered, this time knocking her off balance. The man remained perfectly still, his eyes gleaming in mute laughter.

'Earthquake,' he said with a flick of the hand, and then, 'I'm sorry, but why won't you get me a drink? It's very rude of you.'

'Because I was taught never to speak to strange men,' she said aloud. *And you're about as strange as they come*, she said to herself.

The man cocked his head to one side again and this time giggled. Actually giggled. It was as if the snake had learned how to tell jokes that only *it* found funny.

'I think you should go now. Jake'll be back soon.' As she said it, Elizabeth realized she was *really* hoping this was true.

The creepy man turned his gaze fully on the girl.

'Tell me, Elizabeth, are you warned against speaking to strangers because they might cause you harm?'

'How do you know my name?' said Elizabeth, suspiciously. *If I'm quick enough I can probably make it to the house.*

William James ignored her, reached out and gripped her by the shoulders. She screamed at the sudden livid pain in her shoulders. She could smell the chemical sharpness of acid on skin. Burning. The man's blue eyes glazed to black. The smell of rancid bacon gave way to fish bones rotting in an alley. He leaned in, laughing.

'You were warned correctly,' he said. Then, for Elizabeth, the world went black.

Jake sat on a small hump of rock and moss on the edge of the main path. He was confused, annoyed and feeling forsaken. Stupid William! Stupid Elizabeth! He picked up a pebble and threw it in the air, catching it in one hand. The ground rumbled beneath him. Another earthquake? He placed his hands on the stones and concentrated. He could taste lime and something like chalk. And there was something else there, a taste in the stones that Jake hadn't tasted before. Musty and sour. The stones were *panicking*.

They wailed.

A tremor, much stronger than the first, nearly knocked Jake off his seat. He stood, trying to keep his balance, sensitive to the slightest movements in the ground. He'd been training for weeks to empathize with limestone and now he could feel not only the main shocks, but the hundred miniscule aftershocks that only insects could sense. But *these* tremors were far from slight.

He had an overwhelming urge to find his sister.

He tried to calm the stones nearest to him. After a short while he could get something other than raw panic from their fizzing bones. The stones in spite of their fear – because of it – could give him only the taste of rotten meat, and blackness.

Jake rose slowly, trying to hold the panic at bay, and set off running as the tremors boomed around him.

CHAPTER 27

'How long has she been like this, Jacob?'

Stone circled the prone body. Elizabeth was a rag-doll, her skin so dry it sloughed off in rough flakes as if she were a snake. Every few minutes she convulsed: trapped in a nightmare from which she couldn't escape. She flip-flopped clumsily into a puddle on the cave floor near where Jake had laid her down.

'I don't know, I found her in the garden. It can't have been long – we argued... it was about an hour ago. She was like...*this*... when I found her...' Jake's voice trailed away.

'I brought her here straight away. Was that right? What's wrong with her? Should we go to the hospital?'

The elemental spoke gently, but his voice echoed like a mausoleum.

'Hospitals cannot help her, Jacob. You did right to bring her to me.'

Jake sighed with premature relief. He was still shaking.

'However,' continued the dragon, 'It may be that we are too late.'

'*Late?*'

'Observe her eyes, Jacob.'

Gingerly, Jake lifted the lid of first one eye then the other. They were black like two oily marbles.

'What the...?'

'This kind of intervention is rare. The beast must have great concerns about you.' Stone said. 'It does indeed have a vessel, Jacob. Did you suspect your sister?'

Jake nodded. 'A little bit.'

'As did I. We were wrong. She is a weakness of yours. The beast misdirected us and now it is eliminating everything you hold dear.'

'She's not going to die!' Jake said. It was a statement of fact.

The dragon nodded, grimly. 'Then we must work fast. Your sister is an obstacle the beast has placed in your path. We must remove the obstacle quickly. Now, take out the talisman!'

'Er...' panic flickered across Jake's features.

'The talisman, lad!'

Jake didn't even pretend to fumble in his sports bag.

'I've lost it,' he blurted.

The dragon growled. 'This is *not* good news, Jacob!'

Jake looked down at his sister. She shuddered and snapped open her eyes. It was like looking into an abyss, deep, dark, and unending. (and Jake remembered them close to tears that morning when he'd accused her...)

'We argued,' he said, numbly. 'About the talisman. William said he'd seen her take it. And Bett said she hadn't.' Jake looked up at Stone, his eyes pricking with tears. 'I din't believe her...'

'Well,' said the dragon stonily. 'We shall have to hope that we can have you arguing with each other once more.' And with that he reached into his mouth and broke off a tooth. He winced and passed it to Jake.

'What's this?' Jake asked in a bemused tone, taking the broken canine. Stone rubbed his jaw then brought his tail up in front of him.

The slap was short and brutal.

'Jesus! What the –'

'Your *blood* will give the tooth strength. Time is dangerously short.'

'But what...?'

'NO MORE QUESTIONS!'

The dragon's roar sent Jake to his knees; his stomach pitched then rose. He could feel the blood trickling down his cheekbone and into his mouth. It tasted like copper. He cupped some in a shaking hand

and smeared it all over the tooth. The blood sank into the limestone like water into a sponge. Jake looked to the elemental, bewildered.

'What now?' he asked in a coarse whisper. Stone beckoned him to stand. He held out his tail and gripped a section of it between his claws.

'Here! You must use the tooth and stab down exactly here! Do it once only. Very, *very* hard. Be precise in your aim. I do not want you to tear off my tail!'

'What?! No! I'm not going to stab you!' Jake stood in front of the dragon, sweating and shaking.

In his bones, he could feel the elemental's anger rise.

'Then, Jacob, your sister *WILL* DIE and it *WILL* BE YOUR DOING!' he bellowed, 'Stab now before I lose my patience!'

In a fury of terror Jake brought the tooth up in both hands and stabbed down. It skewered the stone tail like a knife through a watermelon. Golden liquid pooled at the wound's edges. The elemental dragon roared in pain.

Jake didn't know what to do.

Elizabeth writhed on the cold, stone floor, her breathing shallow.

'Now,' hissed Stone. 'You must hold her very still. Keep her mouth open – here, this might help.' He broke a stalactite from the ceiling and passed it over. Jake, knelt down, forced his sister's mouth open and wedged the rock sideways between her teeth. Her breath wrangled in her throat.

The dragon held his wounded tail over her mouth until two drops of the golden liquid slid down onto her tongue. He pulled his tail quickly away.

'Too much,' he said, 'will kill her. Now, remove the stalactite.'

'What is it?' asked Jake, but the dragon shushed him into silence.

'We must wait and see if it has taken,' he said.

It didn't take long. Elizabeth flailed among the puddles and tufa; twice she kicked the stone map at her feet and each time it throbbed an angry warning.

Then, there was the kind of stillness you only ever read about in books or see in films. Not even her chest rose with her breath.

Jake tried to step forward, but the dragon held his arm.

What happened next would haunt Jake for years to come.

From every pore in his sister's skin, from her eyes, ears and mouth, oil streamed like slugs. Black as the devil's heart. It poured over the floor of the cave and shrivelled up or disappeared down fissures in the rock.

Elizabeth didn't move.

Minutes passed.

Eventually the dragon sighed and started to say, 'I am afraid, Jacob... that we were too late, your sist–'

'She moved!'

Jake shook off the dragon's grip and knelt down.

'Bett! Bett! You okay?'

Elizabeth, weak and slick with sweat, sat up coughing. She shivered uncontrollably and sobbed. Jake took his thin raincoat out of his bag and wrapped it around her, mumbling soothing words. He found his water bottle and watched as she took small sips.

'Oh, God,' muttered Elizabeth when she could finally speak.

'What happened?' croaked Jake.

Elizabeth fixed her eyes on Jake's, her bottom lip started to tremble. 'There was this man, Jake. I– I can't remember... there was a man...'

'A man?'

'I knew him. I *know* I did.' Elizabeth shuddered trying to remember. 'He said he *knew* you and– Dad!' Elizabeth's face lit up in terror in the gloom of the cave. 'He looked like Dad!'

'What did he do?'

'I don't remember! He came up and started chatting – just chatty stuff, but a bit creepy. I don't remember anything else.'

She slumped against her brother, then pulled away.

'Urgh. Tastes bad. Feel sick.' She leant over and vomited. A thin, black bile seeped out. She took another sip of water from the bottle.

The dragon stepped forward and brought his head close to

Elizabeth, flicking her hair out of her eyes with his tail.

'I'm afraid, young Elizabeth, you were poisoned,' he said, gently. She pulled back quickly. '*Poisoned*?!'

'Yes. We purged it in time,' said the dragon. 'With thanks to your brother.'

'*Poisoned*,' gasped the girl. 'That man?! Poison?' She tried to wipe her face with her shaking hands.

'The beast,' said Stone. 'It poisoned you with itself. It needs nothing more.'

'That bastard,' hissed Jake.

Elizabeth stared up at Jake and the dragon. She wasn't angry because she'd gone through anger and out the other side.

In the centre of each eye burned a golden flame.

'God!' said Jake startled. 'Her eyes..!'

'What's wrong with my eyes?' Elizabeth asked blinking hard.

'I gave your sister what medicine I could. The blood of an elemental is a powerful thing, Jacob.'

'That was your *blood*–?'

'Blood? What blood? What about my eyes?'

'–What did you think it was, Jacob? It came from my body.'

'WHAT'S *WRONG* WITH MY *EYES*?!'

Jake stopped and stared at his sister. 'Er... they're, sort of, on *fire*,' he said sheepishly. 'You've got flames in 'em.'

'I can't see any flames!' Elizabeth stared around the room blindly and tried to catch a glimpse of fire.

Stone sat back and said in a soothing voice, 'No, lass, and you will not. But quickly, tell us what *can* you see?'

A sudden calm wave passed over her; it fought hard with her natural tendency to be angry at things she didn't understand. She looked around.

'I can see you,' she said, nervously. 'And Jake. I'm in a cave. There's a wall over there and... I can see *through it?* Bones, loads of old bones and shells. And copper.' She blinked hard.

'What does it look like?' whispered Jake.

'It's like, like I'm looking through a tube and around the edges it's all *holographicky* and – Jake! I can see the sea! If I don't look at it straight on I can see the sea!'

Jake looked at the wall. He could see nothing but damp, weathered wall.

Elizabeth closed her eyes tightly, still feeling sick. The feeling of Zen withered like a snowdrop on a sunbed.

'Eyup you, what have you done to me?' she snapped at Stone. He placed his tail on the girl's shoulders.

'You will be fine, lass. It is very powerful stuff,' he chuckled to himself then said, 'You have come across my blood before, lass.'

'I don't think so!'

'In your grandfather's letters. In the moonlight.'

'That invisible ink was your blood? Urgh.'

'Elemental blood is curious and powerful. In all the millennia I have existed not even I am certain I know all of its properties. But it heals. You. And your brother has also benefitted from its powers.'

Jake remembered. 'Your tonic?'

The dragon gave a little nod.

'But you said your blood's molten lava,' Jake added.

'It is that and more. And that is all I will say. Now, we must go, Jacob. It appears that William James – or something like him – has deceived us all.'

'Wait, though, why did I need your tooth? And my blood?'

The dragon stretched open his mouth like a boxer after a bad fight. Jake could see the ravaged canine stub.

'There are very few things that can penetrate my hide, Jacob and my talisman – stone of my stone – is one. This,' he indicated the tooth, 'is a... diluted... version but it sufficed. It may prove useful to you in the fight to come. It pays to be resourceful.'

'What's the other things?' asked Jake boldly. 'What else can penetrate your hide?'

Stone saw no reason to lie. 'Fire and a few of the stronger acids. Now, we must find the vessel.'

'Is it really William?' asked Jake darkly. The dragon's eyes flared red.

'Yes. Whether he intended to or not, he has brought part of the beast here. And if the vessel finds a way into my cave your world will be lost. Perhaps all worlds...'

'He said he was going to see my mother,' said Jake, grimly.

'She will be safe until her return. We must work fast.' The dragon turned to Elizabeth. 'You will stay here. I will bring you food and water...'

'No way! I'm coming with you!' Elizabeth stood up, shakily. 'I'm not staying here!'

'You and your *'ways'*,' growled Stone. He looked at the girl and this time his eyes flared gold. Elizabeth's eyes flared in response. And then she fell down. Fast asleep.

'Move her to the plateau please, Jacob. She will be safe.'

Jake picked her up and carried her to the dry stone ridge covered in moss. It had been carved out of the rock by the persistence of time and the drive of water... *Jake, I can see the sea!*

'What have you done to her?' he asked, looking for something soft to place under her head. He found his jacket crumpled on the floor, and bundled it up.

'I have sent my blood in her veins to sleep,' said the dragon. 'Hers has merely followed in its footsteps. When we return, I will awaken her.'

'What if we don't? Return, I mean?'

'We will.'

Jake looked unconvinced. The dragon stood in front of him and gripped his shoulder.

'Jacob, know this: we *will* be triumphant. We will return.'

'We might not.'

'Then your sister will be glad she is asleep. Now, lad, come. Bring your new 'talisman'.'

Chapter 28

The ground shook.

Jake struggled to keep upright. He felt useless as he watched Stone rise up, his great wings battering the sky. Instinctively he reached into his pocket for the talisman and remembered with frustration that it wasn't there. In his other pocket was the tooth. It wasn't the same, but was it enough? He squeezed it tightly and felt the small pulse of the elemental's power, reassuring.

To his left the mountains loomed, to his right straggly moorland stretched out with nothing but the odd gorse bush and a few trees to protect them.

Above him Stone hovered.

In front of him William James stood staring up at the dragon, his legs apart, his arms outstretched. A sickening grin was glued to his face.

Neither creature moved.

Jake had had little time to think about William and even less to take control of his anger. He felt betrayed.

Stone had said that the thing in front of Jake *wasn't* the man they knew, and that if he *was* still alive, inside the shell of his own body, he should wish himself dead. If he was dead, then he'd been dead for days – maybe even before he'd stolen Jake's map and passed through to this world.

Stone had said all of this on their way to the field, and Jake had believed it. But here, facing the man that he knew and in a strange way trusted, it all seemed... redundant.

The ground shook again and this time the force pulled Jake to his knees. He bit down on his anger and swallowed it whole.

Black clouds clustered above the strange tableau, driving in so quickly that the sky became night. Jake heard thunder close at hand and then another sound, hot and alien. He looked up, and in the nearby distance smoke rose from a dead mountain.

Before Jake had time to think, a blast of wind hit him like a cannonball and threw him onto his back. Breathless, the pain in his gut hot as coals, he lay on his side and looked up just in time to see the dragon swoop.

The vessel howled gleefully as Stone caught him by the shoulders and ascended. Jake smiled grimly as the man's feet kicked and danced like a puppet on a string.

Higher than the mountain tops, stopping short of the black clouds, the elemental dragon flew. Then, with no ceremony or care, he dropped his quarry like an eagle dropping a tortoise onto rocks.

The vessel fell. He didn't scream, didn't howl. The beast angled William's body as if he were hand gliding. When he eventually hit the ground, he would break every bone in his body.

Jake watched, holding his breath. The body landed in silence twenty yards away. Not even the grass cared to make a sound.

Thunder roared. The dead mountain hissed. Then silence.

That was *it*, thought Jake. That's *all* it took? A simple fall?

But Jake had watched enough horror films to know that the crazy baddy always came back. He heaved himself onto his elbows and tried to sit up, settling on a lopsided flop.

A minute that lasted longer than a year passed. Why hadn't the beast got up? Was Jake wrong? Was it *actually* dead?

Stone swept above them, scanning the ground where the vessel had fallen. In the distance, smoke from the mountain started to plume. The black clouds thickened, pregnant with rain.

The dragon hovered, barely moving.

He was singing. Singing the stones to come to him. Jake could feel it in his stomach and his pounding chest. He felt hot as kilned clay.

They came. Sharp, jagged cobs and heavy man-sized boulders, shrapnel pebbles and shards of broken limestone. All singing in reply.

They settled in the air above the prone beast and waited.

The dragon's song deepened. It was the depth of a mining shaft, the bed of an ocean abyss, the low, gut-churning song of hard labour.

The stones dropped.

The impact knocked Jake down: its echoes filtered as far as the town. If the body beneath this cairn had not died when it hit the floor, surely it was dead now, with a hundred tons of limestone weighing it down?

'Is it dead!?' shouted Jake when he got his breath back.

Stone had stopped singing. His eyes glowed white and in the centre of his chest, Jake could see his hide red as molten lava.

The dragon blinked slowly and shook his head: for some reason, it reminded Jake of continents shifting.

'What now?' He shouted against the rolling thunder. The wind ripped at his t-shirt and torn jeans.

He felt the sudden words in his bones. 'I must send it back, Jacob,' said the dragon.

'HOW!!?' shouted Jake.

The rain poured down. A knife of lightning cut through the sky. The dragon struggled to keep his place against the thrusting winds: he was nervous of letting the cairn out of his sight.

'I will take the beast to my cave. We will use my map.'

'No! It's too dangerous!' shouted Jake. He tried to cover his head against the raging storm. At the back of his mind was the image of his sister asleep on a stone plateau.

The black clouds brought not only rain but freezing cold. Jake shivered.

'It's WHAT IT WANTS!' he said, knowing at that moment he was *exactly* right.

'I have contained it in the stones!' bellowed Stone. 'It is weak.'

'Is it?!' Jake screamed, struggling to hear Stone's reply. The dragon made to move, but Jake, terrified and mistrusting, shouted for him to stop.

'Stone! It's not *safe*! I know it. I can *feel* it!'

Rain lashed at the boy's face. He could no longer see the elemental hovering in the black sky. '*Believe* me!' he shouted to the air. Then he caught sight of Stone again as lightning lit up the clouds and the dragon was pinned against the darkness like a moth in a biology lab.

'We... need... the... *map*, Jacob,' Stone said with much effort. 'To... send... it... back!'

Jake, standing now, edged slowly forward. 'I know!' he shouted. 'But it's not the only one! William's got mine. It wasn't destroyed! It's how he got here! In his pocket– I can *feel* it! I can get it!'

'No!' interrupted the dragon. '*That* is too dangerous!'

The rain stung Jake's eyes. He was getting fed up of this.

'It's the only way! If it gets into your cave then it will have the *real* map. Then, that's it! All ended!' Jake was desperate. 'It's the only way! You've got to move the stones!'

Stone railed against the storm and Jake's persistence.

'NO! I cannot,' the elemental bellowed.

'Just a few. If you don't, I'll do it! Trust me!' Jake's voice was hoarse and he couldn't keep the fury down. A new blast of wind and rain hit Stone's body, wrenching him across the sky.

'DO IT NOW!' demanded Jake, and as he heard the elemental's reluctant singing he fought hard to keep his anger in check.

A dozen small stones lifted from the vessel's broken body. Jake crept forward and looked down at the man's unconscious face, blackened and bruised, one eye swollen. One shoulder, twisted back, slowly emerged as the stones shifted, then the man's chest. In a flash Jake was back in the hospital sitting at his father's bedside.

But this wasn't his father. It wasn't.

He swallowed hard and reached out to open William's jacket.

There was the map smeared with blood, poking out from an inside pocket.

A hand shot out like a cobra and grabbed Jake by the wrist.

He'd been half expecting it, but didn't quite believe it. One of the beast's fingers was broken and bent back and as it gripped him, it made gristly clicking noises. The boy squirmed. William's eyes opened.

Jake needed a weapon. He reached quickly into his pocket for the tooth.

It was gone.

He must have dropped it when he fell. He swore out loud. And the beast started to laugh.

'Child,' he hissed. 'You should have left well alone. My plan was infallable.'

The beast, glaring up through the eyes of the vessel, spat black blood at the boy.

'You should have let the elemental take me to its cave,' he said. As he spoke, Jake could hear the grinding of grit in his teeth.

'Now, I must do this the hard way. One-by-one. First your dragon. Then your mother – oh, how tasty. Your sister. This town...'

'You're enjoying this? You have no emotions.' spat Jake.

'I've learned a lot from this body. From humans. I learn quickly. Yes, I am enjoying this.' He laughed again; it sounded like grease down a plughole.

'You I save till last, child. Then you will truly know grief! Losing a father? Hah! *Where* is the grief in that?! You will lose your world today!'

The vessel rose from the cairn as if the stones were made of papier-mâché. He held Jake up to his face, examining him like a butcher examines cuts of meat, and flung him to the ground. Jake bounced roughly and felt a painful wet popping in his ribs.

Above them, Stone cursed and dived. In one swoop he savaged William with his claws and the endless ricochet of his tail. The vessel howled, spitting teeth and black blood. Stone swept up higher and readied himself for another attack.

Lightning, coming from nowhere, skewered the black sky and struck the dragon squarely between shoulder blades.

Stone roared, spiralling downwards. The beast's gleeful cackle rebounded off the fields and mountains.

As the elemental fell, Jake struggled to see through the scathing rain but he could feel something was building, gathering momentum: he could feel the power of the stones surging through the earth.

An inch above the ground, Stone flipped back, oblivious to the pain, and soared once more. In that inch, he gathered up every stone from the cairn. He needed ammunition.

'Jacob!' Stone said softly. 'Jacob, head for the trees.' The words landed in Jake's head like fresh snow. He managed to drag himself up and stagger as best as he could until he reached the scrub of trees. He wasn't sure what protection they would be.

He soon learned.

Stone blasted the beast's vessel with a barrage of stones. And as each one dropped it shot back to be fired again.

Jake watched from behind a birch tree as the vessel deflected one stone after another as if he was flicking away mosquitoes. About one in three found their targets. How the *hell* is he doing that? Jake said to air. The answer was sudden and unwelcome: *it's the wind, he can control the polluted wind.* Jake's heart sank. The dragon's barrage was unrelenting, but useless.

Stone bellowed. The air shook.

Every stone above William's head vibrated, glowing blood-red. Then each pebble, each rock, stole together and in a matter of seconds fused into a slab of limestone fifteen-feet by six. It looked like a headstone against the dark sky.

The dragon roared again.

Jake felt the ground shake. The beast was quicker on the uptake than the boy. It shouted spiky, violent words and a spear of lightning struck out. Stone fell, one wing ravaged, but he didn't stop. He bellowed again.

The ground split open and five more slabs loomed up around the beast. It screamed. One final roar from the dragon and the slabs slammed tightly, fused together and trapped the howling creature inside.

The exhausted dragon slumped impossibly in the sky. His breathing was saw-toothed and rapid, his wing ragged at his side.

Jake hesitated beside the trees, listening to the screaming of the trapped beast. Then a silent pause.

The deathly calm before the storm *truly* began.

What had been merely heavy rain now fell in solid sheets of water. Jake's gaze was fixed on the stone tomb that encased the vessel. He could hear a faint, hypnotic chattering like a thousand wasps at a nest. He gasped, half-drowning in the sleeting rain. The dragon struggled to hover nearby.

'We need to bring the stone map here. It's the best way,' said Jake, then, 'We can trap him here!'

Stone looked doubtful.

'Have you ever tried to move the map?' asked Jake. He wiped streams of water from his face but didn't take his eyes off the tomb. He could already feel the ground becoming mud, slipping beneath him.

'I have never needed to,' came Stone's answer.

Inches of water worked their way up Jake's feet and ankles. If *he* was slipping, what about the tomb?

'I think we need to now!' shouted Jake.

The tomb was shaking.

Then the rain changed again. This time the drops were heavy and black. And hot.

'It's burning!' yelped Jake, slapping at the slashes of rain.

'Burning?'

'Like acid!'

'Stay under the trees! Keep covered!'

Jake stared up at Stone. Where the rain touched the dragon, his hide was dissolving. This was impossible. He was made of stone! Then a realisation struck home. Jake turned his gaze back to the tomb. The stone walls were starting to *erode*. The rain felt like acid because it was acid rain, and as it hit the alkaline of the limestone it melted like an ice-cream in the sun.

From the tomb came low, meaty laughter.

'Stone!' shouted Jake.

'I am fine, Jacob. I re-generate quickly. The tomb, though, cannot. The beast will soon be free. Get to the trees!'

Jake made for the tree-line once more, his journey hampered by the mud and a dull pain in his ribs. He reached out and grabbed a tree to pull him up the last foot. When he was safe, the rain drops bouncing off the canopy above him, he watched helpless as the tomb-cage melted and the vessel stood in its devastated centre.

The rain stopped as quickly as it began. The beast at least knew the limitations of the vessel's skin: it would not do to burn it off the bones. He scanned the positions of the boy and dragon. With the movement of one hand, lightning fired a warning shot to the tree protecting Jake. The boy jumped, terrified, but stood his ground.

Stone shot towards Jake, then, as if caught by some imaginary lasso, stopped abruptly. Except the lasso wasn't imaginary – the roots of a dead tree felled years ago for firewood, had whipped out and caught the dragon by his tail. It catapulted him fifty feet into the air.

'Elementaaaaal!'

The beast stood beside the melted tomb and stared up through the vessel's black eyes. The dragon swung himself back from his forced trajectory and hovered in the air, fighting very hard to stay calm. *Don't feed it, don't give it strength.*

William swaggered over to the melted rock, laughing.

'My, my, elemental,' his smug voice carrying over the chaos of the storm. 'Is this all you have? A stone cage and some missiles?' It pronounced the word 'missal', like the prayer-book.

'Where is the famous molten force of stone? Where is the pressure – millions of years of sedimentary pressure – to be released on the one they call the beast!? Or...' He leered over at Jake. 'Is it the chii-illld? Elemental. Has it weakened you? Are you getting *soft*?'

Stone stared solidly at the creature and, still hovering, batted his wings once, twice, then said, simply, 'You talk too much.'

'Do I?' snarled William.

'Yes.'

Stone charged across the sky.

He hit William with his tail, lifted him fifteen feet into the air and dropped him to the ground. Jake could hear the crack of bones even from this distance, even above the noise of the storm. He grimaced. The vessel rose, his right leg hanging at an odd angle. He bent down and with another crack, wrenched it back into place, not even wincing. He sighed.

'You try to inconvenience me, elemental. But I wonder if you realize of what you are up against.'

The vessel knelt down and smashed the ground. A small dial of cracks emerged, the fist's impact its epicentre. One crack thickened, widened and grew to a fissure. The fissure became a breach and the breach spread out cleaving the ground in two. Earth, stones and bushes fell into the rift. The ground beneath Jake's feet shifted. The rift was at least twenty feet across.

A blast of hot, sulphurous air spewed from the crevasse and knocked Stone off balance amid the rising therms. The vessel laughed again. He pointed with a flourish like a cheap magician at a fun-fair to the cliffs in the distance.

'Ta-daaa' he mouthed and threw a wink in Jake's direction.

A rumble of stones and mud slid down onto the roads below.

'You see, *you* control the stones, elemental. And maybe the dust in the air. But *I*? I control nature as affected by humanity. I have the decayed, vandalized trees, the overheated atmosphere filled with greenhouse gases...'

The vessel spat once more, smacked his lips and continued.

'The skies, filled with the acid of man's pollution. Are they yours elemental? No, they are mine. And lo, let there be volcanoes.' He swept his arms again.

Stone watched as the once dormant mountain slowly and dramatically erupted like in a scene from a disaster movie. At its foot was a car-park full of cars.

Jake screamed. And heard a gristly, wet noise as William snapped his head towards him.

Then Stone struck again. Sweeping in, he lifted the creature by the scruff of his jacket and soared high. If there was a *volcano*, then he, Stone, might have a *weapon*.

He flew low and fast.

And he would have made it, if, at that *exact* moment, the skies hadn't turned blacker than midnight, and a vast, twisting wind hadn't sprung out of nowhere to scoop up the dragon and cast him down, releasing William as it did so. And if the lightning hadn't speared him again, and if the wind (a hurricane now) hadn't carried his body into the troposphere and mocked his broken wing, Stone would have made it.

When he dropped from the sky, the world ended.

Chapter 29

Stone plummeted into the chasm looking for all the world like a broken toy.

The Earth should have screamed. The skies should have collapsed when the land closed over him.

The ripped seams of earth smashed and fused together as if the ground had never been cleft at all.

There was just silence. Pure and complete as though all sound had been stripped from the world; the silence of that first day down by the river. Black rain pattered noiselessly until it too stopped.

Jake held his breath, listening intently, willing every part of his body to sense the dragon. He could no longer feel the pounding of Stone's breath in his own bones.

Track him, said a small voice in his head.

In the funereal drama, the boy bent his mind to the substrata.

There was no trace of the elemental.

Jake could feel limestone around him, even the melted wash that was the tomb, but not Stone himself.

This was impossible! The dragon couldn't be dead! He's immortal!

Jake pushed his mind's eye further, searching deeper through the layers of stone and minerals, past tiny gemstones and solid flints. He felt for the molten core of the dragon's heart, and was found wanting.

The elemental's spine had buckled in the final attack, his wing, already ragged from the fight, had dragged him down into the ground that swallowed him whole. *Nothing* could withstand that.

Jake was numb. That was it, then. It was over. Everything.

He slumped to one knee and felt the grass between his fingers. It felt slick and stubbly after the acid rain.

This was all wrong.

He pressed his hand down hard. Maybe... maybe there was something of the elemental?

Tears streamed down his face (when had he started crying?) and harsh bile burned the back of his throat. He wiped a hand across his snotty nose then pressed down deeper into the earth; limestone splinters dug into his skin.

Stone, please! he begged the ground. *Please!* The pain in Jake's heart throbbed, but his bones felt empty.

The earth's silence was unbearable; in it was the last image of Stone and any hope of defeating the beast. Jake realized the only sound he could hear now was his own sobbing.

And then, the sickly sound of laughter.

Quiet at first, then louder until it became a familiar, high-pitched cackle.

Anger sat on Jake like a fat toad. Still crouching, he turned his head to see the vessel walking towards him.

Stone had been right, this *thing* was not William James; this was a mockery of the man. His eyes were blacker than coal and just as shiny. His mouth split into a grin; at one corner it ran on into his cheek so that Jake could see foetid, bloody tissue and the jaw bone beneath.

As the vessel walked towards him, Jake watched the wounds knitting themselves together. He was drawing his power from somewhere, Jake thought angrily. But where? William stopped a few feet in front of him.

'Seriously, child,' the vessel said in greasy, stoppered tones that slipped and slid over Jake. 'Did you. *Really* think. It. Would end. Differently?' He looked down at Jake and spat black ooze. 'Foolish.'

The beast used William's hand to reach into a torn pocket and produce a small black roll of velvet which he threw to the boy, all the while laughing. As it landed on the ground in front of him a small object fell into the mud.

'My talisman?' Jake hissed, scrabbling to pick it up. '*You* stole it? You bastard!'

'Of course. Child! Did you. Seriously believe your. Own. Sister stole it? You took. This *stranger's* word. Over. Your sister's?' The beast's voice was filled with glee.

Jake had heard of people being so angry they couldn't speak, but he thought it was just a saying until now. He stared, keeping the vessel in his sights. He could feel the nails of one hand dig into his palms as his fist clenched harder, the fingers of the other wrapped tightly around the comb. Just one good punch, that'd do it!

Jake glared at the vessel. Was he getting fatter? He stood in front of him, smiling. He stank of rancid vegetables and rotten meat.

'You bastard!' growled Jake.

'Child. How could I. Open all of the. Doors? Without the key. The true key. Not a wishy. Washy. Simulacrum stolen. From a dream!'

Jake knelt in front of him, fury and fire rising in him like a volcano. William laughed again and flexed his hands. His fingers popped back into place as if they'd never been broken.

'Why didn't you use it then and open the doors? You had my map!' Jake rose slowly.

'Your sketch. Is like whisky without. The alcohol. I desired. And shall have. The limestone map. And the doorways. To *all* the other. Worlds! So much more. Simple with. The elemental. Disposed of. I feel. Your actions have. Greatly. Assisted me!'

'Over my dead body!'

'Of course!' A broken shoulder scrunched under William's coat as bones grinded together in their mending, then he shrugged.

'I said. You *will* die. *Last*. I shall keep. You alive. For a very long. Time.' He gave a long sweep of William James' hand and added, 'I could not. Child. Have done this. Without you.'

Jake swung, putting all his weight behind the punch. The vessel stepped back, laughing. Jake slipped and landed heavily on his knees.

'Goooood,' said William, greasily. 'Anger. So *succulent*.' He laughed again, a nasty little gurgle in the back of its throat.

'When I have. Finished. I may let you. Keep the comb. As a souvenir – for a. Short while. At least.' He reached forward and snatched the comb from Jake's hand. Then he held his stolen arms out wide as if he were a king measuring a kingdom.

'I like your. Anger. Child. Rich with nutrients.' He gestured to the hillside and beyond 'Is it not. Sad. How you have. Let. All this *die*? Trees. Birds. Ah, yes, *otters*. Oh, and *people*. So much. *Fodder*.'

Jake stared, his outrage freezing him where he squatted, his guilt an anchor around his neck.

'Your mother awaits,' said the beast. 'So much grief. Guilt. Regret. So *delicious*.'

The vessel blinked deliberately; the black of his pupils drained away to William's soft blue. His body looked almost healed.

He sighed dramatically. 'Do not. Think of retribution. Or disclosure. Child,' he continued, 'Who will believe you? And *you* have. No weapon. No elemental. I will leave. Unhindered. I have. Hunger, child.'

The beast turned to leave.

'Jake.'

Jake's voice was coarse and low but he spoke calmly. For a second, he remembered Stone's compliment when he'd made the pebble dance in the air; control – that was the key. It felt like a lifetime ago.

He stood slowly unfolding until he was his full height. The beast turned back, still smiling.

'What?'

'Jake,' said Jake louder. 'Not *child*. My name is Jake. My *dad* gave it to me. It was his middle name. It has *responsibilities*. And he gave it to me because he knew I could take them. Because I *am* a *companion*.'

'Your father's name? Child. *He* was not. A companion!'

Jake's heartbeat spiked for a second. 'That was him. I'm me.'

'What!' William snarled, 'Is a companion with. No elemental? You're just a lonely. Little boy.'

Jake could hear the ground tremble.

'No,' he said, calmly.

William stepped forward and Jake heard the faint crack of newly repaired bone breaking again. A look of terror and pain shot across the vessel's face. He wasn't properly healed. It would probably take months of feeding to fully heal. And while the beast had prattled on Jake had found his own anger, guilt and fear and isolated them from his heart. Then, he'd found somewhere to store them. Deep down.

He was calm. Centred. The beast had nothing to feed on.

'Feeling hungry?' said Jake, sarcastically.

'A lonely. Terrified. Child!' snarled the beast.

Jake shrugged holding his hands palm down in front of him. William's blue eyes drained milky then grey.

'No. Y'see, *this* is what you don't understand: *I'm* companion to limestone the *element,* not just to Stone, the elemental.'

This time it was the vessel who felt the ground shift beneath his feet as a wave spread out in increasing circles like ripples from a stone dropped in water.

'I have. No time for this!' William James raised his arms high above his head and started to whisper. The trees bent in sudden winds, and the clouds, still heavy and black, broke into rain, fine at first then gathering weight. Thunder roared once more, lightning struck a nearby tree.

In front of him, Jake could see the wounds on William's face pop open and bruises blossom like night-time flowers. The beast was feeding off its own anger and it couldn't sustain itself.

'Yes,' said Jake softly. 'You *do* have time. That's all we *have* got, now.'

He stumbled but held his ground, and turned his attention to the melted slabs of the beast's former cage.

The fragments rose again, hundreds of little stones. From deep within the earth, a barrage of limestone missiles erupted and joined them: boulders, jagged pebbles, chunks of black and yellow marble, until the air was thick with stone.

They rained down on the beast.

From the old barns in the next field and the dry stone walls edging them, rough-hewn blocks the size of a child's head bombarded the beast once more. The vessel easily batted them aside.

'Do you think–' he hissed, 'That *you* can. Destroy me. Where your elemental. Failed?'

Rage snaked across his oily face. The angrier he became the more he fed off himself, unable to find nourishment from Jake's calm body.

The rain suddenly turned to vicious, sleeting snow.

Jake, half-blinded in the blizzard, concentrated harder.

The elemental hadn't gone far enough. He could *do* this. For Stone.

In his mind's eye, Jake could see nearby caverns. He focused. Stalagmites and stalactites broke off from the floors and roofs and forced their way to him.

Over the noise of the storm, Jake spoke barely above a whisper.

'This is where it ends.'

The beast glared at him. 'Really?' he said, slickly.

'Yes. I have limestone.'

'You think. This game of marbles. Will defeat me.'

'No,' said Jake simply. 'That doesn't interest me. I have the map. I *will* send you back.'

The beast laughed and sent another shard of lightning to the ground inches away from Jake. He didn't even flinch.

'Stupid child. *I* have your map.'

'No. You said it yourself, you have a sketch. *I* have my *map*.'

Jake moved his hands in rapid and complex gestures.

And sang.

Hundreds of small stones flitted towards him, then stopped. A small swoop in the air with his hands, a tiny flick, and they formed a square like a badly fitting jigsaw puzzle on the ground. Circles and triangles etched themselves into the surface: the river; the caves. The domino elemental mark. It glowed.

The vessel watched amazed as more and more stones poured in and fused together, and so the wind dropped slightly and the sleet turned back to rain.

The map was complete. And in every detail *exact*.

Jake's hand slipped to his back pocket.

'*So*, you have. A map,' William James hissed. 'I have. The Key. You need. The flesh of the. Elemental to open. The doorways.' And once again he gave a smug little cackle.

That was it!

Jake shot forward ramming his shoulder into William's stomach. He gagged on the stink of rotten bacon as the vessel doubled over and Jake pinned him to the floor.

'Remember this!' Jake snarled, holding up the talisman. 'Whose flesh is this, then, eh?'

He could feel the anger well up in him and as it did so, the body of the beast grew stronger. He fought hard to calm himself as William rose, struggling to gain some ground. He was winning but it was amazing how quickly the beast could feed off humans.

'How did you get that?' William hissed.

With a final surge of strength, Jake pushed down pinning William onto his back.

'I can *call* it, you idiot! Like the stones! I *know* that now! It comes to me!'

He rammed his arm against the vessel's throat and held the comb like a knife, its bone teeth stabbing into his palm.

'Flesh! You want *flesh*! Have it then!'

He plunged the stone handle into the vessel's soft neck and tried to ignore the gristly resistance of skin and tissue. He felt sick as the stink poured over him.

Then, the man that had been William James slumped beneath him, not even a gurgling rattle to mark the difference between living and dead.

Jake stared at the body and then the comb. It was no mythic sword or enchanted dagger but it *was* a weapon. Stone had been right. He laughed a little hysterical laugh that lent as much to the body beneath him as to the memory of when he'd called the comb *lame*.

He sat back. An oily liquid, stinking of tin and rotten garbage, spurted out of the wound in William's neck as Jake pulled out his comb and dropped it to the ground. His hand was sticky and black. The body started to decay almost immediately like an effect from a cheap horror film: first the chest disintegrated, then the eyes withered, then the hair and skin melted off the skull.

The dragon had been right again; William had been dead for days, maybe weeks.

Jake retched as he crawled away from the gloopy mess of blood and bones. And so he didn't notice the sky getting blacker.

He rolled painfully onto his back and looked up. The black oil that had seeped into the ground from the vessel's body now somehow covered the heavens, making a sky, already dark with clouds, like night. The air oozed.

He hadn't killed the beast, he'd *released* it!

He blinked in the darkness knowing instinctively that now he must return it, must open all the doorways at once and send it away. A bit to *this* world, a bit to that: spread it out so that it was once more weak. *That* much he could remember. What he was struggling with was how to do it.

He looked up. The sky boiled black.

The beast must be looking for another vessel! Would it be him? *Of course it would!*

Think, Jake!

His gaze landed on the comb lying in the vessel's fleshy gloop. The key! Gagging, he reached in, gingerly lifted it out and wiped it unceremoniously on the grass. Well, here goes. He plunged the talisman into the centre of the map, straight through the dragon mark. Now it really did look like the blade in a myth, some Viking saga.

He stood up. Next, he needed the words but he wasn't sure what to say. *Think! Think!*

He couldn't think.

The words wouldn't come.

He'd never really learned them.

He could still hear remnants of laughter. It started to rain fine droplets of black liquid that spattered and stung his face. He clamped his mouth shut and pinched his nose in the hope that the black rain wouldn't get in. Thunder pounded.

He slumped down, and as he did so every stone that he'd brought to the hill, that hadn't made up part of the map but was still circling above him, dropped to the ground with a thud. He hadn't even realised he was keeping them aloft. They scrabbled into the earth, trying to hide. How the map remained whole he had no idea.

Beneath him, the ground thrummed. Jake's body, still dowsed in adrenaline, shuddered: he could feel the aching throb of his back teeth. Then more thunder.

The sky was laughing at him.

His stomach churned in a mocking memory of Stone's voice, and his heart wrenched itself into his throat. He couldn't take any more. He closed his eyes, ready to die.

The ground exploded in a cascade of stone and earth.

And from the new fissure, his body molten-white, erupted Stone.

Like a bullet, the elemental dragon, pierced the oily black shroud. Through the rent, Jake could see sunshine. He heard a roar and realized it was his own voice cheering!

The dragon swooped up and bolted back, puncturing the beast time and again until the black sky was a fragile lace-work of holes. Jake heard a high-pitched screeching like the massacre of rats. Insects fell out of the trees.

Then Stone landed. He looked at the boy with warning in his golden eyes: stand back. The beast, weak and defeated, was pinned to the sky.

The elemental stood over the map, muttering a chant that grew louder and clearer until it became a song, a beautiful familiar song. His eyes flamed red as he bellowed words ancient and powerful.

The whole sky exploded.

Jake gasped as the map swelled forty times its size and sucked in every last scrap of black. The air around him thickened, and the map glowed the same molten colour as the dragon; when Jake closed his eyes he could see its after-image on his eyelids. When he opened them again, the map was its normal size. Jake could feel heat radiating out. The elemental stepped forward and gently, and without ceremony, reached out with his tail and removed the talisman from its centre.

In silent, slow motion the map shattered into a thousand pebbles.

Stone nodded, satisfied, and dropped the comb at Jake's feet. He bent to pick it up.

'No, lad,' Stone said quietly. 'Too hot.'

The familiar, welcome thrum of Stone's voice in Jake's bones pricked his eyes with tears. Heat rose off the dragon's body. Jake heard the steady ping, ping of cooling stone. He wanted to rush forward and wrap himself around Stone, but instead he just stared, dazed.

'I s-saw you...go down,' he whispered, his voice cracked and hoarse. 'What happened?'

'You saved the day, Jacob. The beast has been... extinguished.'

'How?'

'You saw how.'

'I mean...how... *you*?'

Stone blinked a slow that's-enough-now blink. Jake just stared. The sun shone brilliantly in a perfect blue sky, as if nothing had happened. A wood pigeon cooed in the distance. Jake slumped to the floor and Stone shuffled over and sat down. The dragon still radiated warmth, which was fine because Jake suddenly felt very cold. He leaned carefully against the stone body, listening to the rumble of the elemental's very alive heart.

They sat quietly waiting for the world settle. The noises came back in time. The volcano's grumbling landslide slowed to nothing. After a while, Jake turned and, wincing under his broken ribs, peered at the trees. They were still charred where the lightning had struck. It *had* happened then. Already it was beginning to feel unreal.

'I'm glad you're alive,' he said eventually.

'I told you, lad–'

'I know, I know, but I thought... you know.'

The dragon snorted and a fine plume of smoke filled the air.

Jake smiled. 'How did you...?'

'I *repaired* myself.'

'Repaired? How?'

'Let us just say, I found my centre.' The dragon winked one golden eye. 'My core.'

'Core?' said Jake numbly.

Then, a thought, small but powerful, leapt into his mind.

'No! No way! *The* core? No way! *That* would have taken thousands of years. You said!'

A flame flared in Stone's eye and he winked again. 'I am, on occasion, incorrect, lad. But you must believe what you will,' he added, smiling. 'I found time.'

'Time? You can't change time!' said Jake, beaming, all aches and pains drained from his body.

'There are things about the elementals you have yet to learn, lad.'

'No one can change time!'

Stone shrugged, laughed softly and made himself comfortable.

Time passed, unchanged. A small swarm of flies came out of nowhere and buzzed around the dragon's face. He didn't even lift his tail. Eventually he turned his attention to the boy whose weight was comforting slumped against his haunches. He tapped him gently on the shoulder and said, 'We must go now, lad. We have much to do. Jacob? Jacob?'

Jake was sound asleep.

Jake woke to the wind blowing warmly in his face. He coughed then rolled over, and caught himself just in time to stop him plunging hundreds of feet to his death. He didn't know how he'd got there, and he certainly wasn't going to ask, but he was lying on the back of the dragon.

The ground beneath him whisked by, and the clouds fluttered around his face, but he felt as warm as a dry stone wall on a summer's day. As they banked gently he felt the soothing throb of the dragon's voice in his bones.

'You did well, lad.'

Jake smiled and leaned forward, carefully wrapping his arms around Stone's neck. This time the dragon didn't complain, he just kept on flying.

CHAPTER 30

Stone and Jake sat on the topside of the hill looking down at the cottage and the distant town. The training field spread out in front of them, looking bereft of their presence. Jake's bruises had healed nicely and the cut on his face was a yellowed scab. His broken ribs were no longer. Stone breathed easily, contentedly. Every so often he would flick his tail in the direction of the flies more out of habit than annoyance.

Jake played with a blade of grass, running his thumb nail gently along its grain. He'd spent the previous day helping his mother to pack, putting the cottage back to how they'd found it. It was a day of endings and preparations for leaving. They'd be back home by tea-time. After everything that had happened it all felt very small, very tidy.

The heat-wave had finally cracked and now sitting on the hill was a pleasure: a true, concrete, thank-God-we're-alive pleasure. And they *were* alive. Jake could barely believe it. Three days ago he'd faced this amazing, terrifying thing, and he'd *survived*.

He looked at the dragon and said nervously, 'It was *real* wasn't it? I mean... it happened didn't it?'

Stone chuckled gruffly and his eyes flared in a smile. 'Is there reason to doubt it?' he asked.

Jake smiled and shrugged. He flicked the blade of grass onto the ground and picked another. 'It just seems like it was a dream.'

'Jacob, it happened.'

'Yeah... it must've. It was in the newspapers.'

'Newspapers?' asked Stone.

'People notice things like volcanoes and landslides. We were lucky no one was killed.'

'Yes,' nodded the dragon. 'Lucky.'

'They're putting it down to Nature. Freaky Acts of Nature.'

'They always do. Is your sister well?' asked Stone, changing the subject.

'She's still a bit pissed off with you. Sorry.' Jake looked uncomfortable. She was a bit pissed off with him as well, but she'd get over it. She always does.

Stone said nothing for a while, then looked up into the blue.

'Ah, it is a dragon sky today.'

Jake followed his gaze. The sky was like the surface of a brand new swimming pool, perfectly still. Across it, breaking the calm, danced dozens of white clouds, some thick and full like cotton wool and others small and wispy as ghosts.

Jake stared at them. For some people seeing shapes in clouds is difficult, others can't help but populate the sky with cows and tortoises and Santa Claus. Anyone looking at *this* sky would've had to have a very poor imagination *not* to see what Jake saw.

Every single cloud was dragon-shaped.

Two fat dragons played above the tree-tops before a breeze dragged them away; an angry dragon, stiff on its haunches, was shot through with sunlight; others danced and battled.

Jake flung himself on his back and laughed. It was the heartiest laugh he'd had in what seemed like a lifetime. He had to hold his stomach because his ribs ached, and tears streamed down his face. It felt good. *Really* good to laugh.

'They're *all* dragons,' he said, wiping his eyes.

'Yes,' said Stone, chuckling gently. 'All of them. Today, Cloud honours you, lad.'

Jake sat up. 'Me?' he asked, 'Why?'

'She is sentimental,' Stone answered, and didn't add, *and perhaps I asked a favour.*

'Look there, Jacob.' The elemental flicked his tail up towards the sky and pointed.

Jake saw a shape that was clearly a young boy holding in both hands what looked like a dagger, or a sword. Or a comb. The shape stayed just as long as the clouds could carry it and the wind brushed it away.

'Cool,' said Jake, modestly. '...cool.'

'Yes, Jacob. Cool.' It was an odd phrase coming from Stone. He shifted on his haunches and pointed at a thick, heavy set cloud. 'She is always there. In the sky, even at night.'

'Does she have a companion?'

'She has two. A mother and a daughter.'

'Two?'

Stone nodded and said no more. Above them the clouds started to disperse. Jake and Stone watched them go. It was a good moment: a clear, peaceful moment.

It was broken by Jake.

'I've got a couple of questions.'

'You always have, lad,' sighed the dragon still looking up.

'Why was it so... evil? It wasn't just hungry?'

The dragon pulled his gaze away from the clouds and said, 'I am afraid that by taking on the vessel, it took on human qualities...'

'Oh.' Jake nodded, understanding. He added, 'It's not over, is it?'

'Yes, lad. For us it is over. There will be other battles for other elementals. But they are *not* our battles. *Our* battle was *here.*'

'But shouldn't we help!?'

'If we are called upon, we will assist. *If* we are called upon.'

Stone brought his tail around in his familiar way and rested the tip on Jake's shoulder. 'Do you remember that first day, Jacob?'

Jake thought back. Had it really only been six weeks ago?

'I went to take photographs down by the river.' Jake remembered the impression in the grass, the mass moving through the leaves and bracken. The strange silence.

'That was you?!' asked Jake.

Stone smiled and ignored his question. 'Many years ago your father gave you a watch, did he not?'

Jake nodded.

'It is very valuable, Jacob. It keeps time like few other watches and it never stops.'

Jake pulled the battered watch out of his pocket and thumbed the glass. 'You're wrong y'know, it stopped that day I was at the river.'

'*I* stopped it.'

'How?' marvelled Jake.

'Do you remember how I sent your sister to sleep?'

'What, so my watch's dragon-powered!' laughed Jake.

Stone joined. 'Take care of it, Jacob. You might need it one day.'

Jake felt the pressure of the elemental's laughter in his guts. By tea-time he'd be back home and it would be gone. He would miss it.

'That's it then. I'm off home soon. This is all over.'

Stone's eyes flared, puzzled.

'*Over*? No, lad, this is not *over*! We have barely scratched the surface of your training. Perhaps, you can throw the odd stone around and spy on people...' His eyes flared yellow with laughter. '...and perhaps, you can pass through simple limestone that is as weak as rice-paper. But when you can pass through marble – well that will be something to sing about!'

And as the elemental dragon prattled on, Jake settled down, closed his eyes and pictured a scene somewhere in the future: *He's walking to the old meadows he used to go to with his father, and he catches sight of a shadow on the ground that could easily be mistaken for a bird: a goose, perhaps, or a swan. And he looks up and sees above the trees a silhouette. Soaring. Swooping. And utterly impossible.*

The end...

An Epilogue of Sorts

Air rushed around his face and whipped at his clothes and hair. His eyes streamed. He shouted for Stone, but his words were ripped from his throat before they were even half-formed. The air was thin and painful in his chest as, face-down with his arms bent back, he fought against the pressure of the booming air and tried to focus on the ground beneath him.

He was so high up he couldn't even see the roads below. All he could see was cloud. A thick underlay of cloud. He forced himself to will Stone's face into being. But there was no sudden plateau of limestone under his falling body, no fiery roar through the dawn sky.

Jake closed his eyes.

He was terrified. But most of all he was livid!

He'd fought the living force that was the beast, and survived! And after all that he would end up dead after falling from... where *had* he fallen from?

He tried to crane his neck to see behind him but the thrusting air forced his head back. He pulled his arms forward – if he was going to die, at least he'd not look like a squashed scarecrow. His eyes streamed and his jaw ached as he tried to think of what to do.

He reached into his jacket pocket and fumbled inside. His hand closed weakly on the talisman. It was barely warm.

In the distance he could see mountains.

Below him cloud loomed. Jake knew that beneath, and not very *far* beneath at that, was the ground. He stretched his arms out in front of him and tried to clasp the comb with both hands. Velocity increased. The air boomed. His ears popped from the noise and the cold. His fingers half-frozen, couldn't grip the comb properly and it twisted in the air then disappeared; his swearing followed it. He seemed very heavy all of a sudden, and falling very quickly. He gave in and screamed.

And a hand reached out and grabbed his.

Jake stopped falling.

The voice of a girl, two or three years older than he was, laughed.

'I've got you, innit,' she said.

From a bank of cloud reared a head, ancient and beautiful, on the end of a long, slender neck. Its eyes shone blue as a summer sky. Inside each pupil tiny storms swirled.

The dragon's body emerged and on her back stood the owner of the voice, one arm outstretched, holding Jake. He hovered above them like a green and blue balloon until the girl pulled him down behind her, her spiky blonde hair tickling his face as she wrapped his arms around her. She smelled of winter air and jasmine flowers, and she was warm. Jake suddenly felt hot and clammy.

Then, the dragon soared. And as she soared, the girl, like an eagle, screeched and laughed, enjoying herself.

Jake awoke in his bed, his own familiar posters staring down at him.

'What the *hell* was that?!' he said to no one.

His body was chilly and shaking. His hair was damp as dew. Outside, the autumn day filled the sky with wispy clouds and weak sun. He lay back against his pillow, a voice ringing in his ears...

I got you, innit.

His throat hurt and mist clung to his hair, floated in front of his eyes. He laughed, warmly.

'What the hell...?' he said, and grinned.

THE END

331

Author's Notes

Stone's mason mark of the circle bisected by an arrow is made up, although mason marks do exist. It's thought that as well as acting as signatures (which meant masons were paid for their work), the marks were also instructions to builders to ensure they put the correct stone in the correct place, particularly carved stones. There must be nothing more embarrassing than realising you've put a gargoyle's backside where its face should be – or maybe it's hard to tell the difference.

Many of the names that Jake discovers are actual stoneworkers names, and many of these are quite ancient, such as Macun, Stanyer and, of course, Mason. Walker is not typically a stoneworker's name. All of these names are prevalent in the East Midlands. Stanley is a name for someone connected with stone (*stan* in Old English).

The abbey featured early on in the book is a mixture of both Rufford and Newstead abbeys in Nottinghamshire. Although I didn't see any large stone dragon statues at Newstead Abbey it doesn't mean that, to the right eye, there aren't any. There *is* a lovely Japanese garden with stepping stones and shrines though. And swans. Rufford Abbey *does* have a dragon, by the way, a two-headed one made of wood.

Viz Viva – Some 19th Century scientists believed that fossils were not the remains of dinosaurs (and therefore part of the evolutionary process) but a life force in rock that, because of a sort of jealousy, tried desperately to imitate living animals.

The heart of Stone's map lies somewhere in the Bedolina map, Valcamonica, Italy.

The Devil's Arse cave really does exist. It's near Castleton in Derbyshire. There are some things you don't need to make up!